THE
INDIAN DEFENSE

BOOK 5 OF THE ONE HUNDRED YEARS OF WAR SERIES

JAY PERIN

Publisher's Cataloging-In-Publication Data

(Prepared by Cassidy Cataloguing Services, Inc.)

Names: Perin, Jay, author.
Title: The Indian defense / Jay Perin.
Description: [New York, New York] : East River
    Books, [2023] | Series: One hundred years of war
    series
Identifiers: ISBN 978-1-7364680-9-8 (paperback) |
    ISBN 978-1-7364680-8-1 (ebook)
Subjects: LCSH: Ex-presidents--United States--
    History--20th century--Fiction. | United States--
    Politics and government--1989---Fiction. |
    Petroleum industry and trade--History--20th
    century--Fiction. | Nineteen nineties--Fiction. |
    Treason--Fiction. | Murder--Fiction. | Corporate
    power--Fiction. | LCGFT: Political fiction. |
    Thrillers (Fiction) | Historical fiction.
Classification: LCC PS3616.E7443 I54 2023 | DDC
    813/.6--dc23

Editors:
Chase Nottingham
Elizabeth Roderick http://talesfrompurgatory.com/
Cover: www.ebookorprint.com
Maps and illustrations: Murat Bayazit
Video (book trailer): Nauman Gandhi
Special mention: www.GetCovers.com

www.EastRiverBooks.com

To the One They Called God;
To the Best of Men;
To That Goddess of Knowledge;
To the Chronicler.

Table of Contents

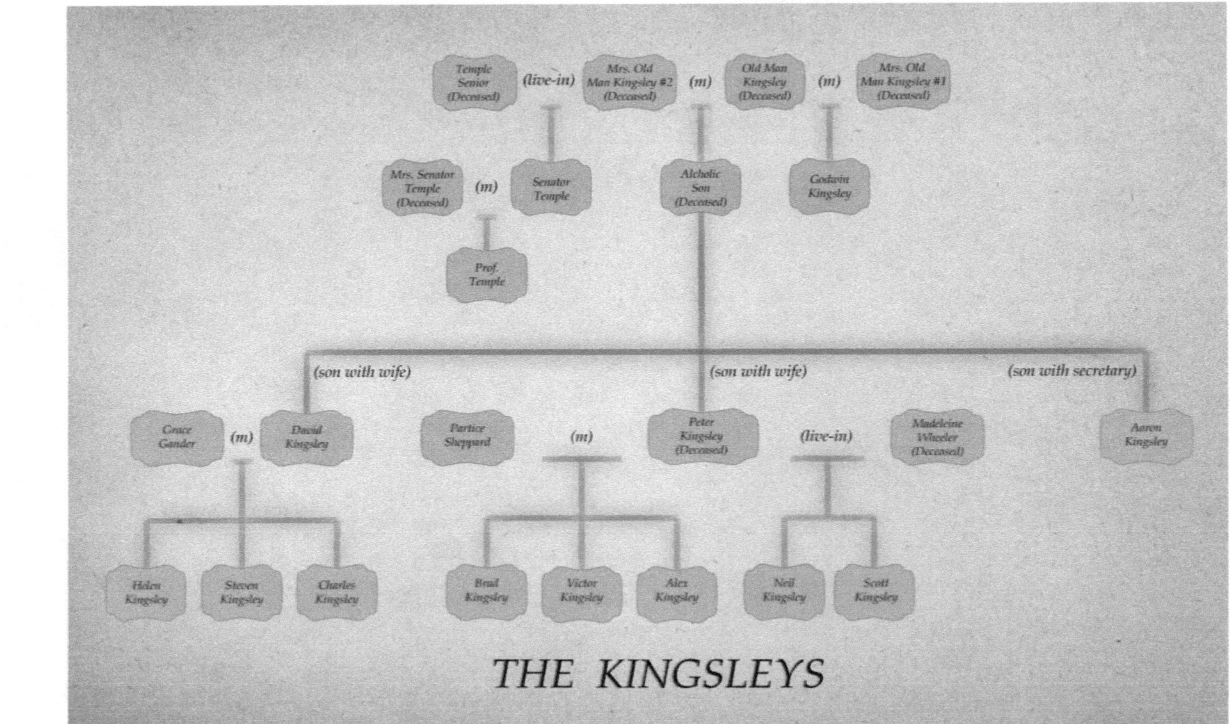

THE KINGSLEYS

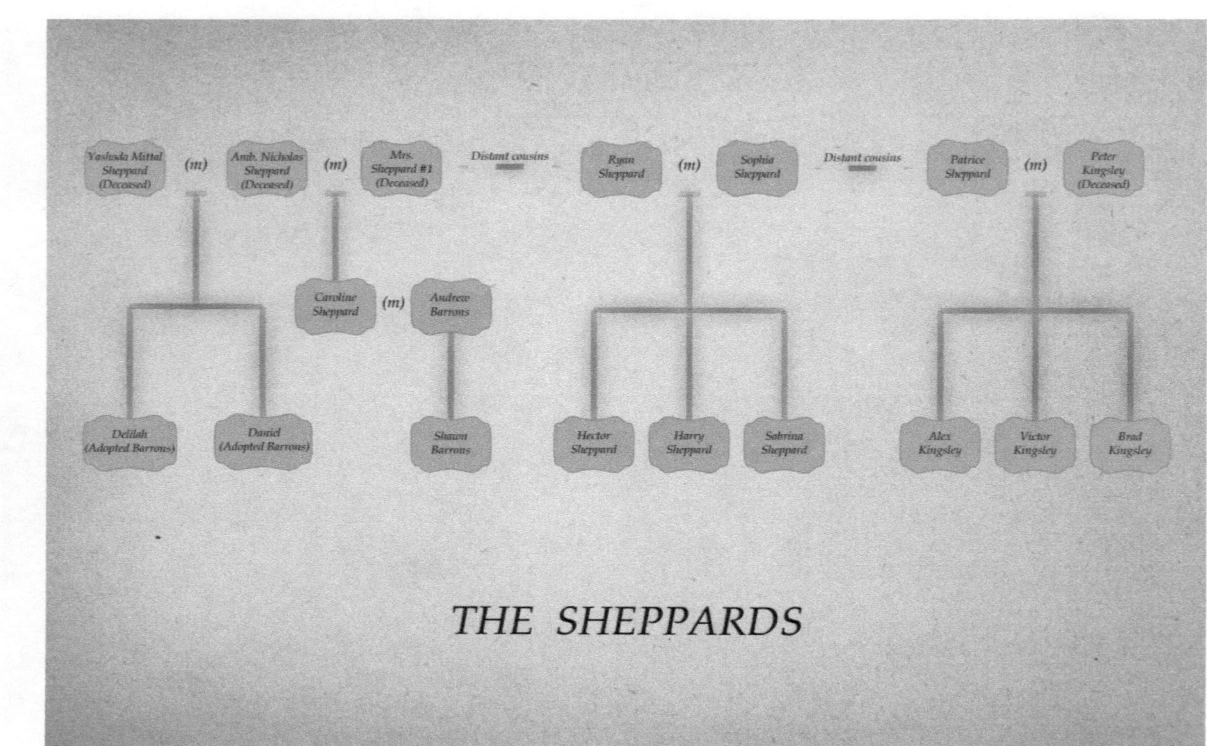

THE SHEPPARDS

Part I

Chapter 1

June 3, 1989

77th Precinct, Crown Heights

Brooklyn, New York

The star-spangled banner fluttered on top of the orange brick building as Temple exited the Cadillac. Squinting against the hot sun hitting his eyes, he glanced at the letters spelling out the identity of the place. The bullet which pierced his skull in the assassination attempt made sure he couldn't read it, but the row of squad cars parked in front and the familiar NYPD emblem on the wall next to the entrance advised Temple as to where he was.

Noah Andersen, friend and former attorney general, had knocked on Temple's bedroom door shortly after daybreak and hustled him into the car. Whatever the problem, if it required the presence of a former American president in a police station, Noah certainly thought it serious.

There were indecipherable murmurs from the cops in uniform as they escorted Temple and his companions inside—Noah and the four secret service officers. Curiosity marked the faces of the staff milling about within. It was to be expected. News of Temple's incapacitation had surely spread through the nation, and people wanted to see for themselves what happened to the erstwhile leader of the free world. Temple wished there were some update he could give.

Day after day after day he'd spent in the hospital, and nothing much changed. Temple could make sounds but not speak any language which could be understood. He didn't comprehend what was said to him. He couldn't read or write. He couldn't even tell the time by looking at the numbers. First the snow outside, then the sprouting grass told him many weeks passed since the shooting. Noah brought a calendar, and the general appearance of the month in question allowed Temple to figure out where they were in the year. There was a therapist of some kind who visited after his discharge. She hadn't come around lately.

Temple knew the woman wasn't returning. He saw the pity in her eyes on the last day, the belief he would never get any better. Growling in frustration, Temple signaled the doctor who traveled with the security team he was free to go... for good. The medic had been part of the crew since their White House days, and he was asked to continue with the former president only because of his advanced age. In the end, there was nothing anyone could do to help.

Raging against his fate, Temple begged Noah to let him die. Of course no one understood what he said, but Temple was constantly watched over the next few weeks by both his friend and his security detail. The secret service officers waited patiently as Temple paced his bedroom, growling in anger. If only the bullet fired by the Kingsley assassin did what it was supposed to do. The Kingsleys... Noah pinned pictures of the entire clan on a corkboard. Somewhere in the middle of the last row was a grainy photograph of the woman who married the eldest Kingsley grandson. Lilah... it didn't matter who her biological parents were. She was Temple's daughter, dammit! And Godwin Kingsley—family patriarch—knew it. He still issued the order to hunt her down. Lilah was now out there somewhere on the run from hitmen.

How could Temple die in peace without knowing what was happening to his child? If the bastards found the young woman, they would tear her apart. Temple couldn't let them get to her.

Perhaps the damage done by the bullet was divine retribution for the things the politician did in his lifetime, the souls he regarded as justifiable sacrifice in his struggle to bring order to the chaotic world. But he could not, *would* not resign himself to being collateral damage in the Kingsley campaign to rule the oil sector. The assassin who fired the gun was unlikely to have been caught, or Noah would've given some indication of it, some way to tell Temple there was hope of getting the Kingsleys for ordering his death.

There was only one weapon remaining which would work against his stepbrother—Godwin Kingsley—the family secret which could bring him down. Temple needed to shout out the truth, to warn the men and women on the streets there was so much more to the tale put about by the media. Somehow... someway... he needed to communicate. He would have to teach himself to talk in a new language which didn't make any sense to him.

Keeping his gaze straight ahead as he accompanied Noah into the precinct, Temple strained to pick up snippets of the various muttered conversations. There were a few common words he'd begun to recognize, but at the current rate of progress, he'd be lucky if he managed to ask for coffee in a couple of years. Tense muscles sent an ache throbbing up the back of Temple's skull, but he caught a familiar name. "...Officer Sheppard..." someone said in hushed tones.

Petty Officer Sheppard? Harry? Why were the cops talking about him? What the hell was going on? Temple glanced at Noah, but he was already striding ahead. Arthritic joints forced Temple to keep his pace slightly slower.

With a small nod directed at a cluster of young cops, the former president followed his friend to the back of the building where yet another official waited at a door. This time, it was someone Temple recognized. He'd met the black gentleman with his partially bald head at a fairly recent event... before the attack by the hitman.

"Commissioner," greeted Temple, nodding again, but the sounds came out garbled and meaningless. Following New York's top cop into the small, windowless room, Temple stopped short at the sight of the tall figure in jeans and a cream tee sitting in a plastic chair, his hands on the metal-top table. Harry and the two men with him—both in business suits—stood to attention. "What's going on?" Temple demanded.

Harry's disheveled dark hair, the urgency in his dark eyes... he didn't say a word, but Temple knew. An enemy trap... Harry was caged.

"Lilah..." said the former president, willing his companions to decode what he was saying. He hobbled around to face Noah. "Get her lawyer here. See where all the Kingsleys are. If any of them has left the country, notify the feds. We need to find her before Godwin does."

Or Delilah Barrons Kingsley, the woman who once ruled the Kingsley oil empire, would die. Temple's child would end up as the final sacrifice in the war he declared so long ago.

Chapter 2

(13 hours ahead of New York City)

June 4, 1989, before dawn

Beijing, People's Republic of China

Alex, Lilah again tried to scream for help, but the hand covering her mouth blocked the sounds. Metal cuffs locked her wrists behind her back, making the pistol tucked into her belt useless. Gunshots, screams, shouts... the crowds in Tiananmen Square continued their rumble, the noise echoing into the hotel stairwell. No one would hear the muffled cries of a woman struggling to escape death.

There was a short grunt in her ear. "I thought I was going to have trouble getting you alone," an unfamiliar voice said, the accent upper-class New York. "The idiot in the square... damn waste of money. But you made my job easy." In a moment of confusion, Lilah had gone running out of her room, straight into the enemy's clutches.

She threw a wild kick rearward, connecting with the assailant's shin. The hand smothering her moved for brief seconds. When she opened her mouth to shriek, cloth was immediately stuffed in, almost choking off her airway. Lilah gagged. She tried to turn, to knee him in the groin.

"Oh, no," he said, wrenching her arms back further. "I saw what you did with Colonel Parker. You're not going to get the same chance with me."

Her eyes teared in pain. Fury surged. *No.* She would *not* die. Not as a victim. Blood pounded in her brain, urging her to fight. With a muffled groan, she made her body limp, and the assailant's hold loosened in reflex response. In the one precious second, she rocketed up with her entire body weight behind the movement and connected the top of her head with his chin. His hands fell away with an accompanying bellow.

Gagged and handcuffed, she limped down the stairwell. When she tumbled, she let herself thump down the steps. Pain, sudden and sharp, rolled over her left shoulder, spreading to every other bone, every joint. Her glasses fell off. She tried to spit out the cloth, to shriek for help. Alex was upstairs. He'd come looking. All she needed to do was hold on until he did. Or if she could get to an exit, if she could get to where the rooms were, someone would witness what was going on.

The assailant caught up with her at the landing and hauled her upright by her hair, still not letting her see his face. Her scalp burned. "I like my women with fight in them," he huffed, one arm punishingly tight around her chest, one clamped across her thighs.

Lilah stomped hard on his foot.

His grip loosened again, but he didn't let go. Hauling her out through the exit at the next floor, the man shouldered a door open. No one was in the hallway to witness what was happening... not a maid or a janitor, not a guest. One shove, and she stumbled into the room. The rumble from the streets increased exponentially in decibel level, drowning out even the war drums in Lilah's mind.

The door slammed shut. She hobbled to the windows... somebody would look up... somebody would see a gagged and handcuffed woman... hands gripped her upper arms from behind and hurled her into the bed. Her face landed on the pillows. Ignoring the screaming nerve endings in the upper part of her left chest, Lilah used her right elbow to support her weight and flipped herself over.

Before she could slide out of the bed, the assailant leaped. His heavy weight landed on her thighs. The pistol tucked into her belt was tossed across the room. A sharp tug on her left arm... something shifted under her muscles. Pain... so much pain... her vision blurred. She was back on her belly, her face smashed into the mattress. She couldn't breathe. Lilah struggled to raise her neck off the bedding.

The cuffs came undone. Again, Lilah used her right elbow as weapon, shoving it backward and connecting with his ribs. There was a roar of anger. Her wrists were wrenched above her head before she was rolled to her back. With a sickening crunch in the shoulder area, her entire left arm went numb and flaccid.

"Say hello, Lilah," said the man, shackling her wrists to the headboard. He sat on her legs, pinning her to the bed.

Her glasses were gone, and there were strands falling across her eyes, but the evil in the watery-blue stare was easy to recognize. The rest of him... a stranger looked down at her... Caucasian with light-brown hair. When she squinted in incomprehension, the back of his hand walloped her across the cheek. More pain... crashing through her skull, making her dizzy. Rage... returning focus to her mind.

Squeezing her mouth open with his fingers, the man tugged the cloth out. "You can scream all you want now. With the kind of noise outside, no one's going to hear you." He yanked the hair away from her eyes. "Recognize me now? JD. Congressman Jack Drummond. Steven Kingsley's brother-in-law."

"Sorry, still don't remember you," snarled Lilah.

His hand gripped her throat. "You will after the next hour or so."

Drummond would be forced to move at least slightly, or he couldn't carry through with his intentions. Lilah waited for her chance.

She got one almost immediately. His face descended toward her, blocking out the light. As soon as he got near enough, she opened her mouth wide and clamped her teeth hard around his lower lip. Blood spurted into her throat. He screamed and reared back, leaving a small chunk of flesh stuck to her teeth.

The weight on her leg lifted. Lilah brought her knee up, slamming it hard into his groin.

His head rolled back. Throat working silently, he slid off the bed.

Spitting out the blood and gore still in her mouth, she grunted, "Bastard. I'm going to make sure you're identified. Whatever you do to me here, Alex and Victor will do to you. None of them—not Neil, not Scott, not even Brad—will let you get away with this. Harry... Harry will kill you, inch by inch." If he were alive to do it... the Kingsleys... Drummond... was Harry also under attack? The enemy would've accounted for him and her brother.

Staggering to his feet, Drummond gurgled, "You'll be dead by then." Rivulets of red gushed from his torn lip and down his chin.

"But you will pay," she swore. She needed to get free... check on what was going on back home. *"Alex,"* she screamed, hoping against hope.

"No one's going to come," said Drummond, his voice thicker still as though the blood was pooling in his mouth.

"Alex," Lilah screamed again.

Then, incredibly, there was a call outside... her name shouted in response. Her desperate mind... was it playing tricks on her?

With a sharp sound of dismay, Drummond spun. He too clearly heard it, even over the cacophony from the streets.

"Lilah," roared someone.

"In here," she yelled.

Drummond's head swiveled between her and the door, his glance going to the windows. He ran and tried to jiggle the panes open.

Another roar... something heavy landed on the door, shaking its hinges.

Drummond wheeled around.

With a loud crack, the hardware broke. Through suddenly foggy eyes, Lilah saw Victor's giant form exploding in. Alex was next, followed by the rest, including Hema.

Lilah sobbed. Then, everything turned black.

Chapter 3

Thumps, thuds, angry rumbles... pain shot down her arm. Screaming, Lilah struggled upright.

"You're okay," said a familiar voice, terror clouding the blue eyes. Neil tried to soothe her back onto the pillows. Standing behind him was Hema, holding Lilah's glasses. "Thank God... you're okay."

Lilah panted, trying to... she looked wildly around. Clunky sounds and shouts came from one corner of the room where three men surrounded the enemy. Curses followed as the Kingsley brothers recognized the attacker as their cousin's husband, Jack Drummond.

"Sonuvabitch will pay," Neil promised. "Lemme check your—" A touch landed on her left shoulder.

An electric shock radiated to her fingertips. Lilah's vision blurred. She fell to the mattress.

"Sorry," Neil muttered. "Looks like it's broken."

Biting her lip hard to focus, Lilah took a few deep breaths. Her wrists seemed to be free, the handcuffs Drummond forced on her nowhere to be seen. Using her intact arm, she attempted to sit again.

"Don't move the joint," Neil warned. "I'll make a sling until we can get you to a hospital to have it fixed. Lemme get you some painkillers for now."

"Stop," said Lilah, swatting him away. "We need to... Neil... get Alex to ask Drummond about Harry and Dan."

Tone calming, Neil said, "Let me make sure you're all right—"

"*Now,*" Lilah insisted.

"Okay, okay," said Neil. "Just stay still, will ya?" When he called out the question, there were more shouts from the corner of the room where the rest of the exiles surrounded Drummond.

Lilah scrambled out of the bed with Hema's help and slipped on her glasses, one of its earpieces twisted at an awkward angle. Blinking to clear her eyesight, she focused on the bearded men pounding away at Drummond. Even Scott was throwing punches, his face ruddy. Brad stood to the side, smoothing back his curly hair. "Some trap for Harry," he said, sounding as refined as always. "Nothing about Dan."

"What trap?" Lilah asked.

"Maybe Steven and Armor tried the same stunt they did with us in Cuba," said Neil, coming up behind. "Steven wouldn't dare try to kill Harry... not this soon after what happened to us... then Temple..." Thanks to Harry's media stunt, there were questions about the role of the Kingsleys in the assassination attempt on the former president. Steven and his accomplices wouldn't want to have Harry killed and trigger further investigation. A trap of some sort made better sense.

"Mr. Harry is not stupid," Hema stated. "Their tricks will not work... he's not going to believe those people. Mr. Dan won't, either."

But would the Kingsleys have sent Drummond without accounting for the two people most likely to seek justice on behalf of Lilah? "Alex," Lilah called. "Ask Drummond..." Alex didn't respond. None of the three men pummeling the criminal responded.

"They can't ask," Brad snapped. "I think the congressman is out cold."

"He should be dead," Neil snarled, tugging off the bandana covering his bright-blond head. "I want my turn with the bastard."

"No more turns." Raising his voice, Brad ordered, "Victor, Alex, Scott! Enough already... or he *will* die."

Neil's jaw dropped. Alex and Scott turned to stare, but Victor continued, either unhearing or uncaring of his brother's command.

"Stop, Victor!" Brad shouted.

Victor stilled. Letting the unconscious Drummond slide down the wall, he straightened. "Bro?"

"He's going to die," Brad repeated.

"So?" Alex asked, tone incredulous. Under the beard, his cheeks were an angry red. "He was about to... to..."

"Rape me," Lilah completed. "Then, kill me." The throbbing in her shoulder returned with increased intensity, reminding Lilah her end would've been unpleasant. Her last moments would've been spent in agony. "He would've killed all of you, too... once you came looking for me."

"Steven would want to get you first," agreed Alex, wiping sweat from his forehead with the back of his hand. Of the six fugitives, Lilah was the only one who could credibly claim in court to be blameless in the Cuba incident which led to this exile. If she demanded Steven return the business to her, the American government could potentially pay attention. "Brad, Steven's behind this for sure, and he ain't sending his sister's husband here by himself. There's a gang, waiting to take us on. Remember the fellow in the square?"

An attempt to snatch Lilah was made only hours before amid the chaos in Tiananmen Square. That attack, Hema's arrival, the possibility of the girl having been followed, the shock of hearing about Harry's marriage to the strip club owner... Lilah's mind had been in complete turmoil when a phone call came. She didn't wait to think. She ran out in search of the switchboard, hoping it was either Harry or one of her brothers calling. Drummond already admitted to hiring the killer in the square, and when the attempt failed, he managed to lure her out.

Alex continued, "Drummond and his buddies would've had a couple of plans ready... diversions... distractions to separate Lilah from the rest of us. But they would've gotten to all of us... eventually. No loose strings, etcetera."

From the corner where Drummond lay crumpled on the floor, there was a groan. His eyes were still closed, and blood trickled down his chin.

"It doesn't matter." Brad glanced away from the unconscious politician and adjusted his round-rimmed glasses. "Drummond's Helen's husband. They have children... a family. Those kids happen to be related to us. More importantly, Drummond's a congressman. *We* cannot afford to kill *him*. Look around the city... the military is everywhere. We can't dispose of the corpse without being spotted. He's not some random criminal, either, for the police will write it off as a mugging gone wrong if we simply leave the body in the room. Don't you think his men will make sure of it?"

"They're going to wait a few minutes before checking on him," Victor said. "Chances are he got paid help, not family or friends. They'll skip town once they figure out he's dead. Also, the whole city's a war zone. Here or outside, he'll be just one more body. No one's gonna care, and we'll be long gone before he's even found by the cops."

"*Steven* will get Beijing police to care," said Brad. "What if he calls the feds and claims Drummond came to China in search of us? Armor's a lawyer. He'll find a way to do it without landing Steven in trouble for not tipping off the authorities about our location. Dead men don't talk... Drummond alone will take the blame for the trip, and we'll be in bigger trouble than we already are." The added charge of murder of a congressman could make a pardon impossible for the exiles. And it wouldn't be only Brad who was accused this time. All the exiles would be implicated in the politician's death, including Lilah. None of them could ever return. Even if the fugitives were never found, Steven would have won.

Victor stared at his older brother for a few seconds as the potential repercussions sank in. "Dammit," he cursed before stepping back. The rest followed.

At Lilah's side, Hema mewled. The intern took one of Lilah's hands in both of hers. A muscle throbbed in Lilah's injured shoulder, bringing tears to her eyes.

"Our best bet is to let Drummond go," Brad declared. "He won't say a word about what happened here. What excuse would he make up for showing up in China in the middle of a political crisis? He can only be blamed for not notifying the feds about us if he were dead. Alive, he won't make things easy for Steven and take the responsibility. Moreover, I'm sure he traveled with fake papers. Both governments will ask questions if they realize he was here. I bet Drummond will sneak out under whatever ID used."

"He *could* claim he came here for something else and saw us accidentally," offered Neil. "If he says we assaulted him..."

"It would be risky for Cousin Steven," Scott murmured.

"True," said Neil. "Murder is not the same as assault. We could fight it in court... maybe show papers from a hospital visit for Lilah. If a court agrees with us, Drummond could be forced to answer questions Steven doesn't like."

Brad nodded. "Also, if Drummond starts a manhunt for us across China, we could be found." The exiles wouldn't die as Steven wanted. They would be extradited to stand trial for treason, not murder of a congressman. Brad might be punished for the stupidities he did as the network's former CEO, but the other five would go free for lack of evidence. After all, they agreed to run as a group only to prevent Brad from facing the death penalty for selling out the nation. With Brad's fate out of her hands, Lilah would be free to battle the Kingsleys. Not something that would suit Steven.

"We need to time it right," mused Victor. "Drummond's men are going to be worried when they don't hear from him. They're going to suspect we have him... or that he's dead. They'll see we're on our guard. Same result... the moment we decamp from the hotel, somebody will pop in to check if he's still alive. They could take him with them, but we can't leave things to chance. I mean, all it takes is one idiot to do away with Drummond and pin it on us. No one's getting a reward from Steven for killing his sister's husband, but he damn well will use the situation."

Brad inclined his head. "The minute we're out the door, we'll notify the hotel manager there's an injured man in one of the rooms. There should be no time for anyone to kill Drummond. Then, we must leave Beijing. Even if the cops ID Drummond, what reason he produces for showing up here won't be our problem... as long as he doesn't mention us... and he won't."

All perfectly logical, Lilah thought bitterly. "Alex," she called. "Before we get out of this place, check what Drummond meant by trap for Harry. Maybe call Uncle Gray." As their lawyer, Grayson Sheppard was the only one with even a slight chance of not being pursued by the feds for aiding accused traitors. Perhaps they could connect through the Indian embassy as they did before.

"We'll need to make Drummond talk," Alex said, shaking his head. "Gonna be impossible to call Grayson. Communications—"

"—are restricted." Brad completed. "Doesn't matter. There will be no waiting around to see what Drummond has to say. We don't want to take the chance of him dying while in our custody. It's not only about him and Steven. Don't forget Prince."

The Burmese drug lord lost all his tussles with the Kingsley brothers so far, their last encounter mere weeks ago in Macau. Prince would know they'd be forced to use the same passports to travel from there to Beijing. He could have tracked them by now. The drug lord couldn't enter China or India because of the criminal cases against him, but his reach extended far into many countries, including these two.

"Not to mention the Chinese government." Tone firm, Brad declared, "The first chance we get, we're leaving." The violence on the streets would have to subside before the exiles dared step out, or the army would shoot them down along with the protestors. But staying in the city a minute beyond wasn't an option. It wouldn't be even if there was no Steven or Drummond, no Prince. The political unrest in the country meant the authorities would likely ask all foreigners to get out. The exiles could well get netted by the American government in the process.

Without warning, Lilah's knees wobbled. It took the last ounce of strength in her to remain standing. Brad was right, of course. In a better frame of mind, she might have even voiced support for his decision. But at the moment, Lilah couldn't care less. "Do what you feel like," she said, fatigue evident in every syllable. "I'll be in my room until we're ready to go."

Chapter 4

"It's not possible," Lilah said to Neil as he helped her to her room. "We don't have time for X-rays." The original plan to escape Beijing was to use Dan's contact to obtain permits to visit Tibet, from there slipping across the border to India. After what happened, they couldn't afford to hang around for the travel documents to be ready.

"No one's leaving the hotel today," Neil argued. "Not without getting crushed by tanks. Time enough to take a look at your shoulder."

With Hema's assistance, he settled Lilah into bed as Alex stood guard at the door. Alex had also retrieved her pistol—the one Drummond tossed across the room during the assault—and located her lost sneaker. Her glasses were broken irreparably, but she carried a couple of spares.

"Yeah, the tanks," Lilah said. "If we can't get out of the city because of the military, how are we going to get to a hospital? And what if the government starts rounding up foreigners?"

Neil placed a gentle hand on her injured arm.

"Ahh—" The stifled scream escaped before she caught herself.

"Lilah," called Alex. "The situation on the streets should be under control by the end of the day, but leaving after dark will be impossible. There will be night patrols. We have at least twenty-four hours remaining. Also, we ain't taking a plane out of China... not unless we want to get arrested. Whatever other route we pick, you need to have use of both arms."

Sweat beading on her upper lip, Lilah considered their options. If not through Tibet... an illegal boat ride to South Korea or Taiwan... a trek across the border to Burma or Laos or Vietnam... through Soviet territory... every route promised to be physically demanding. "Twenty-four hours," she said. "Not a minute more." They needed just enough order on the streets to escape grievous injury but not so much that the government was back in complete control, turning their attention to foreign visitors.

According to what one of the journos hanging around the hotel lobby told Neil, there was a clinic within walking distance. Tucked away in a narrow side alley, the place was marginally safer from being bulldozed by army vehicles, but there were hundreds of injured students waiting to be seen. Every corner reeked of blood and antiseptic.

Neil and Hema stuck close to Lilah, as did Victor who was taking the first turn as guard. Several others in the crowds packing the hallways were clearly tourists. The staff tended to the more seriously injured first, and there were many, many wounded young people. God, so many!

The clock on the wall told Lilah two hours passed since she gave her fake name at the registration desk. Tumult from the streets continued to echo into the building as protesting citizens were plowed down by their own government. The poor students...

their only mistake was to demand the freedoms which should've been their birthright. Their families... *God*, Lilah prayed. The last time the Kingsleys attempted an attack on her, they kept her twin trapped in an airport holding cell on allegations of terrorism. Who knew what the plan was this time? Dan *had* to be alive. Harry *had* to be safe. The handful of people awaiting the return of the exiles... were they all right? Were they watching the news in terror, worrying if their loved ones could be caught in the madness in Beijing?

Four hours... five... six... the side alley might be too narrow for the tanks to get to, but men in military uniform marched in and out. Each time the soldiers showed up, each time they snapped orders at the clinic staff, Lilah's insides coiled into a painfully tight ball. Sweat trickled down her temples. At her side, Hema was visibly stiff, slumping back into her seat only when the soldiers left. The Nepali girl's ponytail was askew, her eyes still red-rimmed.

"Do you need more painkiller?" Neil whispered from the chair on Lilah's right, producing a blister pack from his pocket. The surgeon seemed to carry an unlimited supply of various medicines. Watching her swallowing a pill *sans* water, he added, "Little consolation, but Drummond's gonna suffer in more ways than one."

There was a peculiar note in Neil's tone. Lilah frowned. It had taken him half an hour to find this clinic, during which time his brothers secured Drummond in the room. The prospect of them beating up the criminal further was next to nil. Big brother already declared it over, and his word was sacrosanct to the younger ones.

Before she could ask for an explanation, Neil continued, "The son of a bitch... can't believe he dared show up here himself. I would've thought he'd send another thug like the one in the square."

From his seat on Hema's other side, Victor leaned close. Keeping decibel level low, he said, "Drummond's always been bad news... especially where women are concerned. I've heard a couple of stories around DC. My best guess is he thought he could get away with it. Even if it was proved Lilah was... ahh... assaulted before she died, who would've been left to speak for us? Mr. Temple can't say *any*thing, and whatever Drummond meant about the trap for Harry... Steven and his buddies won't give a damn about what anyone else has to say, including Lilah's family."

"I'm just glad we found you on time," Neil said to her.

"So am I." Blinking on a sudden thought, Lilah asked, "Actually, how *did* you find me?"

Neil gestured with his head toward her former intern. "Hema was trying to catch up with you and saw the whole thing. She was behind you all the way until Drummond dragged you into this room. Then, she dashed back to get the rest of us."

"I told you I could help," said Hema.

Lilah gaped. "You... my God, Hema! If Drummond spotted you..." She would have been his next victim after Lilah. Drummond would've relished every bit of pain he could inflict on either woman. "That's it. First thing we do after getting out of Beijing is putting you on a flight back the States."

Mouth drooping, Hema asked, "Don't you want me around?"

"What I want is immaterial. I told you before... you're not safe with me."

"*You* weren't safe when that other terrible fellow attacked me." The rapist who assaulted Hema during the corporate event in Panama happened on her only in his search for Lilah, but there was no question the young intern would also have perished. "I didn't see you running away. So I'm not going anywhere, either."

"But you shouldn't sacrifice yourself like this—"

"It's not a sacrifice. You always do the right thing, Lilah. So why shouldn't I do the same? I'm gonna be with you until we win this fight."

Win this... Lilah couldn't guarantee *she* would stay alive to declare victory. How was she supposed to protect... "Hema, listen to reason," Lilah pleaded.

"I *am* being reasonable," the intern insisted. "Besides, your brothers haven't given up on you. So why are you asking me to? Mr. Dan would've been here if he didn't need to do stuff for you back in America. You *know* he would. It's the same for me. Lilah... you're the only family I..." Flushing, the girl added, "I know I'm not but..."

Lilah's heart squeezed. "To me, family means love and trust and support. So yes, you *are* family. But I still don't have the right to ask you to die for me."

"If you meant what you said, then you should understand why I want to be here," Hema said, her tone turning mutinous. "Imagine simply going back to New York after what just happened. Thank God I was around to get help!" Careful to avoid the injured shoulder, she wrapped her thin arms around Lilah. "You're fine," said the Nepali girl. "I'm so glad you're fine."

"Shh," said Victor, his eyes darting toward the end of the hallway.

Three soldiers this time. Saying something in loud and irate voices, one of them gestured at the employees transporting a patient with a blood-soaked bandage clutched to his belly. The injured victim didn't appear Chinese. Sandy hair, lean frame... he vaguely resembled Shawn, Lilah's adopted brother.

Heaving up from the chair, Victor moved a couple of feet away to slouch against the wall, concealing the women and Neil from the soldiers. Everyone in the waiting area was watching the interrogation of the dying man. If the soldiers turned their attention to the other foreigners... the exiles couldn't even walk out without drawing notice.

A middle-aged fellow in scrubs showed up and snapped at the employees, motioning them to move the patient into the interior of the clinic. The uniform-clad men conferred among themselves before heading out.

The pattern repeated over and over and over. There was always someone more grievously wounded, someone in dire need of immediate medical attention. Those with minor injuries like Lilah's continued their endless wait. Soldiers walked in and out, a couple of them wounded themselves.

Darkness descended outside the windows at the far end. Night was well underway when Alex relieved Victor. "What's the situation in the hotel?" Lilah asked, nibbling on the candy bar Alex brought along. "The guests?"

He hesitated for a second before answering. "Everyone's getting ready to leave. We do have until daybreak. The rest of the group will be waiting for us in the lobby."

Nodding, she glanced at the clock for the thousandth time— past midnight. Shifting in the uncomfortable chair, Lilah winced. The painkiller was wearing off, reminding her again of what Drummond would've done to her if Hema didn't spot what was going on. The girl could've paid a huge price for her loyalty. She could've died with Lilah today.

The possibility of death had been real to Lilah for years. She became aware of it when Jared Sanders, the tyrant ruler of the oil sector, ordered her and Harry kidnapped. For Sanders, the teens were mere pawns to be sacrificed. The lowly pieces fought back, this time choosing to risk their lives by joining hands with the Kingsleys in an insurrection. The new empress clashed with Godwin Kingsley over the control of the alliance, leading to this exile. Danger pursued her and Harry, but they knowingly and purposefully took the path to war. How could they take chances with the lives of innocents like Hema?

More bloodied protestors straggled in. The girl limping to the registration desk looked nothing like Sabrina, but for a second... Lilah blinked. Worry and fatigue were causing her mind to play tricks on itself. She was starting to picture the faces of her loved ones on the wounded. Not only Harry and Dan, every single person who supported the exiles was in danger. They at least had personal stake in this deadly campaign Lilah waged. The others... the random people who helped the exiles, knowingly or otherwise... she was risking all their lives. Hema believed Lilah always did the right thing, but how could the war she declared be in any way right or just if it ended up sacrificing the same people she claimed to speak for?

There was the private who testified for Lilah in Cuba. She never gave another thought to him until now. The Kingsleys and their minions in the military could do plenty of harm to the poor fellow if they felt so inclined. Victor's contact helped the six people on the run from the American government cross the border to Ecuador. What would happen to that young man called Darwin if the narco traffickers found out what he did? Was his life less valuable than those of the exiles?

Closing her eyes briefly, Lilah bit her lip. It wasn't as though the perils of war were dawning on her for the first time. It wasn't as though she could afford to surrender and let the Kingsleys rule the world. The horror of what was going on in the city and guilt over could've happened to Hema were causing this sudden deluge of doubts. *Harry,* Lilah murmured in her mind. *I wish I could talk to you.* If she could make sure he was all right, that everyone back home was alive and well, then perhaps the storm within her would begin to calm.

Alex was in the chair next to Lilah's, his eyes on a small child sleeping on his father's shoulder. There was a wistful smile on the former sniper's face.

"Did we get anything else out of Drummond?" Lilah asked in a hushed whisper. "About Harry, I mean."

"All we could make out was he's alive," said Alex, turning his attention to her. "There was also something about Will Luce, Verity's dad."

"Huh?" Lilah frowned. What did Harry's former father-in-law have anything to do with it?

"Doesn't make sense," Neil said. "Drummond was probably babbling. He was barely conscious when I—" Oddly, the surgeon flushed, and the strange note was back in his voice.

"Good," Hema said, the single word packed with revulsion. "It means the stupid fellow won't escape."

"He won't," Alex agreed. "Victor rigged the door before he came to the clinic with you, and we... ahh... used the restraints Drummond brought for you. The key was on the floor. Sonuvabitch will stay cuffed to the bed until we alert someone." An anonymous phone call would do the trick.

"We also sh—" Neil started.

Alex coughed.

"You what?" Lilah asked.

"We... umm... shaved him," said Neil, the flush on his face intensifying. "I didn't want to, but they made me do it."

Lilah asked, "What d'you mean you—"

"Excuse me?" called a nurse.

The X-ray confirmed Lilah's shoulder was broken. Her collarbone to be precise. On the stretcher next to hers, a soldier who could barely be out of his teens was getting treated for a scalp wound. He and his comrade paid no mind to the exiles, but neither did the duo show any signs of leaving. The group of Americans talked as little as possible, pretending to be napping most of the time. Alex sat on the floor with his back against a wall, his eyes seemingly closed but hand resting close to where his ankle holster would be. Ten minutes... fifteen minutes... an hour... two hours... the sky outside the windows was just lightening when the doctor showed up to let Lilah know only a sling was needed and not a cast. It would be her second one on the same arm after the elbow injury she suffered when the rapist attacked her in Panama.

Grimy and exhausted, the exiles waited until a group of other patients were exiting the building. Joining the outbound stream of men and women, they got to the entrance of the hotel.

#

Pockets of journalists milled about the lobby, and the decibel level remained high. The rest of the exiles were gathered in the near-right corner as arranged, packed bags in hand.

Lilah sighed in her mind. The risk of capture would remain high until they were out of China... or at least the capital city. Despite every attempt, these five men could never completely fade into the background in Beijing. All were tall and sported dark beards. Neil, too, grew facial hair, but his was blond, a bandana covering his head. Only Scott and Brad wore glasses, and only Alex had the peculiarly translucent brown eyes as opposed to his brothers' blue. Brad's face was currently thunderous.

"What's going on?" Lilah asked Alex, but he was already headed toward his waiting family. "Neil? Do you know?"

"I think Brad heard about Drummond," Neil said, his cheeks once again red.

Lilah halted in the middle of the lobby. "Come clean... what did you do?"

Neil threw his hands in the air. "Like Alex said, we left him handcuffed to the bed."

"And shaved him."

"Umm... yes."

"Go on."

Neil gulped. "We didn't shave his face or his... umm... actual head."

It took a couple of seconds to sink in. Lilah gaped. "You left him—"

"With smoother plumbing than the day he was born." Victor said in a low voice, dragging the luggage toward her. An unrepentant smile adorned his face.

"And just as naked," Alex added, following Victor. "The pink bows on his head were the final touch." Brad and Scott joined the group. "Once the pics hit the papers back home," continued Alex, "Representative Jack Drummond will be known more for his games in the bedroom. I doubt his constituents are going to be happy."

The men—except Brad—laughed silently, their shaking shoulders and ruddy faces revealing how tremendously pleased with themselves they were. Hema's tittering added to the merriment.

Heat exploding in her brain, Lilah shouted, "Were you out of your ever-loving minds?" The noise in the lobby ebbed as the occupants turned toward them.

"Lilah," started Victor. "We wiped the room down. No one gonna know—"

"They just now told me what they did," ground out Brad, "I wasn't around or—"

"Shh," Alex said. Placing a soothing hand on Lilah's shoulder, he urged her toward the exit. "We'll talk outside."

Chest heaving in anger, she shrugged off the hand. Sharp pain radiated across the broken bone. In a lower tone, she said, "You just humiliated the man... the entire world is going to find out no matter how privately you tip off the cops. You destroyed his marriage, his career, his future. He will never, ever forget it."

"After what Drummond tried to do you," Victor said, "we *want* him to remember. There's an added benefit. Now, even if he claims we beat him up, no one's going to believe it. Everyone's going to think he's trying to cover up what he was actually doing in China."

"He wouldn't have said anything about us because Steven wouldn't want him to," Lilah said, thoughts whirling. "Why would you do something so—"

Neil stammered, "We know Drummond's a congressm—"

"He's a criminal," she snapped. "A criminal willing to rape and kill, but he was only following Steven's orders. It would've been better if you simply broke Drummond's neck at the end of your stupid prank. We could've argued it wasn't us... something went wrong in the middle of his kinky games." If they returned to the room now to do the deed, the others in the lobby were likely to remember. It wasn't possible. "Now you've made it personal *and* left him alive. You made sure Drummond's going to return for revenge. Mark my words... we will all regret this day."

One more to add to the long list of villains to hide from—Steven, Godwin, Prince, now the rapist congressman. More danger lying in wait for the exiles and the people who helped them. More bloodshed.

"Let's worry about it later," said Alex. "We need to get out of here."

Not trusting herself to say anything further, Lilah marched to the exit. The rest of the group followed.

Within minutes, they were on their way out of the square, making sure to stay with the crowds at all times and out of sight of TV crews. As they got to Chang'an Avenue, Victor nodded at the column of oncoming army vehicles. "Careful. They're mowing down everyone who gets in the way."

Bright sunlight beat harshly down on the streets. Mostly silent, the citizens of Beijing watched as the tanks rolled along. One man walked out to the middle of the road, carrying a shopping bag. He stood in front of the approaching military vehicles, arms spread wide.

Television cameras whirred. "What's happening?" the news anchor asked the field reporter in confusion. The lead tank attempted to go around the lone protestor. He jogged to the side and blocked their way again. The engines stopped. The army's move was brought to a halt.

Lilah couldn't take her eyes off the man. He looked like a regular chap, perhaps out buying groceries. His clothes weren't stained with dirt and blood. Nor did he appear tired and haggard. There was little likelihood he'd been part of the night's demonstrations. Yet here he was, ready to fight right when failure was imminent.

As he was being removed from the scene, Alex said in an awed tone, "He stopped the goddamn Chinese military. On his own!"

"For about five minutes," said Brad. "What good did it do?"

"He'll pay the price for playing the hero," Victor agreed. "What d'you wanna bet no one's going to see him again?"

Neither Neil nor Scott said anything, continuing to watch in solemn silence. Folded hands held to her mouth, Hema mumbled something in Hindi—a prayer. Her lashes glinted with tears.

Lilah wiped the sudden wetness from her own cheeks. *Be all right*, she murmured in her mind. *Please be all right.*

#

Under the cover of the crowds, Lilah trudged alongside Hema and the Kingsley brothers, only half-listening to their muted discussion. Scott asked once if she were tired, but Lilah merely shrugged in response. Sleep would be a long time coming even if they found a safe place to curl up in.

She simply couldn't get the scene from the square out of her mind. The solitary protestor surely knew he could've died in excruciating pain, crushed under the wheels of a tank. His future promised to be filled with trauma, every living moment a punishment for supporting the students. Yet he chose to go down fighting for them. Would the young men and women condone the sacrifice? Would they have stopped him if they knew what he planned?

A three-hour trek under the blazing hot sun led the exiles to Wudaokou, where the universities were located. Students and international visitors were absent from the neighborhood, with military patrolling the streets. The restaurants, the seedy bars... everything was closed. It took several tries, but at the back door of one of the bars, Alex found a likely prospect.

"We need to get to Kashgar," he said to a sketchy-looking fellow. The town was in Xinjiang province, not far from Soviet territory. Money exchanged hands. "Half the cash now; half at the end."

Three more hours of walking later, the group reached the outskirts of the city where a dented and scratched van waited, its driver the same sketchy character from the bar.

The brothers took turns keeping watch on the ride. Resting her cheek against the glass window, Lilah watched the mostly arid landscape fly past. The driver avoided highways, sometimes taking the van through roads barely wide enough to fit the vehicle. The sleepy little towns where they stopped for gas and food and bathroom breaks hardly had any military presence, with the Chinese government's attention currently fixed on the nation's hotspots.

In three days, the van screeched to a halt outside the dusty slums of Kashgar. Even as he drove off, the driver refused to give them his name, which made Victor doubly sure the vehicle—with its mud-coated license plate—was stolen.

While young people shed blood on the streets of Beijing for their countrymen, one of those same men took advantage of the chaos to make himself a bit of cash. Yet another ordinary citizen showed the courage to put himself in harm's way in support of the students. Their protest was on behalf of all their compatriots, good and bad. The students stood up for regular people who were never given a voice. Their cause was democracy, and their war was just. Except one of those voiceless innocents might be dead by now, killed in a conflict being fought in his name.

Part II

Chapter 5

Earlier

New York, New York

The phone call from Gateway's DC office two days ago about a tanker accident involving one of the deals brokered by Liam had sent him running to the Jeddah Port. To his abject relief, the horrific visions of dead and injured crew failed to materialize, and the puzzled seller informed him the accident required only minor repair work. The vessel had set sail even before Liam landed in Saudi Arabia.

Crediting the mix-up to overzealous junior employees, Liam returned home. When he got to his apartment, he found two policemen waiting in the quiet hallway outside the door.

"Mr. William Luce?" asked one of the cops.

"I go by Liam. But yeah, I'm William Luce. What can I do you for, officers?" Whatever it was, Liam hoped it would be quick. He was sweaty and tired, in need of a shower and a long nap. And some food.

The cop asked, "May we speak inside?"

Frowning, Liam nodded. This was surely about Harry's efforts to bring the exiles home. "Do I need a lawyer?" he asked, only half joking as he unlocked the door and gestured the cops in.

"No, sir," said the second officer. "Please sit."

Bad news. Liam immediately knew it was bad news.

"We regret to inform you..." began the first cop. Will Luce, Liam's father, was dead. Stabbed in the back. And no, they didn't have further information on who or why. Yes, they did have a "person of interest" but couldn't disclose anything else at the moment.

"Has my sister been told?" Liam asked, tone abrupt.

"No, sir," said the policeman. "Since she lives in New York, we did think about contacting her, but we were informed you were probably the best person to be first notified."

"Informed by who?"

The cop hesitated. "Her ex-husband."

Still in shock, Liam didn't think to inquire how Harry had been advised of the death before Will Luce's own children. The next few hours were a blur for Liam... calling work to let his boss know, grabbing a few clean clothes, praying no one got to Verity before he did.

The answering machine was blinking. Almost automatically, he jabbed the button and deleted everything unimportant. Lupe's voice came on. "Liam? *Merde!*" The curse was the entirety of the message. He frowned. For some reason, he didn't erase it.

Even after landing in New York, it didn't occur to Liam to contact his former brother-in-law. Verity took precedence. Liam *needed* to see his sister, to make sure she was all right.

She simply refused to believe the news. Verity made call after frantic call to their father's number and begged his card buddies to check his usual haunts. Sitting on her couch, Liam held his head in his hands and sobbed. When the landline rang, Verity snatched it. Before she could finish saying hello, muffled words came from the receiver.

Her face went white. Without even a squeak, she stood still, holding the phone in her hand.

Liam leaped to his feet and grabbed the receiver. "Who's this?" he snapped.

"Brooklyn police," came a steady voice. "We're trying to reach Mr. Liam Luce... some updates on the matter of his father's death."

Verity's shoulders shook. With a loud wail, she collapsed against her brother's chest. Liam only half heard the cop on the line stating he'd be at the apartment later with some critical information.

Police reports said Harry insisted Lupe called him with a message to meet his former father-in-law, Will Luce, at the address where his corpse was discovered. Liam's friendship with Lupe was known to everyone connected with the club, so the detectives wanted his take on it. He didn't have one. Liam just didn't understand any of it.

While there *were* a couple of calls from the club to Harry's number, no one could corroborate his claim about the content of the message Lupe conveyed. The woman in question was missing. Investigators found a rope made out of sheets hanging from her bedroom window, but Liam didn't get why she needed to sneak out of her own home. Her IDs were also missing. The working assumption was she'd fled the country, her disappearance somehow connected to the murder in Brooklyn.

Harry couldn't be detained any longer without actually being arrested, and the police needed to complete their investigation before throwing anyone in prison. From what Liam understood, Noah Andersen and the former president hustled Harry out and were already working on a defense.

"You got it all wrong," Liam finally managed to say to the detective in the apartment. Verity sat next to him, still pale, still sobbing into a handkerchief. "Harry didn't do it. Lupe wouldn't... she would never..." She'd been Liam's friend for more than a decade. Also, while Luce, Sr. could test the patience of a saint, and Harry was no saint, he didn't have any motive to kill his father-in-law.

The detective sighed. "There is some question of embezzlement." In a few short sentences, he told the siblings about certain financial documents found in Will Luce's Connecticut residence.

"My father was stealing?" Liam asked, shocked to the core. "From Gateway?"

"Yes," said the detective. "We believe Sheppard knew when he went to meet your father. They argued, perhaps. And Mr. Luce ended up dead."

As though the visits from the cops and the trips to the district attorney's office weren't enough, attorneys from Gateway called to consult. The meeting was more like an interrogation with lawyers probing the Luce siblings about the embezzlement.

In the days since the murder, every newspaper in the land and every TV channel discussed it *ad nauseum*. The media shadowed Verity's every move, shoving microphones at her frightened face the minute she stepped outside her luxury apartment. Pictures of her were plastered all over the tabloids, showing the gray-blue eyes she inherited from her father puffy from crying and her platinum-blonde hair disheveled.

Liam dealt with legal formalities and press sideshows every day, returning to stay in his sister's home at her request. She needed... *they* needed the familiarity of each other's company. *Dad... dead... murdered.* By Harry. Sometimes, Liam felt as though he were caught in a nightmare.

#

Next week

Liam pushed through the crowd in front of the Fifth Avenue building where his sister lived, doing his best to ignore the cameras and the shouted questions from journalists. The condo board meeting would start in minutes. Under normal course of events, the board would have made life difficult for the residents bringing unwanted media attention, and left to her own devices, Verity would only have quarreled with the management. *Unsuccessfully* quarreled. Verity's brother reminded the condo board members not so subtly that she was a very wealthy woman and cajoled them into hiring extra security to keep the press and assorted gawkers out. Finding a new home was pressure Verity did not need at the moment.

On their way out of the meeting, Verity whispered, "Let's go to the apartment. There's someone..."

Even before the elevator left the floor, she unlocked her front door and practically dragged him in.

"Wha—"

On the couch was a green-eyed blonde—Sabrina, Harry's sister. Her son was next to her, reading a children's book, *The Polar Express*. The kid was the spitting image of his uncle, except for light-brown gaze which he got from his dad, Alex. Tear tracks stained Sabrina's cheeks. Warily, Liam nodded at her and managed a smile for the boy. He heard Verity shut the door behind them.

"Liam," Sabrina said, wasting no time on preliminaries. "Harry left for DC this morning. He said you weren't picking up his calls, so he asked me to talk to you in person. You need to fly there to meet him. Immediately."

Shaking his head, Liam said, "Sabrina, I'm sorry. But we've been advised not to—"

"No, Liam," she interrupted. "You *have* to go to DC. It's about Lupe Valdez. They found her body."

Chapter 6

Next morning

Washington, DC

"Mr. Sheppard," called a voice.

Harry hadn't been asleep, but he jolted in his seat.

A woman dressed in an austere black suit stood at the door to the waiting room in the morgue, her eyes kindly. The tags clipped to her lapel proclaimed her as an employee. "Are you ready for the identification process," she asked, "or would you prefer to wait for Mr. Liam Luce?"

"Liam should be here any minute. I... uhh..."

Harry couldn't do it on his own. Not when he spent the hours he was detained in the precinct mentally casting Lupe in the role of traitor. Over and over and over, he'd asked the detectives to call Lupe, but they wouldn't.

"Why did you go to the particular building, Mr. Sheppard?" the cop asked.

"For the hundredth time," Harry ground out, "I got a message to meet Will there."

The second officer took a sip from his coffee mug and made notes with his other hand. "So your ex-father-in-law called you—"

"No, he didn't. As I said to your colleague, he called Eden."

"The club in DC?"

"Once again, yes. Contact Lupe... Ms. Valdez. I don't understand why you can't. She will corroborate what I said. Dammit, why are you wasting time instead of talking to her?" Or was she a part of this all along? Did Harry allow himself to be fooled by her sad background, missing the callous greed in her heart?

Noah had called the club, but the manager claimed she was nowhere to be found. Nowhere to be found or hiding? It didn't matter. Harry swore he would hunt her down himself. He wanted to hear her excuses for doing this, for sending him into the enemy's trap. Her cronies made the anonymous call which brought the police to the apartment door minutes after Harry walked in. He trusted Lupe, but she betrayed him. Because of her, Lilah was in danger. Noah and Grayson tried again and again to contact the exiles, but not one call went through. Were they alive? Or was Lilah already killed by the Kingsleys?

"But she called, Harry," Sabrina said, her eyes clouded by fear. "The minute you walked out."

Harry had planned to spend only a couple of minutes at his apartment, reassuring his sister and her son, before leaving for Temple's home to talk to the lawyer hired by Noah. But this new info... Harry shook his head in confusion. "You mean Lupe called after I left to meet Verity's father?"

"Yes!"

A sense of wrongness... dread... the rising awareness of enemy action on a third front. Harry dialed the number of the club and asked to speak to one of the girls. The manager wasn't covering for Lupe. She really was missing.

DC cops didn't want to hear what Harry said. They didn't care Lupe never before left the premises without handing charge to someone she trusted.

Chaos reigned over the next few days. A message arrived notifying Harry about the emergency meeting of the network's board, called by the CEO, Steven Kingsley, to discuss the legal predicaments of its current chairman. Harry would be ousted from chairmanship, of course. Grayson kept trying to make contact with the exiles. There were no direct inquiries from Gateway, but Dante—the company's chief operating officer—brought news he and the other executives were inundated with calls from board members and stockholders. As Harry's older brother, Hector was taking the brunt of it. Far-flung relatives—even those Sheppards who held mere handfuls of shares—forcefully offered their opinion on the man who was suspected of murder. Sharks were circling at the first scent of blood, all of them sensing a chance for payback for every imagined slight from Harry and the unfair advantage he benefited from according to them, including his marriage to Verity.

Harry couldn't bring himself to care about any of it. Calling everyone he knew in DC about Lupe... calling Grayson every few minutes for any update on Lilah... under no circumstances was Harry to leave the country in search of her, Noah ordered. All it would accomplish was to add one more excuse the authorities could use to take official action against him.

Then, Grayson showed up at the apartment. Lilah's twin and her adopted brother were with the lawyer.

"...Congressman Drummond..." Amid the other horrific news from Beijing, there was a snippet in the mainstream papers which noted the presence of the Kingsley son-in-law in the city. Jack Drummond was caught in a hotel under unsavory circumstances. His pictures were in nearly all the tabloids, triggering calls for the politician to resign. Grayson didn't need to say it out loud. The bastard went to Beijing in search of Lilah.

Red hot rage blurred Harry's vision. He barely heard Grayson's insistent voice reminding him if Drummond managed to kill Lilah, the Kingsleys would've made sure those back home heard about it. Even knowing their plan, Harry wouldn't have been able to stop himself from going for Godwin Kingsley's throat. Harry would have been dead before he reached within ten feet of the former justice. With the murder of Will Luce ostensibly at Harry's hands, no one would believe anything he said previously about the Kingsleys being responsible for the assassination attempt on Temple. They would escape blame for Lilah's murder, and Harry's death would be dismissed as a tragic event brought about by his own violent insanity.

"No news is good news," said Grayson. "It means she's alive." He coughed. "Also, the photographs."

The pictures surely meant Alex and his brothers already exacted vengeance on Drummond for what he tried to do to Lilah.

"Son of a bitch," ground out Dan, Lilah's twin. "He should be dead."

Next to him on the couch, Shawn nodded agreement. Sabrina was sobbing out loud. Eyes on the thin silver chain wrapped around his wrist, Harry willed his beloved to stay safe.

One question still remained... where was Lupe? The phone rang the next morning with the answer. She had bled to her death, her corpse stuffed in a trash bag and left for city workers to take to a landfill. The stiletto heel of her shoe poked through the plastic bag, exposing her leg, or her body might never have been found.

Dead? Lupe? Harry didn't believe... he didn't *want* to believe... asking Sabrina to contact Liam, Harry flew to DC and drove straight to the morgue.

The waiting room was restfully furnished, but who could rest in there? Who could take a deep breath? The attendant who talked to Harry before returned in ten minutes to offer him a glass of water, but he declined. Goddamit, where was Liam?

Right when the lady was turning to leave, there was a shuffling noise at the door. Liam walked in, taking a seat as far away from Harry as possible. Harry nodded but didn't attempt to speak. The morgue attendant introduced herself to Liam and told him someone else would be along shortly to help them.

The two men sat in tense stillness for several minutes. Verity's brother resembled her in appearance but not at all in personality. Poor Verity... the divorce, her father's death...

Breaking the silence, Liam asked, "Why did you need me? You're Lupe's—"

"She never wanted anyone to know we got married, so until it becomes absolutely necessary, we'll keep it quiet," Harry said, tone low. He'd asked Grayson to inform Lilah and Alex only because he didn't want them hearing it from anyone else. The news would of course leak to the public at some point, but Harry preferred to postpone the inevitability. Not only to honor Lupe's wishes. He needed to get a clearer picture of the enemy's plot first.

"The cops must know about it already," Liam argued. "Or they wouldn't have contacted you."

"They didn't. They went to the club. Nikki tried to reach both of us and got me first. I thought as Lupe's friend, she'd want you here."

"Mr. Luce?" a softly feminine voice called. "Mr. Sheppard?"

The grief counselor was sympathetic when she explained to them the process of identification and the steps involved before the body could be released for burial. Harry took the clipboard she handed to them. There was a photograph on it, face-down. The counselor let them know Lupe's face would appear bloated, and they would see a knife wound across her throat.

The edge of the photograph was between Harry's thumb and forefinger when Liam said, "Wait. You're not sure, right? Or you wouldn't need us to identify."

Eyes warm, the counselor said the police believed it was Lupe. The identification process was merely a formality at this point.

Without responding, Liam stared hard at the counselor, scratching his unshaven jaw.

"Do you need more time?" asked the counselor.

"Time won't make it any easier," said Liam, swallowing hard.

Harry turned the picture over. As warned, Lupe's face was bloated, and there was a linear wound across her throat, the color an angry red. Her lips were twisted into a smile as though mocking her killer. She died as she lived, defiant to the last second.

Something within Harry crumpled. Sobs tore out of his chest, tears staining the photograph on the clipboard. While he'd been accusing her of treachery, she was lying dead in a dumpster. She sacrificed her life trying to warn him of the danger waiting in the Brooklyn apartment.

Vaguely, he was aware of Liam's harsh weeping, of the grief counselor asking for help. When Nikki called Harry's name, he looked up. The staff apparently contacted the strippers, not knowing how else to get the men out. Stumbling through the door of the chief medical examiner's office, they were greeted by camera flashes, but the questions of the media went unanswered. Harry had no recollection of the ride to Eden or how he got to Lupe's office. He didn't have any idea how long the staff left him and Liam there.

When Nikki returned, Harry was almost surprised to find himself in Lupe's chair. Liam was on the couch by the basement level window.

"The girls want to know," Nikki started, settling into the seat across the desk. Her face was pale, dark circles surrounding her eyes. "What's going to happen to the club?"

Liam sat up, his gaze darting to Harry.

"I..." Harry willed himself to think coherently. Decisions needed to be made. Most of Lupe's employees didn't have any place else to go. "First thing to do is contact her lawyer, but we'll have the manager close the club for a couple of weeks. Where *is* the manager?"

"He's not much help," Nikki said, sniffling. "The fellow didn't want to go to... to identify. He said he was too scared even to go to the morgue to get you. The chief of security told me he and the guards will stay as long as we need, but they're all pretty shook by what happened. A few of the waiters left already."

"After only one week?" Harry asked.

Tone turning awkward, Nikki explained, "They didn't get paid because... umm... Lupe pays them every Friday... used to."

"The waiters come and go, anyway," Liam interjected. "It's not unusual. The security chief... it was under his watch... I get why he's upset. I don't understand about the manager. He's been around since the club first started."

In the end, the manager—a slender man with a Clark Gable mustache and dyed hair slicked back to resemble the actor—said he'd already put in for social security and wanted to retire as soon as possible. Death scared him. He simply didn't want to deal with it.

As the manager walked out, followed by Nikki, Harry frowned. "What do you think?" he asked Liam.

"You mean is it suspicious? Maybe... maybe not... but what *you* did is a lot worse."

Shaking his head, Harry said, "Tell me what I did."

"You wanted access to the club and ended up married to Lupe. You found out my father was stealing from Gateway and arranged to meet him in Brooklyn. You somehow got Lupe to work with you. Maybe you tricked her into it, but she died before she could corroborate your cover."

"If you really believed what you just said," stated Harry, "you wouldn't be in this office alone with me. What if I attacked *you*? Liam, you know damn well it wasn't me. So does Verity. Or why would she let my sister into her apartment?"

Staring hard, Liam stayed silent.

"I didn't know about the embezzlement until the cops told me," Harry tried to explain. "I'd assumed... you've heard the gossip about my argument with Hector. Even if I did know it was your father, not Hector, there were better ways to deal with it. Let's say I did flip out for whatever reason and either went there prepared to kill Will... or it happened in the heat of the moment. My tactical knife—the Ari B'Lilah—is still with the cops because I used it in the Parker incident."

It seemed eons since the fateful night when the network's members first gathered to choose the board and the chairman. The rapist who once assaulted Lilah mounted another attack in the enemy's attempt to kill Harry. Not even a full year had gone by after, and the authorities were still holding on to the weapons they collected as evidence. Harry got himself a new gun but was stubbornly waiting for his beloved knife to be returned.

Harry continued, "So the theory would be somewhere between the time the cops took the blade from me and the night of your father's death, I got myself another knife. But I was carrying my new SIG when the police found me in the apartment. Why would I use the knife when I had a better weapon?"

"A gun would be more traceable," Liam recited. "All you'd need to do with a new knife is wear gloves... or wipe off prints. If you weren't found in the room, no one would've ever known."

"The cops are trying out their shitty theory on you," Harry snapped. "So where are the gloves? Or whatever I used to wipe down the crime scene?" As expected, the investigators couldn't find Harry's fingerprints anywhere in the apartment except along the wall where the light switch was. He never touched anything else with his hands. Noah speculated the cops would argue Harry's training as a SEAL and his rumored work with the CIA meant he'd know how to avoid leaving prints. Whatever he couldn't escape handling—like the knife hilt—a few moments would be enough to clean. Perhaps he used tissue and disposed of it someplace untraceable. Perhaps he flushed it down the toilet. In the septic tank of a big apartment building, such evidence wouldn't be found. Still, crime scene analysts were checking for traces of any tissue. The moment they discovered something, they'd conclude Harry was to blame regardless of the fact any murderer with an ounce of sense could've used the same method. "Please don't blindly believe what they claim," Harry begged.

"I don't know what the hell to—" Liam groaned. "I don't *want* to believe. All of this... my God... the last ten days have been un-fucking-real. You, Dad, Lupe..."

"Yeah, Lupe," said Harry. "How long were you friends? Remember what you know about her. Remember what you know about *me*. If I were to kill someone, I'd make sure he sees my face as he died. I'd want to tell him exactly why he was being killed. I would not stab anyone in the back. Literally or metaphorically."

On the couch by the window, Liam leaned forward to stare hard at Harry.

"Also, Lupe," Harry continued. "Do you believe she would've betrayed your friendship by plotting with me to kill your father?"

Seconds ticked by. "No," Liam finally admitted, voice gravelly. "And she was too damn shrewd to be tricked into it."

"I'm sorry about what happened," Harry said. "But your father was only a pawn in the plan against Brad and his brothers."

"What do you mean?"

"Think about it. Temple cannot do a thing about getting a pardon for Brad. Gateway already stopped me from selling stock to raise money to help Alex and the rest." They were presumed traitors, after all. The Barrons board used the same excuse with Dan. "The press conference Noah and I did was supposed to be insurance against any more attacks on me."

Harry and the former attorney general levelled charges against the Kingsleys, claiming they were behind the chaos at the board meeting in Panama which culminated in the assault on Lilah and the death of the rapist. Then, there was the arrest of the Kingsley brothers and the attack on Harry. Finally, the attempted assassination of President Temple. With the cloud of suspicion hovering over Steven Kingsley, he and his buddies wouldn't have dared try their luck yet another time at eliminating Harry. Not until the media—and the public—forgot all about the Kingsleys and the Sheppards and the Barronses.

Harry had planned to use the reprieve to collect information through Eden's Angels. He would use the evidence to force lawmakers to see things his way. They would see the wisdom in granting a pardon to Brad.

"Now, my credibility's been shot," Harry pointed out. "Even if I try to use the info we got from Eden, no damn politician will care because the public will take whatever I say with a pinch of salt. The pardon's not happening any time soon. Steven Kingsley is hunting Brad and Lilah as we speak. If I try to leave the country to help them in some way, I'll be caught. Killed by the cops in the process, most likely. If the Kingsleys find Lilah, they'll kill her, and they'll have security waiting for my counterattack. If neither of these scenarios happen, they'll simply wait me out."

"The Kingsleys can't kill you right away if you don't give them some sort of opening by trying to leave or by mounting a counterstrike," Liam said, awareness dawning in his eyes. "Without a good excuse for your death, the public might go right back to what you said at the press conference. But time is now on *their* side since you can't do shit about a pardon. They'll use the opportunity to set the scene for your death some other way."

Harry nodded. "If the police feel they have enough evidence against me, I'll be arrested. Even if they don't, the Kingsleys will make sure the media plays up your father's case. What do you want to bet there will be plenty of readers who decide I'm guilty? No one will believe it if I claim Steven's behind Will's murder. Every paper in the country will jump to conclusion I'm only trying to get out of trouble. Public opinion will continue to shift away from me. Things will get to a point where what I said at the press conference will be dismissed even if I end up dead—even if all the exiles end up dead."

Lilah would be targeted the same time as Harry. If he were to be killed first, she and the five brothers would know there would never be a pardon. Lilah would return, perhaps accompanied by one or more of Brad's brothers since there was no evidence against them. Attacking her on American soil might bring attention back to what Harry said at the press conference, so the enemy wouldn't dare touch her. She would fight them in court... if the Kingsleys allowed her to return. No, she'd go the same time as Harry and the five brothers, perhaps dying in a convenient accident in some corner of the world where the officials could easily be bribed into looking the other way.

"One madman who already killed someone, a few traitors," murmured Liam. "Who's going to give a damn? And Lupe? Was it coincidence?"

"Got to be the Kingsleys." Standing, Harry shoved the swivel chair back with all the savagery in his mind. It hit the wall behind with a thump and crashed to the floor. When he turned to right the damned thing, he came face to face with the icon of Virgin Mary. The statue was still shuddering from the force of the collision between the piece of furniture and the wall. The votive candle in front was lit as always. Harry stared at the serene face of the mother of God for a second. Did the deity witness what happened to poor Lupe? The figure stopped vibrating and settled in a slightly lopsided position. As though...

"But why would the Kingsleys—" asked Liam. "I don't get it."

Putting the chair back in place, Harry collapsed into it. "The cops traced Lupe's last phone calls to you and me. The first one, I attended. It's when she gave me the message to go to Brooklyn. Sabrina took the second call. She says Lupe insisted there was some kind of emergency. Then, there was a call to my cell which I didn't get... I wasn't carrying it. The last call was to you, but you were conveniently sent out of town."

"She left a message," Liam murmured.

"What?!" Harry asked, jerking up.

"*Merde!*' It was all she said. She figured out something, didn't she?"

"Must have." Deflated, Harry sank back. "She didn't say anything to anyone else in the club premises, not even to the guards. She simply left the club to find a way to warn me."

"The bastards got to her before she could do anything," Liam said, hand over his mouth. His shoulders shook in a fresh bout of grief. "They killed my father to get you. Whatever his crimes, he didn't deserve to die the way he did. Neither did Lupe."

"The Kingsleys won't get away with it," Harry swore. "I'll stop them." Until he did, the exiles needed to stay safely hidden.

He and Liam did a quick check of the room, intending to do the same with Lupe's upstairs apartment. The cops had already been through the building twice, first when they believed she was absconding, then after her body was found. There was no evidence. Of course there wouldn't be. Whoever killed her would've made sure not to leave any.

On their way out of the office, Harry turned off the lights. The votive candle still glowed. The Virgin Mary icon was still tilted to one side.

"Wait a second," Liam said the same moment Harry was about to stride back in.

There was a folded piece of paper under the icon, which apparently escaped the notice of both the criminals and the cops. Liam opened the note and quickly scanned it. Handing it to Harry, Liam said, "Not for us."

No, not for Liam or Harry. No answers to their quest for justice. It was only a letter Lupe wrote to a woman she never met.

Part III

Chapter 7

Two weeks later, late June 1989

Long Island, New York

The blinds in the library were usually kept drawn to prevent sun damage to the books. Today, Temple was glad to have the light and the warmth of the summer sky beating down on his back as he perused the photographs spread on the table next to the window. Only, he didn't have a clue how he would accomplish what he wanted without being able to speak, read, write, or even understand the digits on a clock.

The therapist who used to visit did try to teach Temple what he assumed was sign language, using Braille since he couldn't visually recognize any writing. His brain refused to interpret what his fingers sensed. Eventually, the lady coached him and Noah as well as the secret service officers on a few gestures—motions of the head and hands to signal yes and no, to indicate hunger and thirst, to identify common objects and actions. Simple movements to carry out basic communication. How could a nod or a wave be enough to tell the tale Temple needed to tell? How could he be expected to understand any of what was going on?

Murder... Noah had shown Temple a newspaper. There was a photograph of a corpse with a blade sticking out from its back along with a face shot of the victim. It took the politician a day or so to place the fellow and only after seeing a picture of Verity Luce in the papers. Temple met Will Luce exactly once, and it was sometime after Harry's wedding. The one certainty was it was arranged by Godwin Kingsley to trap Harry.

Temple's former protégé had visited a couple of times after he was let out of police custody, which meant no arrest warrant was issued yet. The relieved smiles on the faces of Grayson Sheppard and Noah told Temple Lilah somehow escaped. Only then was the former president able to take a deep breath.

The day before, Noah held a meeting in this same library with Harry and Dante, the COO of Gateway. A flamboyant fellow attended. The unknown guest wore rings on every finger, and his gray hair was puffed up to stand on end all around his dark face as though he'd just been electrocuted. With him was a lawyer who interned with Temple back when he was a senator. The youngish chap and three of his comrades during internship had visited a few times when Temple was in the hospital. The former president recognized all of them, which meant his memory wasn't affected by the bullet.

If only Temple could spit out what he remembered. *Amber*, he whispered in his mind. If only he spoke up then for a dead girl, Will Luce wouldn't have died, and Harry wouldn't be in his current predicament.

The colorful lawyer probably arrived to discuss the case. A senior partner in some high-powered firm, from the deference shown by Temple's former intern. They would make sure nothing happened to Harry.

Today, Sabrina also showed up to talk to Noah. Her son was in tow. While the adults sat on the couch to discuss their concerns, the child wandered up and down the library. The boy's gaze was more solemn than it should've been for his age. Stopping at the coffee table in the center of the room, he poked a finger at the musical instruments much cherished by Noah. The mandolin was Noah's first love, but he also played the flute.

Miracle of miracles, Noah didn't seem bothered by the child's antics. They had all been changed by the events of the last few months. Well... some changes were for the better. Noah had given up on dyeing his hair the ludicrous jet black, letting the gray show through.

The boy picked up the wooden flute, peering through each hole in turn. He put his lips to the blowhole and puffed hard. The resulting sound was piercing. Startled, he dropped the flute onto the hardwood floor. Sabrina clucked and gesticulated at her son to put the flute back next to the mandolin.

Temple laughed. When the lad glanced toward the window, Temple gestured him closer, wanting a look at Alex's son. The boy padded to Temple's chair.

What was the child's name? Temple had made it a point to learn the names of the next generation of Kingsleys. Victor's son was called Gabriel, and this lad was... "Michael," Temple said.

Eyes grave, the boy nodded.

Temple sat up, his spine ramrod-straight. "Michael," he repeated, careful to keep his voice low.

The boy nodded a second time.

Excitement bubbling, Temple tried, "How old are you?" Maybe it had returned, whatever "it" was.

Face scrunched up, the boy stared.

Temple's shoulders sagged. Nothing was back. He'd misunderstood the boy's response. "Michael," he muttered.

Pointing at his own chest with a finger, the boy said, "Michael. Mike."

Temple heard the name quite clearly... and its diminutive. His mind soared. Scrambling through the pile of photographs on the table, he stabbed at a picture of Alex in military fatigues.

Face lighting up, the boy said something.

Temple gestured at the child to sit in the chair across the table, then pointed at Alex's image a second time. Temple watched the boy's lips move. Two syllables. With concentrated effort, Temple moved his mouth and tongue to mimic. "Da-ddy."

Michael seemed to catch on. Slowly, he repeated the word.

Sabrina called out, her tone distracted, and returned to her conversation with Noah. Temple put a finger to his lips, and Michael nodded. Decibel level way down, he repeated the word, allowing Temple the time to follow the movements of his mouth. Sabrina once again said something, and the boy turned. With an apologetic glance at Temple, she directed her son to a chair.

"No," Temple tried to say. "Let him stay. I want to talk to him." Noah was instantly at Temple's side, placing a pacifying hand on his shoulder. The sharp green eyes were concerned as though Noah expected Temple to have another breakdown any moment... a frequent expression over the last few months. The former attorney general had moved into Temple's home. Noah didn't have any close relatives left alive to visit, and he also seemed to have completely given up on his travels, something he claimed helped him keep his finger on the pulse of global politics. While Temple was extremely glad for the support and the company, there were times when ungrateful thoughts abounded. Shrugging away the hand, he said, "What you need, my friend, is a punch to your noggin. I'm not an idiot. Stop treating me like one."

But of course, no one understood him. Both Noah and Sabrina bustled around Temple, and she fetched him a pillow. Only the kindness in her gaze stopped Temple from hurling the offending thing across the room. Except for this problem with language in any form—spoken or written—the bullet did no damage Temple could see. He could fetch his own damned pillows.

From the other chair, the little boy grinned conspiratorially, the solemnity in his eyes vanishing for a moment. In perfect empathy, Temple grinned back.

It got worse. Noah picked up the flute and started to play. Not as if Temple minded music. Far from it. He simply never imagined there would be a day he found himself wanting to smash the Sinatra records over his own head.

The boy turned to Noah, saying something. Noah started showing the child the correct way to hold the cross flute—horizontally, with mouth against the blow hole on the side. When Michael took the instrument from Noah's hand and put it to his lips, Temple braced himself. With Noah's long fingers directing the boy's pudgy ones, a recognizable rendition of "Hot Cross Buns" flowed out, smoother than expected for a first-timer.

From the expression on Noah's face, he was impressed, and Noah Andersen wasn't easily impressed.

"Not bad, young man," said Temple, clapping. Flute magic aside, Michael managed to teach Temple two words in one morning.

Although he knew he wouldn't find what he wanted, Temple dug through the pictures again. There was one of himself and his secretary with a very young Lilah when she interned for him. The salt-and-pepper hair of the then-senator was now completely gray, and the blue eyes which stared back at him in the mornings from the bathroom mirror had witnessed a fair share of tragedies. Lilah... the beauty and the glamor shone through even in the blurry Polaroid. The blue-black waves were held in a ponytail, a serious look in her hazel eyes and a haughty tilt to her chin. There was a book in her hands, fatherly pride in Temple's gaze. Some things changed hardly at all in the years since the snapshot was taken. He smiled and set it aside.

There was a formal picture of Temple's mother with Godwin's father in the gardens of the Kingsley mansion on their wedding day. Godwin stood with the three sons of his dead half-brother in a black-and-white photograph. Peter with Patrice at their nuptials, a portrait of their sons next to the fireplace. Richard had his arms around the shoulders of his adoptive parents at his graduation from West Point. Armor Sr., the Kingsley chauffeur, had sent the copy at Temple's request. An awkward-looking Steven and a grinning Charles posed with their sister, Helen, at her engagement party. Andrew Barrons stared up from a photograph with Temple on his first inauguration as president. No Amber Barrons and not the one other person Temple wanted to see—the living, breathing evidence Amber left behind as evidence of Kingsley treachery.

Chapter 8

A few minutes later

The valet Temple believed was hired by Sabrina came in, urging the former president out of the library and into the bedroom where a black suit waited on the mattress. Temple frowned. No matter where they were headed, he was going to be subjected to curious stares. A fact Noah was aware of, so the trip was certainly something he considered important.

"Where?" Temple asked the valet, using his hand to convey the meaning.

The response of course made no sense to Temple, but at the end of thirty minutes, he was better dressed than he'd been during his time in the White House. His shoes never gleamed so bright, and his pants were never creased this crisp. Even his eyebrows were brushed to perfection.

In the Cadillac, Noah handed Temple a black-rimmed card. Funeral announcement. Temple had seen enough of them to recognize one. Round face, blond combover, gray-blue eyes... Will Luce, of course. There was surely a point to Noah's idea of attending the burial of the man whose untimely death Harry seemed to be accused of, but Temple wasn't looking forward to it. Grimly, he smiled. Funerals were never anything to look forward to, but he'd gotten to the age when it happened with distressing frequency. Last month, his former chief of staff had passed, leaving behind Temple and his personal secretary, Wilma, from the trio which started out together in politics so many decades ago. Plus, Noah. Temple glanced at his loyal friend, but Noah was peering through the car window.

The Cadillac exited the highway in Brooklyn and rolled up to a pair of ornate Victorian gates. *So many years*, Temple thought. So many years had passed since he last visited this particular burial ground.

#

Seventeen years ago, March 1972

Green-Wood Cemetery

Brooklyn, New York

Shoes squelching grassy mud, Senator Temple struggled to open the umbrella. The wind whistling through the trees kept whipping the black fabric the wrong way. Chilly rain drizzled down his scalp to his collar, dampening his clothes. In the pond by the clearing, a duck squawked.

"Today of all days," muttered Temple, keeping a wary eye on the three young men by Peter Kingsley's grave. They clearly hadn't shown up to attend the funeral going on some distance away. Nor did they appear to be mourning the passing of their father so long ago. The lads were dutifully on their knees, but they were chatting. A gust of air carried their indistinct voices to Temple's ears. He hoped they'd leave soon. He didn't want any Kingsleys sighting him with Andrew Barrons, much less overhear their conversation. At least Shawn—Andrew's son—didn't seem to be around. He, of all people, could not be allowed to hear what the senator had to say.

Temple even asked his assistant to wait in the car at some distance, or he'd have had some help with the damned... the umbrella opened. Finally! Keeping himself hidden behind the sassafras trees, Temple switched his attention to the funeral happening a few feet to his right.

The service was almost over. Andrew Barrons would be along any minute. The departed souls might have been his father-in-law and his second wife, but for Andrew, nothing took priority over business. Sure enough, his own umbrella held open in one hand, he was making his way to the back of the group even as the minister was concluding his remarks. Thoroughly disgruntled, Temple noted Andrew's brown hair was perfectly dry, and there was not a damp spot to be found on his suit.

"Sorry I couldn't take your calls, Senator." Andrew's voice boomed over the subdued prayers and the pitter-patter of the spring shower. "As you can see, I was busy. Paying respects to the dead takes precedence over meeting with politicians."

Gritting his teeth, Temple resisted the urge to tell the businessman where he could put the *faux* virtue. Pettiness was all it was. He'd been prone to such outbursts of pique since their attempt to create a Kingsley-Barrons alliance fell apart more than twenty years ago. Andrew Barrons was not especially vindictive, but neither was he inclined to forgive and forget unless he saw some benefit to him.

His loud voice had already drawn attention. A few of the mourners turned in their direction. Spotting a familiar face, Temple almost groaned. Ryan Sheppard. The departed ambassador had been a partner in Ryan's company. Temple needed to do this quickly before Ryan—or anyone else—came close enough to eavesdrop.

"Look, Andrew," Temple said, keeping his voice low. "Right now, I'm wondering why, but I came here to do you a favor. Your son visited my office last week."

Instantly, Andrew's blue eyes sharpened. "What did he want?"

"Information," Temple said. "About Amber."

Shoulders bunching, Andrew asked, "That's it? He's been curious about her since he graduated high school."

"I know. He said you were relieved 'a fag like him' wasn't... how could you, Andrew? He was only seventeen at the time!"

Andrew shrugged. "He said he wouldn't go to West Point if it meant he would have to pretend to like women. Can you believe he wanted to learn computers? But my shock treatment worked."

"Yeah, it did." Temple snarled. "For a couple of years. Then, he got kicked out for wearing his mother's beads. He wants to know all about the girl who owned them."

"What did you say?" Andrew asked, the rain pelting the umbrellas not concealing the worry in his tone.

Pinning Andrew with his gaze, Temple said, "I told your son Amber never took any names. I lied... I said she might have been battling the Kingsleys, but she and I didn't run into each other much even though I'm Godwin's step-brother."

Relief. The emotion on Andrew's face was abject relief. Not spite. Not speculation. Not even curiosity.

"You think you made a mistake telling Shawn, don't you?" Temple asked, eyes narrowing. "You don't want him finding out anything about his biological father."

"Would you?" asked Andrew. "The one favor the girl did me was to keep her mouth shut. She didn't tell even *me*."

"You never asked around?" Temple inquired, almost holding his breath. All these years, and he never dared bring it up with Andrew. Now, Shawn had given Temple the perfect opening. He needed to figure out how much Andrew knew.

"No. I didn't care. It was probably the boyfriend Godwin mentioned to the police." The one she reportedly tried to play against Temple's half-brother.

Temple loosened his tight grip on the umbrella handle. "If you don't care, why are you still holding this grudge against the Kingsleys?"

"Because whatever the circumstances, Godwin should have made the drunk marry her, dammit. Do you realize how many plans fell through once the Kingsleys withdrew? The amount of losses I was forced to take! Not to mention Jared Sanders is still out there."

Shaking his head, Temple said, "But it allowed you to pretend—"

"I already had other plans." Gesturing sharply at the group mourning the dead, Andrew said, "I was keeping an eye out for someone presentable who was desperate enough. In a few years, I found Caroline. She wanted out after her father brought home his second wife. She was fine with whatever I asked. It wasn't much... a simple lie in exchange for a luxurious home and her own hefty bank account."

Temple began to understand. "You were simply waiting for the right woman to agree to your conditions... thus letting you play the role of supportive husband to infertile wife. Then, Shawn happened, and you couldn't help grabbing the chance... Caroline came later. If the truth ever gets out, people will question the story Caroline put about. They might hear about your old war injury."

Andrew admitted, "I did make a mistake by telling Shawn. Senator, get him to drop this foolish search."

Temple nodded. He got what he came here for and could afford to be generous. Andrew Barrons didn't have a clue about the real story. The Kingsleys were safe.

"There are more problems for us to worry about," Andrew continued. "Sanders made an offer for Genesis."

"Gen—" Ryan Sheppard's company.

"Yup," Andrew said quickly, eyes darting around.

Temple swore under his breath. He'd feared this day a long time. "Sanders was bad enough twenty-five years ago. Now, there's also Gaddafi to worry about. Ryan needs to get out of Libya."

Andrew shook his head. "I'm not getting through to Ryan. Sanders is a dangerous man. The Sheppards are better off selling it to whoever and leaving the business altogether."

Not easy to do when "it" was all you possessed, but Andrew had a point. Unfortunately, while Ryan Sheppard was nowhere as wealthy as Andrew, he was as prone to putting business over people. And Temple was as bad, accepting campaign cash from Andrew in return for little favors here and there.

Distant laughter made Temple turn. The Kingsley boys. He'd almost forgotten. Victor seemed to be wrestling his brothers to the ground.

From the far end of the funeral group, the string quartet struck up a hymn. "Nearer, My God, to Thee."

"Almost done," Andrew muttered. "I'd better—"

Someone shouted, "Hey." It was Alex, the youngest of Peter and Patrice's boys. The three lads finally appeared to have noticed there was a funeral going on not too far away. They'd stopped messing around and were headed out. Well... Brad and Victor were, but Alex was staring toward the funeral group.

Temple followed the young man's gaze. There was a ripple within the small crowd. A dark-haired boy pushed through, his arm around the shoulders of a girl in a black skirt suit. Her face was buried in his chest, but the coltish gait announced her youth. Rain plastered long, dark hair to her scalp.

"The ambassador's family?" Temple asked Andrew.

"His daughter with the second wife... the Indian lady. There's a boy, too. Daniel. A fine young lad. They're twins."

Temple nodded at the duo. "Him?"

"Heh? Oh, you mean—no, he's Harry. Ryan's son."

The boy suddenly looked up, his intense dark eyes colliding with Temple's, holding his gaze for a couple of seconds. The lad inclined his head, dismissing both Temple and Barrons from his consciousness before walking off with the girl.

They brushed past Alex, neither noticing him. Victor and Brad had already left. Something fell out of the boy's pocket. Alex picked up what seemed to be a white handkerchief, studying it carefully.

"Bro," shouted Victor, jogging back. "Let's go."

The ambassador's daughter had disappeared into a grove with Ryan Sheppard's son.

Alex followed his brother out, dropping the kerchief into the garbage can a few feet down the path.

"What's her name?" asked Temple, feeling sorry for the child.

"Delilah," said Andrew. "But everyone calls her Lilah."

"How old?"

"Fifteen," Andrew said. "You know, while you're here, I'd like to introduce her brother, Daniel, to you."

As though the funeral of a child's parents was an appropriate venue. "Another time, perhaps."

Andrew shrugged. "Sure. You're going to meet him sooner or later. I'm hoping to adopt him."

Taken aback, Temple asked, "Only him? What about the girl?"

"Temple, I'm not as callous as you imagine. She can also stay with us. It will only be a couple of years before she leaves for good."

Temple shook his head, banishing Lilah and the indifferent fate awaiting her from his mind. He wasn't likely to encounter her another time. Nor was he likely to run into Harry Sheppard, the boy with the peculiarly direct gaze.

#

Back in the present, late June 1989

Green-Wood Cemetery

Brooklyn, New York

Unlike the wet spring day so long ago, this afternoon was bright and sunny. *And warm,* thought Temple, sweating under his collar. Across the crowd around the grave, he met Harry's eyes and nodded. The group with him included Dan Barrons, Liam Luce, and Verity, Harry's wife—his *former* wife. At least Verity Luce had to be former, or Harry couldn't have married the stylish woman he brought to Temple's home. Temple still didn't understand the marriage, much less approve of it. His main concern was for Lilah, not Harry's new or former wives.

Verity was sobbing softly into a tissue, her brother patting her head. His face was blotchy, as well. There was no accusation to be seen whenever the siblings glanced at Harry, which caused Temple to heave a small sigh of relief. Dan looked upset, but he was staring straight ahead in silence. With his dark hair and eyes, he resembled his half-sister—Andrew's wife—more than his twin. Chic, too, like Mrs. Barrons. All of which would've suited the oil driller's purposes very well.

Not long after, Harry trod across the grass to Temple's side, Liam and Dan following. There were quite a few heads turning toward them. Half a dozen cops stood to the side, their grim glares fixed on Harry.

Something rustled. Noah handed Temple a newspaper clipping. The same black-and-white picture of Will Luce with a knife sticking out from the spine. "The cops think Harry did it," Temple said. He'd deduced as much already.

Noah couldn't have understood what his old friend said, but he dug into his pocket and brought out another card—a second funeral notice. It carried the picture of the extraordinary young woman who'd married Harry in Temple's library.

"My God," Temple whispered.

Chapter 9

Later the same day

Back in his home, Temple collected the discarded photographs. He'd have to get the valet to put them back in the album. Later. Right now, his thoughts were whirling.

He'd firmly believed he was doing the right thing. The lessons taught him by his father... his mother, the fisherman's daughter who agreed to be the live-in lover of the senator from New

Jersey... both achieved what they wanted from the union. She became a movie star and the goddess of every man's dreams, going on to marry a wealthy admirer with a first wife locked up in a mental hospital. The politician got his son and heir without having to find himself a wife. Temple was in his teens when he heard how his mother met Godwin's father. Disgust was Temple's first reaction to the story, but adulthood brought with it some understanding of his parents' motives. When he announced his intention to run for his first elected office as a congressman, it was with full certainty of what he wanted to do with his life. The task begun by Temple, Sr. and Sylvia Fontaine would be completed by their son.

World War I was long over by then. The robber barons who moved the puppet strings on the elected representatives in DC and elsewhere were being brought to heel, but the economy was suffering. Anyone with half a brain realized cheap and plentiful fuel would be critical in getting the nation out of the downturn. Factories, automobiles, construction... the United States needed to maintain control over the energy sector, and Temple was determined to make it happen. Only, someone unknown waited in the shadows, someone as shrewd as the robber barons and far more brutal. A man named Jared Sanders. The Austrian immigrant became a force to be reckoned with toward the end of the Great Depression. By the time the Allies declared victory in the second world war, Sanders was the *de facto* ruler of the oil sector. He created an empire which spanned the planet, himself its ruthless sovereign. Those who opposed him were viciously cut down. Women, children... no one was exempt from the sharp edge of Sanders's sword.

The tyrant needed to be dethroned. An alliance of companies would rise up in revolt against the rule of corporate monsters like

Sanders. The cause was emancipation, and the conflict would be a last-ditch effort to restore balance.

Three men were invited to the meeting at Temple's office in New Jersey—Godwin Kingsley, Andrew Barrons, and Ryan Sheppard. Godwin held fast to his rigid ideas on society and hierarchy, but Temple had nevertheless come to appreciate his stepbrother's intellect and integrity. The other two members of the alliance were a generation behind Godwin and had only recently assumed charge of their respective businesses. Still, Barrons O & G was a giant in the sector, and Andrew showed every sign of being an astute leader. The Sheppards' drilling enterprise was profitable at the time, and the family reproduced at an astoundingly high rate, their progeny stationed in every corner of the American government. With the three clans united, they would have a reasonable chance of success against Sanders.

A way around the laws which forbade collusion... regulatory authorities wouldn't have any reason to poke noses into marriages between private citizens even if they happened to hold shares in certain businesses. All involved would keep their heads down to evade Sanders's watchful eye until it was time to render judgment on his crimes. The only outsider who was privy to the details of the scheme was Temple's old friend and confidante, Noah Andersen.

When Andrew's cousin, Amber, died, the first attempt at forming a partnership faltered, coming apart completely a few years later with the failure of the Peter Kingsley-Patrice Sheppard marriage. Temple still harbored hopes of resuming their unfinished work someday. Besides, the life which was lost was never coming back, and an otherwise exceptional man did not need to be condemned for eternity for the one sin he committed. Temple deliberately shoved away his grief and remorse over the dead girl, the first casualty of a war she was lured into joining. No one would learn the secret she left behind with Andrew Barrons, not even Noah.

Temple's silence on the tragedy... he was complicit in what happened to Lilah. Will Luce and the young woman who married Harry were gone today because Temple refused to speak up against the monster who hounded Amber to death only to protect his reputation. Now... Temple didn't have a choice. Not unless he planned to sacrifice Amber yet again.

Noah said something, drawing Temple from his thoughts. The former attorney general walked to the table and scrutinized the pictures. Picking up the one with Andrew in it, he glanced speculatively at Temple.

"No," Temple croaked, trying to convey his intention with a vehement shake of his head. "Don't do anything."

Noah didn't know the full story. Until Temple was able to communicate clearly what exactly the connection between Shawn Barrons and the Kingsley family was, they couldn't risk it. Or ignorant of his importance in this saga, Shawn would set out to investigate. Without being adequately prepared for an attack, he'd encounter a psychopath willing to slaughter everyone in his way. Even being seen with Temple would be enough to put a bull's-eye on Shawn's back.

I'm sorry, Lilah, Temple murmured in his mind. He would continue to try... every day he had left on this earth, he would battle his own brain and try to spit out the secret which could bring down the Kingsleys. Even if he failed, Lilah already knew who her enemies were. With wide-open eyes, she saw the possibility of death and embraced it. Delilah Barrons was forged by the flames at the Egypt-Libya border. She was a fire-borne princess who took on the mantle of empress.

Harry was in trouble at the moment, but the former SEAL wouldn't stop until he found a way to bring her home. He and Lilah rode at the forefront of the army they willingly led.

Shawn was not aware of the dangers lying in wait. He never volunteered to join this fight. He didn't have anyone to stand between him and his enemies except an old politician who already failed his mother.

Stay safe, Temple said to his daughter. *Wherever you are, stay safe until Harry finds you.*

Part IV

Chapter 10

Four months later, October 1989

Kashgar, Xinjiang Uyghur Autonomous Region

People's Republic of China

Soldiers in riot gear were everywhere, a couple in front of the large mosque with its mustard-yellow walls. "Keep moving," Alex muttered to his two companions. Mentally, he cursed. The fellow who promised to help the exiles insisted on meeting at a place he deemed the most secure. If not for the demand, Alex wouldn't have taken the risk of venturing out of their hiding spot, let alone brought Scott and Lilah along.

The Chinese military had increased its presence in the region, monitoring for terrorist activity and conducting random checks. Recent events in Beijing aside, Xinjiang province witnessed its own unrest in the last couple of months. The threat of capture remained high every moment the exiles spent outside... no, every moment they were forced to spend in China.

At least they fit in better in this town. Alex and Scott wore embroidered *doppas*—the square hats favored by locals. Their pants and shirts were also bought locally. The clothes and the facial hair would somewhat help them blend in. Luckily for the exiles, Caucasian features and build were common in the western-most frontier of China... as well as Han faces and Central Asian and innumerable mixes.

The black shirt and skirt covered almost all of Lilah's form except for her hands and sneakered feet. Her hair was concealed by a deep red scarf, the end of which was pulled over the lower half of her face. *Niqab,* she'd called it. A lot of the ladies in this Muslim-heavy region of China covered up, so she wouldn't stand out. Familiar hazel eyes glinted behind plastic-framed glasses.

It took the trio an hour to get to the Sunday Bazaar. The crowd in the covered part of the market was almost shoulder to shoulder, adding sweat and noise to the relatively warm evening weather. A donkey cart creaked alongside Alex as he strode to his destination, the clippety-clop of the beast's hooves punctuated by an occasional bray of protest. Somewhere to the front, there was radio music coming from one of the stores.

Walking between the two men, Lilah kept her eyes straight ahead, but Scott was squinting through his glasses at the stalls lining the path. Lampshades and lanterns, stone cups and tumblers, baskets of dried fruits... there was even a shop with mandolins of various sizes displayed in front.

Satiny fabric hung in neat rows in a stall minded by a young boy with apple-red cheeks. The lad called out something to someone behind and turned an impromptu cartwheel. Alex laughed quietly. Michael... he was a few years behind the kid in the shop. Ignoring the sudden, sharp squeeze in his chest, Alex continued his march. In a few minutes, they'd meet his contact, perhaps the only man who could get the exiles out of China.

"Over there," said a husky voice. Lilah tilted her head in a slight nod.

Alex darted a casual glance in the direction of her gaze. Camo-clad figures stood in front of a spice stall, carrying rifles in their hands. They were pulling men and women from the crowd, seemingly at random, and asking for identification. The customers in the barber shop next door were peering at the scene, their feet still tapping to the fast-paced duet from the store.

Muscles tightened in Alex's shoulders. The three of them did have fake papers identifying them as locals, but they'd be pegged for foreigners the moment they were unable to understand questions in the language. Lilah's hand went to her waist, dropping after a moment or two. The pistol tucked into her belt would not be of much use under the circumstances. Alex's was secured to his ankle.

"Stick close," he ordered. Keeping his gait purposeful but not too hurried, he walked into the store selling dried fruits and nuts. Speech wasn't needed to signal the young fellow minding the store they wanted roasted cashews and almonds. As the shopkeeper counted coins, Scott nibbled on the nuts and wrinkled apricots. Lilah couldn't eat anything without removing her face covering.

If Alex knew anything about the man he was to meet, there would be someone tailing the exiles. The shadow would somehow intervene. There would be some opportunity, an opening provided for escape. *If* the initial offer of help was made in good faith.

Sweat trickled down the back of Alex's neck as he did a quick visual sweep of the covered bazaar. There... a flicker of a movement across the path. A young man—perhaps a teenager—was strolling into the barber shop. Something about the lad's movements... the way he was glancing across to the other side... Alex tilted his head slightly.

One second, two seconds... four... six... without warning, the music from the store blasted through the covered pathway. Sound waves crashed into walls, setting them vibrating. The ground almost shook. Shouts of alarm, the donkey braying... shoppers and shopkeepers alike rushed to check what was happening. The soldiers, too.

The bag with nuts and apricots dropped from Scott's hand, and he goggled at the scene. "Now!" said Alex, tone low. Slipping behind the crowd gathered at the entrance to the barber shop, the trio strode out. Not a single word was said until they exited the bazaar, not a look exchanged. The young fellow who rescued them would likely make up some silly excuse for the ruckus he created. If the soldiers were in a pissy mood, he'd spend a night or two in jail... at worst. Even if it happened to be more, the lad would prefer the punishment meted out by the Chinese military rather than report failure to the man who sent him.

Fifteen minutes later, the Americans were at their destination—a stone building at the end of a narrow lane. The man who answered Alex's knock didn't bother to check the visitors for weapons. It wasn't necessary. They would be significantly outnumbered. Sneakers discarded at the door, the three of them followed their guide to a room at the back of the building.

Dust particles danced in the beam of sunlight coming through the only window on the dirty stone wall. The men seated on mats around the room muttered, one of them shouting an order to an unseen subordinate. The language didn't sound like Arabic, and there was no change in Lilah's stance to suggest she sensed trouble.

"Alex Kingsley," said the man directly in front of the former sniper. The British accent was quite proper. "I didn't think we would meet again."

"Neither did I." At a signal from Alex, his companions lowered themselves to the floor and sat on folded legs. He gestured toward the leader of the group in the room.

White tunic, loose pants, long beard... Pathans were an ethnic group spread mainly across Afghanistan and Pakistan. This particular fellow's blue eyes and fair skin proclaimed European genes, which some claimed was a gift left by Alexander the Great's soldiers on their way to India. He was also educated in one of England's best private schools.

"Yasser Afridi," introduced Alex. *Mujahideen* chief, Islamist Afghan guerilla, known slave trader and sex trafficker.

#

Alex first met the Pathan during his years in Pakistan. To be precise, they met during Alex's forays into Afghan territory to battle Soviet troops. According to the CIA, Yasser left the opium business to his comrades after his younger brother fell prey to heroin. The Pathan's other interests were bad enough... most notably, the training and arming of Uyghurs to conduct terrorist activities as well as the slave trade which financed such activities. Limited options were available to the American intelligence agency to stop the advancement of Russians into a geopolitically sensitive part of the world, and Captain Alex Kingsley was brusquely told to fit himself with internal blinkers. Or he could follow in the path of other soldiers who started with naïve idealism and ended up mentally crippled, sometimes even blowing their own brains out. Alex decided on day one he intended to come out alive and reasonably sane no matter how many times he was forced to accept the Pathan's assistance.

In Yasser's company, Alex and a couple of his men even slipped across the border into China a few times to gather intelligence. Soon after, certain Russian commanders were forced to bid *adieu* to this world, courtesy of a sniper's rifle. Alex had enjoyed taking the same route trodden by Marco Polo, but he never imagined bringing his family—not to mention Lilah and her intern—to the same places. The Pathan leader's continued existence had been relegated to the back of Alex's mind until chaos erupted in Beijing.

Eight weeks ago, he led the rest of the exiles through the slums of Kashgar to a house he remembered. Yasser Afridi's Uyghur colleague recognized Alex. He was able to connect with the Pathan, who asked them to wait in town for his arrival.

The group was confined to two small rooms in the crumbling courtyard house of a local separatist, but they remained safe from Chinese authorities. They could also eat three times a day without access to their money. Contacting the Swiss bank Lilah used was impossible with the political unrest going on in the country, and every penny left after the journey from Macau to Beijing and then to Kashgar needed to be saved for what lay ahead. Nor could they communicate with anyone back home, not even Grayson. The exiles wouldn't know what the hell was happening back in the U.S. with Harry before they got out of China.

The fake passports and visas obtained by the exiles so long ago in Ecuador couldn't be used when there was a good chance the documents were what led the Burmese drug lord, Prince, to them in Macau. Without question he *and* Steven would know the fugitives were still in China. Alex wished like hell they got the chance to collect the new set of papers from Dan's contact before fleeing Beijing. Asking the mujahideen for different travel documents would give them an opening to keep track of the group of seven. Not the greatest idea, but it was their only option. The separatists also provided fake IDs the exiles might need in town. It still didn't mean they could cross the border to Afghanistan with impunity. To evade the authorities, the Pathan's help would be crucial.

Weeks went by while they waited for Yasser to show up. Their host assured them the Chinese authorities didn't have a clue he was associated with the separatist movement. Any house-to-house searches by the ever-present military was unlikely to involve their particular abode. But as Victor said to the rest of his family later, there was a huge difference between "unlikely" and "not gonna happen."

He and Alex took turns standing guard in the room assigned to the ladies. No one objected, not Brad, not Hema, not even Lilah. Besides the impatience at the delay in their departure from China, the living arrangements gave Alex something new to worry about. Day after day, Lilah stayed in her corner, breaking her silence only to discuss plans. Every remaining moment seemed to be spent in thought. Oh, she'd been cold and angry with the Kingsley brothers since the beginning of the exile, and she slept in snatches, sitting up in her cot the rest of the time. But there was a new restlessness in the way she talked... the way she moved. Alex couldn't put his finger on what exactly changed.

"*Shock,*" Victor decided. He believed it was because of the attempted rape by the bastard, Drummond.

Alex didn't agree. This was a woman who'd kept her composure under military interrogation. This was a woman who took everything life threw at her and still refused to bend. Lilah stuck with the husband she plainly loathed only to ensure the empire built on her back was returned to her. She couldn't—none of them could—stomach seeing it in the hands of a criminal like Steven. Did Drummond's attack finally break her will? Alex didn't buy it.

Before he gathered the courage to ask, a message arrived. Yasser Afridi was in town and was ready to grant an audience. Afridi was a busy man. With the help of the West, the mujahideen drove Russian troops out of Afghanistan only a few months ago. The information Alex got from his sources was at least a year old—before the events which led to the exile—but the American military was keeping an eye on their former allies, the guerrillas. Radicals from all over the world had congregated in the region, and talk was the terrorists planned to use the country as base to target the U.S. next. There was a new group called Qaedat al-Jihad or al-Qaeda, bank-rolled by wealthy Arabs, but Afridi's focus remained on the Uyghurs.

The Pathan spoke the English of upper-crust Britons, but Alex would be at a disadvantage without a CIA linguist to help gauge the collective mood of the separatist group. Lilah at least spoke Arabic which some of the mujahideen used. If the Pathan was surprised when a woman showed up with Alex, he didn't say anything.

#

Chipped porcelain dishes containing fragrant lamb noodle soup were set beside the three Americans. Each attendee at the meeting was handed a similar bowl of food. Alex muttered his thanks to the young girl serving the group. Who knew if the poor child was on the sex trafficker's list, slated to be sold to the highest bidder?

"You're married by now, I assume?" Yasser asked. "Children?"

"Yes and yes," said Alex, averting his gaze from the serving girl. He couldn't afford to feel guilty, couldn't afford anger. "One boy, and I'd like to return to him. How much longer do you think we need to hide in this town?"

"Patience," the Pathan said as the girl left the room. "We're going to wait until the summer traffic dies down. Taking a group of novices through checkpoints will not be the same as helping a single sniper cross the border. There are seven of you... the larger the crowd, the more likely it is someone will do something to draw attention. I don't want the Chinese military capturing us because of anyone's foolish mistake."

The voices of the other men rose in agreement.

"The military is precisely what I'm worried about," Alex muttered. "They're everywhere in this town. Also, the longer we wait, the colder it will get." The mountain passes they'd have to take were more than ten-thousand feet above sea level.

"Freezing," the Pathan admitted. "But believe me there will be less chance of getting caught. The Chinese will only ship you and your family back to America. Me, they will kill. I don't intend to die any time soon. So tell your sister-in-law it's going to be a few more days. Provided all of you stay inside until we're ready to leave, we should be okay." He completely ignored Scott's presence but flicked a glance at Lilah, eyes lingering for a couple of moments on the scarf covering her face and her modest outfit. To his colleagues, he said something Alex didn't understand. Yasser turned back to Alex and smiled. "We have entertainment arranged for the evening. Would you care to attend? You should be safe enough here."

With effort, Alex forced his shoulders to relax. "Another time. It's nearly sunset. My brother will be anxious to see his wife back safe and sound."

When the Americans exited into the courtyard, twilight was fast giving way to the darkness of the night, taking the temperature down. The plaintive sounds of the Islamic call to prayer echoed in, but those gathered didn't seem to be in the mood to heed it. Sweet hookah smoke swirled all around. Three women clad in glittery bras and sequined hip scarves wiggled their bodies in time with Middle Eastern music coming from a boom box. Belly dancing... the ordinary citizens of Kashgar were forbidden by cultural norms to indulge in such pastimes, and they'd be shocked if they knew what went on in their town behind their backs.

There was a sudden clatter, causing Alex to glance behind. The men from the meeting pushed through a door and gathered in a circle around the ladies. Most were pulling on blazers to protect themselves from the cold.

On their way out, Lilah halted, watching the performance from the back of the small audience. Drums rolled. Cymbals crashed melodiously. Flute music began. The dancers spun, rocking their hips at furious tempos, their bellies rippling and torsos moving from side to side. The men whistled and clapped in appreciation. Cash was thrown at the performers.

"Looks tough," Scott said. He was peering hard at the ladies, blue eyes blinking rapidly. "But very nice."

"Nice," agreed Lilah. There was a note in her tone... a grimness...

One of the dancers shimmied her way through the spectators, stopping to undulate her body against Alex's. He staggered a step or two to the rear.

Her companions followed her, and the audience turned. The first one ran a finger along Alex's shoulders and spun all around him, letting her breasts brush against his chest with each turn. He got farther from Lilah and Scott with each little push. The men around hooted and cheered.

"No," said Alex, his hands on the dancer's upper arms as he pushed her away gently. Within seconds, he returned to Lilah's side. "We need to go."

Once again, not one of the three Americans said anything as they made their way back through the dwindling crowds in the bazaar. It wasn't until Alex was reasonably sure no one could overhear that he asked, "Did you get anything?"

"A few snippets here and there," said Lilah. "Mostly what we would expect... a couple of names... Abdullah Azzam, bin Laden... other terrorists, I assume. Your friend doesn't seem to agree with their priorities. He thinks they should focus on Asia, not the West. And yeah... he said something to his men about seeing my pictures in newspapers from the U.S."

#

There was no electricity in the accommodations assigned to the exiles. From his spot on the dusty floor next to the door, Alex stared out through the barred window on the wall across the narrow hallway. A full moon hung in the sky, and there was only the muted breathing of slumbering humans in the room. Those humans who weren't Alex Kingsley, anyway. Shifting, he glanced at the shadowy forms of Brad and the twins. None of the men had cots, having given up the two allotted to the group to the ladies. A rolled-up coat served as Alex's pillow, and there was no blanket to protect him from the cold, but sleep would've been a long time coming even if he were covered by silk sheets. They'd made plans. Victor ordered everyone in the group to be prepared for trouble and to keep their weapons ready at all times. Still... Afridi's remark about Lilah's pictures... a sex trafficker... and this unholy deal with the devil was their only way out of China.

"Alex," came Victor's voice from the hallway, tone low. He was supposed to be on bodyguard duty in Lilah and Hema's room tonight.

Grabbing the gun next to his head, Alex leaped to his feet.

"Shh," said Victor. The top part of his giant figure was leaning out of the women's chamber into the shadowed passage.

A couple of strides, and Alex was next to Victor. Keeping an eye on the narrow entrance to his brothers' room, Alex asked in a hushed whisper, "What's up?"

Victor jerked his head toward the cots inside. Lilah was sitting up on her bed. Two feet away, Hema slept on the second twin mattress.

"I've talked to Victor," Lilah said, her tone abrupt. "He'll give you the details."

"About?" asked Alex.

Lilah stood from her cot. "About Afridi... we're going to play the Indian Defense."

Chapter 11

A few weeks later, December 1989

Hell was not a firepit. It was a mountain range frozen solid, where the devil and his minions preyed on the weak and the helpless. Alex took one last glance behind at the twisting streets and squat buildings of the Kashgar slums as they followed the Pathan into his domain, a wild terrain beyond the reach of the Chinese government. There would be no turning back, no escape from hell except death.

Five hours to the border, Alex said to himself, climbing into the back of the truck crammed with cows. There was barely enough space for the five men and two women, but the arrangement would help them pass for Tajik herders headed back home to Tashkurgan, the westernmost settlement in Xinjiang province. It would only be the first leg of their journey into the devil's kingdom.

The women were seated to the right of Alex with Victor on their other side. Lilah's hair had grown back to her shoulders now. The nose ring she got in Macau was in place as were the glasses. Both she and Hema covered their heads with scarves, heavy sweaters and long skirts completing the disguise. The trekking boots were military issue, a gift from the Pathan. *American* military. Alex didn't ask how the mujahideen leader came by them. The men only needed thick jeans and the cheap but warm winter coats worn by most locals. Brad was at the extreme right, as usual leaving bodyguard duties to Alex and Victor. Neil and Scott were the closest to the cab of the truck where the Pathan sat in the passenger seat.

The Karakoram Highway wound alongside a river strewn with rocks, and snow-capped mountains towered on either side in all their harsh majesty. This section of the road was well-paved, and the drive was smooth except for the thin air and the brutally cold wind.

Lilah was staring straight ahead. She shifted as though aware of Alex's scrutiny and tilted her head in a slight nod. Alex glanced at the cab where Yasser Afridi was. The local square hat and his nape were the only visible parts.

The group hid in a home in Tashkurgan for one night. The brothers were supposed to take turns keeping watch, but Alex hardly slept more than five minutes at a time. At every small noise, at every change in wind direction, his muscles tightened. Each time his eyes snapped open, he saw Victor sitting, pacing, or studying the landscape outside the window.

The westward trek resumed early next morning. Up a rocky stream, the exiles joined a group of Tajik men on their way to help fellow herders collect the yaks and goats and return to town for the winter. The twenty miles to the border might as well have been two hundred for the people trudging through three feet of snow in the valley, far out of sight of roads paved and unpaved. Uncaring of the fears of the humans, unperturbed by the painful thundering of their hearts, the Pamir mountains witnessed their journey.

It was sunset by the time they reached a collection of *yurts*. The Pathan led them to the one in the center. The inside of the circular tent was colorful with warm red rugs adorning the ground. The chief of the nomadic herders offered them zesty noodle soup cooked by his wife over a dung-fueled tin stove. The chief told Alex he was thirty-two, his weather-beaten face at odds with his relatively young age. His wife jangled with even the slightest movement from coins sewn onto her scarf... not to mention the silver pendants and bracelets dripping from her neck and arms.

After dinner, the Pathan announced, "Time to change clothes." His glinting eyes lingered on Lilah's behind as she left with Hema.

As soon as the rest went to their allotted yurts, Alex approached the chief and offered a fistful of American money. With much giggling, the chief's wife handed him a pouch heavy with part of her jewelry. Tucking the treasure into his backpack, Alex joined Victor standing guard outside the yurt to the right.

When they were all assembled, Scott pushed his glasses up his nose and blinked at the sky. Tone satisfied, he announced, "I can't see the moon." There was supposed to be a mere sliver visible, but even that appeared to be hidden tonight. Also, the temperature dropping to soul-freezing levels meant no sane guard would be outside only to patrol the border for illegal traffic.

"Are we ready to go, Afridi?" asked Victor.

"Behind me," ordered the Pathan. "No talking and no stopping for anything."

There would be no turning back from hell.

#

Unforgiving wind whistled through the mountain ranges, creating ominous music as it slapped the faces of the travelers with ice-cold fingers. Accompanying it was the drumming in Alex's brain as he and the rest plodded on behind the Pathan through knee-deep snow. Only the terrorist leader wore night-vision equipment—Soviet make—but Alex's eyes had adjusted enough to the dim glow from distant stars. The entire earth seemed blanketed in white... or at least as far as his vision extended. Even under the woolen scarf protecting his mouth and nose, his skin cracked from the painful cold. His lungs burned.

At the muffled cough next to him, Alex turned his head. "You need help?" he asked Hema, eyeing the backpack she carried.

"No," she said, blowing white clouds with each breath. "I'm a child of the mountains, Mr. Alex."

From the front of the group, the Pathan raised a hand. "Shh!"

Looking up and down, Victor muttered, "No Chinese military... so far."

The moment the words were out, the Pathan said in a low tone, "I hear something. Down!"

None of the exiles paused to ask questions. They dropped to the ground and made themselves flat. The white ski jackets and snow pants would help them blend into the landscape and were waterproof.

Seconds turned to minutes. Wind continued to howl in the dark night. Sheets of snow blew across with ominous speeds, settling on the humans lying perfectly still. Alex strained to listen for extraneous noise. The ability to perceive and localize sounds was part of what made him a damned good sniper, but he never heard what the Pathan did. Was there a laugh in the distance? Maybe the rumble of a military vehicle? Funny... he could almost visualize a Jeep hurtling toward them. Alex blinked hard. He couldn't let his mind play tricks on him. Focus was never a problem when he went on covert operations for the military, and he couldn't let it slip right when he needed it the most.

Next to him was Hema. Alex moved his gloved hand an inch, patting hers lightly. Lilah would be between her intern and Victor. When Hema shifted her head to glance at Alex, he nodded reassuringly. The fear in the young woman's eyes didn't abate, but she nodded back.

Eons seemed to pass before the Pathan raised his arm in a go-ahead signal. Once again, they lumbered through the snow and the wind. Twice more, they were forced to drop to the ground, holding their breaths and praying whoever it was would fail to spot them. The last time, a lone sheep galloped across a few feet from them, bleating furiously. In a couple of minutes, there was a roar not far away... one of the snow leopards native to the Pamirs was on the hunt. Alex's hand shot to the weapon tucked into his jacket. Before he could bring out the gun, the bleating stopped abruptly.

It didn't take long after for them to get to the fence. Only barbed wire separated China from Tajikistan. With thickly gloved fingers, the Pathan tugged the steel cables apart and clambered to the other side. Victor was next, followed by Neil, Brad, Lilah, Hema, Scott, and finally, Alex. In under five minutes, they were all on Tajik land.

"This is it?" Scott asked, turning a three-sixty.

"What were you expecting?" Victor chuckled, but the tension in his voice was unmissable. "Gunfire and background music?"

The wind gusted, its pitch rising. Everyone glanced toward the mountains for a moment or two. The pounding in Alex's head sped up. Adrenaline... preparing him for what lay ahead.

"We may still get gunfire," Alex cautioned, willing his brothers not to forget what they were told. The Pathan had promised to have transportation waiting not too far from the border. The men who brought the vehicles would carry heavy-duty weapons. Those weapons could be used either to protect the exiles or to keep them captive.

Yasser turned toward Alex in an abrupt movement. It was hard to see anyone's expression in the darkness, but the sudden increase in the Pathan's alertness was clear in the set of his shoulders. After a moment or two, he visibly relaxed.

Alex frowned. Tone calm, he added, "Remember, this is Soviet territory. Got some miles to go before we're in Afghanistan. So be on guard for Russian troops."

"Keep moving," ordered Yasser.

With a quick nod at his brothers, Victor fell in next to the Pathan, dwarfing the fellow as they led the way. Neither man talked. The ladies were as always in the middle of the group with Neil and Scott on either side and Alex and Brad bringing up the rear.

Hiking along, Alex stared holes into the back of Yasser's head. There was something in the Pathan's demeanor... perhaps it was wariness... a response to Alex's admonition to his brothers to remain on guard. *No.* Every instinct he developed as a sniper warned him the enemy was convinced his attack plan would work. But what was the strategy? Where was the strike coming from? Continuing to march forward, Alex turned a three-sixty.

Between looming peaks, the valley stretched endlessly into the dark horizon. The desolate silence of the night was broken only by the sounds of nature... of air gusting, of a small rock or two rolling downhill, of wildlife. Scott stumbled, falling sideways onto Lilah and knocking her to her knees. Except for a tiny hmph, she didn't utter a word.

Scooping her up, Alex carried her to a rock on the right. Her gloved hands slid down the front of his coat as he set her on the low boulder. "I'm fine," she said, her voice loud enough for only Alex to hear.

There was a sound of irritation from Yasser. "Keeping moving," he ground out.

"Wait one minute," said Neil. "Let's at least make sure she—"

The Pathan snarled, "Shut up and *keep moving.* We need to get to my village before dawn."

Startled at the sudden aggression, Neil took half a step back.

"There's no time for breaks," agreed Brad, his tone sharp. "Lilah can rest once we're safe in the village."

The Pathan agreed with alacrity, "Absolutely correct."

Helping Lilah to her feet, Alex murmured close to her ear, "Something's up." An offensive strike was imminent, coming a lot sooner than they expected.

She inclined her head slightly. Neither glanced toward Victor, but the former boxer would've already picked up on the vibes.

The group continued their trek. Falling in next to Alex, Scott whispered, "What's going on?"

"Got to be careful," Alex said, tone steady but his gaze on the Pathan's back. "Russian territory."

With every step forward, his eyes darted around, looking for strange shadows. He listened for human sounds... a shift in the air... the stench of a killer... something to help him pinpoint the location of the enemy's army. The other terrorist leaders whose names Lilah heard mentioned at their initial meeting with Yasser...

were they waiting to ambush the exiles? Under Alex's skin, blood ran hot. Muscles tightened.

It must have been an hour before they spotted another of the yurts. Two Humvees—the latest in American military's utility vehicles—waited next to the tent, four men standing next to the flap. The rifles in their hands were pointed at the approaching group.

Alex cursed hard in his mind. So this was the plan. *Two trucks*... Yasser meant to separate the exiles long before they got to the village. There were also more terrorists to deal with than Alex and Victor anticipated. It seemed the Pathan didn't care as much about a larger crowd drawing attention now that he was on safer territory, and he and his men would be carrying enough artillery to ensure the cooperation of their prisoners. Five terrorists, all armed to their teeth, against a sniper, a boxer, three men who never saw combat, and two women.

First calling out to his comrades to identify himself, the slave trader commanded the Kingsleys, "Get in."

His pals came forward, cigarettes glowing red between their teeth. The sweet smell of tobacco wafted to Alex's nostrils. The weapons remained pointed at the exiles.

"Why the guards, Afridi?" Victor asked, his manner quite casual.

"Don't worry," soothed the Pathan. "We need them for protection from the Russians. Nothing more." Bringing out a gun from his backpack, he stood to one side of the vehicle's rear with two of the guards while the remaining two positioned themselves on the other side. "Both of you," Yasser ordered the ladies. "In here."

The sharp hitch in Lilah's breath was audible. Without saying a word, she looked toward Victor. Slowly, he inclined his head. Three feet behind Victor, Alex waited as the women clambered in. A pulse pounded hard in his ears. Despite the sub-zero cold, sweat trickled down between his shoulder blades. The terrain seemed to sharpen, with the surrounding peaks and the trees stark against blindingly white snow. A chance... an opening... some way to stop the sex traffickers...

"You two in the second truck," instructed the Pathan, gesturing at Alex and Victor with his gun. "The rest can split up."

No way could the ladies be left without protection from either Alex or Victor. A shootout... by now, Brad and the twins would also have picked up on what was going on. They were drilled over and over on keeping their weapons easily accessible. Still, the chances of them winning a gun battle... the women were already inside the vehicle. They could lock the doors and secure themselves... but only if the terrorists could be drawn away for a critical few seconds. Lilah wouldn't drive off and leave the rest to die, and she could use the truck as a weapon. Timing was everything. Alex needed to buy her a few seconds—

Victor crouched, scrambling in the snow.

"What are you doing?" asked Yasser. "Get inside."

"I dropped something," explained Victor. "My wedding ring, I think."

"You're not going to find it here," said the Pathan, bending down.

"Now, Alex!" Victor snapped out the command as his arm clamped around the terrorist's neck.

"*Ahh*—" shrieked the Pathan, tumbling to the ground.

A quick move, and the gun tucked inside Alex's jacket was in his hands.

With a yell, one of Afridi's guards pointed his rifle. Gunfire thundered. Roaring, Victor fell to his side and took the Pathan with him. They rolled.

Two more shots came in rapid succession from two different guns... inside the Humvee, smoke curled from Lilah's pistol.

"Victor!" Alex shouted, not daring to turn his weapon from the two remaining terrorists. "Are you okay?"

"What's—" came Brad's voice, sounding confused.

"Victor!" Alex shouted a second time. "You'd *better* be okay. Brad, Neil, Scott... one of you help him! Get a lock on Afridi."

But it wasn't needed. Victor roared again. His knee was on the Pathan's back, his hand driving the terrorist's face into the snow. Afridi's limbs thrashed about in his desperate attempt to escape.

"Run," Victor snarled at the remaining thugs, his hand driving Yasser's mouth and nose deeper into the white powder.

Breath coming in loud gasps, the terrorist guards glanced wildly around. They were now outnumbered. A step to the side... two steps... one of them turned and ran, his friend following. Alex fired two more shots in rapid succession. With high-pitched shrieks, both thugs pitched forward, one rolling a few feet down the slope.

On the ground, the Pathan's legs convulsed one last time, then became still.

Chapter 12

Squatting next to the Pathan's corpse, Alex gave the head a light tap. It lolled.

"What the hell?" Brad shouted. "What did you do?"

Neil and Scott were still gaping. Heaving himself up from the snow, Victor limped to his family. "You all right?" Alex asked, scanning his brother for signs of a gunshot wound.

"I'm good," said Victor. "Ripped my coat is all."

The hole was near the collar. An inch closer, and the bullet would've torn through his neck. If the projectile hit the carotid artery, there would've been no time to even try to staunch the bleeding. Victor would've... Alex blinked.

Turning to Brad, Victor added, "What did I do? Got us out of the terrorist's clutches. You can thank me later."

"Oh, my God," Brad gasped, smoothing a gloved hand over his head. "How are we going to get out of here? Did you even stop to think—"

"Yes, I did," said Victor. Tone turning conciliatory, he reminded, "Bro, our friend here did sex trafficking on the side. We couldn't risk the ladies."

"The ladies?" Brad ground out. "So you decided to condemn the whole lot of us to die in the mountains? Couldn't you wait until we got to Afghanistan?"

Hema muttered something under her breath, but Lilah simply looked away. Neither woman said anything to Brad. *'Need to know only,"* Lilah had insisted when she ordered Yasser Afridi's execution. There was no room for dissension. Oh, all the exiles were on the lookout for tricks from the Pathan, but the fact he was slated to be killed no matter what was known to only three people.

Yasser would've thought the same as Brad... the fugitives needed help to get out of the mountains. As soon as the other terrorists joined the group, the Pathan would've imagined himself safe from attacks. So the death sentence would be carried out the moment he got them the promised transportation. The exiles couldn't afford to wait until Afghanistan.

A ruthless strategy... their enemy was lulled into the belief he won while the black queen's army waited to deliver the kill blow. There would be no mercy shown, no opportunity for Yasser to escape. He would get no benefit of the doubt.

Victor asked, "Brad, do you seriously think... Hema and Lilah... rape would've been the least of it. The rest of us... Afridi would've helped us reach Afghanistan... *maybe*. The 'village' he was talking about? Whad'ya wanna bet it's a terrorist camp? Dozens if not hundreds of men like him. We couldn't battle all of them. We would either be forced to leave the women with Afridi or die all together. Our best bet was to take care of him and his buddies before."

"Shit," muttered Neil, his breathing heavy and irregular.

Brad snapped, "Yeah, things have been bad for a while. Yeah, it's been worse for Lilah, the daughter of a *billionaire* like Andrew Barrons. No other woman in the universe as unfortunate as the delicate princess, of course. One tumble, and she needs someone to carry her around. So I won't get upset about trivial things like getting out alive and getting our business back."

Carry her... Of course Brad didn't like what Alex did, but all he wanted was to alert Lilah as to what he suspected.

"Don't worry about reaching Afghanistan," said Victor. "*Two* Humvees... there's the equipment from Afridi and his pals. And I'm sure we'll find maps in the vehicles... would be stupid not to use them in this terrain. We simply need to keep going southeast. Also, our expert guide might be dead, but Alex has some familiarity with this region."

Dusting snow from his clothes, Alex stood. "Brad, we needed Yasser's help at least this far, and *he* was too worried about the Chinese government to try very hard at kidnapping the women straight from Kashgar. There was no way in hell we could trust him any further. See the trick he tried to pull? Two trucks, with him and his buddies ready to shoot us if we ran. Even if he did everything he promised, do we want to owe one to a terrorist? Take my word for it... he agreed to help because he saw benefit for himself. Lilah and Hema for one, and the possibility of blackmailing us for the rest of our lives."

"You didn't want to be obligated to Prince," Victor reminded Brad. "What's the difference between him and the Pathan?"

"Very little," said Brad, "but there's this thing called timing. You two... if you stopped to think... and what happens when the people at the terrorist camp realize Afridi's dead?"

"We timed it perfectly," insisted Victor. "Afridi believed he had the advantage up until the moment we chose to strike. As for his pals at his village... they're not going to worry for at least a couple of days. Delays happen when you're trying to avoid the Russian military. We do need to be out of here before they start looking."

Brad shook his head. "What's done is done, I suppose. Let's get in the trucks and start driving. You'd better not start any more trouble."

#

The men in the group rifled through the pockets of the dead terrorists and robbed the corpses of everything useful. Besides the night vision equipment used by the Pathan, there was one more set in each automobile. The dollar notes in the Pathan's pocket, the weapons... even the cigarettes would come in handy.

"Take a look at this," invited Victor, tossing a colored rock in his palm—deep cherry for the most part, with purplish blue at the bottom. "Why the hell was Afridi carrying around quartz?"

"Quartz?" echoed Alex. He blinked. A vague memory resurfaced. "Stop playing with it for a minute. Lemme see. It might be a ruby."

Victor laughed. "C'mon, bro."

"Seriously," said Alex. "There are several mines in the area controlled by terrorist groups." The information had completely slipped his mind until now. "Never been to one myself, but I've seen the mujahideen use stones like this as currency."

Victor handed the rock to Lilah. "You're the chemical engineer. What do you think? Plain old quartz or worth something?"

"Not precisely my specialty," Lilah said, studying the stone with the aid of a flashlight. "However, I do believe Alex is right. This is ruby." Nature had given the jewel the rough shape of a flower with a violet stalk. "So yeah... worth something. Check if there's more in their pockets."

There were a total of three such rocks. Watching Victor pass his haul to her, Brad's face turned thunderous. Without a word, she ceded the gems to her husband.

The group divided the remainder of what they found. If they somehow got separated, the guns and the cash would be critical to survival. In half an hour, they left the corpses on the snow and set out, Alex and Scott with the women in one vehicle, the rest in the second.

"This truck," Scott said from the back. "Uhh... it looks tough."

"Military vehicles need to be," Alex responded. Under his hands, the wheel stayed steady, but he kept his gaze on the snow-covered terrain. There would be no clear path for some distance.

After a second, Scott asked, *"U.S. military?"*

Alex nodded. "Likely stolen... or faked as stolen. The rest of the equipment... the smaller stuff could even have been supplied legitimately."

"The military-industrial complex," Lilah murmured from the passenger seat. "They don't care who gets hurt as long as they get theirs."

Corrupt businessmen made much moolah out of miring the nation in endless wars. The blood spilled by American soldiers was merely the cost of doing business for the bastards. Trading technology to terrorists would also be considered the same. *This* was what the Kingsley brothers were accused of, what Alex was accused of. Except, on a much larger scale with nuclear arms. Captain Alex Kingsley was now a traitor in the eyes of the nation he once served. Blinking a couple of times, Alex told himself to focus on getting the group to safety.

A soft croon came from the back... Scott, singing under his breath. As the Humvee bounced along a bumpy stretch, Alex said, "Sorry."

Slumbering in the back seat, Hema's only response was a tiny snore. Scott didn't bother to break his song. In the passenger seat, Lilah stayed silent, her eyes on the moonless sky outside.

"They call this region *bam-e-duniya.*" Alex said. "The roof of the world."

"Heaven?" she asked.

"Guess so," he muttered, feeling foolishly pleased she responded to something so trivial.

From the back, Scott contributed, "This area is the junction of multiple mountain ranges." He rattled off a few names and numbers.

With a lazy sigh, Lilah said, "It feels peaceful, Scott. I imagine heaven would be."

"Yes." After a second or two, Scott added, "The plan with the terrorist... it was good."

"Mostly Victor's idea," said Lilah.

"He's a good man," Scott said, leaving it at that.

There wasn't much conversation after. In a couple of hours, they saw lights moving along a curve ten feet below. "Road," Alex said. "We have to stop and wait for the morning when there's more traffic. On our own, there's a higher risk of getting pulled over."

"The delay," said Scott. "What about Afridi's friends in his village?"

Alex nodded. "No helping it. We can't afford to draw attention from the cops, either." Also, who knew if some of them were in cahoots with the terror groups?

Alex volunteering to take the first watch, the exiles napped in the parked trucks. When Lilah needed to stretch her legs, he accompanied her as guard as she stomped to a tall, pointy rock.

Turning back at the boulder, she started to return to the rest of the group. Alex tugged down the scarf covering his nose and mouth. "Wait a second," he called. "I need to talk to you."

A muffled sound came from behind her clothes, an inflection at the end. Impatiently jerking the wool aside with a gloved finger, she repeated, "What?"

He scanned the landscape... only snow as far as the eyes could see and the road below. Except for the Humvees, there was no place to sit. "The ground will have to do," he said, pulling her down with him.

"It's cold," she complained, cupping her hands together over her nose and mouth.

"I know. But there's no privacy inside... Lilah, what's going on?"

"Heh? What do you mean?"

"You're... different. Not angry or depressed... something else."

"So?" she asked. "We're in a difficult situation. I'm sure you've had your moments, too."

"I know you better than most people, but even I don't understand..." Dammit, there was no good way to ask. Lilah's restlessness started after she got word of Harry's marriage. The bond between them went beyond the affection of a shared childhood. How could it not when they'd been to hell and back together in Libya? Alex was perhaps one of the few people aware of the whole story of what happened to the duo, and Harry had made it clear he and Lilah agreed not to take their friendship any further. Still, who could tell what Lilah actually thought? "You're not upset about Harry, are you?" Alex blurted. "Er... about him getting married?"

She stilled for a second. "What if I am? We're out here, and he..."

"Upset enough to have second thoughts about the network... this exile... all of it? No, I ain't buying the idea. You're too smart to let your personal feelings blind you that much."

Lilah growled as though annoyed with herself. "Of course it isn't because of Harry. There must be some explanation for what he did."

"Then what?" asked Alex. "Victor thinks the attack in Beijing might have been something like a shock to the system. Maybe it's making you regret your decision to follow us. I hope you're not giving up."

"And if I do?"

No one could blame her for it, but Alex couldn't bring himself to believe this second explanation, either. "Don't," he begged. "Without you, we wouldn't... Brad won't be able to... Harry won't..." Mentally, Alex cringed. Definitely not what he meant to say.

"Harry won't let the likes of Steven control the network," Lilah said, tone hardening. "Then there's you, his brother-in-law. He's not going to stop helping simply because I got cold feet. Alex, it's just... I've been wondering what gives any leader the right to sacrifice innocent bystanders. The military-industrial complex... they cook up plenty of excuses, too. What makes us different from them?"

"The military-indus—" Alex started. "C'mon! Are you buying into what Armor and Steven said about us in court? Yes, my brothers and I got a lot of things wrong, but we didn't set out to hurt anyone. Lilah, I used to be... none of us would *dream* of selling out the nation. No way in hell!"

She shook her head. "I'm not talking about Brad's stupid deal. What happens going forward? We are the ones in exile, but there are other people involved in this war besides us. They have plenty to lose, perhaps much more than us. Remember the private I called as witness in Cuba? What do you think Steven and Armor will do to him?"

"Nothing," snapped Alex. "Because the military won't let them."

"God, Alex... you're too trusting. Okay, what about Hema? She got attacked in Panama because of me. Drummond would've killed *her*, too. And Afridi... do you think he would've let her go? Poor girl is in trouble only because of us... because she chose to join us. We can't treat people like cannon fodder."

"We're not," Alex said. "What we're doing is for people like Hema, too. Letting Steven and Armor run the network is too damn dangerous for everyone. You just said so yourself!"

"But..." Stopping, Lilah huffed. "I did say it, and it's true, so why... maybe it's because I'm tired."

"You're not tired," Alex charged. "You *are* upset about Lupe and taking it out on us." As soon as the words were out, Alex shoved gloved fingers into his hair. His hand encountered the hood of the ski jacket and fell. He could've kicked himself. Accusing Lilah of being jealous and self-centered was probably not the right way to persuade her to stay the course.

With a mirthless laugh, Lilah said, "As though you and your brothers haven't done anything for me to get upset!"

"And we're trying to make up for it," Alex snapped. He and Victor even made sure Brad didn't get a chance to object to her plan for the terrorist leader. Raising his hands in surrender, Alex continued, "Lilah, I'm trying to remind you the network is something we built together. If you leave, it will be all of us—including you—losing. There *are* other people involved in the network... our employees, partners, everyone who's relying on us. Just don't make any decisions... look, you used to talk about power and duty and dereliction of duty. Did you stop believing it?"

She made a movement which might have been a shrug, but it was difficult to tell under the bulky clothes. "No. Power should always be about duty, and those in authority simply cannot refuse to do their jobs under whatever pretext. Thing is every war has casualties of some sort. Ours will, too. I'm trying to understand what the limits are where others are concerned. Where do I draw the line? Without that line, how can I call what we're doing a just war?"

Alex sighed. "I get what you're saying. It's been a rough few months... *years* for you, and now we don't know what's happening with Harry. My wife and son, your brothers, everyone else we left behind... poor Mother... she must be scared out of her mind. You're scared, too... wondering if it's all worth the risk to them. Trust me... I've had the same thoughts. Why not try to put the stuff out of your mind for a few hours? Get some rest. Things will look better in the morning."

"What do you think is going to change by morning?" Lilah mocked. She brought her knees up to her chest, tightly hugging her legs. "And how exactly do I 'put stuff out of my mind'?"

Alex managed a smile, frantically hoping he'd be able to break through. "I have something that might help." From the inside of his jacket, he drew out the pouch and set it between them.

As though confused at the sudden change in topic, she stared for a couple of moments before shaking her head. "What is it?"

"Bought it from the chief's wife. At the border." He leaned back, resting on his elbows.

She took the pouch, a small smile blooming as she recognized the jangling sound. "Her jewelry?"

"Better than simply rubies," Alex claimed in a smug tone. "Jewelry... from heaven."

Lilah laughed quietly. "Thank you. This is... umm... very thoughtful... thank you." Leaning down to the side, she brushed cold lips against his cheek.

One of his elbows slid on the slippery snow, and he fell backward, his flailing hand catching her shoulder. When she collapsed on top of him, he sputtered, "Sorry." Wrapping his arms around her, he flipped her onto her back, intending to stand and haul her up with him.

"Cold!" she complained, laughing out loud. "I've got snow in my ear!"

"Careful," said Alex, clambering up and extending a hand. "We don't want Brad to come out here and check what's going on. You heard his little crack about me carrying you. If he sees the jewelry—"

It took Alex a couple of seconds to recognize the fury in her stillness. A muted snarl escaped her mouth, and she scrambled around, searching for something.

"Sorry," he said quickly. "It came out the wrong way. Lilah, I—"

With a violent jangle, she hurled the jewelry pouch toward him. Her glasses fell off in the action. "Don't talk to me," she snapped. "This is exactly what you did when I told you about Godwin. Your priority was protecting your grandfather at all costs. Not Harry's life or my safety. You cowardly little—"

Slipping and sliding, Lilah heaved herself from the snow and looked Alex straight in the eye. One deep breath, and it was as though a curtain of ice dropped between them. Without saying another word, she limped to the Humvee.

Alex managed to get through the next hour sitting in the driver's seat next to her. Her glasses were in his pocket, but he didn't dare offer them back. Staring into the dark night outside, Alex asked the image of his wife what was so damned wrong with what he said. Yeah, Lilah was as much a part of the family as Brad, and no, she was clearly not interested in tolerating her husband's weaknesses, but Alex couldn't abandon his brother.

Her accusations about Godwin's involvement in the murder attempts on Harry were laughable when the Kingsley patriarch had nothing but praises for his grandsons' friend and well-wisher. Grandfather was helpless to do anything on their behalf in the military court in Cuba. Didn't matter if everyone knew Steven tricked Brad into the nuclear deal. There was no actual proof of Steven's treachery, and a former supreme court justice was obligated to uphold the law regardless of his personal feelings.

Dammit, Lilah was a lawyer herself! She should've understood Godwin's dilemma better than anyone else.

"My turn," came Scott's voice.

Startled, Alex sat up. Hours had flown by, and his watch was done. "Come to the front, will you? And drive for a while. I'm gonna go to the other truck and send Victor to you. Got to talk some things over with Brad. Passports and stuff." Surreptitiously, Alex tossed the glasses onto Lilah's lap before leaping out.

Even when morning came, and they joined the traffic on the road going east, Alex remained in the second vehicle. He stayed with Neil and Brad while they drove along the border road in the direction of Shuroobod, the barely guarded town he remembered from his days as a platoon leader. The Humvees got them some cash, as did the cigarettes. It wasn't much, but added to the small amount left over from Macau, the money would get them to their destination. A boatman with a makeshift raft agreed to transport the exiles across the river for the price of the weapons stolen from the terrorists.

Once in Afghanistan, it wasn't difficult to locate a driver to take them to Kabul. The locals were used to Western tourists and their crazy antics. In the Afghani capital, the exiles used Canadian passports provided by the dead mujahideen leader to sign up with a tour company organizing trips across the Hippie Trail. The rickety bus belonging to the company took the group to the city of Quetta in Balochistan province of Pakistan. Then, it was Karachi, followed by Lahore, and finally, the bus rumbled across the border with India.

The exiles' route out of China - part 1 (markings made later by the CIA)

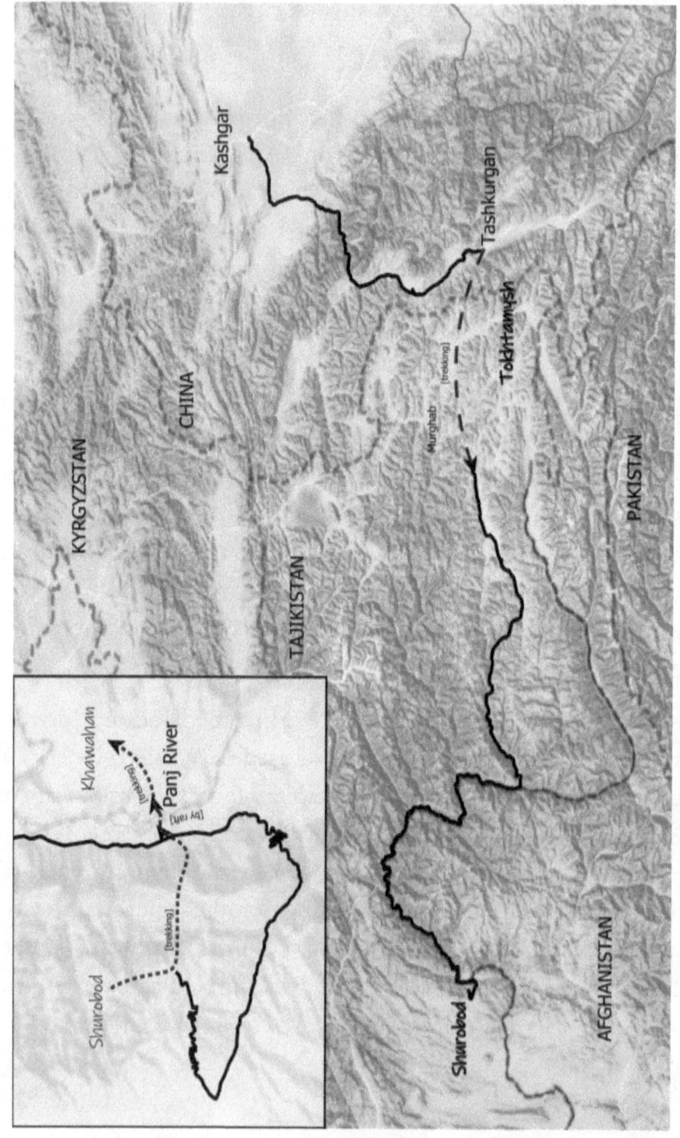

The exiles' route out of China - part 2 (markings made later by the CIA)

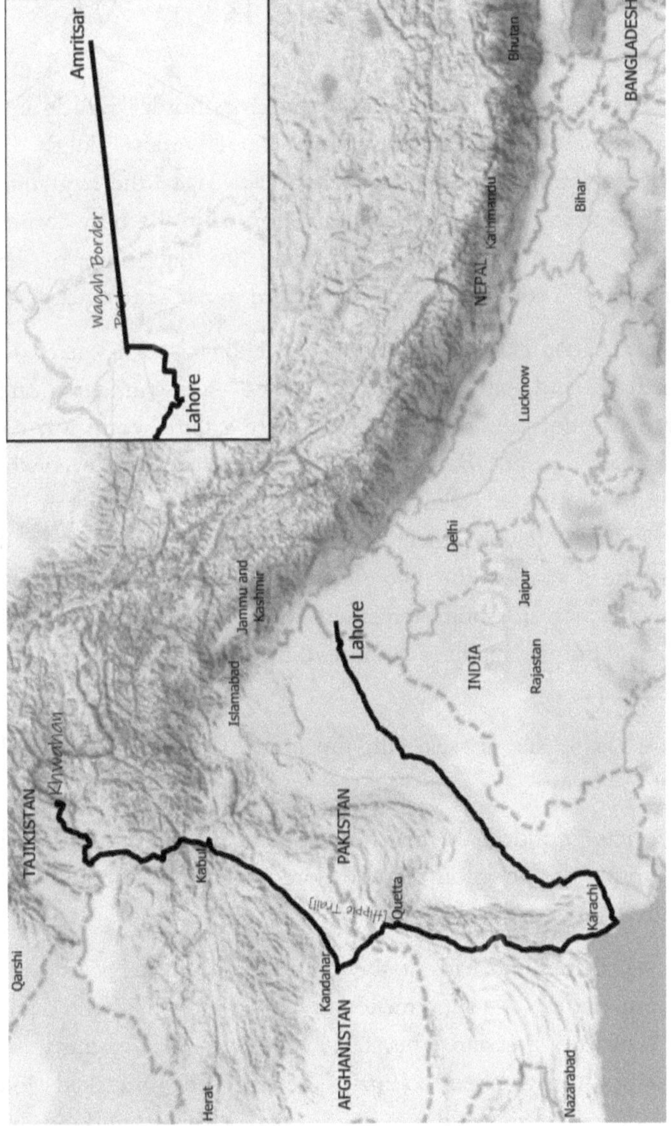

Chapter 13

Backpackers tumbled out of the cross-border vehicle into a terminal crowded with automobiles of various kinds. The sweltering heat, loud chatter in many languages, the fragrance of roasting peanuts from somewhere... no one in the busy corner of the city of Amritsar paid any mind to the group of seven Americans. Yet the exiles couldn't afford to relax their guard.

This conflict-ridden region—extending north across the Himalayas and south to the Arabian Sea—was considered one of the major hotspots on the planet where a third world war could potentially erupt. Border security officers were everywhere. Groups of men in green and khaki uniforms drove past in Jeeps, and quite a few of their comrades patrolled the streets. The hostilities between the two neighboring countries meant every potential incursion point remained heavily guarded. Any suspicious activity, and the fugitives could end up being hauled in to answer questions.

Cleaning his glasses with the hem of his shirt, Scott asked Victor, "Now?"

Victor nodded, darting a quick glance at the trio of soldiers striding in the direction of an armored truck. "Be careful," Victor muttered. "Don't get caught."

As though he had all the time in the world, Scott ambled toward a group of young men with long, matted hair who'd joined the tour from Pakistan. Their talk in the bus suggested this was not their first trip to either country. The stench of unwashed clothes and tobacco smoke and weed permeated the air around the chaps.

In a couple of minutes, a cheerful voice said, "Sure, mate. We'll take you to him."

Alex accompanied Scott while the rest followed several feet behind. Scott carried on a stumbling conversation with their guide, one of the young fellows from the bus. Surreptitiously, Alex kept an eye out for the military, the police... any potential threat to their safety. First sign of trouble, and Victor would get the rest to a pre-arranged spot—a hotel they picked out of a map. Alex and Scott, if they escaped unscathed, would join the group there.

Half an hour later, they were in the middle of what appeared to be a market. Except for a traffic cop arguing with a taxi driver, there didn't appear to be any security around. Many tourists were wandering the narrow lanes, peering curiously into the stalls.

"This is the place," said the exiles' guide.

At the back of the spice store was a turbaned fellow with a bushy beard. Dollar notes traded hands, followed by a bag of quality hash and another of cocaine. "Thanks, man," Scott said to the guide. "I can take it from here." Scott waited until the young fellow disappeared into the street outside. The rest of the group would be waiting in the tea stall next door. Clearing his throat, Scott inclined his head at the drug dealer. "One other thing..."

The exiles were forced to stick around the market until the evening when the dealer's friend, the travel agent, officially closed shop for the day. It took another two days and one of the rocks stolen from the terrorists for expedited delivery of brand-new passports... American, Canadian, and Jamaican. The drugs were already flushed down the toilet in the cheap lodgings suggested by the agent/counterfeiter, but none of the fugitives could sleep more than a few minutes at a stretch in the thirty-six hours they spent in the city. They were wide awake when they boarded yet another tour bus, this one bound for Agra.

#

A day later

The white marble of the Taj Mahal gleamed brightly against the cloudless sky, thousands streaming in and out of its doors. The monument and the city which housed it would be prime target for any miscreant, but law enforcement presence was not as ubiquitous here as it had been at the Indo-Pak border. A tourist guide motioned a group of children in school uniforms and their teachers to go around Alex as he waited outside the phone booth. Inside, Lilah was in conversation with Grayson Sheppard.

Before fleeing their home, the exiles had arranged for Gray to visit Temple's residence in Long Island daily to wait for their call. The former president's phone line was unlikely to be tapped. If anyone dared try—including the Kingsleys—the Secret Service would track down the culprit. Steven would be in deep shit with the American government.

Any time Lilah and the Kingsley brothers changed hiding spots, they called Temple's number from a payphone, leaving carefully worded messages on the answering machine. Grayson would know what the message meant, and he would personally answer a second call at the time mentioned. They would use the former president's line to continue communicating on a regular basis.

Unfortunately, this would be the last such contact between the fugitives and their lawyer unless it happened to be a true life-or-death emergency. Nor could Grayson know exactly where they would hide. The exiles were tracked down three times. Chances were the fake passports they got in Ecuador gave them away, but they couldn't simply hope to escape unscathed a fourth time. To go deeper into hiding, there would be no more talks with Grayson, no more updating him on where they took shelter.

Tugging at his collar, Alex huffed. The heat was near to intolerable after the bone-chilling cold of the Pamirs. He wondered how the women could possibly endure the head-to-toe coverings. In addition to the faded red tunic and printed leggings, Lilah's hair was wrapped in a long scarf, one of its ends pulled across the lower half of her face to conceal her identity. Hema was at a vending cart with Neil, trying to tempt him into testing out Indian street food. The other three of their group were in the budget hotel, sleeping off their exhausting trip.

"Alex," Neil called from the food cart, shaking his head as he laughingly declined whatever dish the vendor was offering. "You eat this. I can't take the spice."

With a wave of his hand, Alex dismissed his brother. He was in no mood for food. The rest of their problems aside, he needed to put an end to this chilliness between him and Lilah. Alex hoped like hell the news from Grayson would soothe her fears about Harry's safety. Once she felt a little less unsettled, she might be more inclined to talk to Alex.

Inside the booth, Lilah's face blanched. Her gaze flew to Alex. Sudden fear jolting his heart, he gestured at her to open the door. It seemed eons before she finally hung up and stumbled out.

"What happened?" Alex asked. "What did Grayson say?"

Eyes skittering unseeingly, she mumbled something.

"What did you say?"

"I need to go to Kedarnath."

Confused, Alex asked, "Where?"

"It's where the mountain is," she said, voice cracking. "The Swargarohini Peak. You said I need to think clearly."

"*What?* Lilah, what exactly did Grayson tell you?"

"Jack Drummond threatened Lupe with deportation," Lilah said, face getting paler by the second. "Harry married her to keep her in the country."

Alex bit back a cluck of impatience. This was the part they knew already. "And?"

Words barely audible, Lilah said, "Lupe died six months ago... murdered... for helping Harry. Uncle Gray said police are going to arrest Harry... for killing Will Luce, Verity's father."

#

There wasn't much quiet to be had in the travel lodge next to the railway station, what with the back-to-back train horns and engine rumbles and myriad noises from the street. Inside Brad's room, silence prevailed as the seven people sitting around weighed options. Some way to survive until the mess back home was sorted out... Alex slouched against the wall next to the closed door and sifted through ideas in his mind.

"How long does it take for such cases to go through the court?" Neil finally asked.

"A few months at least," Lilah whispered, seated on a plastic chair, her folded hands at her chin. "Years, sometimes."

Tone somber, Victor said, "Keep in mind the possibility of a guilty verdict."

Alex shifted in place. *Years?* Sabrina... Michael... Patrice... how long was Alex expected to stay away from his wife and son? And Harry... he was at risk of serving time only because he supported the exiles in their fight. On the other hand, there were the treason charges on Brad. *What am I supposed to do?* Alex asked silently.

The other men in the room were glancing at each other, discomfort on all their faces. So was Hema. Lilah's eyes were closed as though in prayer, her lashes stark against pale cheeks.

"So what's our next step?" Neil asked. "We can't give up and return. Brad will get arrested. But how long can we keep running?"

If Brad were to be convicted, there was a high chance he would get the death penalty. Treason was not a small crime. Alex shook his head. Sabrina and Michael were alive and safe back in the States, and one more year or so spent apart wasn't going to kill any of them.

"Harry can appeal," Scott said. He turned to the lawyer in the group. "Right, Lilah?"

"Yes," she agreed almost tonelessly.

"It's gonna take more time," said Neil. "And cash... which Harry doesn't have. We don't, either." Allies of the exiles found themselves cornered financially, forbidden from selling their stock to raise money. Only Shawn had enough assets to help support Lilah and the five brothers, the funds deposited into her Swiss bank account.

Yeah, the government in Berne didn't usually entertain demands from Uncle Sam to divulge info on the customers of their financial institutions. Still, being tracked down three times left the fugitives wary of accessing the Swiss bank funds and perhaps leaving a trail for their enemies to follow. Of the gemstones stolen from the Afghan terrorists, two remained, but to use those, the group would need to find yet another criminal buyer. This time, one with enough loose cash to fork out in exchange for the jewels. More risk.

"It might get to a point where the only option will be to return," said Brad. At the murmurs from his brothers, he raised a hand. "Didn't you read Grandfather's interview? All he wants is peace in the family. I could agree to permanently hand over control to Steven. Then, Grandfather can help me get a pardon. He will. Right now, he can't do a single thing because Steven's the CEO, and he calls the shots. Steven won't care what Grandfather does as long as it doesn't cost him the position."

Putting her hands down on the armrests, Lilah sat up in the chair. "*You* will agree to hand over control?" she asked. "To Steven? What happens to all the people who helped us? What about Harry and... and Lupe... and everyone else who sacrificed? What about justice for me?"

Voice irate, Brad started, "What do *you* suggest—"

"Bro, it's not a decision we need to make right away," interjected Victor. "So what's the point of fighting about it now? Let the case go through the courts. In the meantime, we'll do what we meant to do anyway—hide."

"I'm with Victor on this," said Alex. "It may look hopeless now, but Harry will find a way. He's Petty Officer First Class Harry Sheppard. They gave him the Medal of Honor for a reason. No one's going to lock him up for long for something he didn't do. He can't make any moves at the moment without inviting attention, but my bet is he's waiting for an opening. He'll strike the first chance he gets."

"How is he going to get *any* chances if he's found guilty?" asked Brad. "He'll be in prison!"

"Won't be easy," Alex admitted. "And I don't know how long it will take—"

"Five years," Lilah interjected. Everyone else looked toward her. "From what Grayson said, it will be five years in custody before Harry can apply for parole."

"The first opening he gets." Neil huffed. "Shit. What a mess."

Mess? It didn't begin to describe… Alex couldn't speak for a couple of seconds. Five years away from Sabrina… half a damned decade. Not merely a few more months. Michael would be almost twelve by the time Alex returned. How could any father possibly—

Brad nodded. "How are we going to hide anywhere for five years without money?"

"There's really no other option," Victor said. "Yeah, Steven might let Grandfather ask for a pardon if we agree to give up all claims on the business. What happens if he doesn't? Our cousins would rather not have us around at all. Also, remember what they were like before. Back when we were kids… Steven said he wanted a truce, and we took him at his word. Think about where it got us. What happens if he lures us back home, then gets Brad arrested?"

Death penalty… Alex raked his hair with his hand. *I'm sorry,* he said to the woman whose image he carried in his heart. How could he be happy with his wife and kid, knowing his brother died in the trap they stupidly let him walk into?

"I get it," said Brad. "But where do we go that we won't be found in a matter of weeks?"

Ignoring the splinter of guilt and pain, Alex offered, "Getting help from Lilah's Indian relatives is a possibility, but it's one of the first places anyone would think to look for us. Same for help from people we know in the Gateway office in Bombay. Or…"

"Or?" Brad prompted.

Alex pushed off from the wall. "We could go someplace our enemies won't imagine us picking. Someplace right under their noses."

Part V

Chapter 14

A week later, December 1989

World Trade Center, New York City

"Even in court, there is presumption of innocence," Harry argued.

The conference room was packed. Not a single board member failed to show up. At the head of the table was Ryan Sheppard, Harry's father. He hadn't spoken a word since the beginning of the meeting. His once-dark hair and beard appeared to have turned completely gray over the past few months. On Ryan's left sat Sophia, Harry's mother. Sophia Sheppard had semi-retired since the business took off, but she couldn't stay away this afternoon. The wrinkles on her face bore witness to the stress she suffered. Harry's brother was seated to the right of their father, doing all the talking.

"So what do you propose we do?" Hector asked. "Wait until the police arrest you and some court rules on the case? Do you realize how long it could take? What do you imagine will happen to Gateway in the meantime? No, Harry. You are my brother, and I owe you my personal loyalty. But as an executive in the company, I have a fiduciary duty to the stockholders to put their interests first. Allowing you to continue as part of Gateway will be detrimental to the prospects of the organization. It won't be fair to anyone... partners, management, or employees."

"What about fairness to me?" Harry asked. This hall... the row of windows overlooking downtown Manhattan... the ocean beyond the island... he'd been part of the company from its inception. He'd shut up as ordered while Lilah sacrificed her future so the Sheppards could save their sorry asses from Sanders. Harry stood by their side through every deal big and small, clinked glasses after every loan repayment to Andrew Barrons. When they moved from the old office in Brooklyn to their current digs in the South Tower, Harry carried box after box into trucks, folder after folder, and the last pencil lying forlorn under the radiator.

"Oh, I think we've been more than fair to you," said Hector. "Father and I made it clear we couldn't let you sell your stock to support people accused of treason, and you decided you could no longer abide by the rules of the organization. Instead of turning in your resignation, you took a long leave of absence. You then went to the press with your cockamamie theories about the Kingsleys. You purposefully and deliberately leveled unsubstantiated accusations against a partner company while officially still a part of Gateway. You maligned the image of the network merely because your favored candidate lost. Correction: Brad Kingsley gambled the network away. In spite of it, you continue to support him. Do you believe any of our employees who did the same would have been allowed to work another day for Gateway? Now, this thing with Will Luce's death. The network voted you out, and our board will decide whether to do the same."

"Hector," called Dante Maro, the COO of Gateway. The tall, lanky African-American was aging rapidly as well, his hair now thin and face lined profusely. "Your brother never claimed to be speaking for Gateway in any of his dealings with the media. I don't believe the company has any right to dictate to any employee what he or she should do with private time."

Hector flushed. He might be the CEO's eldest son, but Dante outranked him at work. "Of course my brother has his rights as a citizen of the country, but don't Gateway's shareholders have a right to expect the executives to refrain from behavior detrimental to the organization? Besides, it's not as if he'll be left destitute without his paycheck."

"I agree," said a voice. A hefty businessman tapped his glasses on the pile of papers in front of him. "As you said, Hector, no other executive would've been given the latitude Harry enjoyed. The line has to be drawn. If not at murder, then where? If the Sheppards decide he's entitled to behave as he pleases on account of his connection to the CEO, I can guarantee the company won't last much longer. What do you say, Ryan? You built this firm. Surely, you're not going to stand by and watch while your boy destroys it all."

"Uhh..." Ryan Sheppard attempted to sit up in his chair, his movements clumsy. The once-tall form appeared to have shrunk. His wife was biting her lip, her blue eyes watery. Gray-streaked blonde strands escaped the usually neat bun. Hector resembled her in appearance, and his suit was high end, but his stance betrayed the fighter within the commodities broker. "Harry," Ryan called. "Son... if you continue... I shouldn't have to tell you..."

Chapter 15

Ten minutes later

"Mr. Sheppard," a television reporter shouted the moment Harry exited the World Trade Center and stepped out on to the street in front of the South Tower. She thrust a microphone under Harry's nose, her cameraman filming.

Despite the freezing weather, there were more of her colleagues waiting their turns, some smoking, some drinking coffee from Styrofoam cups. Pedestrians hurried on to their destinations, many audibly complaining about the press presence.

"Your liaison with Ms. Valdez was big news in the tabloids," continued the TV reporter. Liaison... investigators assigned to Lupe's death remained unaware of her marriage, and the few people in the know did not volunteer the information. "Could you tell us more about her?" asked the journalist.

"There will never be anyone else like Lupe," Harry responded automatically.

Sabrina's car was pulling in, Liam getting out from the passenger side. She was at the wheel, glaring at the gathered journos. Michael would be in the back seat. Harry shook his head slightly. If the press recognized them, there would be more personal questions about the exiles, about Harry's divorce from Verity, about Luce, Sr.'s death, about Lupe.

Right on cue, another journalist called, "Harry... any updates on the Luce murder?"

"I've been advised by my legal team not to talk about it." There *were* no answers Harry could offer... at least, no answers which could be shared with the world.

The info he got from the club revealed Charles Kingsley showed up the night of Lupe's disappearance. DC cops dismissed his presence as nothing out of the ordinary, and Harry's theory she went outside to find a way to warn him was not something New York's law enforcement wanted to hear. The latest assumption was she left the club for reasons no one knew and was killed in a mugging gone wrong. Crime wasn't exactly unknown in the capital of the United States. Neither Harry nor Liam bought the idea. It wasn't coincidence Drummond went to Beijing the same time. One woman escaped, and the other ended up dead. Both men would pay. Someday.

There was also the embezzling. Liam was looking into the co-conspirators for clues to his father's murder. Harry insisted Liam put it out how he was merely investigating the theft to clear the Luce name, but the Kingsleys would see his continued support of Harry for what it was... a threat to their safety. The enemy didn't have cause to worry yet. Liam's investigations yielded nothing... except for a few inexplicable details.

The apartment meant for low-income New Yorkers where Luce, Sr. was found was rented under his name. He had a perfectly good home of his own in his very high-income Connecticut neighborhood, which authorities verified he had not lost at cards. They claimed Luce might have wanted the place in Brooklyn as base for his illicit activities or perhaps to meet his debtors. More curious was the pizza box left at the scene of the crime, with the crumpled tissue inside. There was no receipt to be found. The owner of the deli right next to the subway station confirmed Harry wasn't carrying the pie with him when he bought water from the store right after he got out of the train. Nor was there enough time for him to have ordered a late-night snack and consumed it even as he stuck a knife into the victim's back. The official assumption was Luce bought the food... but days ago since there was no trace of it in the stomach contents. There were also no fingerprints on the box. Despite Harry's denial, the police believed he wiped the container, and what reason would Luce, Sr. have to clean it up?

The response Liam got from the New York City Department of Corrections was even more concerning. The one solid lead he and Harry thought they had in the matter of the embezzlement was James McCoy. The man once attempted to poison Neil Kingsley and Dan Barrons to hide the discrepancies in his books. McCoy surely knew something which could help... except, he'd somehow managed to secure post-conviction bail sometime before Luce's death.

Bail after conviction? Almost unheard of, according to Harry's own lawyer. No question there was an attorney helping McCoy, someone with the legal knowledge, the clout, and the motive to aid the criminal. Someone perhaps like Major Richard Armor, the Kingsley attack dog who interrogated Lilah in Cuba. There was McCoy's alibi for the day of the Luce murder. According to the police, McCoy was in Las Vegas. He produced the permission slip from the official supervising him and hotel receipts as proof. Also, there was nothing linking him to the Kingsleys.

The crowd of reporters outside the South Tower didn't appear to notice when Sabrina's car took off quietly. "All right," said the journo who asked for updates on the Luce case. "What about the latest theory on the Temple assassination attempt? Your comment?"

Impatient mutters rose from other reporters. The shooting happened little more than a year ago, but it was already fading from the public mind. There was juicier stuff for the press to cover.

"Do I believe it was a random act by a mentally unstable person?" Harry smiled grimly. "No, but I'm holding on to my faith in the nation's investigating agencies. I hope they don't simply close the book on the crime."

Unfortunately, there was nothing to suggest any other motive. Some note explaining reasons, a phone call to the media... there was nothing heard from any radical group, and why else would anyone want to kill a former American president? Harry dismissed the FBI's assumptions. The shooter couldn't have gotten away from Times Square without help. Perhaps there was assistance from someone in official capacity... which meant a pre-planned attack. Then again, the cops couldn't find any evidence Temple was followed which would've been an essential part of any such plan. But neither Harry nor Liam would stop looking.

"What about the situation in Gateway?" the reporter pressed. "You have already lost support from the Kingsleys and the Barronses. Rumor has it you will soon be relieved of your responsibilities in the family business... if it hasn't been done already at today's board meeting."

"The Barronses have not commented one way or the other," Harry countered. "As for the Sheppards—" Harry hesitated, suddenly unsure of what he wanted to say.

"Gateway put out a press statement last week stating they vehemently oppose your allegations regarding the Kingsley family," the reporter reminded Harry. "There are many in the company who believe the oil network is better off under Steven Kingsley. They support the network's action in ousting you from the chairmanship. They support the expected restructuring of the network so Brad Kingsley—your candidate—would not get back to being CEO even if he got pardoned. Steven Kingsley will now be both chairman and CEO. Your own brother signed the statement."

"I can't answer for Hector," responded Harry. Hector Sheppard trusted Steven more than anyone else in the world. Even Ryan and Sophia... they were hurting terribly, but Harry wasn't sure his parents believed his protestations of innocence in the Luce matter.

If only there was some evidence he could show his family. McCoy was thus far the only solid lead unearthed by Liam and Harry's investigations. All they needed was one thread connecting the embezzler to the Kingsleys. One death to pin on them... just one of the murders... the entire conspiracy would unravel. Until then, no one would buy Harry's claims. Until then, Liam would need to lay low.

"What I *can* say is this," Harry continued. "The network was meant to help stabilize the sector, and the only way we're going to achieve it is through Brad. Steven is not a fit leader."

"You seem to have an incredible amount of faith in Brad Kingsley's leadership," said the reporter. "Enough to go against your own family."

"They're Brad's family, too, in a circuitous way. Alex is married to my sister."

The reporter smiled. "You must be the world's best brother-in-law."

For a second, Harry couldn't speak. Lupe once said the same to him. "Alex and his brothers were wronged, and I want justice for them. Also, Alex is not merely my brother-in-law... he's a friend. I'm willing to give up anything—my parents, my siblings, whatever I have—to make sure he returns."

It could take years. Harry would need to bide his time until he found incontrovertible proof of enemy involvement in his legal troubles… or of his innocence. Until it happened, any funny business from him or anyone connected with him to implicate his adversaries would be taken as further evidence of his own guilt. There was absolutely nothing else he could do with all eyes boring into him.

Still, the government, the media, the Kingsleys… they would blink at some point. Only when they looked away would Harry get the chance to strike back. He needed to wait at least until then.

If Harry couldn't find the restraint to take the long and hard road, he wouldn't be the only one suffering. Lilah might not be able to return. Sabrina might never see her husband again, and their little boy could lose his father. The massive network of oil companies would permanently end up in the hands of the Kingsley crooks, with anyone who dared object slaughtered mercilessly. *Patience,* Harry admonished himself for the millionth time.

Chapter 16

A day later

Chicago, Illinois

Wild applause erupted in the basketball court, the two young lads next to Harry jumping up and down in excitement. "Careful, Gabe," Harry said to Victor Kingsley's seven-year-old son who was clambering to stand on his seat with a half-eaten hot dog in his hand. Ketchup decorated Gabriel's face and hair.

Michael, too, leaped onto his chair, screaming loud enough to shatter eardrums. His soda cup dropped to the floor. Paying the spilled drink no mind, the boy yelled, *"Michael!"* as the Bulls' star player, Michael Jordan, faced off with the legendary Magic Johnson. Whistles and shouts abounded all around.

Dammit... Harry would've loved to scream along. He didn't even dare plan a day out with the lads without making sure there was another adult with them. Dan and Shawn were on the other side of the boys... in case Harry was called away unexpectedly on the matter of Luce, Sr.'s murder.

At least the two cousins seemed to have forgotten their worries in the thrill of watching the game. In August, two months after Will Luce's funeral, Sabrina received news of a death in California. Eddie Garcia, the man who fostered Victor's son, passed without warning from a heart attack. *Señora* Garcia was sickly herself and could hardly deal with Gabriel on her own. Victor's wife, Luisa, was at a loss on what to do with a stepson she barely knew. Even his own father couldn't claim to know young Gabriel well.

Sabrina first invited Gabriel to spend Thanksgiving. It was a squeeze with all of them in Harry's two-bedroom, but the cousins had a great time together. Michael perked up quite a bit with the other boy around, and the sullen look on Gabriel's face vanished in a couple of days. Both lads were immensely interested in Harry's motorcycle, his medals, and his weapons. They were thrilled when he let them take turns on the driver's seat of the parked Harley, listening intently as he explained the various parts and their functions. Michael even asked about shooting lessons. The outrage on Sabrina's face on hearing the question made the two boys howl with mirth. It was damned good to see them laugh, but there were moments... muted mutters between the lads... Harry didn't need to ask what they were talking about.

Once Christmas vacation was at an end, Gabriel would return to San Diego and finish his school year while his foster mother completed some paperwork. Afterward, Gabriel Kingsley was moving to New York to live with Sabrina and Michael. She was already looking for a house big enough for the three of them. There was one she particularly liked, right next to Temple's Long Island residence.

They would be safer there. Harry needed time and privacy to plan his activities. Besides, the boys were better off away from the constant reminders of the problems in the family. This game in Chicago was supposed to be a break for them. Except, there was the presence of Lilah's brothers... the young lads liked Dan and Shawn, but their company wouldn't have been necessary if not for the threat of the government inviting Harry to be their guest any day now.

"Did you see it?" screamed Gabriel. "Another three-pointer!"

The boys leaped down from their chairs and did a little victory dance. Even Dan and Shawn were red-faced in excitement, shouting cheers for their respective teams. Shawn wore a yellow-billed Lakers cap while Dan sported a Bulls jersey.

Harry couldn't tell what the hell he missed. He didn't even know the score. An arrest... it was coming any day now. Petty Officer Harry Sheppard would be in prison, counted among the worst of humanity.

The criminal defense attorney hired by Noah was excellent at his job, Harry told himself. The gent was personally handling the high-profile case with an entire team of junior lawyers assisting him. They all admitted an arrest was imminent. Under normal circumstances, the state was unlikely to slap charges on Harry with the pitiful little evidence found thus far, but there was simply too much media attention, too much political pressure for the government not to make a move.

The chairman of the Peter Kingsley Network was caught standing over a dead body, blood from the murdered man staining his shoes. Every politician looking to beef up his reputation—egged on, no doubt, by the Kingsleys—was calling on law enforcement to get Harry. The case was being compared to those of the young black men from the same impoverished Crown Heights neighborhood who were serving life sentences on much weaker evidence. If they could go to prison, why not a billionaire oil broker? Several members of the network chimed in, virtuously proclaiming support for equal justice. If Jared Sanders—an immigrant who was only pursuing the American dream—could be thrown in jail for deaths which happened under his watch, why not Harry?

Newspapers spent pages and pages speculating if the authorities would turn a blind eye to the violent crime committed by one of the nation's elite. A sense of disbelief permeated the articles about Harry's claims to be innocent even in publications usually friendly to him. Means, motive, opportunity... police statements made it clear to the press Harry had all three to kill Will Luce. Not to mention the fact there were no other suspects. No one who might want Luce, Sr. dead was spotted anywhere near the apartment building where the body was found. Public opinion had already tilted against Harry.

Any day now, the district attorney would call the defense lawyer and ask Harry to turn himself in.

"*Go!*" roared the crowd, rising from chairs.

Harry jolted. Once again, he didn't have a clue what just happened, but he stood with the rest of the audience as they applauded. Across the court were a couple of uniformed cops. Eyes narrowing, Harry studied them. The two men disappeared through a doorway. The pounding behind Harry's brow decreased in intensity. No... they weren't at the game to pick him up. The defense attorney had said the state would prefer to avoid a public arrest in high-profile cases like Harry's. He would get a message to show up at the DA's office.

The entire family was desperate for the circus to be over, but Harry's legal team advised him to prepare for the case to drag on for months. The prosecution's theory had more holes than Swiss cheese, and the defense would point each one out to the jury. A dozen random people from different walks of life... popular sentiment was not supposed to guide them. Unfortunately for the defense team, the twelve men and women deciding their client's fate were unlikely to be completely ignorant of what was being written in the press.

Nor would the jury be allowed to hear Harry's theories about Steven and the rest of the Kingsleys. Any evidence offered in support of the enemy's prior malfeasance would be dismissed as irrelevant since there was no link—none whatsoever—connecting the Kingsley family to Will Luce's death.

The defense lawyer had already warned Harry about the possibility of losing. But they could and would appeal. Once the nation inevitably turned its attention to the next salacious story, it would be easier for them to... it would also be easier for the Kingsleys to ensure Harry's demise after a guilty verdict. The enemy would be planning, anticipating counterattacks—

Something flashed in the periphery of Harry's visual field. A man holding a TV camera was walking along just outside the sideline of the court. He was filming the audience, not the game. Did the fellow spot Harry and the rest of the group?

There were more men in uniform walking alongside the videographer. Security wasn't unusual at sporting events, but why were they following the media? One of the guards seemed to be looking directly at the boys but showed no sign of recognition.

Pinching the bridge of his nose, Harry stared straight ahead. He wasn't doing anything at the game which could've drawn the attention of the guards. And if the journo did indeed recognize Harry, he'd have to return some other day for a comment. The boys didn't need to hear any more of the shit than they already had.

Glancing again at the two lads celebrating the Bulls' narrow victory, Harry swore in his mind. His mistake cost them the fathers who should've been at the game with them, and there was nothing he could do to atone for his sins. Not right now.

The Kingsleys couldn't use the legal system to keep him shackled for eternity. At some point, the media would get bored with the story. At some point, the authorities would turn their attention to other crimes. The instant it happened, Harry would be ready. A loose aggressive strategy... a targeted assault to force the enemy into a tight spot.

Patience, Harry told himself again. The game he was forced into playing was going to be a long one, and the only way to win was to do nothing at the moment. He would use the time to study the enemy until he knew them better than they did themselves. He would plan and prepare, and he would wait for the right moment to launch his attack. All the while, he would be in prison, counted among rapists and murderers and drug dealers.

Harry rolled his shoulders. Truth without valor to defend it was useless, and valor without sacrifice was meaningless. It was his turn to sacrifice.

Walking out of the arena into the crowded street, Gabriel belted out Queen's rock anthem, "We Will Rock You."

After a beat or two, Harry joined the singing, howling his lungs off at the heavens and making Michael laugh. The six-year-old gave it his best shot as well, with Dan and Shawn guffawing. The people on the street either chuckled or paid no mind as they continued on their way.

"Mr. Sheppard," came a voice from somewhere to the right.

Some reporters simply didn't respect even family time. Ignoring the summons, Harry continued his clown act. The boys did the same, but Dan peered sideways. The mirth on his face vanished instantly.

"Mr. Sheppard," the voice called again, tone peremptory. There was a frisson of fear in Harry's chest, but he continued singing as he turned. A few men were waiting, all in business suits. "Police," said the leader of the team.

Stopping his performance, Harry inclined his head at Dan and Shawn. "The boys..."

"Let's go, kids," said Shawn. "Your uncle can talk to the officers while we get some pizza."

"Call Liam," Harry instructed Dan before the group walked away. "He'll know what to do."

The cops didn't wait for the kids to be out of earshot. "Harry Sheppard," started the lead officer. "You're under arrest for the murder of William Luce. You have the right to remain silent. Anything you say..."

Part VI

Chapter 17

Next week, December 1989

Upper East Side, New York City

Richard did a quick three-sixty of the conference hall in the Kingsley residence. The Gilded Age mansion boasted of six stories, not including the basement. This particular chamber, meant for media interaction, showed little of the fabulous opulence of the rest of the dwelling. Looked like any press room in any damned hotel, Richard decided. State-of-the-art equipment, of course. Nothing less than the best for the likes of the Kingsleys.

"Mr. Armor," a nasal voice called from the inner door. The ancient butler waited there, his skinny back held erect. Except for the maids and the cleaning people who came and went, most of Godwin Kingsley's retainers were as old as dirt. In their mid-seventies, Richard's own adoptive parents were among the younger ones. Why they stuck with the arrogant patriarch was something Richard would never understand. "Mr. Steven requests that you join him and the family in the breakfast room since the press conference doesn't start for an hour," informed the butler.

His tone was even, betraying none of his feelings on the invitation. The rest of the servants didn't have much to do with Richard when he lived in the apartment over the garage with his parents. Even as a boy, he knew his destiny was different and never bothered to interact with the staff, which left him friendless because the rich brats in the neighborhood wanted nothing to do with him. Then, Steven Kingsley offered Richard the hand of friendship.

When time brought the changes of manhood with it, the maids in the mansion started noticing Richard. Their encounters with him usually ended in mutual pleasure, but he always made it clear there would be no offer of matrimony. His eyes were set far, far above what they would ever dare imagine. Yet the heiresses he met in Steven's company maintained the façade of affability only as long as the Kingsley scion stuck around. The rich bitches never cared to acknowledge Richard otherwise... except of course when they were naked under him in the privacy of their rooms.

Someday, Richard had sworn. Someday, the bastard adopted by the Kingsley chauffeur and his wife would make his mark in the world. Someday, the arrogant princesses would be begging *him* for acknowledgment. He'd prove to them he was better than the men in their families—their daddies, their brothers, their spineless boyfriends and husbands. Better than Alex, the Kingsley golden boy, who got everything on a platter.

Richard worked hard for everything he achieved—West Point, his promotions, law school, the drilling business he eventually bought. He owed his success to no one except himself.

"Mr. Armor?" the butler called again.

Mister, not Major. To Godwin Kingsley and his servants, Richard would remain a mere mister no matter what he achieved in life. The only one in the household to ever treat him as an equal was Steven. If it weren't for their friendship, Richard would not have put up with the slight.

#

Fifteen minutes later

"Do you understand what Godwin could do to you?" Richard asked, battling the urge to hurl Charles's aristocratic ass out through the window of the six-story mansion.

Brown hair disheveled and reeking of gin, Charles Kingsley—Steven's little brother—slumped in his chair at the breakfast table. He was in no shape to respond. Steven's parents had already left on some errand or the other, giving their elder son and Richard a few minutes to grapple with this new problem created by Charles.

"One day!" Steven shouted at his brother. "I told Grandfather even you could manage to control yourself for one damn day."

"Keep it down, Steven," Richard said, glancing toward the arched doorway leading to this magnificent corner of the house bearing the modest label of breakfast nook. Maids were always walking in and out, bringing fresh coffee, clearing the sideboard, or cleaning up. Richard didn't want to take the chance of anyone overhearing what he and Steven had to say to Charles. Not when the topic was the death of the DC madam at Charles's hands and Godwin's ultimatum to make the loser behave or else.

"How the hell do I—" Steven started. He looked around the sun-drenched room as though making sure none of the domestic staff was within earshot. "Thanks to you," Steven said to his useless brother, "we can't cut JD loose."

The sleazy congressman had sworn he'd travel to Beijing himself. There were trusted men in his employ whom he could set after Lilah. Steven and Richard of course knew JD would try to have his fun before finishing her off. They simply didn't imagine he'd be incompetent enough to get caught.

The politician claimed to Steven there were people stationed inside the strip club who would make sure the Valdez woman didn't get a chance to warn Sheppard. Charles was only supposed to show her his mug as a reminder of JD. Once Sheppard got arrested, the woman could've been cowed into continuing her cooperative attitude. Even after Charles returned from DC and took off on another of his exotic vacations, Steven and Richard didn't know what happened. Then, merely days after the Luce murder, news reports came on television, announcing Lupe Valdez's violent demise.

Both Richard and Steven immediately realized who was responsible. In the six months since, the two of them just about managed to make Charles avoid the kind of behavior which could cause DC cops to train their sights on him. It would be a short line to draw from the idiot Kingsley to the rest of his family.

"Charlie, how could you be dumb enough not to realize you were JD's insurance?" Steven asked.

The politician didn't mention the exiles to the authorities or the media, but if someone made the connection independently, the Kingsleys couldn't use JD as patsy. Charles had insisted JD never told him what to do. Of course he didn't. But a hint here... a sly suggestion... the shady politician knew exactly what would happen. He had the Kingsleys exactly where he wanted them.

The minute Steven tried to blame his brother-in-law for any mishaps... even if the family simply failed to express continued support... JD would threaten to reveal Charles's part in Lupe Valdez's death. Pinning a second murder on Harry Sheppard was not possible when he was hundreds of miles away in Brooklyn. Charles was in town, in the club building. If the cops decided to dig further—

Slouching in his own chair, Steven groaned. "Dammit, *I* need a drink. God only knows what Grandfather's going to say when he hears what Charlie's done now."

Steven's big fear after news of Lupe Valdez's death broke was Godwin Kingsley might decide to get rid of both problems in one swoop—JD and Charles. The former supreme court justice was already in a towering rage about the setback they suffered because of the congressman's incompetence, and Charles's worth was reduced to a negative in Godwin's book. Those who got on said list weren't slated for a long and happy life.

Steven didn't give a damn about his sister's husband, but Charles was another matter. Steven loved his loser brother.

"Stick to coffee for the time being," Richard said. He took a healthy gulp of the creamy brew and grimaced. Black with no sugar was how he preferred his caffeine. "But we're both getting smashed after the presser." Glaring at the Kingsley idiot, he called, "Charlie."

The drunk merely snorted in response.

"Charlie," repeated Richard. "Pay attention, please." When the idiot finally looked up, Richard continued, "Do you not understand the only reason you're still alive is your brother?"

Steven was Godwin's front man for the Kingsley takeover of the network, the fall guy if things went south. Knowing it, Steven still agreed to his grandfather's plan for a coup because Brad was a damned fool who didn't deserve the position he found himself in. It didn't matter Steven was now in charge of both the Peter Kingsley Company and the wider network. When Godwin issued commands, he expected them obeyed. If anyone ever felt tempted to challenge the old man, all he'd have to do was remember what happened to Brad's wife.

"Yeah," muttered Charles.

Steven had presented a story for the Kingsley lawyer to recount to the detectives investigating the Lupe Valdez case. Charles went to the strip club for the same purpose as every other male—to see some skin. He'd been to Eden before, and it wasn't as if his weakness for women was not known.

Charles was the diametric opposite of Steven who was more circumspect in his appreciation of the fairer sex. Oh, both Steven and Richard had also visited Eden, but not the one in DC. And neither ever caused women to shudder in revulsion, unlike Charles. The useless piece of shit was blessed with both money and the Kingsley looks like the rest of the men in the family. He inherited the height, the brown hair, the gray eyes. Charles also possessed the degree from West Point paid for with Godwin's cash. The ladies would've put up with a lot from Charles Kingsley, but he seemed to have an uncontrollable need to... especially when said women were not in a position of power. Not to mention the drinking and the lack of anything resembling a brain.

In Godwin's presence, Charles was instructed not to talk to any cop without his lawyer present. Richard obtained for the Kingsley patriarch a copy of police report which showed the victim was still alive and accounted for when Charles left the club. Harry Sheppard did try telling the investigators the Kingsleys arranged the murder, but the claim was ignored.

Godwin ordered Steven to keep his brother on the straight and narrow until the uproar subsided, until they devised an alternate strategy to deal with the exiles. There would be no more drinking for Charles, no strippers, no complaints from any quarter about unwelcome sexual advances. Neither Steven nor Richard dared ask or else what. There weren't many men Richard feared, but the former supreme court justice and Kingsley patriarch made the cut.

"After everything we talked about, how could you possibly—" Richard started. "Never mind. Steven, let's figure out how to handle this so your grandfather doesn't get to know."

"One thing," Steven said, biting into a piece of toast with force. "Charlie, you had one thing to do. Do you realize your name is already on the press invites?"

Both brothers and Richard were supposed to attend the presser scheduled less than an hour from now. Even after Sheppard's arrest, stories circulated in certain parts of the media which designated Steven as the villain of the entire saga. A public show of support from his own family was needed at today's event where a crucial topic was sure to be brought up. Steven's father, David, was nearly blind and uncomfortable in such settings. Godwin couldn't be seen giving legitimacy to his grandson's rule of the oil sector when the capture of power was supposed to have been Steven's handiwork alone, something the former supreme court justice was supposedly against. Aaron Kingsley, Steven's uncle, always took Brad's side. Richard could almost feel sorry for Steven, having only Charles to play supportive relative.

Godwin warned Steven against hauling his brother along for the news conference. Steven insisted Charles knew better than to break the rules when they were this close to a complete victory. Except the Kingsley loser turned up hungover.

"Maybe we should just let him sleep it off," Richard suggested, eyeing the drunk. "I doubt any of the reporters is going to ask about Charlie, but if they do, we can tell them he caught the flu."

Shaking his head, Steven said, "Can't risk it. The staff saw him coming in. Grandfather's going to hear what happened, and he's going to want to know why we changed our minds about having Charlie with us. We're gonna have to make sure he gets through the press conference somehow so there's no way for anyone to claim he's a weak link."

"If he says something..." objected Richard.

"We'll jump in," said Steven. "Charlie, you stupid little shit, I'll get someone to clean you up. Just sit at the table and don't say a word. Rich and I will handle everything."

Huffing, Richard took another sip of the coffee. The loser had thirty minutes to make himself presentable to the media.

Richard wished they'd handled everything right from the beginning instead of involving JD and Charles. The Kingsleys should've been celebrating the downfall of all their enemies in one smooth move. Major Richard Armor should've been reveling in his triumph over Harry Sheppard, former SEAL and Medal of Honor winner.

"No matter what, I will not let Grandfather do anything to..." Steven paused. "There are some things I value more than Kingsley Corp."

Yeah, Richard knew. Steven would battle the patriarch himself for his parents and his siblings... and for his best friend, the Kingsley chauffeur's adopted son.

#

Less than an hour later

Cameras flashed as Richard took his seat at the conference table. The image would be in papers and television screens, and the nation would witness Major Richard Armor sitting alongside the Kingsley brothers as their equal.

As promised, Charles had been cleaned up, bloodshot eyes the only evidence of his wild partying the night before. On his other side was Steven, face slightly pale but pose relaxed.

"Mr. Kingsley," one of the reporters called Steven. "Anything new from the state department regarding the Panama situation?"

As CEO of the network, Steven was informed in advance about many events, including the invasion of Panama by American forces which started the week before. "The state department can give its own updates," Steven said. "As for the network... Panama remains our headquarters on paper for now, but most of our operations were moved to the U.S. a few years ago." It had been done by the ousted executives, but Steven didn't mention the little detail. "Which means there isn't much we need to worry about in terms of mitigation."

There were more questions about goings-on around the world, every one of them directed to Steven. Richard was an important part of the Kingsley circle, but Steven's word as CEO was considered final. None of the journalists even glanced at Charles.

"What about Berlin?" a reporter asked. The wall which divided the city was no more, and German reunification was expected any day now. Soviet Union supplied a third of the gasoline West Germany required, which Ronald Reagan, another American president, had warned against. There were businesses in both nations which were part of the network.

"Politics is of course an unavoidable reality for the network," Steven admitted. "But we..." He went on to explain the systems in place which would help maintain stability in the markets in case the friction between countries ever devolved beyond verbal warfare.

There were approving nods from the gathered pressmen. Doubts still lingered about how Steven came to be in the CEO position, but the feeling he was growing into his role was gathering strength. Yeah, with Noah Andersen still insinuating misbehavior on Steven's part, there were holdouts, but the scales were beginning to tilt to the Kingsley side. Soon, the media would ask certain questions, the answers to which could determine whether Steven got to keep his job.

It didn't take long. "Your comments on Mr. Sheppard's arrest?" asked the *Wall Street Journal* reporter.

"Would you accept 'none' for an answer?" Steven asked, drawing mild laughter from the group. "Anything I say will seem like payback." After all, it was only months ago when Harry Sheppard called his own press conference to accuse the Kingsleys—Steven in particular—of tricking Brad and the rest into the deal which eventually led to the transfer of power. Sheppard went as far as insinuating Steven's hand in the assassination attempt on Temple. A defamation suit could've brought attention to Steven's past deeds, and all he could do was soldier on in the hope law enforcement didn't buy the idea. Which they didn't. Instead, Sheppard was now facing jail time. Steven glanced toward Richard. "My friend and colleague, Major Armor, is monitoring the situation for me. Rich, would you mind?"

"Mr. Sheppard was not simply the chairman of the network," reminded the reporter. "He had a huge role in building it."

Richard inclined his head. "Justice is supposed to be blind. Under Steven's leadership, the network will work with the authorities to make sure the law takes its course no matter who is accused of the crime."

There was no trace of any expression on the journalist's face. Richard was still learning his way around press types, but if he wasn't mistaken, the same reporter once wrote a series on Petty Officer First Class Harry Sheppard and his rise in the oil sector.

"My point was more about the credibility of the charges, Major," stated the journo. "As acting executives of the network, do you really believe someone like Mr. Sheppard would have committed such a foolish crime? Even with Jared Sanders—the man considered responsible for the loss of Genesis, the Sheppard family's old drilling company—Harry didn't go as far as physical attacks. My colleagues might not know this yet... Mr. Sheppard donated the money he got from the fall of Sanders, Incorporated. A highly reliable source within Gateway mentioned this to me."

Dryly, Richard said, "Sanders is currently sitting in a federal prison. I doubt he feels grateful to Sheppard for sparing his life."

Ignoring the mild ripple of mirth in the room, the *Journal* reporter continued, "Regardless, there's no direct evidence against Mr. Sheppard in the Luce case. Given the scenario, why did the network oust him without waiting for the courts to rule? I mean... even the arrest was only last month. The trial still has to happen. A jury has yet to give its verdict."

Elbows on the table, Richard leaned forward. "Direct evidence is not always necessary when everything else points to one person—and only the same one person—as the culprit. The victim clearly didn't knife himself in the back. According to the police, there is no one besides Petty Officer Sheppard who could've done the crime."

"But—" objected the reporter.

"Sheppard served the nation well in several roles," Richard continued as though there had been no interruption, "beginning with his time in the navy. Then, the work he put in building the alliance. None of it gives him any more rights than the average citizen. Which brings us to the network's stance on the matter. Neither we nor the justice system can afford even the appearance of favoritism... not if we are to keep the public's trust. Hence we decided Mr. Sheppard could not continue to serve as chairman."

Murmurs rose among the other reporters. "It's been hard to believe for a few in the press," dismissed a pretty young thing with her hair in a ponytail. "He was on good terms with many of the old-timers."

"Harry convinced a lot of veterans in the media of many things," agreed Steven. "If the recent articles I read can be taken as proof, people are waking up to the fact he duped them. Finally!"

Chairs scraped the carpeted floor as the journalists shifted to glance at each other. A few whispers, frowns... Richard bit back a smile of satisfaction.

"The accused must either prove his innocence in court or serve time for the crime he committed," announced Steven. "Anything less will destroy the nation's faith in the legal system. We can discuss Harry's role in the network once he returns."

Except Petty Officer First Class Harry Sheppard would never return from prison.

Chapter 18

A week later, January 1990

Brighton Beach, Brooklyn

The waistcoated accordion player in front of the bakery swayed to his own song. Tourists and locals alike halted to dance along to Eastern European music, many wandering into the warm interior to sample pastries. *"Spasibo,"* the musician said to the tippers, thanking them in Russian as they dropped dollar notes into the upturned Yankees cap on the chair next to him.

Most of the stores lining the street announced their names in the same language. There was some Italian, Spanish…

"Shit," muttered Steven, shouldering his way through the evening crowd. Steam curled out of his mouth with every breath. Temperature was dropping fast in anticipation of the night, but the residents of the neighborhood refused to stay in their homes. Wrinkled old ladies with bright-red makeup and voluminous fur coats hobbled toward produce stores and salons. Men played cards in front of a video shop advertising tapes from the old country, eyeing pretty girls as they flirted with tattooed chaps. The rumble of cars, a couple quarreling somewhere, teenagers on their way back from school, visitors clicking pictures… how the hell was Steven supposed to find Richard in the middle of the chaos?

There were no guards to help look. Within the United States, safety was not considered a big issue for someone in Steven's position as long as he kept his lips zipped about his schedule. The feds were unlikely to be gentle with any miscreant who caused trouble in the markets by attacking the network's acting CEO, and the one man who would've ignored the diktats of the American government was behind bars, unable to even take a piss without being monitored. More importantly, there was the objective of tonight's trip, the second part of their offensive strategy against Harry Sheppard.

The fellow in charge of the new plan insisted on at least peripheral involvement from Steven. The presence of Steven Kingsley in the club—the designated meeting place—was supposed to be insurance against any attempt at deception.

"Get lost," snapped a female voice, adding a couple of words unintelligible to Steven.

Of course it was directed at Charles. He'd stopped to leer at a woman and her friend, and the ladies apparently didn't appreciate whatever it was he said.

Steven didn't wait to apologize and hauled his brother by the collar back into the crowd. "Stupid commies," Charles muttered. "JD said you need to show cash to—"

"Can you not do anything dumb for one whole minute, Charlie?" Steven asked. "You'll get us killed."

"In here," someone said next to Steven.

With a jolt, Steven stopped. It took him a moment to notice the familiar light-blue eyes. "Rich, you nearly gave me a stroke."

"You passed me at the intersection," said Richard.

No disguises this time, even though he was once again about to meet someone with questionable allegiance to the rule of law. It wouldn't do for the Kingsley men to be seen with Rickie Brennan, the Irish mechanic who recruited James McCoy from prison to trap Harry. The winter clothes Richard wore would've been suited to any upscale eatery in Manhattan, and a fur-lined aviator hat sat on his blond head. Steven and Charles were in business suits. As far as any onlooker was concerned, the three men were merely out to enjoy an evening after a hard day at work.

Richard nodded at Charles. "The less importance you give to what JD says, the better for you... for all of us."

The former congressman was barely tolerable in regular times, but he was looking for blood these days. From the five brothers and Lilah, specifically. After he was forced to resign in disgrace, his political career was completely dead, and his wife—Steven and Charles's sister—was said to be considering divorce. JD would likely lose any custody battle over their children. Who knew what he would urge Charles to do in his quest for revenge?

"Huh?" Charles's confusion at Richard's unusually sharp tone was clear.

Steven didn't bother to explain. He shoved Charles into the building Richard pointed to—a restaurant and nightclub.

Blinking to adjust his vision to the darkness, Steven looked around. Polyester suits were everywhere in spite of having gone out of favor years ago. Women in shiny dresses smoked cigarettes, sending the smell of tobacco swirling around the room. In a few minutes, they were at their table.

"This is Brooklyn, Charlie," Steven said once the waiter left with their order. "Not the Upper East Side. Try to remember it. I don't want to explain to Grandfather how we got shot at by the Russian mob."

Swirling vodka in his glass, Richard said, "Charlie's not the only one. Most of America doesn't seem to understand anything about this place."

John Wilkes Booth, Son of Sam, Al Capone... many such delinquents boasted of ties to the borough. Mobsters of every ethnicity were drawn here... the Irish, the Italians, the Greeks, the Israelis, and more. The Bratva—the brotherhood of criminals with roots in the Soviet Union—was a recent arrival but ruled this particular neighborhood.

"People get killed in front of witnesses," Richard continued explaining, the prior annoyance in his blue eyes replaced by remarkable patience. "The cops can't seem to put anyone away." Only a few years ago, a mob boss was riddled with bullets right outside his apartment. "Then, Reznikov... he was supposed to be an effective killer. He got shot by the Italians outside this same nightclub. Don't mess with anyone here."

"Trust me... they're not going to care you're a Kingsley," warned Steven.

"Might even make things worse," said Richard.

He threw a glance in Steven's direction, but neither said anything further to Charles. Who knew what he'd blurt to whom when under the influence? One of the main businesses of the Bratva was gasoline bootlegging. Taxable transactions to retailers were camouflaged as tax-free business between wholesalers with dummy companies producing fake records. Said dummies would promptly declare bankruptcy when the internal revenue service showed up for its share. There was also the matter of number two oil purchased tax-free by companies pretending to be home heating oil buyers, which would then be sold as diesel fuel to retailers, the supposed taxes going straight into the pockets of the criminals. The mob, of course, took a cut. The loss to the government was estimated to be close to a billion dollars from the tri-state area alone.

Major Phillip Potts, son of the former dean of West Point, who was currently on assignment with the U.S. Army's criminal investigation department had mentioned an ongoing probe involving some big names in the oil sector. Even if he didn't, the feds would've alerted the CEO of the network of the new development. A major indictment was in the offing. Getty Terminals Corp. was in for an unpleasant surprise sometime soon. The powerful people under scrutiny would pull many tricks to make it all go away. An informant had been found strangled in New Jersey not too long ago.

There were also the malcontents from the Middle East. Phillip had heard chatter about Arabs who helped the U.S. drive communists out of Afghanistan now recruiting in America to fight the West. A refugee center located on Atlantic Avenue in Brooklyn was being monitored by the authorities.

Steven Kingsley blundering into some sort of trouble on their turf? Terror groups would relish the opportunity to kill him and send the markets reeling. The mafia tended to be a bit more pragmatic. They wouldn't want to draw undue attention from the federal government, and they welcomed a good economy as much as the average person. But yeah... any mobster worth his name would still smell opportunity.

On the stage, the show started. Laser lights, dry ice fog, cabaret... "Las Vegas," Steven said.

"Almost," agreed Richard. He leaned back in his chair.

They watched for a couple of minutes, Charles gorging on caviar. As the dancers shimmied their way out, a singer walked in and broke into an accented rendition of "Karma Chameleon."

"So?" Steven eventually asked. "Are we good to go?"

Richard nodded. "Finally. Your cousin's wife might be cunning, but it won't be enough to save her and her male harem from this particular group of people."

Steven once again reminded himself there was no reason to feel guilty. Lilah might not have been party to her husband's idiocy, but her support enabled him. "She got her chance to switch sides," Steven muttered.

Raising an eyebrow, Richard asked, "You mean before they decided to run? Yeah." Steven had asked her to work with him, but she refused and preferred to go on exile with the five losers. Lilah surely knew she was inviting trouble by sticking with Brad. If she didn't realize it before JD showed up in China, she certainly did now.

When the congressman flew to Beijing, Steven and Richard imagined two possible scenarios unfolding. In both cases, Lilah needed to go first, along with the five brothers, something JD was supposed to ensure. The security officers hired by the Kingsleys were prepared for an attack from Harry. Even if he retained enough sense not to try a suicide mission, his destiny would've been the same, waiting only for him to get to prison. Deaths happened to inmates quite frequently, sometimes officially sanctioned, sometimes not. The public would dismiss it as a sad fact of criminal life.

"Harem," Charles echoed, giggling. "Brad and the rest, Sheppard... who else do you think did her?"

"Charlie," snapped Steven.

Richard held up a hand. "Listen to me carefully, Charles. You and JD created enough problems for us already."

The congressman's incompetence made sure Lilah was still alive and back in hiding. Harry's press conference with Noah Andersen remained a roadblock in any plans the Kingsleys might now make to eliminate their main enemy, but once the former SEAL went to prison, the perception of him as a military hero would change. He could be killed after a slight delay without the death causing a ruckus in the press. But Lilah...

Harry couldn't be touched until Lilah's demise was guaranteed. Or she would immediately conclude no pardon was forthcoming to save her idiot husband. She would hotfoot it to the United States, perhaps with Alex in tow.

Within American borders, the ousted empress of the oil sector wouldn't be as easy to kill without suspicion falling on her enemies. Also, since she wasn't legally implicated in Brad's stupidity which led to the exile, she could and would start a battle in courts over control of the network. There was at least a reasonable chance Steven could lose. Then, she would proceed to avenge her friend's death. Too big a risk... Lilah needed to be located before anything could be done about Harry.

"The operation is at a critical stage," Richard explained to Charles. "We cannot afford any distractions from you. One more screwup, and I don't know if even Steven can save you from your grandfather. We need to be done with the problem of Mrs. Kingsley once and for all."

Which was what brought Steven to Brighton Beach in Brooklyn, where the Russian mafia ruled the streets. "This wouldn't be necessary if we knew where they were," he brooded. "How the hell did seven people leave China without anyone noticing?"

When Grayson Sheppard, the exiles' attorney, traveled to Kathmandu with Lilah's former intern, Steven assumed it was simply to take the girl home. The lawyer returned to New York, and no one bothered to track where Hemalatha Rai went from Nepal. A junior staffer was too insignificant to bother about. Mistake... after the exiles vanished from China, Steven's investigators learned she got on a plane to Beijing. The girl surely joined her former boss, bringing their numbers up to seven. Not an unnoticeably small group. Because of the outside attention, the government was monitoring foreigners at all entry and exit points. If the fugitives tried other fake passports, they would've gotten tagged.

"China's a big country," said Richard. "All we can know for sure is they're not in Beijing. Or my contact would've found them by now. But yeah... they could've taken one of the many unconventional routes out of there."

"Which leaves us with only the rest of the planet to watch." Steven huffed. "At least we now have the time to take care of it." Harry was locked up, expected to be convicted. There was nothing he could do to stop Steven from restructuring the management hierarchy of the network to ensure Brad wouldn't become CEO even if he got a pardon. The Kingsleys could not afford to relax until they knew for sure there were no more threats to their control over the empire, but they got enough breathing room to plot their moves.

"Time is a weapon which can cut both ways," said Richard. "As your grandfather would say, the longer an enemy is allowed to stay in the game, the more likely he will mount a defense. Mrs. Kingsley needs to be taken out at the first available opportunity." He held up a finger. "Step one... putting Sheppard in prison."

"Already done," said Steven.

"Step two," Richard gestured with his head toward their left. At a table across the room were two men, one of whom Steven recognized—Phillip Potts. Actually, Steven wasn't sure he would've identified his friend of many years if he weren't looking specifically for him. Major Potts could make himself unnoticeable at will—something about the body language—a skill which got him the job at the CID headquarters in Quantico, Virginia. Like his father, Phillip was a firm Kingsley ally. The general would've fallen on any sword to help Godwin protect the family name. Not so the general's son. Hence, the insistence on Steven showing up tonight. "The fellow Phillip is talking to?" murmured Richard.

Not a regular ol' civilian for sure. Even while sitting, the stance seemed coiled. It didn't matter who he was. An officer with the CID could talk to any criminal element without arousing suspicions. "Yeah?" said Steven.

"He's our man inside the prison. The moment he's done, we'll go to step three. Your cousins are not going to see the Bratva coming."

Part VII

Chapter 19

A month later, February 1990

Goa, India

"Tourists, the navy, the mafia..." recited Rekha, the transgender woman Lilah once stayed with in Bombay. They were mostly concealed by the coconut palms bordering the moonlit shore, but she had to holler to be heard over the sounds of the wild party on the sands. "Be careful."

Eyes on the almost otherworldly scene, Lilah nodded. The sea glowed a magical blue under the full moon, fluorescent light emitted by lamps hanging haphazardly from trees adding to the eerie appearance. Bare-chested men with guitars and drums blasted psychedelic music from a corner of Vagator Beach while revelers gyrated, kicking up golden dust.

"The mafia?" Victor asked from behind Lilah. "Local or from outside?"

She had paused between the shadowed trees only for a moment's respite from the bulky travel backpack, but the rest of the exiles followed suit. The pleasing breeze from the ocean swept across her face and neck, drying the sweat. Bliss... closing her eyes for a moment, she took a deep breath... and was immediately hit by fumes from weed and tobacco.

Vigorously nodding, Rekha said, "From all countries. British, Israeli, so many Russians these days. Communism gone, and *poof!* They get out of country. Some of them visit and go. Some stay. The Bratva is bad... very bad." Rekha's hometown was in Goa, and she clearly kept up with local news.

"Alex?" called Victor. "Did you run into anyone in the Russian mob before?"

"Not to my knowledge," Alex said. "Soviet military and intelligence... yeah, sure." When the exiles were hiding out in Kashgar, he'd given the rest a succinct version of what he did during his time in the army. The Russians had lost quite a few of their key personnel thanks to Captain Alex Kingsley. When the same Alex Kingsley showed up to negotiate deals on behalf of the oil network, the KGB kept an eye on him. The intelligence agency's dirt on Alex and Harry was used by the Kingsleys in the military court in Cuba. "I don't believe any of my... ahh... encounters with them involved the mafia."

"Still..." brooded Victor.

"Yeah, be careful," Rekha repeated her warning. "The police take bribes from gangs."

"The navy?" Alex asked. Goa was home to India's largest naval airbase. "Are they also on the take?"

Rekha shrugged. "I dunno, but be—"

"—careful," Scott finished.

She'd been saying that since showing up in Agra to meet the exiles. The group was forced to hide in the travel lodge near the Taj Mahal for more than a month while they located Rekha. Contacting any of Lilah's family wasn't possible. It wouldn't be only the cops from India and the U.S. monitoring. After their last encounter in Macau with the drug lord named Prince, there was a good chance he would keep an eye on all the people and places connected with his enemies. He couldn't set foot in India because of the criminal cases against him, but his minions were sure to be watching the movements of those who helped the Kingsleys before, one of who was Rekha.

As far as Lilah knew, Rekha still worked as security guard for Gateway's Bombay office, but calling her there would be dangerous. Neither Lilah nor Alex could remember the number to the woman's home, and in any case, there was a chance of that particular line also being tapped.

Call after call was made to landmarks Lilah remembered around the transgender colony. Finally, the puzzled fellow at the ticket office of a local movie theater hauled Rekha in to answer. The next morning, she clambered off the bus in Agra. Alex asked her a question... something he remembered Rekha mentioning during the India part of the network's expansion, which he handled.

A two-day train ride... not a single cop in uniform or soldier was around, but Lilah's belly clenched each time someone paid the group a little too much attention. What if her red hair dye and clip-on nose ring proved not to be enough? What if the glasses and brown contacts failed to conceal her identity? Then, Rekha or Hema would move, shielding Lilah from curious eyes. The men still wore their beards as disguise, and Hema could pass herself off as a passenger from one of the northeastern states where far-east Asian features weren't uncommon. But not one of them could relax even when they got off the train, even in the relative seclusion of the taxi drive to the beach. They couldn't begin to breathe easy until they got to the promised sanctuary. *If* they found sanctuary.

Nor did they get the time and privacy required for this briefing from Rekha on the situation on ground. Not until they started walking down the unpaved path by the shore.

"The mafia... the navy..." Neil shifted on his feet, peering at the throng dancing on the sands. "I wish we picked a different place."

There was a tiny gulp from Lilah's side. Tilting her head, she gave Hema—her former intern—a reassuring smile.

"Goa is our best option," Alex said to his brothers. It was the one place no one would think to look for them. No one would dream the exiles would dare hide in their enemy's backyard.

"We're going to keep to ourselves as much as possible," Brad promised Rekha.

"None of us will do anything to draw attention," agreed Victor. Nodding in the direction of the beach, he added, "And look... most of them are tourists. We'll fit right in."

Few in the crowd in fact appeared local. Of course there were the vendors serving *chai* and snacks to stoners who couldn't seem to figure out where on their faces their mouths were located.

Most of the partiers wore loose cotton clothing like the exiles, some dressed in saffron sarongs printed with religious symbols. Several of the ladies were topless. One naked man with hip-long dreadlocks was running up and down, screaming for God.

"Freaks," commented Rekha. "Trippin' on acid. LSD *free* at rave parties. Brown sugar, too. Old hippies, tourists... some now stay for years." She pointed toward a skinny man with a deeply wrinkled face and thin hair. He appeared to be meditating on the sand amid the chaos, young people surrounding him with folded hands. A couple of dogs were running around the group and snapping up scraps thrown by the humans. "Eight-finger Eddie," said Rekha, rolling her eyes. "He was the first of the hippies who came here... back in the 'sixties. Eddie's American." With a nervous glance over her shoulder, Rekha said, "Let's go. No waiting here. Maybe not the mafia, but what if somebody saw your pictures in papers?"

#

Lilah kept pace with Rekha, Alex on her other side. The rest still straggled, stopping to peer at the wild party every few minutes in bemusement. The noise didn't abate one iota.

With a quick glance over his shoulder, Alex said, "You decided against it... thank God."

Since the phone call to Grayson, Lilah barely uttered two words to Alex. She wished he'd let the silence continue. "Decided against what?"

"I think you wanted to split. It would've been the perfect opening after Grayson told us about Harry's arrest. Instead, you were arguing against Brad when he suggested returning."

Lilah took a look behind her, making sure the others remained out of earshot. "I'm not going anywhere." She couldn't. The network was built because Lilah allowed herself to be used as linchpin, and it was her responsibility to bring down the monstrous creature she created. Fear, anger, doubt, resolve... despite all the conflicting emotions, she wouldn't give up. There was also a strange new sensation of being cut loose from the beliefs which anchored her actions. So many painful thoughts crowded Lilah's mind about the murder rap on Harry, about Lupe, about why she sacrificed her life.

"So why are you still so..." Alex asked. "You're simply not yourself."

"I'm not sure," Lilah whispered. She desperately needed to go to the mountains, to roar her questions into the vast silence.

"Not sure about *what?* The network? The exile? The collateral damage?"

"Alex, I—"

"Almost there," Rekha huffed, pointing to a well-lit group of red-roofed, whitewashed buildings... the resort she mentioned. "The house is right behind."

Alex nodded but continued talking to Lilah. "You gave up so much... we all did. I thought it was for a cause you believed in. Don't you want the network back? Isn't it why you put up with Brad this long?"

She didn't toss Brad out on his ear because her agreement to go on this exile with him was part of the deal with the Kingsleys. Unless she helped him return home a free man, his brothers would refuse to cooperate with her plans for the network. Lilah convinced Harry of the need, but now...

There was no capital punishment in New York. Also, on her last phone call to Grayson Sheppard, he'd said the district attorney couldn't find enough evidence to get Harry on straight-up murder. The theory was Harry somehow found out about Will Luce's embezzling activities—perhaps through the strip club—and went to the apartment to confront him. An argument left the embezzler dead. First-degree manslaughter was the planned charge.

Harry's lawyer was supposed to be one of the top defense attorneys in the country, but people got convicted on less evidence all the time despite the best legal help money could buy. Grayson didn't know who would argue the case for the prosecution. New York State would surely send its finest to court, especially since the Kingsleys would work behind the scenes to make it happen. A bench trial, where verdict would be delivered by a judge, was deemed too risky for the same reason. The former supreme court justice, Godwin Kingsley, could whisper in a few ears, and Harry would end up before a judge sure to find him guilty. The defense opted to stick with a jury trial.

Twelve random people stood a better chance of delivering an uncorrupted verdict, if not a fair one. They would not hear what Harry had to say about the Kingsleys. Such claims would be dismissed by the court as irrelevant to the murder case. The jurors would only see the evidence considered admissible in the trial. And regardless of the instructions the twelve men and women got from the judge, they might or might not have read the tabloids. They might or might not have already formed an opinion on the case. They might or might not be swayed by their own life experiences. Those twelve as-yet-unknown citizens would pronounce the verdict.

If convicted, Harry could be in prison for twenty-five years. The defense attorney would appeal of course, but it could take a long time. Even the first chance for parole would come up only after five long years in jail. Harry, caged like a wild animal... Lilah blinked, shoving away the images.

"Or were you fooling everyone with your talk about the responsibilities of power?" Alex challenged, breaking her train of thoughts. "Maybe Brad was right. Maybe you simply want revenge."

Choosing not to respond, Lilah followed Rekha through a small gate set to the side of a walled compound, in the middle of which stood the brightly lit buildings of the resort. There were several couples making out under the swaying coconut palms, unmindful of the crowds thronging the large pool and the open-air bar. Neon lamps announced the presence of a casino on site.

"All our efforts this far... you realized what could happen when you go looking for revenge and got cold feet," Alex finished, tone bitter.

Curling her fingers into tight fists, Lilah pinned him with her eyes.

Sighing, he said, "Of course I didn't mean it. I was only trying to get through to you. You're always wanting to do the right thing."

Yes, the right thing... the just war she was intent on waging could end in Harry's death. There would be no attempts to kill him until the trial was done, or suspicion would turn to the Kingsleys. The death of a convicted killer would play differently in the media than the death of a man merely accused of the crime. Conspiracy theories would pop up, and this time, they would be right. If Lilah were to return and force an investigation partly on the basis of those rumors...

But once Harry was officially labeled a killer and locked up for good... once the case faded from the public mind... Grayson insisted over and over Harry could take care of himself. Lilah already knew it, but the knowledge did little to soothe her fears.

There was the network. With the board ousting him from chairmanship, Harry no longer possessed the clout to get Brad back in the CEO spot, let alone to get him to dismantle the organization. But Grayson had assured Lilah her old friend was determined to continue the fight against the network. Grayson didn't mention anything about how exactly Harry planned to fight the Kingsleys. The elderly lawyer very likely didn't know. Harry would be waiting, watching. Unless someone came up with proof of his innocence, the first window he got to do anything would be during his parole.

Grayson also reported the cops dismissed the idea of Charles Kingsley's involvement in Lupe's death, but Harry believed she was killed to stop her from warning him. The actual criminals would walk away scot-free in both murders.

Lupe Valdez... tucked into the front pocket of the backpack, Lilah carried the grainy clipping of Harry with the strip club owner. The war against the Kingsley clan had already claimed its first victim.

Why? Lilah repeated the question she'd been asking the past few weeks. Harry was at least as tangled in the network as the exiles, and his legal problems were a result of that. She'd assumed Lupe's involvement was limited to providing him an avenue to collect information. Perhaps he offered her something in return as they did with the owner of the tabloid, *The Big Apple Reporter,* who was instrumental in bringing about the fall of Jared Sanders. Risk was involved... but surely nothing which would require Lupe to put herself directly in the path of danger. Except she went to the extent of marrying Harry... and died in her attempt to save him. Why? Why did she sacrifice herself?

"I don't know." Alex shrugged. "Lupe is... was a strong woman. Maybe she was also trying to do the right thing."

Startled, Lilah straightened, only just realizing she muttered her question out loud. "How do *you* know she was strong? Did you go to her club?"

Alex flushed. "I lived a long time before I got married. So yes, I've enjoyed meeting a woman or two here and there."

"Not that marriage made any difference in your life," Lilah snapped. "No woman ever will. Your wife, your son... how many times have you thought about them in the last few months? Brad always takes priority. And of course, Godwin."

Alex's face blanched, but his gaze never left Lilah's. "It's not true," he whispered. "And what's more, you know it."

Rekha led them to the back of the compound, where there was a row of very functional-appearing two-story structures. Her eyes were on the buildings, but there was no way she could miss hearing the conversation between the other two.

"Really?" Lilah asked Alex. "You strong-armed me to get your brother what he wanted... it's what got us into this exile. All of you agreed to follow Brad, no questions asked. So why would you now start caring about Sabrina and Mikey?"

"*I do care*—" Lowering his voice again, Alex continued, "Yes, I made a stupid mistake trusting Brad would know how to deal with Steven and his uncle. Yes, we lost the business. I'm trying my best to make up for it. I—we've given up everything to—"

"You keep talking about what 'we' gave up," Lilah said through gritted teeth. "But neither you nor your brothers exactly volunteered for this trip around the world. Your 'stupid mistake' *forced* us into this situation. Poor Lupe! As though what she did for us and what you... let me see you actually sacrifice something for a change."

As Alex fell silent, Lilah turned away.

#

A few minutes later

At the front door of one of the houses in the back of the compound, Rekha argued with an Indian man with dark circles around his eyes and streaks of gray in his hair. A tee and shorts hung loosely on his skinny frame. He and his wife managed the independent resort they built on land inherited from his parents. Behind the resort proper were buildings housing the staff, one of which was used by the couple. Terrible for the employees to be forced to live amid the constant noise, but Goa would be one heck of an expensive location for someone on a regular salary, and basic staff accommodations likely came at a steep discount.

Mouth turned down, Rekha returned to them. "There's a little problem," she announced. "The manager says they moved the male employees to someplace a little far away in town. A couple of them harassed the tourist women... not good for business. Only ladies can stay in the hostel now. His wife is very strict about it."

"But on the phone, he..." Victor huffed. "The hostel's not a good option. Lilah and Hema alone will be too risky. Did you tell the manager he won't need to let any of us men stay with his female staff? We can rent one of the houses in the compound."

Either Victor or Alex would join the two women, while the remainder of the group moved into separate residences. When Steven or anyone else looked for a band of seven people in any of the likely cities, he wasn't going to find one.

Rekha shook her head. "Houses only for married senior staff," she said. "You're not senior. Single girl junior staff go to the hostel. Single men, somewhere else. Manager's wife insists."

Neil muttered a curse. "What now?"

"Return to Bombay with me?" Rekha offered, her tone doubtful.

"Not possible," Lilah said. "Bombay will be one of the first cities they check. Also, Prince." He was the reason they were at this particular resort. "Guess we don't have a choice but to find some other town."

"Wait a second," said Alex. "The resort manager's objection is to all men? Not just straight?"

"To men... straight, gay..." said Rekha, nodding.

"In that case," Alex said, "tell him I'm trans. Like you."

Chapter 20

Tra... trans? Lilah gawked. Around her, everyone else erupted in a chorus of exclamations.

"We can't go around India, looking for a place to stay," Alex said, shoving fingers through his hair. "Not gonna happen without selling the rocks, but each contact we make could land us in trouble later. The resort idea is better, so let's find a way to make it work."

Victor objected, "But—"

Alex was adamant. "We'll split up as planned. I can stay with Lilah and Hema. It won't be difficult for the rest of you to find places, I'm sure." Turning to Rekha, he added, "I need to shave."

Farther into the interior of the town was a tiny hotel grandiosely named Paradise Resort. Alex used the room to get rid of the beard which had been part of his disguise for more than a year. He borrowed clothes and makeup from Rekha. For the next thirty minutes or so, thuds and grunts and loud complaints abounded from the attached bathroom, accompanied by Rekha's scolding.

The Kingsley brothers—sprawled in various positions over the twin beds and on the floor—were silent. Hema dozed in the plastic chair by the window. Next to her, Lilah sat in the second chair, clutching her backpack to her chest. On the ceiling, a fan twirled, moving warm air around the small room.

The door creaked as Rekha finally exited the bathroom. Sweeping her arms grandly toward the opening, she said, "Ta-da."

Alex stepped out. Eyes lined with kohl, cheeks lightly rouged, lips painted wild red. One of the wigs Lilah bought in Macau now covered his scalp, the thick, brown braid hanging between his shoulder blades. His tall and muscled form was attired in a long-sleeved orange tunic and matching sarong.

Shaking a fist, he warned his brothers, "Say a word."

Brad simply stared. Holding up both hands, Victor bowed.

A single snicker. From Scott. "I'm sorry," he said, muffling it.

Then, the sound was echoed by Victor. Neil followed, the mild laughter soon devolving into wild guffaws.

Tossing the backpack to the floor, Lilah rose from her chair. Three steps, and she was face-to-face with Alex. "Why?" she asked.

The laughter in the room sputtered to a stop.

"I told you," Alex said. "You can't stay in the hostel by yourself. You need some kind of protection. Also, the Russians. If there's someone in the local Bratva who knows about me, this getup will be better disguise."

Shaking her head, Lilah repeated, "Why? It's likely to be at least five years before we get to return. At a *minimum*. Looking for some other town might be easier in the long run."

Not to mention Brad's reaction. Given their situation, he wouldn't have an option but to agree to this scheme, but he'd most certainly make his displeasure clear. Alex would know it.

Alex's hand went to his hair, encountering the wig and falling back down. "If Lupe could sacrifice her life..." He waved a hand, indicating his clothes. "I can put up with this for however long it takes."

#

Sometime later in the morning

A flock of seagulls flew across an impossibly blue sky while other birds watched from thickly leaved trees, tweeting and cawing their greetings. The sun beat down on the streets, conspiring with the nearby sea and the wind to make humans sweat. Enjoying the salty smell of the ocean, Lilah glanced around. It had been too dark when they first arrived to actually see the place.

The green... oh, God, the green... weeds on the roadside, wild shrubs in the yards, tall coconut trees... Mother Nature had lavished love on Goa. The brightly painted houses in town looked very colonial even to her untrained eye... mostly Portuguese in style as Rekha explained. There were also the homes which were local in design with pristine white walls and tiled roofs. Hotels, beach shacks selling seafood and alcohol... the rave party was done, and only a few tourists remained on the shore. Most were sunbathing. The naked dreadlock guy from the night before snored on a sheet while a couple of his friends sat in yoga poses nearby.

The nocturnal beach scene wouldn't be the image of India most carried in their minds, and there would be a Goa beyond the tourists and the parties, a place which was as strongly rooted in tradition as the rest of the nation. A place where regular families lived and raised their children, to whom brown sugar meant a cooking ingredient, not cheap heroin.

"Mathur *saab,*" called Rekha.

They were again at the door to the house from the night before. Next to it was the ladies' hostel. It was only then that Lilah noticed the metal plate on the wall, proclaiming the name of the building. *Lakshmi Nivas* or home of Lakshmi, the goddess of prosperity and consort to Hari, a.k.a. God. Someone inside was playing the flute, the melody both teasing and welcoming. Almost as though the edifice was asking the new arrivals what took them so long. Lilah smiled a little—an island of peace in the midst of a frenzied ocean of indulgence.

A short minute later, the owner/manager invited the group of four in, looking them up and down. His wife was in the resort, busy with the day's work, and wouldn't be around to overhear the discussion. She couldn't be allowed to know any of it, the manager insisted.

"Jews," Rekha started, going over their cover story. "From New York. They speak English, and the ladies know a little bit of Hindi." Israeli tourists who arrived with no expectations of leaving weren't uncommon in Goa, and American Jews could get away with not knowing the language. Still, thanks to Lilah's early childhood in Tel Aviv with her diplomat father, she was fluent in both Hebrew and Arabic. "They want to learn Hinduism," Rekha finished.

The manager said something in the local language though he'd spoken in precise English only moments ago.

"He wants to know the names you're going to use," translated Rekha. "And what kind of work you can do."

"Barbara," Alex blurted.

Lilah just about stopped herself from gaping. Brad's secretary's name? At least it wasn't Sabrina. Or Lilah.

He continued, "I... ahh... I can shoo—I mean, I can dance."

"Dance?" the manager asked, suddenly sitting forward in the chair in the living room. The visitors were on the couch. "What type of dance?"

Alex smirked. "Swing, Latin, waltz, whatever."

Rekha gawked, looking mildly worried, but Alex wasn't making it up. When Lilah first met him, they'd danced together the entire evening. Later, she learned from Patrice that while all the Kingsley boys took lessons, Alex and Victor excelled at it—which they obviously used to impress the ladies.

"Can you teach?" the manager asked.

"Sure, I can," Alex said.

"Like Bollywood movies?" asked the manager.

"Absolutely," said Alex, not missing a beat.

Lilah nearly rolled her eyes. As good as Alex was at most kinds of dancing, she was sure he had no clue what the manager fellow was talking about.

"Good." The manager nodded. "This could work out well." He turned and called to someone, voice suddenly sweet and loving.

A little girl appeared at the inner door, poking her tongue through the gap in her upper teeth. Her white slip dress was stained with a variety of foods. The promise of beauty was evident in the child, with eyes ever so slightly tilted up at the corners. The glinting black irises and angled eyebrows and the messy black hair gave her the appearance of having been up to no good.

"Tara," introduced the manager. "My daughter." She was the couple's only child. "Some movie people who stayed at the resort asked my wife about Tara," claimed the proud papa. "They think she would look good on screen." Young Tara scowled, but her father didn't appear to notice.

Being able to dance was apparently crucial for success in Indian movies, and the manager's wife was looking for a teacher. There was also the demand for Bollywood-style lessons from foreign tourists. The manager would tell his wife he'd found a candidate who could do both. Of course, Lilah and Hema would be given other jobs in the resort.

Alex gestured the child to him. "Hi, Tara." It came out sounding like Terr-ah.

The child's brows drew together. "Tara," she instructed. "Thaa-rah."

"It means star," contributed Rekha.

"I'm eight," Tara informed them.

"Are you?" asked Alex. "I have a son who's almost seven."

"Where is he?" she demanded. "And what's his name?"

"Mi—" Alex coughed. "My son is called Max. He lives with his mother."

"What's *your* name?" the child asked Alex.

"Barbara," said Alex.

"Barbie?" the child asked, mouth falling open.

"No, I'm—"

"Barbie." The child nodded, finally smiling.

"Dance Master Barbie," the manager corrected.

Lilah bit the inside of her cheek until her eyes teared, trying not to laugh.

Hurriedly, Alex suggested to the child, "How 'bout you call me *maestro*? It's Italian for master. Sounds cooler, doesn't it?"

The child shrugged, apparently unconcerned about such nuances.

On her way out, Rekha muttered to Alex, "I hope you actually know how to dance."

After her departure, the manager turned toward the other guests. "What about you?" He looked Hema up and down. "You won't pass for Jewish."

"No, I'm keeping my own name—Hema." It was a common enough moniker in India, so the girl had decided to stick with it. "I'm from Sikkim state." It would explain the mix of Indian and Chinese features. "Hindu. I... umm... went to New York two years ago." Pointing a finger at Lilah, Hema added, "To work for her."

"And I'm Barbie's cousin," said Lilah. "Hair and makeup artist."

"My wife's going to want to see IDs," brooded the manager. "Is it going to say Barbie?"

"We have our passports." Digging into her bag, Lilah came up with the fake documents they got after their arrival in India. "You can tell your wife Barbie's name is Arjun."

Alex elaborated on his story. He underwent only one official name change at the time he got interested in Hinduism thanks to Hema. The... ahh... realization he wanted to be a woman came later, but he didn't get around to making a second formal change in documents.

"And you?" the manager asked Lilah.

"I'm Krishna," said Lilah. For as long as it took, Alex Kingsley would live in Lakshmi Nivas—the ladies' hostel—as Arjun. Lilah would be Krishna.

"Let's talk about your side of the bargain now," said the manager.

Lilah nodded. At her side, Alex stayed still, his face expressionless. They would all do what they needed to do.

"You're going to help me get my wife's cousin out of my business," the manager stated. "The next time he shows up here, get rid of him."

Yes, the tourist resort called The Mermaid was the one place none of their enemies would think to look for the exiles. No one would imagine they would take refuge in the resort owned and operated by the brother-in-law of the Burmese drug lord called Prince.

Part VIII

Chapter 21

Five hundred million dollars... in Harry's childhood, it would've seemed like an ungodly amount of money. As an adult, his net worth grew to a lot more... wealth the Sheppards got by bartering Lilah.

"A defendant with his resources and connections?" the prosecutor asked at the bail hearing soon after Harry's arrest. "He's a flight risk." The defense lawyer had imagined the district attorney would allow the accused to turn himself in when the time came. Yet the NYPD crossed state lines, cornering Harry in a public place in the presence of his family. Now, the absurd bail.

Five hundred million was still an ungodly amount when he couldn't touch it.

"I begged Hector," Sabrina sobbed, sitting across the table from Harry in the visiting area at Rikers Island, the prison where New York City detained pretrial defendants. "So did Dante." Not saying a word in response, Harry glanced around the room. Most of the gray plastic chairs were occupied, with couples holding hands over the table and families chatting.

Forget selling stock to raise the bail amount, Hector Sheppard had refused to release even the cash they needed to conduct an independent investigation into Will Luce's death. The elder Sheppard son never forgot Harry accused him of embezzlement and attempted murder when the discrepancies in the company's accounts were first discovered. Sabrina and Michael would have their dividends to live on, Hector pointed out. As for Harry, the stay in prison was exactly what he deserved for his deeds thus far.

Without the money, he had little hope of proving his innocence. Without the money, he *would* go to jail. It would be at least five years of incarceration before Harry got parole, before he got to see the outside world.

"Father and Mother," Sabrina continued. Michael sat silently at her side. Harry didn't like the idea of the lad visiting Rikers, but his mother said he got agitated when she was about to leave alone. "God, Harry... they look so old now. They don't seem to have any say. It's Hector all the way."

Holding his wife in his arms, Ryan Sheppard wept all through the couple's one and only trip to see Harry. Their family was coming apart. *"Karma,"* Sophia Sheppard mumbled over and over in a voice dulled by grief. For everything they did, for all the people they hurt. Harry asked them not to return. He didn't want them seeing him in there, clad in the prison uniform of gray jumpsuit and flip-flops, surrounded by guards.

He soothed his parents with the information Noah Andersen was taking care of the lawyer's fees. Any appeal would also be financed by Noah. Without being allowed to sell stock, none of the rest—Sabrina, Liam, Dan Barrons—had anywhere near enough loose cash to help. Shawn's resources amounted only to a fraction of everyone else's, and whatever he had was already earmarked for the exiles, sent to Lilah's Swiss bank account. Neither Temple nor Grayson ever bothered to put aside more funds than what would be required for a quiet retirement life, and Harry couldn't let the elderly men deplete their savings.

Gateway also managed to tie up future dividends from Harry's stock under the pretext of some internal review of the events which led to the murder. After all, the whole affair revolved around the business. The cash Harry made from dismembering Sanders, Incorporated was long gone, donated to charities around the world. It was blood money, and he didn't want a single penny. Victor and Alex followed Harry's lead and donated good chunks of their profit from the episode to oil sector workers who lost their jobs in the ensuing market crash. There was plenty left to keep their families in comfort but nowhere close enough to pay for Harry's bail.

Still, there were other business holdings and properties Harry could put up for sale. The cash would go to Eden as he once promised Lupe. Traffic to the clubs had dwindled after the demise of the glamorous proprietress, and the employees needed a way to make a living. Liam was in the process of converting the clubs to a restaurant chain. Nothing fancy—there wasn't enough money for it—merely a project guaranteed to bring steady income for Lupe's girls. Only what remained could be used to fund a private investigation into Will Luce's death.

Five years... if Harry didn't win on appeal by then, he would ask for parole. No matter what the cost to him, he would put his plan into action. It would still be five long years before Harry could do anything to help the exiles. Five years... if the enemy didn't get to him in prison, if he found a way to evade the eyes of the Kingsleys and the authorities after.

"I threw the first punch," Michael admitted, glaring across the table at Harry.

"He won't tell me why," Sabrina said, her lashes wet with tears. "His teachers, the principal, Shawn, Dan... nuh-huh... Mikey won't talk to anyone except Gabriel."

"Mike," the lad corrected. "And Gabe gets it. You told him to stay with Mr. Andersen and play Gameboy."

"Because I don't want him making excuses for you with Uncle Harry," *snapped Sabrina.*

In silence, Harry pinned Michael with his eyes. Michael glowered back.

"His teachers want to move him up a couple of grades," Sabrina said. "He's gifted, but I don't want him to... he shouldn't miss out on his social development. I got him a computer for his birthday, and he's already almost as good as me in several things. Noah's been teaching him how to play the flute. He wants to send Mikey to Juilliard. What Mikey prefers to do is get into fights."

"Mike," the boy said again, his tone long-suffering. "And I wasn't looking for a fight, Ma."

"Then why—" started Sabrina.

"All right," Harry said. "We'll sign you up for boxing and taekwondo. Also, some shooting lessons. The best defense for a man who wants to stay out of trouble is to make sure no one dares pick a fight with him. You do *want to stay out of trouble... right, Mike?"*

The lad's gaze darted between his mother and his uncle for a few moments. His sneakered foot started tapping a nervous rhythm on the floor. "They said something," he finally blurted. "Those boys."

Neither Harry nor Sabrina needed to ask what was said. As promised, Liam and Dan started taking Michael and Gabriel to martial arts classes and the boxing ring. The lads were enrolled in the junior program at the same shooting range their fathers once went to. And yeah, there were still no calls from Hector Sheppard to check on his nephew or ask how his sister was doing.

"Be careful," Harry said to his sister, keeping his tone low. Sabrina was alone on this visit. They needed to be to discuss her special project, the virus. What was originally intended to help the Barrons brothers track financial

transactions of certain people who opposed the exiles could well be modified to leave a fake money trail.

Programming a precision-strike weapon would take time and effort. Unlike the movies where a magical hacker could solve every problem, Sabrina would need to code, test, and refine over and over and over until she was reasonably certain the virus would do the job quickly and completely without alerting the intended targets. There would be no room for errors, no second chances. A failed attack could well warn the Kingsleys what their enemies were up to. Steven and his best buddy, Major Armor, would strengthen their flanks with enough digital barricades to counter even Sabrina and Shawn's combined expertise. Harry's defense strategy would collapse. The programmer who designed the virus would also be thrown in prison.

"Do not even think of deploying it yourself," Harry said to Sabrina. "Times have changed since you last went hacking into FBI's systems. There are laws against it now."

"Instead of me, Shawn will get into trouble." Sabrina hissed. "So will you... for something I did. Not cool, Harry."

"Neither Shawn nor I have children to worry about."

If there was ever a hint of wrongdoing on her part, Godwin Kingsley could use it to take Gabriel and Michael away. Sabrina had assigned guardianship to Dan Barrons... in case something happened to her as well as Harry and the exiles. She didn't trust her own parents not to cave to the Kingsleys on the boys' custody. Nor could she depend on Patrice, the lads' paternal grandmother, not to put her affection for Major Armor—son of the Kingsley chauffeur—ahead of her own grandchildren's welfare. Especially not if it came out the weapon Sabrina designed was aimed squarely at Armor.

No, it couldn't be her fingers setting the digital virus loose. Shawn had contacts spread across the globe who could do the job for them—hackers, located in places beyond the reach of Uncle Sam. Breadcrumbs needed to be carefully laid, leading the cops where Harry wanted them.

Except none of it could be done now when the eyes of the authorities were fixed firmly on Harry and those who might help him. Nothing could be done while the case went through the courts. Harry could make no move which jeopardized his parole. He needed to be outside when the culprits behind the deaths of Will Luce and Lupe Valdez were exposed. Harry needed the freedom to talk to the media, to force recalcitrant politicians into supporting a pardon for the exiles. Sabrina had exactly five years to build the perfect weapon.

Michael would turn twelve by the time Alex and the rest returned home... if they got lucky and every piece fell into place. Half a decade would pass before Lupe's spirit got justice, before Liam and Verity got closure for their father's untimely death.

"I'm not going," Liam said to Harry over the phone. No matter what Hector had to say, Liam was not traveling to Saudi Arabia to check on Gateway's office.

With Saddam Hussein having invaded Kuwait, the situation was tense, but the company's employees were all accounted for. Business from the Jeddah port was suffering, but they were making do. The trip was surely planned as a way to get Liam away from DC on the crucial day when Drummond was attempting a takeover of Lupe's clubs on the pretext of paying off her bank loans. What he and the Kingsleys wanted was to make absolutely certain Eden and its angels never dared help Harry.

Liam purposely missed his flight to Jeddah. Two hours prior to the hearing at the Superior Court for the District of Columbia, he politely declined the use of Gateway's jet, which meant Liam would soon find himself unemployed. Didn't matter. Either Shawn or Dan Barrons would give Liam a job. Besides, he wanted to witness the shock on the enemy's face when he announced to the probate division of the court that there was someone with a stronger claim on Lupe's estate. Her bereaved husband, Harry Sheppard.

The Kingsleys and Drummond did get a shock, and the media exploded in excitement, but they weren't the only ones.

"Did you already know," Andersen asked, "that Ms. Valdez's father was one of the Puelche tribe in Neuquén?"

Harry jolted, causing the guards to move closer to the table. The presence of a former president and his entourage meant the correctional facility was forced to clear the visiting schedule because of safety concerns. The prisoner they showed up to see was also considered one of those security threats.

The tragedy in Argentina was still not public knowledge, Noah assured Harry. Godwin Kingsley would also be implicated in the incident, and he'd never let his criminal grandsons in on the secret.

Harry didn't know what to make of Lupe's connection with the Puelche. In all their conversations, she never even hinted... Noah said the tribe didn't approve of her father's dalliance with an outsider. The fellow eventually went back home with his tail between his legs. After her mother's death, Lupe lived briefly with him but got kicked out at the age of fourteen for what the tribe deemed unacceptable behavior. Lupe didn't return even when the man who sired her died in an accident a few years before Harry and Alex arrived on scene, setting fire to the entire village.

Was it why you helped me? Harry asked Lupe's ghost. *Did you know it was us?*

Or perhaps the universe was having the last laugh, picking the perfect weapon to deliver punishment for the crimes he did commit. Except Lupe didn't realize she would serve as the instrument of judgment.

The defense lawyer's arguments about the pieces of evidence which didn't fit were pooh-poohed. New York State didn't have the responsibility to satisfactorily explain everything found on the crime scene. Will Luce's death was clearly not by his own hand. The only other person who could've done it was Harry. Means, motive, opportunity... he had all three, and there were no alternative explanations to the murder.

"We find the defendant guilty," the jury foreman announced.

Chapter 22

June 1992

(2 ½ years after Harry's arrest and 3 ½ after the exile began)

New York

Cameras flashed in the courtroom. A furor erupted among the watching press, drowning out the sobs coming from Temple's right. He'd caught only a word or two of what the judge was saying, but the tears pouring down Sabrina's face told the story.

Harry's sentence was not light. It couldn't be death penalty; capital punishment had been abolished in New York years ago except in cases where the murder victim was a police officer. The length of the prison term depended on the charge slapped on the former SEAL.

Temple had hoped... he tried to keep track of the passage of time, tried to keep up with the case from the few words he understood. Only a matter of following the legal process, he'd believed. Whatever evidence the Kingsleys cooked up, the court would demand that Harry's guilt be proven beyond reasonable doubt. Which wouldn't happen. He wasn't stupid enough to get caught knifing his former father-in-law. All the waiting... the last couple of years... the nights Temple stared into the darkness, telling himself Harry would soon be free... what would happen to Lilah now?

Fear balled into a heavy knot at the center of Temple's chest. *Breathe,* his mind ordered. He couldn't afford to succumb, not before his child was brought back home. There would be an appeal... parole... even if Temple couldn't help, there were others who would.

More harsh sobs joined Sabrina's. On her other side were Ryan and Sophia Sheppard. Holding on to each other, the couple wept. Liam Luce sat behind Temple and Noah and the Sheppards. The Barrons brothers were with Liam, a red-haired young woman hugging Dan from the side. His lady friend, perhaps. The boys—Gabriel and Michael—had been left behind in their Long Island residence, the house next to Temple's that Sabrina moved into not long after Harry's arrest. The lads were safe in the care of a babysitter and security guards.

Other than court officials and cops and the defendant's supporters, only the media seemed to be present. The press crowd was smaller than Temple would've expected. Of course Noah would've informed the court of Temple's intended attendance, which explained the limited number of spectators allowed.

Cops flanking him, Harry rose from his chair as his parents stumbled toward their son. Whatever he said to soothe the couple served only to make them weep harder. A hand on Sophia's shoulder, Shawn Barrons said something, but Dan hung back as did Liam.

"...twenty-five..." said Shawn.

Temple blinked. He caught that. *Twenty-five* years? There was a roaring sound in his brain. Harry would be in prison for twenty-five years? Without him, Brad didn't have a prayer of being pardoned. No one else on their side possessed the skill set, the sheer will to achieve the impossible. Lilah's twin adored her, but the young man wouldn't last a week in a war with Godwin. There would be no presidential amnesty for the oldest Kingsley brother, and the younger ones would not agree to return without him. Without support from any of them, Lilah wouldn't be able to dismantle the network. Still clinging to the hope of destroying the oil empire someday, she would keep running.

Would the Kingsleys even allow her to live as long? They'd be waiting... watching...

My child, Temple pleaded in his mind. *Hide well. Whatever happens, don't come out. Not until Harry finds a way.*

Petty Officer First Class Harry Sheppard would never admit defeat. He would have a plan even if Temple didn't know what the hell it was... *if* he survived whatever other traps waited for him in prison.

Temple clambered to his feet, the secret service officers standing with him. He needed to ask Harry... no one would understand what the former president said, but he needed to somehow warn... Shawn Barrons was still talking to Harry and his parents.

The former president couldn't be spotted anywhere near Shawn. With the aid of photographs, Temple had managed to make it clear to Noah only a few were allowed to visit him at home. The Barrons brothers were not on the list. Temple didn't care what they thought of the omission. Even when he ran into Shawn at a public place, Temple took care not to be seen near the lad. Until the day Temple could shout out the darkest chapter in Kingsley family history, Shawn would be in danger merely from being in the vicinity of the one man who knew what happened to his mother.

Silently, Temple willed Shawn and Daniel to leave so Harry could talk to his former mentor. Instead, the cops seemed to be urging the prisoner to walk. Harry tilted his head in Temple's direction before striding away.

The roaring within his skull getting louder, Temple turned. At the back of the courtroom, standing in one corner, was someone he didn't expect. Patrice Kingsley once wanted nothing to do with the Sheppards, but her face was pale with anxiety as she watched Harry leave the room. There was more gray in her hair than Temple remembered. Her last visit to him had been a while ago, while he was admitted in the hospital after the assassination attempt. Much time had passed since then, time she would've spent worrying about her sons... about *all* her sons.

"I'm sorry," Temple whispered. No one would've understood what he said, but Patrice glanced toward him as though she heard. When she approached, Temple murmured again, "I'm so sorry."

Noah said something to Patrice, but her gaze skittered away. She didn't wait much longer before departing. Patrice didn't acknowledge the Sheppard parents on her way out. She didn't even attempt to talk to her daughter-in-law, Sabrina, who was consoling her father and mother.

In Patrice's eyes, the politician saw the reflection of his own guilt. If only she spoke up before... if only she confessed the mistake of her childhood... if only blood recognized blood... Peter Kingsley's sons were on the run because of her silence.

If only Temple could speak... if only he could confess his sins... the woman he considered the daughter of his heart was now paying the price for what he failed to do. Harry might die in prison because of Temple's mistakes.

Chapter 23

Same evening

Sing Sing Correctional Facility

Ossining, New York

Light barely filtered in through the dirty panes of the barred windows, trapping the inmates of A-block in gloom and insane monotony. Rows of horizontal bars stretched down the inside of the building, creating the optical illusion of terrifying infinity. Myriad sounds came from every direction. Voices rose in anger on one side, ricocheting off the thick, gray walls. Lewd suggestions were screamed at the patrolling guards. The first notes of "I'm Too Sexy" blasted out from the floor above. Harry winced. Over the last few weeks at Rikers, the song had been played incessantly. The officers there were big fans of the band, Right Said Fred.

Clearly, they were also fans of shipping prisoners out without delay once sentences were announced. It took barely an hour for Harry to be transported to this maximum-security facility in upstate New York.

Sing Sing seemed to have no air-conditioning. Perspiration glued the dark-green polyester uniform to Harry's chest and back as he shuffled down the gallery with the guard propelling him along. The building stank with sweat from more than five-hundred male bodies.

Muddy water splashed when Harry stepped on a puddle, rain still dripping from the leaky roof. Something flew from a cell on his right, and Harry came to an abrupt stop as the guard yelled obscenities at the inmate who'd thrown soiled toilet paper at them. The foulness of her language matched that of the prisoner she was threatening. The guard banged on the bars with her baton and promised the inmate in the next cell she would shove the dirty tissue into his mouth if he didn't stop cackling. Her form was lean, but the muscles revealed by the rolled-up sleeves and the cruelty in her eyes made it clear she could and would do what she said.

When she'd had enough, she shoved Harry forward. "Move along, pretty boy. I don't have all day."

#

Later in the afternoon

"Get a move on, pretty boy," said the correction officer, tone bored. A young man this time. His hand landed on Harry's back, thrusting him forward. It had only been around 2 p.m. when he got to the prison, but dinner came early for the inmates.

Without responding, Harry scuffled along the long line at the mess hall. In front, hungry prisoners bellowed, throwing curses indiscriminately. Kitchen staff dished out thin, unappetizing beef stew from a large cauldron. Guards cleared rows of detainees minutes after they sat.

A brawl broke out at the other end of the hall when a prisoner called a guard a particularly foul name. "Shut—the—fuck—up," bellowed the officer closest to Harry, running to the scene.

Everyone in the large hall was staring in the direction of the commotion. With a casual glance at the ruckus and a quick scan of the room, Harry returned his eyes to the front of the line where the servers were gaping at the stupid inmate who'd picked a fight with the officers.

There it was. A hitch in the breath behind him, the stench of a predator. A blade hissed.

Half a foot to the right.

The assailant pitched forward, off balance.

Every guard around was focused on the loud brawl. On this side of the mess hall, no one uttered a word. Studiously averted eyes were fixed on other things.

Harry grabbed the attacker's knife arm, pulling it across his back. Bone popped violently out of socket. The prisoner screamed before dropping to the floor.

Heads pivoted. The prison officials came running back. Before they could shoulder their way through to see what happened, Harry stepped over the fallen man and waited patiently at the counter for his food.

He ate every morsel of the soggy mess on the metal tray. There were other inmates at the table, but on either side of him were man-sized gaps. No one attempted to talk to him.

Inmates were allowed to take classes in the evening or attend gym. Not wanting to do either, Harry made for his cell right after finishing the meal. A fat orange tabby sat at the top of the stairs, washing itself. When they made eye contact, it scampered down the steps with a high-pitched "meow."

The yowl almost obscured the hiss from Harry's right. Inside a cell were three men, frantically gesturing at him. Harry hesitated, not wanting to go in.

"All right, stay there then," the impatient man muttered. "Do you know whose arm you broke, Pretty Boy?"

The Kingsley assassin. His name didn't matter. And apparently, Harry was stuck with a new moniker.

The inmate doing the talking was black and large in size with a bulging belly. The tattoo of a dagger curved over his shaved scalp, the handle behind one ear and the tip ending close to the brow. An ugly X-shaped scar marred one cheek. "He was one of the Rivals' men in here. They'll kill you for what you did. Get them before they get you. The yard is the best place."

"A gang?" Harry finally asked, having taken a few seconds to understand the Rivals were not *his* rivals, the Kingsleys.

"What're you? Retarded or somethin'? Yeah, a gang. Someone paid them to get you."

The man's comrades again gestured Harry in, cackling when he chose to stay at the door. Quickly, they dragged a small box from beneath the cot in the cell.

"Here," the leader said, handing him a scalpel. "Stole it from the clinic."

Harry twisted the knife around in his hand, staring in silence at each of the three in turn.

Voice casual, the leader asked, "You know how to put a blade in a man?"

Harry got a fifteen-minute tutorial on how to kill an adult human with a doctor's scalpel. As the prisoner lectured on, Harry eyed the vital points on the leader, calculating how long it would take him to bleed to death from each injury.

Bundles of old newspapers were handed over, along with a food tray. One of the sidekicks added a roll of duct tape to the pile. "Tape the tray to your front... like a shield. Leave the newspapers for the sides and back."

"Don't talk if you get caught," the leader said, rubbing fingers over the scar on his face. "The Blades never forget."

Ahh. Harry was meant to be the Blades' instrument of revenge for the scar. Thanking them, he took the knife. On the way back to his cell, he used the fabric of the uniform to rub off any prints before tossing the blade to the ground. No evidence of any sort of misbehavior could be attributed to Harry for the duration of his stay in the place.

The six-by-nine cell held a narrow cot with a thin, lumpy mattress. There was a small desk to the left and a commode as well as a sink toward the back. Stripping off his shirt, Harry hung it on the wall hook above the desk. *Strange,* he thought, glancing down at the scar on his left chest. It was the result of the altercation with the rapist at the network's board meeting more than three years ago. Once the wound healed, Harry didn't pay much attention to it, but there had been no hair around the line going down his pectoral skin for a while. Then, a white swirl appeared.

Collapsing into the bed, Harry wished he'd been allowed to bring a few more personal items. Memories of happier times, like the silver chain and Eiffel Tower pendant wrapped around his wrist until the day of his arrest. As he did every evening since then, he brought its image to his mind... the innocence, the joy.

"Did you miss me?" Harry asked, his heart full at the sight of her. They hadn't seen each other since her parents' deaths. After more than a year of only phone calls to keep them content, his parents invited Lilah to Libya for Thanksgiving break.

Wrinkling her nose, she said, "Not even a bit. I was too busy spending Andrew's money."

"Too bad," Harry murmured. "'Cause I missed you like hell, habibti.*"*

Eyes wide open, Harry smiled.

The shouts and roars in the prison eventually died down to the occasional loud snores, punctuated by a quiet mutter or two. Guards chatted with each other on nightly rounds, their footsteps fading away shortly. Even if there had been a moon in the sky, the structure of the prison block would not have let the light in.

Outside the bars of Harry's cell, a shadow separated from the rest. Senses snapping back to the present, Harry lay still as the door opened. Not an amateur like the first one, he decided. Not a sound, not even of breathing. No wasted movements. The door closed as silently as it opened, leaving the shadow inside. Only a slight change in the draft from some unseen vent told Harry the intruder was close.

A hand descended on his face without warning, the latex glove rubbery against his skin. Air whooshed as the hitman raised his other arm to sink the blade into his target's chest. Harry clamped his teeth around the flesh of the assassin's palm, using both hands to pull the knife-wielding arm to the left side of the cot. Raising his knee, he struck hard against the killer's abdomen.

The killer grunted, falling on top. He withdrew his hand from Harry's mouth and used it to push against the bed in an attempt to free himself, legs scrambling comically on one side of the cot.

Harry didn't let go until he felt the knife drop. When the blade fell to the mattress, he freed one of his own hands to grab the assassin in a headlock and rolled with him to the right. They tumbled off the bed into the cramped space between the cot and the desk, Harry on top.

In silence, the two men struggled. The stakes were high. Only the winner would get to live, but discovery would bring more trouble than death. Harry wrapped his legs around the killer's, pinning him to the floor.

The assassin arched up, using his free hand to try and push Harry away at the hip. When it failed, the thug tried to flip Harry by the shoulders, but there wasn't enough space.

Harry slammed the hitman's right arm to the ground, the head still wrapped in a lock.

With his other arm, the assassin underhooked Harry's elbow, trying to break the headlock.

Drawing up his right knee, Harry crushed it into his opponent's crotch. Other than a loud grunt, the killer did not make a sound, but the head wrapped in Harry's arm was suddenly soaking wet. The small cell stank of piss and sweat.

While the thug was still gasping for air, Harry let go of the man's knife arm and brought his own left arm to the killer's head. Hands slipping against sweat-drenched hair, Harry brought his right knee up to the opponent's chest. Breath came in a massive whoosh when Harry yanked the man's neck forward, lifting his shoulders off the floor. One violent twist to the side. Vertebrae fractured. The body under his stopped the gulping breaths. It convulsed for a few seconds, then shrank into itself.

Harry pushed the flaccid limbs aside and lurched up. He stood by the corpse and wiped the sweat from his lip with his sleeve. A small gasp from outside caught his attention. There was barely any light, but he could make out a few forms.

He dove for the knife on the bed. "First one inside gets it," he snarled, blade in his right hand.

Running footsteps sounded, but not all the shadows left. "You not bad, Pretty Boy," said a slightly nasal voice, tone appreciative.

"The Blades. Were you behind this?"

The leader slipped in, arms raised. "No. We heard somethin's up and came to check."

"The Rivals?"

"Not them, neither. A badge. The badass-est sumbitch."

Harry cursed fluently. He needed to get rid of the body. The gloves on the killer, too. They would carry his dental imprint.

"Listen," said the leader of the Blades. "I gotta deal for you."

Within a couple of minutes, the corpse was dragged out and left in the hallway, right in front of the cell where the Rivals' boss resided. The assassin's gloves were shredded with the knife, the weapon then wiped. The pieces of latex would be flushed down the toilet. The sole eyewitness to the process was the tabby cat Harry saw earlier, and the feline wasn't about to snitch.

Quietly, the men returned to their beds. "How did you manage to get out of your cell?" Harry asked on their way back.

The leader laughed. The snort should have been comical, but it wasn't. "This is Sing Sing, Pretty Boy. Not television. Some of them who run the place are my people."

#

In the morning, the prison complex was in uproar. All the men in the block were questioned. The investigation team was led by a fellow directly deputized by the chief of corrections.

"Sheppard," a female voice bellowed, and a black officer marched to the table in the interrogation room. Behind her was a male colleague. The female officer was lean and average in height, but she moved with the toughness of an athlete. The same guard had escorted Harry to his cell when he first arrived. Spite shooting from her brown eyes, she slammed a hard hand on Harry's neck. A forceful tug at his collar... he stood, taking care to keep his fingers loosely curled, and focused his gaze on the top of her head. "Spit out the truth, Pretty Boy," she snarled, "or you'll pay for it." Turning to the investigator on the other side of the table, she added, "The deceased looked up his cell number yesterday."

"And you are?" the lead investigator asked, a hint of command in his tone. At the beginning of the interview, the tall, slender man sent his subordinates off on other tasks before mentioning he knew Noah Andersen well. So did the corrections chief. The three men occasionally played golf together. The day Harry was first arrested, the former attorney general had made a call to his golf partners to keep an eye on any problems involving the high-profile prisoner. The conversation in the interrogation room would've been heard by the people listening in from outside, but nothing illegal was said. Still, it explained the interruption.

The guard flushed. "Sorry, sir. I should've introduced myself." Not dropping her hold on Harry's collar, she added, "Officer Regina Berra." Her male colleague stood ready, his eyes alert for the slightest hint of trouble from the prisoner.

"Thank you, Officer Berra," the investigator said. "We started the interview only a few minutes ago. I would've gotten to the question you asked myself... at a time and in a manner *I* picked."

With an impatient huff, the officer said, "The inmate should be cuffed while—"

The door opened again to let through a large man. Unlike the correction officers, the newcomer was dressed in a brown suit, his gut spilling over his belt. His face was clean shaven, but there were brown tufts on his earlobes, matching the hair on his head.

A few steps, and he was at the table. The fellow presented himself to the investigator. "Arthur Berra. I'm the warden."

Berra? Neither the warden nor the guard acknowledged any connection. The warden was white and middle-aged while Officer Berra... there was a slight resemblance to their features. Father and daughter?

Blue eyes sharp, Warden Berra nodded. "We don't offer special privileges in Sing Sing to the rich and the well-connected. Moreover, this particular inmate should be considered prime suspect... I believe it was what Officer Berra was trying to tell you. Therefore, he's even more of a safety risk and needs to be cuffed. Once the interview is done, he'll be moved to solitary."

Harry stiffened. First, the enemy sent an amateur to try his luck. When he failed, the professional showed up. Now, solitary confinement... a prison within the prison. Was Harry about to be put in a trap he couldn't possibly escape from?

The investigator smiled, but there was no amusement in his eyes. "Your decision, Warden Berra, but let me warn you... I have an obligation to inform the department chief about this. The fact the dead man looked up where an inmate was located hardly suggests anything nefarious on the inmate's part. There is also good reason to suspect the killing was related to prison gang activity... something you're supposed to prevent, Mr. Berra. The warden cannot blame his failings on a random prisoner. I don't see justification for putting Mr. Sheppard in solitary at this time."

Warden Berra glowered for a moment or two before inclining his head and marching back. Officer Regina Berra followed but not before glaring at Harry, her narrowed eyes promising retribution.

The investigation team conducted more interviews with the rest of the prisoners. If there were other correction officers involved in the murder attempt, they wouldn't dare accuse Harry and unmask themselves. Instead, the Rivals lost their leader in Sing Sing. Where he disappeared to and in what shape, no one bothered to ask. Not long after, more fights broke out between the Blades and the Rivals, leading to a few broken ribs, a few knife wounds. Without their leader, the Rivals soon fell to the Blades. The chief of the Blades made sure everyone in A-block knew Harry Sheppard was considered an ally and not to be messed with.

Part IX

Chapter 24

Five months later, November 1992

(nearly 3 years after Harry's arrest and 4 after the exile began)

Upper East Side, New York City

The ABC news anchor speculated breathlessly on a Bill Clinton presidency. The nation wouldn't learn the outcome of the election until later in the night, but it was clear what the media wanted. In Godwin Kingsley's home office, the group of men watched television in silence. Well... everyone except Godwin. He was still reading *The New York Times* article on the currency trader who brought down the British pound only a few weeks ago and created confusion about the European Union project. It didn't really matter to such businessmen—including the Kingsleys— which political party occupied the White House. Politicians around the world would have no choice but to heed the dictates of the real rulers, the ones who wielded authority from outside the spotlight. The former supreme court justice often said real power was that which was exercised behind the scenes and beyond scrutiny.

Keeping only one eye on the screen, Richard concealed himself in the shadows next to the window and monitored the movements of the woman in the garden. Patrice Kingsley was too far away to hear anything discussed inside, but Richard didn't want her spotting him at all. He felt like an idiot, hiding from her like this, but she was already far too involved in his life. His parents' lives to be accurate.

Richard had suspected for a while she was spying on him through his parents, but as far as he could figure out, all they discussed were personal details which bore no relevance whatsoever to the situation her sons and daughter-in-law found themselves in. There was never any talk of the Kingsleys, of Steven, or even of Richard's own troubles with the damned labor contractor hired by Armor Drilling Co. who was now under investigation for trafficking minors. The issue didn't make headlines, but a couple of newspapers did report the story. The senior Armors expected the FBI to find their son—the proprietor of said drilling company—blameless, so perhaps they didn't deem it necessary to seek counsel from the lady of the manor.

Still, Patrice succeeded where Richard failed. She convinced his mother to see a decent doctor for her diabetes instead of the incompetent idiot she so far relied on. And now, *Miss Patrice* was at the door to the garage where her servants lived, waiting patiently under the overcast sky. At least the rain which soaked New York City all morning had let up for a while.

"Steven, I hope you have your people talking to the Clinton team?" the tall figure of Justice Kingsley inquired from the leather chair behind the desk. Folding the newspaper and sliding it to one side, the family patriarch sat back. White haired tied at his nape with a leather thong, Godwin projected the strength of a much younger man. His white beard was always neatly trimmed, and the gray eyes were just as sharp as Richard remembered from his childhood.

Not far from Richard, Steven paced the carpet. "Of course." It was the bare minimum expected of the network's chief executive. "You don't need to ask."

"Oh, but I do," Godwin said, tone calm. "Nothing you assumed responsibility for has gone right thus far."

Steven stopped pacing, his face flushed. "I work damn hard—"

"Setbacks happen," Richard interjected.

On the couch against the wall were Phillip Potts—son of General Potts—and Charles. Thankfully, the Kingsley idiot stayed silent. "Unbelievable," Phillip mused. "The fellow was supposed to be one of the best."

With a derisive chuckle, Godwin Kingsley said, "Major Potts, you brought an entire team with you and couldn't manage to take down Harry." Petty Officer Sheppard survived the attempt on his life which was arranged to coincide with the interrogation of the Kingsley brothers and Lilah in Cuba. "What made you think a single officer would be enough this time around?"

Phillip sat up, looking every inch the soldier he was. The brown hair and eyes made him nondescript only as long as Phillip himself decided he didn't want to be noticed. "With all due respect, sir," he addressed the Kingsley patriarch. "What happened before was precisely why I decided to tread carefully. We're talking about a mission inside Sing Sing. It would've been idiotic to simply put out a hit. Too much uncertainty... too many men involved... I'd end up in trouble. You have enough grandsons, so one or two dead or in prison doesn't make a difference, I suppose. My father has only me. It's been the two of us since my mother passed, and I intend to stay alive and out of jail for the old man's sake."

Godwin's countenance darkened at the blatant insubordination. Richard made a mental note to warn Phillip to be careful. They would all be safe until the day the exiles and Harry died. Afterward...

"See what happened?" Phillip continued. "Even a professional didn't succeed, but at least there's no one left to snitch. And I hope you're not seriously claiming it's possible to go after Sheppard with a whole team of professionals inside a maximum-security prison. The one I hired for the job is gone. It takes time to vet someone else and even more time to arrange a situation where suspicion doesn't fall on us... but rest assured we'll get it done. It's simply a matter of locating a chap with sufficient motive... could be money, could be something else."

"I've been around a lot longer than you, Mr. Potts," said Godwin. "Like all Kingsley men before me, I served in the military before returning to the family business. I expect I've forgotten a lot more missions than you've even been a part of." The former justice turned to Richard. "Mr. Armor, you brought up this idea of attacking Harry to lure Lilah and the rest."

A cartload of cash was delivered to the Bratva to have men ready to go at every major international airport in every possible country the exiles could've taken refuge in. When news of Sheppard's death broke, Mrs. Kingsley and the Kingsley golden boy would've come flying out of their hiding hole. Lilah Kingsley would've been killed before she even boarded the plane back home, and her entourage would follow soon after. An expensive operation, and timing would've been critical, but the Russian mafia swore they could make it work. Except, Petty Officer Sheppard refused to cooperate.

"How in God's name did you fail to realize Harry would anticipate exactly what you did?" Godwin growled. "Useless! A major! The army is fortunate you decided to go into business, instead."

Humiliation, anger... a painful pulse pounded behind Richard's eye. Turning away from the window, he bit out, "Any competent officer would anticipate enemy response. Both Major Potts and I understood Sheppard would be on the lookout for attacks, but we had to operate within the constraints of the—"

"'On the lookout'?" taunted Godwin. "So how did you not realize a direct attack like your hitman tried would in fact be suicidal? You either have to catch Harry by surprise or be absolutely certain to leave him no chance of escaping."

"Give me time," Phillip repeated, "and I *will* find someone. The Russians I hired have men in every continent watching for Brad and the rest to resurface." They would only know Phillip Potts wanted payback for what he considered his father's defeat in the court in Cuba. As far as the mobsters knew, Phillip was angry about traitors escaping justice, and the payments he made to the mafia came out of his investments in the oil business.

"I still think we should first look for Cousin Brad," Charles said, tone sulky. "JD really wants to. He says at least one of them's gotta go because of him. Brad or one of the rest, Lilah, Harry... even one of their brats will do."

Ignoring Charles's recommendation, Richard swore to Godwin, "It will get done. Sheppard's not going anywhere, so it *is* merely a matter of time." The trickster could not escape again. Major Armor would not be demeaned again in this household.

"The more time you give them—" Godwin snapped.

"Grandfather," called Steven. "I get what you're saying, but a pardon's out of the question unless Harry somehow manages to get himself exonerated first. Both he and my cousins are stuck in position, wherever they are. They can't make any moves. Only we can."

"Twenty-five years in prison," said Godwin, "five until parole... which will come up in two more years. He's planning something, and it's not going to be for twenty-five years from now. The only reason he's been lying low is the media attention. It won't be the same when he comes out on parole. Mark my words... he's going to have his plan ready."

"But until then, we will know where he is every moment," pointed Steven.

"Something positive," agreed Godwin.

It didn't seem to occur to the Kingsley patriarch his maker might call him back before the scheme to deal with the problem of Harry Sheppard came to fruition. But then, the Kingsleys who weren't stupid enough to invite death stayed hale and hearty into their nineties, several even making it to a century. Godwin Kingsley was eighty-seven and still able in both mind and body. Besides, the former justice already achieved what he wanted—Kingsley dominance of the oil sector. Now, it was merely a matter of continuing to move the puppet strings from six feet under.

At least Richard was not one of the old man's puppets. Taking a deep breath, Richard cast another glance through the window, in the direction of the garage.

"Two years should give us enough time to permanently take care of even Harry," Steven said.

Godwin shook a finger at his heir. "You cannot afford to relax your guard until it's all over. Harry can't make any moves, but he has men on his side who can. Luce's son has been asking questions. The Barronses... if they find something to help Harry..."

"Luce, Jr. is not going to get anywhere," said Richard. "Any investigation into the McCoy connection will lead to the Sheppards, not the Kingsleys. I guarantee you."

"Good," said the patriarch. "There's no way we can get rid of the young man at this point without having the cops reopen Will Luce's murder. And keep an eye on Lilah's family... both her brothers. Daniel is her twin, but the other one got her out of trouble in Cuba."

Shawn Barrons was an acknowledged expert in technology circles and the number one suspect for having rigged Lilah Kingsley's computer so the evidence against her was inadvertently destroyed. It was also Shawn who sold his tech stock and sent money to her Swiss bank account when everyone else turned their backs.

"All of them are being watched," said Richard, "but Andersen is the one to worry about."

The former attorney general made sure everyone in Sing Sing knew Harry had allies. Then, there were the interviews. A hint here, a second one there... anytime Steven's actions won media approval, Andersen would say something to drag the Kingsley heir back to square one. The public was frequently reminded of Steven's role in the Cuba episode and of Charles's assault on Lilah Kingsley. Even Stanley Gander, Steven's uncle who merely followed orders, didn't escape Andersen's wrath. Surprisingly, Andersen had given Major Armor a wide berth thus far. Perhaps the chauffeur's son wasn't deemed important enough. Not so surprisingly, Godwin's name was never mentioned among the villains. Anyone who suggested the revered former supreme court justice had been part of a conspiracy to steal his own grandson's business empire would be counted among tinfoil hatters.

The grandiose tales about Brad Kingsley's goodness were laughable. Damned kissass... there was nothing he did to deserve... he lost the empire he never earned on a roll of dice. Whatever Andersen and Sheppard now thought of the man they picked for the throne, they were forced to sing his praises to justify his return to power.

"Andersen's definitely a problem—" started Godwin.

"What about the other lawyer?" Charles piped up again. "We should make him talk. I heard you say he knows where Brad and the rest are. So all this other stuff won't matter. We kill them first and finish Harry later."

Richard grimaced.

"Imbecile," muttered the patriarch, not bothering to elaborate.

"For God's sake, Charlie," said Steven.

"A former chairman of NYSE?" Richard asked. The old fellow came out of retirement to act as the chief legal advisor for Brad's company. After the Cuba debacle, Grayson Sheppard became personal lawyer for the exiles. The feds would investigate anything happening to someone like him. It wouldn't be the same as Harry Sheppard accusing the Kingsleys or even Andersen saying anything. After what happened to Temple, another suspicious death in their team or the disappearance of someone with a stellar reputation like Grayson Sheppard or Noah Andersen would create enormous uproar.

"N-Y-what?" asked Charles.

"NYSE," Richard said. "New York Stock Exchange." Out of the corner of his eye, he saw Patrice Kingsley head up the path to the house. Must have been a short visit with the Armors. He held up a hand, warning the rest in the room to be silent.

Steven joined Richard at the window. "Aunt Patrice? She's going to Uncle Aaron's wing... too far to hear anything."

Shaking his head, Richard said, "Wait a couple of minutes."

They watched her trudge along, holding the edges of her coat tight against her chin, the wind whipping her hair around her face. She reached a fork and turned right toward Aaron Kingsley's apartment. Richard hoped the fool woman would have enough sense to stay out of the rain and the chilly wind for the rest of the evening.

When Richard turned back, Godwin Kingsley was staring at him, a small smile on his face. With difficulty, Richard hid a frown. Those at the receiving end of the former justice's good humor had more to worry about than those subjected to the sharp edge of his hostility.

Chapter 25

A month later, Christmas Day, 1992

Upper East Side, New York City

Patrice's room in Aaron Kingsley's apartment was spacious and quite private. Her living arrangements raised quite a few eyebrows, but she'd survived society gossip before. Aaron was hardly ever home in any case, spending most nights at his lady friend's place.

When Patrice first moved in, she'd been happy about getting to see Richard when he visited his adoptive parents. Of course she worried about her sons with Peter, but so many people were trying to help them, including a former president. Even after Temple got shot, she didn't panic. There was Daniel Barrons, who clearly loved his twin. He would move heaven and earth to bring her home. Harry was a Sheppard, and Patrice couldn't trust any of the family, but his sister was married to Alex. No matter what, Harry would bring the exiles back.

Then, Andersen visited, telling her all about his nasty suspicions of Richard. The former attorney general insisted she stay where she was. For one, she could pick up useful info from the Kingsleys and their staff. For another, Godwin knew her little secret. If she left, if the old man got the faintest hint she would talk, he could well hurt Richard.

Patrice would never have moved in with Sabrina. It was a Sheppard home, after all. Nor did Patrice dare leave the Kingsley mansion to live on her own. She did as Andersen asked, but in the four years since her sons went on exile, there was nothing she learned which could be of use to them. The lawyer made his disappointment clear each time Patrice said she didn't have anything new to report.

It was the truth! There was nothing to implicate Richard in any of Steven's crimes, but Andersen refused to believe it.

The day she heard about Will Luce's murder... Harry's arrest... when the judge announced the sentence, Patrice almost couldn't breathe. Andersen said they would appeal, but it would take time. Meanwhile, her boys were out there somewhere in the world, unable to come home, unable to see their families. Lilah, too. What could Dan Barrons do for her on his own? Would he even dare after what happened to Harry and Temple?

Pacing the carpeted floor, Patrice willed the jitters to go away. Perhaps she shouldn't have agreed to help at the holiday dinner organized for the homeless by the Temple Foundation. It wasn't as though she didn't care about the less fortunate. It wasn't as though she didn't understand Noah Andersen's point about presenting a united front before the media. The tabloid owner who once helped Patrice's boys defeat Sanders—the bald-headed fellow called Eugene Bishop—was there, clicking pictures of the former president and his friend as well as the rest of their circle.

Liam Luce showed up, as did the Barrons brothers. There was the same red-haired young woman Patrice saw with Dan before—his secretary. The girl's name was Amy, and they were shacking up without the benefit of matrimony. Daniel had clearly decided to brave his adoptive father's disapproval for love. Shawn, on the other hand, changed partners with dizzying frequency. Lilah's brothers adored her, but their lives didn't come to a standstill in her absence.

The ones who suffered the most were an abandoned wife and two young boys. Sabrina, Michael, and Gabriel helped the volunteers carry trays of food back and forth, chatting and laughing with everyone as though there was nothing wrong.

Patrice went to the event mainly to see her grandsons. She talked to Michael and Gabriel every week on the phone, but it had been a long time since she actually met the boys. After the unfortunate run-in with Richard on a New Year's Eve visit to Patrice, Sabrina balked at bringing the kids to the Kingsley mansion. She never expressed overt annoyance at Patrice's refusal to visit their home in Long Island, but nor did Sabrina bother to hide her puzzlement at her mother-in-law's behavior.

Then, there was Noah Andersen. The former attorney general didn't say a word to Patrice at the food bank event. He didn't need to. The presence of her grandsons did it for him. The boys should've been celebrating Christmas with their fathers. Instead, they...

She wasn't doing anything wrong, Patrice assured herself. Not a day went by when she didn't plead with God to bring her children home. She prayed every night for Harry's freedom... for *Ryan Sheppard's* son. Lilah... the poor girl was suffering only because she married into the Kingsley family. Patrice wished there was something she could do to help, but there wasn't. Abandoning Richard yet again would only break her heart anew without accomplishing anything useful.

Still... Michael and Gabriel's chatter... they didn't mention their dads even once in Patrice's hearing. Perhaps it was out of consideration for her, but her conscience wasn't letting up.

What she was hoping to get from visiting Richard's adoptive mother, Patrice didn't know. It wasn't as though she could confess anything to the lady.

Ringing the doorbell, Patrice waited. There was nothing other than cheerful friendliness on Mrs. Armor's face when she let Patrice in. Prattling about Richard's latest offer of a townhouse in Williamsburg, his mother led Patrice to the kitchen.

Accepting the offer of a seat at the countertop, Patrice asked, "Don't you *want* to move?"

Mrs. Armor shrugged, tucking her gray bun under a polythene cap. She was very meticulous when she cooked. "Not really. Richie says all the neighbors would be doctors and lawyers and teachers. What would we do in a place like that? Here, we have our friends among the staff."

Delicately, Patrice said, "But it can't be easy here. You and Mr. Armor must be..."

"Seventy-five and seventy-seven," said Mrs. Armor, brown eyes twinkling. "We were in our thirties when Richard was born."

"I didn't mean to pry," Patrice said.

Mrs. Armor's short, plump form shook with laughter. "I'm old enough not to mind. When we get too weak to be of any use, we'll move to a nursing home. Someplace where it won't matter what we used to do for a living."

"Richard won't agree," Patrice said instantly.

"Oh, I know," said Mrs. Armor. "He never liked being called 'the chauffeur's son.' I don't know where the boy learned his ego. Mr. Armor and I... we didn't teach Richie to be ashamed of his background, but he is. If we move in with him, he's going to want us to lie about our work. Neither his pa nor I will agree to do it. So a nursing home it will be for us." She sighed. "Poor Richie... too clever for his lot in life. Too strong, too proud, too handsome, too everything. Things got even worse after he made friends with Mister Steven. Miss Patrice, I wish you'd never left the family home. If your boys were around when my Richie was growing up, *they* could've been friends."

"Maybe," Patrice murmured, her heart squeezing. Instead of being friends, Richard joined forces with Steven to attack her sons. No, she corrected herself. Richard was merely the lawyer.

Flushing, Mrs. Armor said, "I never thanked you for not holding it against him. It can't be easy, seeing him here while Mister Brad and Mister Victor and Mister Alex are out there, God knows where."

Tears smarted Patrice's eyes. "Who knows if they're even alive?" she whispered.

Mrs. Armor hurried around the counter to wrap Patrice in a silent hug.

"I'm all right," Patrice said, shrugging loose. "And you *should* think about moving in with Richard. He's all alone in his apartment."

Returning to her cake mix, Mrs. Armor huffed in exasperation. "He says he meets plenty of women, but what kind of young ladies were they if he never brought them home to visit me? The boy doesn't seem to want to get married. He needs a wife to take care of him."

"Does he have a housekeeping service? Sabrina—Alex's wife—uses an agency, but they're not very good."

"Oh, I personally checked out Richard's cleaning service," said Mrs. Armor, rattling off a name. "The girls do a great job."

Patrice wasn't sure why the rather mundane information stuck with her, but it did. Months later, she would pick up the phone and whisper what she learned to someone.

Part X

Chapter 26

Two months later, February 1993

Long Island, New York

Michael kicked the floor and rolled his chair back until it hit the wall by the window. He cursed a blue streak, every foul word he knew tripping fluently off his tongue. Though his ma didn't have a clue, he'd overheard plenty of off-color language from his dad when he was around and from assorted uncles.

Fingers curled into a tight fist, Michael prepared himself to bloody his opponent's nose. If only there were one... but he and Gabriel were the sole occupants of the large bedroom overlooking the garden.

"Dumb woman," muttered Gabriel, hurling the magazine in his hands to the floor. He wasn't talking about any of the ladies featured in the glossy.

The mom of one of Michael's classmates had asked him if Lilah were his stepmother. He'd barely managed to limit himself to a no before going in search of the one other boy in the school who also faced similar questions. In the afternoon, Gabriel dug out some old periodicals from under his mattress. All carried pictures of Lilah with Michael's daddy and his uncles. The writers talked breathlessly about a weird family which didn't sound like them at all. The names were the same, but the rest...

Gabriel collapsed onto the bed and pulled the cap over his face. At eleven, he was only a year older than his cousin, but he was practically a giant for a fifth grader. The coach at school even suggested he try out for the football team.

"She gotta be dumb," Gabriel insisted. "Or she wouldn't repeat such stupid shit."

"If you know it's stupid," Michael ground out, "why are you keeping the magazines?"

Face still covered by the cap, Gabriel shrugged. "My father's in them. He called only a couple of times a month, so I got all the papers I could find."

Photographs of his long-dead mother were displayed openly on the desk as were those of the Garcias, the family he lived with before moving to New York. Mrs. Garcia cried when he left, but her husband had died, and she was ill herself, which meant she couldn't take care of Gabriel any longer. There was some *really* weird stuff she sent with Gabriel. Talismans meant to protect him from evil spirits were scattered around the room. Gabriel actually believed the stupid stories about gods and visions and magic but not the ones in the tabloids.

The only other image to be honored with a place in the room was one of Gabriel with Michael and his ma. Oh, and the giant poster of Maradona, the soccer player, which hung over the desk.

"I used to wish all the time Uncle Alex was my dad," Gabriel continued. "At least he kept you with him."

Michael laughed, hating how small and pathetic he sounded. "Yeah, they're both not around now, are they?"

"It's been more than four years," supplied Gabriel.

Michael couldn't even remember his father's face without looking at a picture or some such. "We have Ma," he insisted. "And Uncle Harry."

Sitting up, Gabriel nodded vigorously. He was all Kingsley while Michael's mug was more Sheppard... Harry, specifically. Except, everyone said Michael got his father's weird brown eyes. "And Mr. Temple, Mr. Andersen, Uncle Liam, Uncle Shawn, Uncle Dan..." tallied Gabriel. "Uncle Grayson, too."

Even Harry's former secretary—Natasha—visited a couple of times. When Harry left Gateway, she went to work for *his* boss, the COO.

"Don't forget Mr. Dante," said Michael.

Dante was a serious man, always asking Michael about school. His son was cool, though. Virgil was an aeronautical engineer. He built airplanes. But of all the people helping them, Andersen who lived next door with the former president was the coolest. He once pretended to pull candy from behind Gabriel's ear. Plus, there were the flute lessons... Michael loved them. He reciprocated by showing Mr. Andersen how to use chat rooms on the internet. The old fellow was fascinated, declaring it was a good way to keep his "finger on the pulse of the world" even if he couldn't travel any longer and leave his friend—Mr. Temple—all alone.

Temple was nice, too. Also, it was kinda neat knowing actual secret service officers. Michael's mother once muttered that Mr. Temple's son needed his backside kicked for never visiting his father, and Andersen didn't have any close family left alive. The two elderly men popped into Michael's home almost every day, and Temple usually left his friend talking to Sabrina to make straight for the boys' playroom. He'd pore over their old picture books, stabbing with his finger at each word until Michael or

Gabriel read it out loud. Temple would then mimic each sound. Andersen interrupted them once and asked the boys if they ever told anyone about the sessions. There was relief in his eyes when Gabriel said no. Michael clicked his heels together and saluted. Of course they wouldn't blab... not even to friends at school. This was a secret mission from the president of the United States.

"Where do you think they are?" Gabriel asked, tone subdued. The "they" didn't need to be named.

"Doesn't matter," said Michael. "We're getting along fine on our own."

"But they're still our dads. Aren't we supposed to make them proud or something? I mean... they were soldiers... officers."

"I'd rather make my ma proud." Michael would actually be the kind of hero she bragged his dad was. Even if the Kingsley brothers never returned, Michael would win back everything they lost. He'd make the enemy face justice for their crimes. Major Armor would pay for what he did to Michael's family. And Michael would never, ever leave his wife and kid to fend for themselves.

#

A week later, 26ᵗʰ February 1993, 11:50 AM

New York, New York

Sir-Mix-a-Lot rapped "Baby Got Back" on the car radio.

Dancing along in the back seat, Michael peered out the window. "How tall are they?" His eyes followed the Twin Towers all the way up to gray clouds. Inside Liam's Toyota, it was warm, but white air puffed out from the mouths of the pedestrians making their way through the crowded sidewalks of Lower Manhattan. Snowflakes drifted down on their puffy coats.

"More than a thousand feet, I think," said Liam. "Listen, buddy. Your principal wasn't too happy I pulled you out, so get all your lessons done before you go to school on Monday, okay?"

The fourth-grade math teacher whose class Michael was supposed to be in right now would also not be thrilled by his absence. He shrugged. "Yeah, but I really want to see where Uncle Harry used to work." Since Liam left his job with the Sheppards to work for Shawn's company, he could only take Michael to visit Gateway when the place was open for business. The Peter Kingsley Company also used to have offices in the same building. Still did... except the other Kingsleys were in charge.

Perhaps Michael could stop at the floor and at least take a look from the outside. He hadn't said the second part to his mother, or she'd have refused to grant the request, his tenth birthday or not.

A yellow van with black letters proclaiming the name of the rental company, Ryder, swung into the garage ahead of them. "I don't have regular parking here, anymore," said Liam. The Ryder van in front pulled into a spot on level B2. Another car parked next to it. Liam cursed. "Idiots. It's not a legal parking space."

"Forget them, Uncle Liam," Michael said. "Let's go."

First, they needed to meet one of Liam's friends who worked in the North Tower. Afterward, they'd go to the South Tower to Gateway's offices. Once they were there, Michael would persuade Liam to let him get a glimpse of his family's former kingdom. After all, he planned to be sitting in the same office some day in the future while the Kingsleys languished in prison for their crimes.

12:05 PM

The Port Authority's cafeteria was crowded. Munching on his cheeseburger, Michael wished Liam would hurry up and finish talking to his contact.

"There has to be some way to figure out if it was the same man who took the flight," Liam said, sweeping his hair back over his head. "Security cameras are our best bet. I have a hard time buying the hotel simply tossed the tapes out."

James McCoy was again the topic of discussion. Michael had heard the name a few hundred times over the last few years. Everyone around was quite certain McCoy was responsible for putting Harry in prison. The defense lawyer had brought up the possibility in the trial, then in the appeals process, but there was simply no proof.

"I'm trying," said Liam's contact. "What we need is an inside man—someone who could help us locate the tapes. I've put out some feelers."

When Michael finished his burger and slurped up the last of his lemonade, Liam said there was one more "contact" to meet before going on to Gateway's office.

12:18 PM

They exited the elevator right outside a door. "Mike," Liam started, his hand on the knob. "Your Uncle Hector's going to be—"

Something slammed into Michael, lifting him off his feet. He opened his mouth to scream for Liam, but breath wouldn't come out. His head struck a wall. Then, he was thrown back down.

Shouts and shrieks filled the hallway. "Earthquake," someone yelled. Men and women stampeded toward the stairwell. Through the painful haze in front of his eyes, Michael looked for Liam. Running bodies merged into each other in a colorful blur. The walls of the building shuddered, making his tummy churn.

A hand grabbed his arm and hauled him upright. "Let's go, Mike," Liam ordered, voice urgent.

"What happened?" Michael asked, feeling dazed.

"No idea, and we're not waiting to find out." They joined the crowd headed for the stairs. Smoke rose, thick and black. "Don't let go of my hand," ordered Liam.

Coughing, Michael let himself be hustled down the steps. The dark smoke got thicker... so heavy... he couldn't see his own hand. The sounds of hundreds of footsteps, the blaring alarms from every floor, the screams... Michael's heart started racing, each thump painful. His breath came in gasps. Ma. He wanted his ma.

"Hold on, Mike," said Liam, wrapping an arm around his shoulders. Michael was on the left, sandwiched between the wall and Liam. "We'll make it out of here."

Michael whimpered. The last time his insides hurt this bad was back in Panama during the raid when Major Richard Armor's icy eyes landed on him. Michael had only been a baby at the time, but he'd never forgotten the horrible feeling.

Liam staggered against him, muffling a groan.

"What?" Michael asked.

"My chest," said Liam. "Something fell on me when the... thing went off."

"Is it broken?" Michael asked, voice trembling. "A bone or something?"

"Don't know. Listen, Mike. If we run into a cop or a firefighter, I want you to go with them."

Leave Liam to make his way out on his own? *If* he made his way out. "No," said Michael, his shoulders tightening. His breathing slowed to normal. His pulse steadied.

"This is not the time to arg—"

"The military leaves no man behind," recited Michael.

With a strangled laugh, Liam asked, "Where did you learn the gem? Your dad?"

"Uncle Harry," Michael said, his tone sounding strangely calm. His vision sharpened until he could see the forms within the smoke. His ears heard their sobs. Over the smoke, he smelled the fear, the panic. Something solidified within him. The will to survive. The resolve to rescue. "We're going to get you out of here, sir."

"Mike..." Liam huffed. "No point in debating it unless we do see an officer. I'm going to hold on to the wall next to you, all right, buddy? *You* need to—my belt, maybe."

The belt was soon wound tight around Michael's wrist and one of Liam's pant loops. Limping and stumbling, they inched their way down. Michael didn't know how long it took. What he knew was he was drenched in sweat, that his every breath smelled of smoke. That Liam's gait was getting more and more clumsy. Grabbing his arm, Michael wrapped it around his shoulders and tried to take some of the weight.

A tendril of cold air hit his nostrils. Michael opened his mouth to say something to Liam when more fresh air drifted around him. He took deep, gulping breaths. Everyone in the crowd was doing the same. Excited chatter rose.

Another flight down, and they saw daylight. There were cops and firemen outside, guiding people to safety.

"Officer," Michael called, his voice slightly high. "My uncle—"

"Injured man here," hollered the officer.

Soon, Liam was strapped onto a stretcher. Michael was allowed in the ambulance with him. When they got to St. Vincent's Hospital, Liam refused to let anyone treat him until Michael's ma arrived to pick him up. With all the commotion on the streets, Liam's sister who lived in Manhattan was the first to reach them. Verity stayed in the waiting room with Michael and sniffled into her kerchief, but she did tell him what happened at the World Trade Center was no earthquake. There was an explosion in the garage. The FBI was investigating.

When Michael's mother got to the hospital, she came flying across the room to haul him out of his chair. His breath whooshed out. The tight grip she had around his torso would have made any wrestler salute in awe. His right shoulder was soon soaking wet with her tears.

"You're crushing him," teased Andersen, walking to them with a white-faced Gabriel.

They waited with Verity until Liam was out of surgery. From his bed, he saluted Michael. "You did well, soldier."

Michael clicked his heels together and saluted back. "I'm glad you're safe, sir."

"Thank God," his mother mumbled. "Oh, Mikey... my baby..." She hugged him again, then shook a finger in his face. "Don't you *ever* dare... don't you do this again... a bombing! I was worrying about your father, and you... stay safe, you hear me? We *all* have to stay safe."

Over her shoulder, Michael exchanged glances with Gabriel. All... meaning the men who didn't call even once in the last few years to check on their families. Michael's narrow escape wasn't gonna be enough to make them call, either. *If* they heard about it wherever they were.

Chapter 27

Four months later, June 1993

Goa, India

The air was thick with the feel of impending rain, but it was nowhere near strong enough to dispel the heat hanging over the flea market. Monsoon clouds rolled over gray sky. Whistling wind set the tall coconut palms dotting the landscape swaying gracefully, the green leaves now rendered a darker shade by the gloom. Summer was off-season, so there would be no live band or fire dancers or any of the food stalls which popped up to cater to tourists. Visitors on tight budgets still trekked to Goa, which meant there was money to be made.

Rocking to the rebellious Hindi song blasting out of a boombox, aging hippies and local entrepreneurs continued hawking flimsy cotton bikinis and macramé jewelry and dresses made from cut-up old saris. Silver trinkets and silly souvenirs were laid out on the ground. Neither the vendors nor the shoppers showed signs of running for shelter from the approaching storm.

Between the rows of stalls, Tara marched alongside Krishna and Maestro Arjun on their way to the alternative medicine clinic where one of their friends worked. Maestro took Tara there almost all Saturdays. It was a busy night at the resort for her parents, and Maestro minded Tara the entire evening.

Scratching her sweaty neck, Tara eyed the group of white backpackers sauntering past. All of them were huffing and puffing in the humid heat and chatting among themselves. The language sounded like Russian to Tara's ears. It wasn't Portuguese, which she learned in school in addition to English thanks to Goa's colonial past. Not French, either, which she could kinda, sorta understand after hanging around the resort all her life and running into all kinds of nationalities. One of the backpackers bumped into a trash can, muttering, *"Blin."*

Yeah, Russian. Tara recognized the curse word.

"The bowl looks cool," Maestro said, hustling Tara and Krishna to a stall on the other side of the path. "How much?" Maestro Arjun asked the vendor.

Tara rolled her eyes. As though she couldn't see through the ruse. They were dodging the Russians like Maestro always did. The resort staff had been muttering about the growing influence of the Bratva for months now, and Tara's father didn't believe in keeping secrets from her. What if she ran into one of the mafia people at The Mermaid and did something stupid because she didn't know who she was talking to? Her papa often pointed out faces in the restaurant and the casino, coaching her on whom to avoid. The Russian mafia was now a part of almost every kind of business in the state, and the police looked the other way. The bad men scammed the tourists, starting with taxi rides from the airport. They sold drugs, women, guns... you name it. Trans prostitutes were in demand. No wonder Maestro tried to stay away from anyone who looked even a bit Russian.

Maybe that was the reason Maestro Arjun didn't bother dressing up a little more. The silly wigs were gone, thankfully. Maestro's own hair was now tied in a low ponytail reaching all the way to mid-back. The coiffure and the makeup were fine, but the long-sleeved orange shirt and sarong were quite unisex for someone who insisted she was a woman. He also wore sunglasses, the wraparound kind. A long garland of *rudraksha* beads—dried fruit stones used in prayer—hung around his neck. All in all, a twentieth-century guru look. There was the way he walked... talked... Tara cringed. *She! Not he!* Fashion choices aside, Maestro had every right to decide who *she* was.

Ignoring the fake haggling Maestro was carrying on with the poor vendor, Tara turned her attention back to other shoppers. Four men in naval uniforms followed the Russians. Maybe they were following-following, Tara speculated. Like a spy movie or something. Sadly, the sailors' eyes were on a food cart a few feet away. With a distant thought that the outfits could use improvement, Tara dismissed them. Sailors were also not an unusual sight in Goa due to India's biggest naval airbase being located a mere forty kilometers from Vagator, where Tara lived. Which, of course, meant military helicopters frequently flew the blue skies.

The two people Tara was currently with acted way weirder than any visitor or sailor. Krishna kept her hair wrapped in a saffron-colored scarf, the fabric printed with religious symbols. The ends of the scarf were knotted around her loose braid. Large sunglasses perched on her nose, and a *tilak*—marking made with vermillion powder—decorated her forehead. Even the side-slit tunic and loose trousers were made of the same printed saffron cloth. And yeah... she had her own *rudraksha* beads. Very tourist-chic, practically screaming, "I am one of the many foreigners here in search of Indian spirituality."

Except Tara didn't buy it. Oh, Krishna knew her Hinduism... among a couple of other isms. Still, there was something.

Of course without buying any bowls, the group of three left the stoneware stall and resumed their walk to the alternative medicine clinic where Maestro's friend worked. "Why do you always cover your hair?" Tara asked Krishna.

"To prevent damage," came the pat response, the voice husky as always.

Tara turned her snort into a wheezing cough. If there was anything she learned to recognize in her eleven years on this earth spying on the guests at the resort, it was how to recognize fakeness... fake body parts, dye, cosmetics, eye color. Escaping from under Krishna's scarf were tendrils in a sun-kissed shade of red... which totally came from a bottle. What Tara didn't get was why the woman would then conceal it. Also, Krishna rarely ventured out of the ladies' hostel without all her gear and wore the tinted glasses every single minute. Her figure was perfect even with the shapeless clothes, but why hide it to begin with?

Tara skipped over a broken seashell necklace lying forgotten on the ground. Someone probably forked out a fistful of cash for the thing before it fell apart. The market was wildly successful in parting tourists from their money, and they actually seemed to enjoy getting fleeced. Krishna claimed it was part of the Goa experience.

Not that Krishna ever went around Goa to experience it. She didn't go *anywhere* alone. Maestro Arjun accompanied Krishna and Hema even on their shift at the salon in the resort. When Maestro gave dance lessons, Chef Vikram showed up to guard Krishna. He, too, worked at the resort. Maestro and Vikram did whatever heavy work there was in the salon—moving and carrying equipment and cleaning—so the supervisor didn't mind.

Tara grinned to herself. Most of the salon staff nursed crushes on the giant with the shaved head. They got super jealous of all the attention he gave Krishna. Vikram *was* a total babe, with his faded jeans and rolled-up sleeves and easy laugh. A couple of the salon girls commented in Tara's hearing how Vikram was too nice for a snooty woman like Krishna. The lady did her job without a single complaint—hair, makeup, sweeping, dusting, scrubbing the shampoo bowls. But just like with Maestro, there was something weird about the way Krishna walked... talked... as though she were a princess.

The cheeky men who braved the presence of a glowering Maestro and a hulking Vikram to try and chat up Krishna were usually met with a dismissive glance. Tara bit back a chuckle. She needed to try out the attitude on some of the silly boys at school. Chin tilted up, a look of "Beat it, peasant!"

"Five years," muttered Maestro. Thunder rumbled.

"What?" asked Tara.

"Ahh," said Maestro. "I was saying we've been away from home nearly five years."

Yeah... Maestro had family back in America. "I bet Max misses you," Tara said.

"Max... yes, champ," agreed Maestro. "I bet he does."

Max's dad sure missed him a lot. Tara became "champ" whenever Maestro remembered his son. *Her!* Tara chided herself. *Not his!*

Shaking her head at the puzzling inability to remember the important detail, Tara heard her name called. Only then did she realize her two companions had stopped a few feet behind.

"We're here," said Maestro.

Tara retraced her steps to the side street she just walked past. The coconut trees lining the path continued their crazy dance in the wind. It was after hours, so there were no patients queueing up in the tiny yard before the single-story building housing the alternative medicine clinic. The neighborhood was close enough to the beach but was nicely protected from all the chaos by a maze of narrow lanes, so there was relative quiet even in the thick of the tourist season.

Lightning forked the sky just as Tara and Krishna followed Maestro into the clinic's waiting area. Thunder rumbled again. The chair behind the small desk where the clerk would've been sat empty. A familiar stray dog—a puppy really—curled under the table. One of Maestro's friends constantly fed it scraps, and the mutt seemed to have adopted the clinic as his home.

Without further ado, Maestro shoved open the half-door to the doctor's office. Rain lashed the single window of the exam room, causing the man behind the desk to glance that way before turning to the visitors with a dazzling smile. Blond, blue-eyed Nakul also dressed like a guru... a doctor-guru who wore saffron robes instead of a lab coat.

The doctor worked as an assistant in a hospital lab. A few times a week, he ran the clinic advertised as following alternative medicine, like so many similar ones promising magical cures. Tara's mother once declared any government official trying to put a stop to the unlicensed miracle workers would be chased through the streets like mad dogs.

Tara didn't find anything "alternative" or "magical" about Doctor Nakul's advice on vaccinations and antibiotics, but he did seem divine. She stared at the glass door of the medicine cupboard, studying his reflection. Tara saw him without his bandana and tinted glasses only once, and it was enough. Even his bushy beard was beautiful.

Instead of the robes, Tara would outfit him in khaki pants, a white tee, and a blue-gray blazer. On a yacht, winding whipping his—no, clean-shaven. Without the headscarf. The lovely hair cut in layers, touching his collar. A female model would be next to him, her long legs set off by a dusty-red one-piece and matching translucent sarong. Tara frowned. What kind of woman would she have to be to look good next to male perfection like the doctor-guru? Someone around Krishna's height... five feet eight if Tara estimated correctly.

The half-door swung open. Chef Vikram walked in, shaking a wet umbrella and tossing it into the metal pail next to the trash can. "How can it be hotter in here?" muttered Vikram, mournful eyes on the ceiling fan as though he were pleading with the rusty old thing to speed up.

Tara giggled, prompting a wink from the giant chef.

Behind him was the man in rounded glasses Tara nicknamed "That Guy." His Hindu name was Raj. Stopping by the clerk's desk, he tossed dog biscuits to the mutt waiting underneath. A couple of pats to the pup's head, and Raj, too, walked into the inner room.

He'd arrived in Goa to trace his roots... his Portuguese-Jewish forefather showed up in the neighborhood centuries ago. Raj's mother was from New York. Not a practicing Jew, Maestro had said, so Raj didn't know much about the religion, but he was keen on tracing how his ancestors got to India, then to the U.S. The local art museum agreed to pay him a stipend to study and catalog their documents. Raj also worked a couple of hours a week at The Mermaid's casino.

Tara had tried what she usually did—sketched Raj in clothes she thought would suit his looks. Sadly, she couldn't come up with anything more exciting than the buttoned-up shirts and flat-front pants he already wore. He wasn't a bad looker, really. The curly, brown hair and blue eyes should have been cute, but even the beard couldn't entirely hide the discontent in his glance whenever it landed on Maestro and Krishna. Maestro usually responded with soothing noises, but Krishna turned stonily silent as though she were wishing herself anywhere but there.

Tara wondered why the group called themselves friends when it was obvious at least two of them—Raj and Krishna—couldn't stand each other. Raj was always present at the Saturday meetings in the clinic. The violin teacher friend of Maestro's usually joined them, but today, he was either late or not planning to show.

Strange how they all turned up in Goa around the same time. As far as Tara could figure out, apart from Maestro and Krishna and Hema, the rest stayed in different places. Only Vikram visited Maestro and the ladies and that, too, only in the salon where Krishna and Hema worked. Not in the ladies' hostel. And when Raj showed up for his part-time job at the casino, he never ventured anywhere near his friends. Even the weekly gatherings in the clinic were done when there was no one around to see except Tara, and she was just a child in their eyes.

Really, really weird, especially when Vikram, Raj, and the violin instructor looked like each other. If Tara noticed it, other people would have, too. Or maybe not. Her art teacher at school said she saw details no one else did because she was always looking at people and trying to sketch clothes for them. Unfortunately, the theory couldn't be put to test when no one else saw the five men together.

Four men! Maestro was a woman, and Tara needed to remember that! She didn't know why she couldn't even after all these years.

#

Within minutes, the storm ended, and there was a call from outside. Dr. Nakul went to the entrance, returning with a bundle of papers. The tattoo parlor next door doubled as a newsstand carrying the kind of international publications not available at the resort—tabloids and such. Of course, Tara was presented with magazines featuring the latest of styles for both men and women. She'd made it very clear fashion was her true love. Dancing was fun, but she endured the thrice weekly lessons only to keep her parents happy. Tara stifled another snort. *Movie star!* Nah, not for her. She did a couple of ads, which was enough! Her mother still got her to do two or three photoshoots, the pictures going up on the walls of the resort's salon.

Soon, the adults in the room were perusing the papers. "Nothing in *The New York Times* about the appeal," Krishna muttered from the chair between Maestro and Raj. "The media's still talking about the blast at the World Trade Center."

"The bastards got caught," Maestro said, tone satisfied.

Krishna shook her head. "A truck bomb. The papers say both towers could've been destroyed. Thousands of people work there! They could all have died. Dan... thank God, nothing happened to... umm... anyone we know."

Tara made it a point to hang out at the salon. It was the best place to pick up pointers on what cosmetics suited which type of clothes. When the news of the attack came on TV, Krishna had gasped and run to Maestro. Tara couldn't hear the whispered conversation, but both left, claiming a family emergency. A white-faced Krishna and Maestro Arjun returned a couple of hours later, relief clear in their demeanor. Tara didn't know quite what to make of it all.

Only a month after, there were blasts in India, too—in Bombay. Everyone said it was some kind of religious violence. Goa was spared thus far, but Tara's father said they had their own problems. Even before the Bratva showed up, drugs were sold openly. Sex trade... the mafia... the Russians were merely the latest group on scene. The collaboration between foreign criminals and local law enforcement was an open secret.

Mama's face would turn dark each time she overheard Papa talking to Tara about it. She knew why. A part of Mama's family came from Mizoram, in the northeast region of India, and they maintained ties to some person in Burma called Prince. *Myanmar,* Tara corrected herself. The country had renamed itself.

The Myanmarese fellow apparently helped with a loan when Tara's parents were building the resort on the land Papa inherited from his grandfather. Prince also took complete advantage of the situation after, using the place to conduct illegal activities like selling drugs. If Papa objected, Prince's people would come visiting. Papa would lose everything he possessed. If there was one thing he and Mama constantly argued over, it was this Prince. Mama didn't think they needed to worry. Prince carried enough clout with the local officials to prevent any legal trouble for the Mathurs and their resort. Also, if something like a raid did happen, the owners could claim ignorance since there was no actual proof of their involvement in anything nefarious. Besides, why didn't Papa think about all this before he took cash from her family? He would grit his teeth and fall silent.

Tara was told to stay silent, too, or they could all land in jail. Thank God, she never met the Prince fellow. He was wanted by the Indian government and hadn't been able to show up in person in Goa for years. If he accidentally got photographed by some tourist, even his friends in Goan police would get into trouble. The men who called the resort to do business on his behalf were bad enough. Papa called them Prince juniors.

"I wish the store carried *The Big Apple Reporter,*" Maestro said, startling Tara from her uneasy musings. "Dammit! If we could call Rekha..."

Rekha was the woman who approached Tara's papa about jobs for Krishna and Maestro Arjun. From what conversations Tara managed to eavesdrop on, it seemed the Rekha lady didn't know Papa personally. She'd heard something of his problems with the resort through her old friends in Goa, the ones who did the weekly drag show. Then, Rekha contacted Papa about Krishna and Maestro, although what the duo had to do with the situation, Tara couldn't tell.

Money, she decided. All her parents' troubles had to do with money. As far as Tara could figure out, most people's problems boiled down to money or boyfriends. The girls who worked in the salon were always complaining about the men in their lives.

On the stool next to the cupboard, Tara turned studious eyes to the glossy on her lap. Puzzling over the group's secretive behavior was far more relaxing than worrying about her parents' cash flow problems.

Doctor Nakul was on the other side of the desk, with Vikram peering over his shoulder. "Wait," said Vikram. "The *Journal* has something."

Maestro plucked the paper out of the doctor-guru's hands. "About Mr. Temple... his visits to his protégé in Sing Sing." His eyes darted side to side until he reached the bottom of the sheet, then he flung it to the desk to rummage through the pile. "There has to be more. Something to tell us..."

There wasn't. "Five years since we left," Raj said, tone frustrated. "And nothing."

Maestro consoled, "But only *four* years since he was... all we have to do is hold on until he gets an opening... one more year now."

Vikram said, "Appeal is taking time. Especially since he doesn't have the kind of money it takes to do an independent investigation."

Money, again! And who's this 'he' they keep talking about? The older Tara got, the more careful the group became about what they said around her, but they still slipped up occasionally. She wished she could crane her neck and take a peek at the paper.

"What if he doesn't get an opening?" asked Raj. "The sentence is *twenty-five* years. Also, what happens if he does get out before?

We thought the plan was to use the club, but it's gone. There's no cash. How is he going to do anything for us? Even if I... even if the pardon comes through, what then? Without him as chairman, we're not going to get the network back. I think it's time we called Grandfather. We can have him tell Steven we're ready to give up. Maybe they'll let us live in peace."

"Your grandfather?" Shoving back her chair, Krishna stood. Voice shaking, she asked, "All these years, and you still don't understand what Godwin... why am I even bothering? None of you will ever admit Godwin did anything wrong. He nearly got me thrown in jail where your cousins would've... but no, Grandfather didn't mean any harm."

"Things are not black and white as you make them seem," Raj said shortly. "Grandfather loves us, but he was... *is* obligated to uphold the law. It's all he did during the interrogation. He also has a fiduciary duty to do what's best for the company. But if we agree to a truce with Steven, he won't care if Grandfather asks for a pardon. Which means our legal problems will be solved."

"What about all the sacrifices... the lives lost thus far... the people who helped us?" asked Krishna. "Lupe Valdez... I still don't get why she... was it all for nothing?"

"Which part of what I said don't you understand?" exclaimed Raj, still sitting.

"I understand well enough." Krishna tore off her scarf and grabbed her braid in one hand, shoving it in Raj's face. "You weren't the one dragged by your hair. You're not the one looking at *twenty-five years* in prison for a crime you didn't commit. You're not the employee who's been forced to work under a crook like Steven. You didn't make any of it to begin with, so you don't value it."

Tara started. She'd never heard Krishna's husky voice raised.

"How dare you?" asked Raj, mouth twisted into a snarl. "The company was—*is*—mine. Nobody values it more than me."

"Oh?" countered Krishna, stabbing at the air with a finger. "What did you sacrifice for it? Did you spend years and years away from your family like your brothers did?"

Maestro stood, inserting himself between the two combatants. "Lil—Krishna, we can't do this here."

"Out of my way," ordered Krishna.

Standing, Raj shoved Maestro aside. "My brothers worked for me; they did what they were supposed to do. It is *my* legacy, and it's *my* decision what to do with it."

On her stool, Tara stayed very, very still, not even daring to breathe.

Krishna threw her head back and laughed, ridiculing Raj with every note. "You're delusional; nothing else explains that statement."

"And you're out of control," said Raj.

"*I'm* out of control?" Krishna asked. "Where was your self-control when you decided to stake the livelihood of every man, woman, and child in the company on one stupid idea? Whose permission did you get?"

"Stop, please," begged Vikram. "Both of you."

Neither paid him any mind. "I had every right to do what I wanted," said Raj. "Win or lose, I didn't need anyone's permission."

"My God!" said Krishna. "You still don't get it, do you? Leadership signifies trust, not possession. What you lost was not your personal property. Your words and your actions are the most glaring evidence of why power should never be concentrated in the hands of a few."

"I still have the same power," Raj ground out. "My brothers are not going to do anything I don't want them to. And I think it's stupid to waste time over a fight we can't win."

"You're insecure *and* manipulative," Krishna spat. "You always guilt-trip your family into doing what you want just to prove to everyone you're the lord and master. You'd rather watch them all die than admit you had no right. You were ready to let me go to prison."

"As though *you're* a saint," Raj accused. "In fact, if it weren't for you, none of it would've happened."

"How's any of this my fault?" asked Krishna.

Raj said, "It wasn't enough for you to have every man you met slobbering all over you. My own brother for God's sake! And acting like you ran the company! In front of clients, employees... even my own family. You made me look like a fool. Let me tell you something, my dear. *You* are the fool. Do you really think those men were impressed with your *mind?* There was only one thing they wanted from you."

Tara snarled. It was warm in the room, but she shook violently. Maestro was at her side in two strides, going down on haunches next to the stool.

"You decided to teach me a lesson," Krishna stated, her voice trembling in fury. "You destroyed all our lives to satisfy your *ego.* "

Pushing his glasses up the bridge of his nose, Raj asked, "Destroyed? Only because the offer turned out to be a trap. If it had been real, everyone would've been talking about me."

"They promised to double our profits!" Krishna said, fingertip to her brow. "How could you possibly think it was real? You couldn't see it because you were out to prove your manhood."

"I didn't see it," Raj agreed. "But not because of ego. Because I was distracted by your perverted games."

"Know something?" asked Krishna. "I don't even care enough to deny it." She turned to the rest. Pointing her finger at each in turn, she said, "As for all of you... remember, we're defined not only by what we do but also by what we fail to do. So go ahead... blindly follow him exactly like you did before. Don't say a word to stop him. History will judge you... your own children... the people you left behind."

Voice full of the same tender concern he always showed Krishna, Chef Vikram said, "I *know* what I did, and I will regret it to the day I die. I have to fix things. Or I won't be able to face my wife and son... and there's Mother."

Through her anger at Raj, Tara digested the new information. Vikram was married. The ladies at the salon would be disappointed.

"What are you?" Raj hissed. "Her new lover?"

"Bro," chided Vikram. "Come on. My son's eleven. I haven't seen him in... since he was six. All because I... and you still have doubts about my loyalty?"

Breathing hard, Raj glared at Vikram. Then, he wheeled around and stalked out, leaving the half-door swinging violently on its hinges. The surprised face of the clerk was visible in the waiting area.

There was a whine from under the tiny reception desk, and the pup scampered out. The clerk's head swiveled between the departing man and the group inside the doctor's office.

"I thought you went home for the day," Nakul called out, tone sharp.

"I return only two minutes... forgot my purse," the clerk said and poked the upper part of his body in, his eyes on Krishna who was quickly wrapping the scarf back around her head. "Speak nicely."

Krishna jerked back. "Excuse me?"

"You lady," the clerk said. "Speak nicely."

Krishna stiffened, but the silly man launched into a lecture in a combination of English and Hindi and the local language. It was all about ancient Indian culture and decent women and how they behaved with men. According to him, Krishna wouldn't find a husband unless she changed her attitude.

"Stop," Nakul snapped at the clerk before there was another explosion from Krishna. "Return home before it gets any later. Your wife will be waiting."

Shaking his head in disapproval, the clerk left.

"Forget him," Vikram said to Krishna. "Actually, forget what Br—Raj said, too. He doesn't really want to give up. He's frustrated. All of us, to be honest. The people back in New York..."

"Patrice must be sick with worry," muttered Nakul. "Sc—Dev and I were talking about her the other day." Dev was the violin teacher who was absent from the meeting.

"What about me?" asked Krishna. "Don't you think I feel frustrated, too? Five of you are at least together, but *I* haven't seen my own bro—" She heaved in a breath. "But then, I remember Lupe. After all these years, I'm still trying to understand why. I think about... about Tank Man. Don't you remember him? Haven't you wondered what made him—"

"Enough, all of you," ordered Maestro. "All of us are homesick. All of us miss our families and friends. *My* son is ten. I already lost five years of his life. I miss Sab... but we can't..." Glancing meaningfully toward Tara, Maestro added, "Let's discuss this another time. Tara has her dance lessons. Right, champ?"

#

Few minutes later

Tara was still fuming about Raj—rechristened That Idiot Guy—when she got to The Mermaid with Maestro and Krishna. There was a police jeep in front. Tara frowned. Drug overdose? Such incidents did happen, especially after one of the rave parties. June was off-season, and there had been no beach party the night before, but addicts paid no mind to schedules. The media reported on these events with relish.

Ignoring the police vehicle, they made for the employee entrance in the back. Tara scowled. She was practically *melting* in the heat, and the two adults wanted to walk all the way around the building. Oh, she was also supposed to use the door meant for staff, but no one ever stopped her from running in or out through the huge lobby. Except of course Maestro and Krishna. Tara simply couldn't figure them out. So many secrets and such annoying sticklers for rules! At least the air-conditioning was on full blast inside.

Strange... Papa was waiting by the glass doors of the salon. Normally, Maestro would've delivered Tara to the office section where her mother worked.

"Everything all right?" Maestro asked.

Squinting at the feeble smile Papa directed toward her, Tara wondered if the police jeep parked by the main entrance had brought new troubles. He threw a quick glance over his shoulder. The ladies in the salon all seemed to be busy with guests. There was no one else around.

"Be careful," Papa muttered to Maestro Arjun. "His men are here. There's a meeting with some police fellows."

"His—" Maestro stiffened. "You think he'll show up?"

"He usually calls ahead." Papa said, scratching at his chin hard enough to take the skin off. "But it was before... ahh... he got into trouble with the government."

Tara frowned. Who were they talking about?

Krishna inclined her head. "We'll be ready," she said, her husky voice quite firm.

"Wait," said Papa. "The policemen brought a couple of Russians with them... the Bratva."

Huffing out a breath, Maestro said, "Shit."

"Yeah." Papa nodded. "Get to the hostel before any of them spots you. The element of surprise—"

"Hey," someone shouted from behind.

All the three adults with Tara suddenly froze. Stumbling to the salon doors was a lanky fellow.

Tara's heart thumped unpleasantly hard. Drunk guests were not unusual, so why was Papa looking so panicked? Employees were always getting stopped by visitors needing help, so for what reason was Maestro Arjun stepping in front of Krishna, shielding her from sight? Why was Tara's skin so hot as though she were still on the beach under a blazing sun?

"Where's the manager?" the guest demanded in a loud voice, the accent sorta North American. "The bartender said he's here."

It took a couple of seconds, but Papa said, "I'm the manager. How may I help you?"

"I need beer," the guest grumbled. "Not this feni shit."

Papa pasted on his professional smile. "The bar carries beer."

"Not the kind I want," the guest explained morosely.

"Sorry to hear that, sir," Papa said. "Room service can get what you want from the local liquor store."

The troublesome fellow wouldn't leave until he got the manager to call the liquor store from the salon phone. Standing at the glass doors, Tara peered in the direction of the staff exit through which Maestro and Krishna were disappearing.

Later, Tara sang Michael Jackson's "Dangerous" and break-danced her way through the lobby to the office section while Papa laughed and followed.

Halting a few feet from the hall where the clerical staff did their work, he said, "Tara girl, don't mention what happened to your mom, okay?"

"Why not?" she asked.

Papa shrugged. "Your dance teacher and Krishna are not from India, and I don't want them getting into trouble with the mafia or the local cops. So I warned them... but you know how your mother gets when I talk about such things."

Yeah, Tara knew.

Chapter 28

A few months later, November 1993

(4 years after Harry's arrest and 5 after the exile began)

Central Park, New York

Sitting under the pastel murals decorating the ceiling of the Tavern on the Green, Richard took a sip of fine whiskey and exhaled in appreciation. Around him, glasses clinked, and silverware clanked. A roar of laughter came from the other end of the Crystal Room, and Richard cast a casual glance in the direction of the correction officers occupying the tables. Some of New York's boldest were celebrating the retirement of one among them in the famed Central Park restaurant. Arthur Berra, Warden of Sing Sing, was standing with his glass raised. His speech was unintelligible to Richard, but the officers greeted the warden's words with whistles and hoots and thundering applause.

Tucked inside Richard's blazer was a copy of the press release put out by the New York State Department of Corrections the summer before. Once again, he took it out and perused the list of Medal of Honor recipients. He paused for a moment at a name—Officer Regina Berra, daughter of Warden Berra.

Richard had gotten into the habit of sizing up the people he employed in person. Not always directly, of course. It would be foolish to give away his identity to a certain type of man, but it was important to evaluate a potential partner at least from a distance. Perhaps the habit rose from the trouble he got into with the contractor he hired in Texas. As a new business, Armor Drilling Co. had needed cheap labor, and said contractor provided what Richard asked.

Illegal immigrant workers were being used as indentured servants, said the FBI officials who visited Richard's office. Rumor had it the women—some of them underaged—provided sex as part of the deal. Richard had made sure there was no paper trail leading to him, and he swore to the feds he wasn't aware of the contractor's crimes. The story wasn't widely reported, and the couple of articles which did pop up here and there seemed to echo Richard's own thoughts on the matter. The immigrants could've easily gone to the cops. They didn't simply because the arrangement was mutually beneficial. But of all the incompetent... what arrangements the contractor made with the immigrants was not Richard's problem. The bungling was what bothered him.

Since then, he made it a point to visually gauge a potential associate's worth. A lot could be said from a man's body language, the way he spoke, the way he moved. Glancing again in the direction of the retirement party, Richard nodded in satisfaction.

He spent a few more minutes at the restaurant. It wouldn't do to get up and walk out in haste. There was no place he needed to get to in a hurry, anyway. The plan for the exiles was ready to go at a moment's notice, and the call to the Bratva would be made only when news of Harry Sheppard's demise reached Major Armor's ears.

It was damned difficult to believe. For years, a group of five men and two women managed to evade not only the American government but also every thug they ever rubbed the wrong way and the entire Russian mafia. One of Phillip Potts's informers worked at a refugee center in Brooklyn which functioned as a front for terrorist recruitment. The snitch tossed a few carefully casual questions around about suspicious sightings. Nothing at all... the exiles were not spotted in any of the major cities in Asia or the Middle East.

Either they escaped the continent altogether, or they were hiding in a smaller town. It would be someplace which wouldn't occur to others right away but with enough European and American expats and tourists so they wouldn't stand out. Still, it was hard to believe there was nothing even in the media. In the initial years, tabloids had claimed sightings which turned out to be false alarms. A few months after the sentencing of Petty Officer Sheppard, those also died down.

Shitty luck for Steven, but Richard would rectify the situation with help from Phillip Potts. Only one more year was left before the former SEAL got his conditional release from prison. Richard would make sure the con artist was killed before the deadline. Very soon, a web of former criminals from the old Soviet Union would be placed on high alert, waiting for the reemergence of a certain Lilah Kingsley.

Glass of whiskey still in his hand, Richard stood. At the door, he drained the smoky drink to the last drop and beckoned a waiter to take the empty tumbler.

"Excuse me," said a clipped female voice. "You're blocking my way."

Richard turned. He froze for half a second before stepping aside for the athletic-looking black woman with closely cropped curls and impatience in her sharp brown eyes.

"Thank you," said Officer Regina Berra, striding toward the corrections department party without a backward glance.

Part XI

Chapter 29

Four months later, March 1994

(nine months to go before parole)

Sing Sing Correctional Facility

Ossining, New York

Michael kept his gaze averted from the female guard, his brain hurting with the effort to stay silent. Harry's eyes warned both Michael and Gabriel not to react. Liam was staring hard at the floor. None of the other inmates or their visitors paid any mind to the drama. They all knew what the Cub was like. Yeah... it was her name among both prison staff and inmates.

"Better not take too long, Sheppard," she warned, "or you're going to be on septic tank duty the next two weeks." Satisfied how she'd humiliated the prisoner enough in front of his nephews, the guard wheeled around.

As she strode away, Gabriel muttered, "Bitch."

"Don't let your aunt hear you," said Liam.

"Why not?" spat out Michael, taking care to keep his voice low. "She would agree. I don't know how... Uncle Harry, how can you... you're acting like a wuss. I hate it."

"Different circumstances call for different tactics," Harry said, his tone only slightly harsh. "Compliance is the best weapon when dealing with Officer Berra."

"How do you stop yourself from punching her in the face?" Gabriel asked, eyes hot. "Don't you think about it, like *every minute?*"

Harry laughed, but he didn't sound amused, and there were white lines around his mouth. "Gabe, I do what I need to survive while others are doing the work on my behalf. Liam for one. Finding his father's killer is all he's thought about all this time. As for my life in here... when I'm doing the job I'm assigned, there's hardly a chance to think. If I get a free moment or two, I find something else to do. The gym, library books..."

"Still," muttered Michael.

"Oh, there are days..." Harry admitted. Tone distant, he said, "I close my eyes and pretend I'm Harry Sheppard, the son of Ryan Sheppard, proprietor of Genesis Oil."

"When you were a boy?" Gabriel asked.

Harry nodded. "Back in Libya."

"Did you have the Harley then?" Michael asked eagerly. As soon as he turned sixteen, he planned to get his license. His ma wasn't thrilled at his announcement. "Mr. al-Obeidi said you and him used to ride around Tripoli."

Saeed al-Obeidi was Harry's old friend from when the Sheppards ran their drilling company in the Middle East. Mrs. al-Obeidi often called Michael's mother to ask about updates on Uncle Harry and the exiles. So did a couple of Lilah's school friends.

Harry smiled. "Business was barely breaking even at the time... no money for Harleys. I owned a second-hand Honda. Saeed never went with me to the desert, though."

"Did you ever take any girls there?" Gabriel asked, eyes wide and mouth slightly open.

With a crack of laughter, Harry said, "I wanted to. But just one girl. A princess."

It was Michael's turn to goggle at Harry. "No shit! You're making it up."

Holding a hand to his heart, Harry said, "All true. I wanted to take her to the sand dunes someday and scare the hell out of her by going too fast. The winds can get terrible in the Sahara."

"If she was anything like Ma," Michael said, "she'd have dumped you for it."

Harry's eyes crinkled. "Oh, she'd have been spitting mad, but she wouldn't have dumped me. Only I knew the way to the oasis."

"Huh?" said Gabriel. "Where they have water?"

"Not merely water. There was a coffee shop there. They had their special baklava, all flaky and buttery with walnut flavor. One bite, and you'd be in heaven."

"I want some," Gabriel said, voice rapt.

As Michael and Liam snickered, Harry admitted, "Point is I was lucky enough to have a happy childhood. You two... if I don't keep myself out of trouble, parole... appeal... everything will be affected. Your fathers might not be able to return home. So whatever job the officer assigns me, I'll do it." Harry laughed again. "Besides, it's about the only time she lets me be. No one gets within twenty feet when I'm cleaning the septic tank. Perfect peace."

"Gimme a break, Uncle Harry," said Michael. "Gabe and I are not babies. You don't have to make it sound as if you're cool with it."

"No, you're not babies," acknowledged Harry. "What I'm trying to do is make you both understand why I... discipline is the key, Michael. SEAL training taught me patience and discipline, and I got the chance to watch Mr. Temple in action. He waited years... planning, strategizing, recalibrating as needed. The enemy we're dealing with is no less patient, no less intelligent than Temple. If I don't show the same discipline, we won't win. If I let Officer Regina Berra get to me, your dads won't make it back home."

"That her name?" Michael asked. "Berra?"

"Why do you want to know?" Liam narrowed his eyes. "Better not try anything stupid. Remember... you're only eleven."

"I'm not going to be eleven forever," said Michael.

"No matter what age... you need to practice patience." Harry leaned forward. "We'll talk more about it later. Let's discuss your ma's concerns for now. Gabe, about the hair on your face... I thought Dan showed you how to shave. Remember, the ladies generally prefer men to be well-groomed. Including *Sports Illustrated* models."

Everyone at the table guffawed, drawing a few looks from the people around. Gabriel complained, "Wasn't me who got the magazine."

"Like you didn't look," Michael taunted.

"Bro," said Gabriel, tone lofty. "I was only reading the article on Emmitt Smith." At the collective scoff of derision, he added, "Anyway, those chicks ain't my type. There was one last year... great abs!"

Liam groaned. "Neither of these dumbasses is going to survive until you get back home, Harry. Sabrina will kill them both herself."

"Shh," said Gabriel. "Mike promised her he wouldn't look at another girl."

Amid all the howls of mirth, Michael managed to explain, "Ma wouldn't believe us when we said we respected women." He really did, but girls were nice to look at.

The art of discretion when admiring women, schoolwork, Michael's interest in digital technology... Gabriel making the football team was their big news for the week. Neither he nor Michael played soccer, but both were crazy excited about the upcoming world cup. Since the U.S. didn't have a prayer of winning, they planned to root for Mexico. Both boys were enrolled in boxing and martial arts classes as well as shooting lessons, but Gabriel didn't share Michael's dream of going to West Point. Talking to his uncle, Michael even forgot for a while they were in the visiting room at the prison.

"Being an effective warrior involves a lot more than decent aim," Harry counseled. "It involves a lot more than getting Liam out of a dangerous situation. It takes the heart and the will to sacrifice for people you've never met. People who may never feel gratitude. People who may even hate you for what you do. Sometimes, you could end up hating your own self. Mike, getting your hands dirty to keep the nation safe takes a toll on a man."

"I get it, sir," Michael said. "I think." He wasn't sure how to put the ideas in his brain into words. "I feel like I should... I mean... someone should put things right, so why not me? I want to help the good guys win. Nothing more; nothing less." The events at the World Trade Center merely showed he possessed the will to go with the ambition.

Harry smiled. "Just war."

Frowning, Michael asked, "What?"

"Military ethics," Harry explained. "When you get to West Point, they'll teach you. The cause has to be good and just for the war to be moral. It can't be fought purely for self-interest. A just war can only be the last resort and should have a reasonable chance of success. It should always be declared by an entity with the authority to do so. The authority is conferred by the people—"

A guard announced there were only a few minutes remaining.

"Harry," called Liam. "I was going to tell you before the charming Officer Berra interrupted us. We have an update on James McCoy. Maybe something, maybe not. The surveillance camera footage..."

"You got something?" Harry frowned. "After all this time?"

Michael knew the story. His mother always gave him and Gabriel enough information on what was going on. Leaving the boys in the dark would be more dangerous, handicapping them with no idea of who not to trust and what not to say.

Liam spent several years trying to track the McCoy fellow's movements in Las Vegas on the night of the murder. The hotel McCoy was staying in insisted to Liam the security tapes were missing. They didn't generally bother to keep recordings from uneventful days, and no, it wasn't unusual to have cassettes vanish. Nor were the cops interested. James McCoy was not their suspect... Harry was.

Liam grimaced. "I was right... bastard owner didn't want to get involved in the case. So he simply ordered the staff to hide the damn tapes. Thank God they didn't get thrown out. You know... worry about destroying evidence and all. If the cops did eventually ask, the hotel planned to produce it."

"But not for us," Harry said, tone frustrated. "How did you finally manage to convince them?"

"I didn't." Liam smirked. "The men I asked to keep an eye out for news on McCoy and the Kingsleys... one of them's a former infantryman who works at the World Trade Center. He heard about another veteran who moved to Vegas. The fellow got a job as a guard at one of the hotel chains. Took him a while to find someone willing to help in the fancy place McCoy picked. We watched the whole thing together... the entire twenty-four hours' worth of recordings. Now... the guest room floors and elevators don't have cameras, but the rest of the hotel is under constant surveillance."

"And?"

"Not a single picture of McCoy."

"Not possible," said Harry. "Not if he were actually there. Are you sure you got the entire film?"

"Positive," Liam said. "Everything's time-stamped. But McCoy's got receipts from those couple of days. Also, the hotel confirmed the booking. I suppose he can claim he never went to any of the restaurants or to the casino, but how did he escape the cameras at the exits?"

Harry asked, "What about the Kingsleys? Any of them show up in the videos?"

"I wish."

"Too much to expect, I suppose," Harry brooded. "After I accused them of arranging the trap, the cops did ask for their whereabouts."

Liam nodded. Steven and Charles had claimed they were at the family home, with their grandfather. Major Armor said he stayed home with a cold.

"They could've lied," Harry continued, "but I'm assuming not. I can't imagine Godwin Kingsley letting his heirs take the risk. Richard Armor? Was he on the tapes?"

"Unfortunately, no," said Liam. "I followed up on every guest in the hotel the night my dad was killed and compared pictures to the camera footage. The only one I wasn't able to track down is a mechanic, Rickie Brennan. His description doesn't fit Armor or any of the Kingsleys. But you know how these pictures are... not always very clear."

"Doesn't matter," said Harry. "If *McCoy* had been there, he would've popped up in the video. And if he wasn't there, someone else arranged to make it appear as though he were. Not Steven; Godwin wouldn't have let him. There are only a couple of men who would go to such lengths for Steven Kingsley."

"Major Armor," supplied Liam.

"Yes," agreed Harry. "And Phillip Potts, I believe. But Armor's more likely. Forget the alibis they gave the cops. Check again on both of them."

Tone bitter, Liam said, "McCoy's out there, walking free after everything he did."

James McCoy had apparently come up with the cash to appeal the poisoning case. Liam was certain the Kingsleys paid for it, but there was no evidence. The experts hired by McCoy's lawyer argued the arsenic in the wine which poisoned Neil Kingsley and Dan Barrons was a contaminant from the cask... which somehow showed only in their glasses. The judge still bought the explanation, and McCoy was exonerated. Oh, yeah, Harry and Liam were convinced Steven Kingsley's lawyer friend, Major Richard Armor, was behind the scheme.

McCoy was only tried for the attempted murder, never for the embezzlement. Gateway didn't press charges initially because there was evidence Hector's division was involved in the thievery, and Harry had accused Hector himself of orchestrating it all. Now, nobody in the company was interested in revisiting the issue because Will Luce turned out to be the culprit, and he was allegedly killed by Harry.

After a few moments of silence, Harry said, "Liam, be careful. I'm sure the Kingsleys are tracking how far you've gotten in your investigation. I hope you're keeping Verity far away from it all. You know what happened to Lupe when she got in their way."

Liam leaned forward, an angry expression on his face. "Don't you think this is for her, too? She was my friend before she ever met any of you. Nikki and I are going to Macau next week. The last of our trips with Lupe's ashes. It's the least we can do for her."

"The least you can do is stay safe," reiterated Uncle Harry. "She wouldn't have wanted anything happening to you. The minute you find something concrete on McCoy, bring it to me... or

Noah. Do not... I repeat, do not... try to pursue it all on your own."

Worriedly, Michael asked, "You'll be okay, Uncle Harry?"

Smiling reassuringly, Harry said, "Yes, Mike. I'll be all right, and as long as I'm fine, your dad and the rest will be safe. You have to practice patience. The appeals process takes time, and the defense attorney is doing his best. If not, I have one more year until I can apply for parole. Then, we'll see."

"You have an idea or something about the Kingsleys?" Gabriel asked.

"Or something," said Harry, glancing at Liam.

Inclining his head slightly, Liam said, "We'll be ready on time."

Chapter 30

Two hours later

Special Housing Unit a.k.a. The Box (solitary confinement)

Sing Sing Correctional Facility

Ossining, New York

From the outside, the Box was only a red-brick building with two levels, but the massive metal door gave it the appearance of a walk-in freezer. Except it was sweltering inside with high-pitched screeching coming from one of the cells on the top floor. The air reeked of violent insanity.

"Why am I being put here?" Harry demanded, heart thundering. If one of the guards attacked him in this place... even if he escaped, the fact he committed an infraction which earned him time in solitary would jeopardize parole. "I didn't do anything."

With a hard hand, a muscle-bound officer shoved the prisoner forward. "Oh, yeah? You didn't call Officer Berra a 'bitch'?"

"No, I didn't."

"Could've sworn it was you," said Officer Berra, joining them. "Or was it one of your visitors?"

Gabriel. "It's not a crime to call someone a name," Harry said through clenched teeth.

"Not outside the prison," she agreed, tone completely pleasant. "In here, we have rules. Whoever it was, he violated our rules. For one of *them*, it would be disorderly conduct."

"You're lying," Harry accused. She had to be.

Officer Berra shrugged. "He could always call his lawyer. In the morning. As long as someone posts bond, he'd be out tomorrow."

A twelve-year-old boy arrested from his home... parole... the exiles... all the plans... Gabriel would be in jail for one whole night. His life would never again be the same. "I did it," Harry said.

The smile on the guard's face was full of malice. "Thought so. Ninety days, Sheppard."

As the muscle-bound guard walked toward a booth, Officer Berra stayed, a mocking look on her face. Harry gripped the bars so tightly he wouldn't have been surprised to see blood seeping through his skin.

One snap of their fingers, and the Kingsleys had destroyed years of planning. They put him in a brig with no escape hatches.

He'd die like a caged rat. After his death, they'd wait for Lilah to surface. Harry snarled. "You go tell your bosses she'll find a way."

Narrowing her eyes, Officer Berra said, "What are you talking about?"

"I knew a woman who called herself a whore." Harry would suffer. For his insolence, the correction officer would make sure he suffered to the last drop of blood, but he didn't care. "But you... you *are* one. You sold yourself to the Kingsleys."

"I sold—" Baring her teeth, Officer Berra shook a finger at him through the bars. She wasn't supposed to get within arm's reach of any prisoner, but spite and triumph made her forget the rules. "Listen, you son of a bitch. I'll kill you."

Harry laughed, the sound deranged even to his own ears. "But you'll never get *her.* Even if I die, Alex will never let you get anywhere near her."

"What the actual hell? Who's Alex? And who's 'her'? You're crazy."

A high-pitched alarm rang through the gallery. Red light flashed from the wall. The officer who'd escorted Harry in exploded out of the booth, bellowing.

Officer Berra wheeled around. Over the ear-splitting sound, she shouted, "What's going on?"

"Riot in A-block," her colleague shouted back.

"You can't leave," screeched Officer Berra. "Not until your relief gets here. It's against procedure." As the male officer sprinted toward the door in disregard of "procedure," she took a step forward.

Through the bars, Harry reached with his left hand and hauled her back by the elbow. "You're not going anywhere," he spat.

Her other arm—the left—was flailing. Air whooshed. Her baton landed on Harry's hand.

Pain, white-hot, ran up his nerves to his eyes, nearly blinding him, but he wouldn't let go. "You will die tonight."

Through the bars, the baton rammed into his chest. She screamed for help, but every inmate on the floor was now screaming. The alarm blasted nonstop. When she aimed the baton at his chest a second time, Harry shot out his right hand and caught her by the jaw, hauling her against the bars.

She grunted on impact, her screams cut off for a moment. Her breath came in rapid gasps. Fear. He could smell her fear. It was intoxicating. If he squeezed tighter, her face would turn red, then blue. Her life force would drain out into his hands.

"Daddy," she whimpered, her eyes glazing over.

At that one word, Harry's grip loosened. The guard booth was empty, its door open. There were no officers anywhere. No Warden Berra. There were stairs leading to the lower level, but no one ran up the steps to see what was going on.

The officer's body became lax, and Harry's hand slipped from her throat to her shoulder. With his other hand on her elbow, he managed to keep her semi-upright. Around them, pandemonium continued. The worst of New York's criminals were housed in this building, and they were all yelling, demanding Harry finish the job.

"Kill the bitch," raged the one on Harry's left.

"Wait," shouted a second one, adding a lewd suggestion about what else Harry could do to her through the bars.

Harry had become a hero to rapists and serial killers. A hero to monsters. "I'm not..." he croaked. "I don't..." Harry once held his girl in his arms and wept blood while he prayed for her to live. He'd saved children from sex trade. He rescued hostages from terrorists. Harry wore the SEAL Trident with pride and lived the life of a defender of his nation and its people. "I am Petty Officer First Class Harry Sheppard."

Before he could take his hand away, someone thundered in... a large man with a shaved head, dressed in the gray polyester of New York State Department of Corrections. He stopped short at the sight of his colleague in Harry's grip. Cursing, Harry hauled her partially conscious form upright to use as shield. He might spend the rest of his days in prison after the attempted murder of a guard, but he would see if he could at least negotiate his way out of instant death.

To Harry's surprise, the new guard smiled. "You want out, Sheppard?"

The fellow's sleeves were rolled up to the middle of his bulging biceps, but unlike the other men Harry knew who worked in the Box, this one did not have trousers tucked into his boots. Eyeing both Officer Berra and the male guard, Harry calculated. Finally, he nodded.

The guard went to the booth and with his right hand, pulled one of the handles protruding from the wall. The cell door opened. It wasn't easy maneuvering the limp form of Officer Berra in front, but Harry got himself and the unconscious officer to the booth. "What about her?"

"You'll have to kill the Cub," said the male guard. "Or I'm not letting you walk out of here."

Around them, the inmates watched the drama in morbid fascination.

"Why?" Harry asked. "You can always say I used her as a hostage. Why do I need to kill her? And why are you letting me out?"

"I don't give a damn about you." The booth door was open, with the male guard standing at the entrance. "But Papa Bear and his Cub owe me a few *debts*, shall we say? I'm sure you understand."

Harry let Officer Berra fall to the floor. Then, he bent as though preparing to finish her off. One fast sweep of his arm around the male guard's right ankle... with a roar, the guard tumbled backward, his head hitting the wall of the booth. He struggled to get his right leg out of Harry's grip, kicking out with his left. The heavy boot connected with Harry's ribs. With sweat-slick fingers, Harry tugged the pant leg up. There it was. The ankle holster. Within seconds, the Glock 19 was in Harry's hands.

Two shots. The guard's shoulders lifted off the floor, and his mouth opened in shock. Blood trickled from a hole in his neck and from another in his chest. He fell back, his body collapsing into itself.

A rumble started from the cells. "Let us out," screamed an inmate. Others joined him in a chorus. The siren continued to blast through the building. The red light on the wall continued to flash. Stepping around the corpse, Harry checked the levers on the wall. Gates, main door, cell doors. He made sure everything was locked. No one could get out, and no one could get in.

Outside the booth, he crouched next to Officer Berra. "I know you're awake."

Her brown eyes opened. Words tripping over each other, she said, "You don't need to kill me. If they see me with you, they'll let you leave."

Take her hostage? For a few seconds, Harry considered it. "Might have taken you up on it *if* I'd been planning to escape." He added, "I'm not going to kill you, either. It was only... I lost it for a minute or two. Temporary insanity. Shouldn't have happened."

Warily, she eyed him.

"I swear. Or I'd have shot you right after I shot your friend in the booth. At least dragged you out with me. I wouldn't be wasting time like this, waking you from your fake faint."

Finally, she asked, "How did you know I was..."

"I used to be a SEAL," he said dryly. "I can usually tell when someone's faking a blackout. What were you planning to do?"

"Get you to let go of my throat," she admitted. "But then—" She sat up and glanced at the dead guard. "*He* walked in and asked you to kill me."

"What about us?" screamed one of the prisoners.

Harry groaned. "Can't you shut them up?"

Officer Berra got to her feet. "My baton?"

"Next to my cell, probably."

In less than five minutes, the woman was back to terrorizing the prisoners. At least now she was careful enough to stay out of their reach. Harry sat on the floor and watched, his back against the front of the booth, the Glock still in his hands.

When the Cub returned, she eyed the corpse in the booth with distaste and sat next to Harry. "The safest place for us is in here."

"I agree," Harry said. "Any idea how long it might take for help to show up?"

"They're almost certainly already here," Officer Berra said. "Outside the walls. Getting inside the prison is a different matter. I'm betting the rioters have taken hostages."

"Your father?"

A look of relief passed over her face. "Wife number three is having her baby. He's at the hospital with her. Probably worrying to death about me." According to gossip Harry picked up, Warden Berra harbored a fascination for black supermodels. How he got them to give him the time of day was a matter of mystery to the world. Officer Regina Berra was his child with the first Mrs. Berra.

The alarm continued unabated. The inmates of the Box added to the cacophony. "So we could be here a few days?" Harry asked.

"Most likely. Why don't you use the time to explain a few things?"

"Someone's trying to kill me," Harry admitted.

"You and ninety percent of the inmates in Sing Sing. Give me something more."

"Okay. Some very powerful people want me dead."

"The Kingsleys?"

"Yes." Harry elaborated, "They're in oil—"

"Yeah, yeah... I read the papers... and I read your case file. I know who the Kingsleys are. Why do they want you dead? And what's with all the politicians who come here? What do they have to do with it?"

"One politician," Harry corrected. "Noah's not in politics... not on paper, anyway. It's only Temple. He would like to keep me alive."

She slammed the baton on the floor. "Don't act cute, Pretty Boy."

Bitterly, Harry laughed. "Will you believe me if I tell you I'm innocent? Isn't every inmate in Sing Sing innocent?"

"First, I want to know why you didn't kill me."

"I'd already decided it was a bad idea to kill you. Then, the dead sonuvabitch came in and asked me if I wanted out. Why would a guard make the offer?"

"He had something else in mind."

"Exactly," Harry said. "Then, *he* asked me to kill you."

"Because I owed him," she said, lips twisting into a snarl.

"Do you?" Harry asked.

"Probably," Officer Berra admitted, "but that's beside the point."

"You are..." Harry bowed. "...something else. He was encouraging me to kill his colleague and make a run for it. What if I got caught outside? What if I named him?"

She agreed, "He never planned to let you go. As soon as you killed me, he'd have killed you and claimed self-defense." Forensics would've pointed to Harry as Regina Berra's killer, bolstering the assassin's story. "But how did you know he had a gun? We're not allowed to carry inside the prison."

"I wasn't sure he did, but he had to have something, or he wouldn't have been confident in suggesting the deal. It's when I decided he was the Kingsley assassin. Or why would he bring a weapon in here? As you said, it's not allowed. Besides, I noticed his pants. Most of the men here act like they're going on an armed raid. Sleeves rolled up... trousers tucked inside boots."

"But not his," mused Officer Berra. "His boots were covered. So you decided that's where he hid his weapon."

"Right."

"You figured it all out in those couple of minutes?"

"Told you I used to be a SEAL. I even have a Medal of Honor."

"So do I," she said.

"From the U.S. Congress?" he challenged.

"From the Department of Corrections and Community Supervision," she countered, chin held high.

Harry wasn't quite sure how to respond. Finally, he said, "You haven't asked me to give you the Glock."

Dryly, she said, "Oh, at this point, I don't think you're going to kill me. So you can hold on to it until we get rescued. Protection from the big, bad Officer Berra."

"You're not bad," he allowed. "Just tripping on power."

She didn't deny it. "Now, tell me why these Kingsleys sent an assassin after you."

Gesturing with the gun, Harry said, "I don't know how much you heard about the Peter Kingsley Network and what you got from my case file, but I used to have... I mean I still have shares in Gateway. It's the family oil trading company. With President Temple's help, Gateway and a couple of other companies created a merger of sorts... the network. We became very successful. Unfortunately, Steven Kingsley decided he was entitled to all of it. He tricked our CEO into signing a paper which made it look like he was dealing in nuclear weapons."

"The case file said the deceased stole money from your family business. Only a couple of lines about you claiming the Kingsleys framed you."

"Setting people up is clearly a pattern with the Kingsley lot," said Harry.

"Or a pattern with you and your friends pretending you were conned into criminal activities." At Harry's steady stare, she acknowledged, "All right. Maybe you've given me some reason to doubt the verdict... in *your* case. But how do you know the CEO was tricked? Got any proof?"

Harry opened his mouth to object, then snapped it shut. "Brad wouldn't..." Harry started. "None of them would... I *know* them, all right? Anyway, he was forced to leave the country. President Temple and I were trying to bring him and his family back. Then, Temple got shot."

"And you got arrested."

"In a nutshell."

"This is where you once again insist you were framed," she said, lips pursed.

"I *was* framed," he said. "I'm not a murderer."

Angling her head to the side, she indicated the corpse in the booth.

"He was different," Harry said. "Will Luce was my father-in... my *former* father-in-law. He was embezzling from Gateway. The cops claimed in court I lured him there and killed him for revenge. I won't pretend I'm incapable of hurting a fly, but knifing someone in the back is not something I'd do."

She glared at him for a moment or two as though weighing his trustworthiness. "You have someone working the case?"

"Yes and no," Harry said. "Money is a problem."

She mocked, "For a businessman with connections to a former president?"

"It's complicated. Temple's not rich." American presidents tended to either come into the office wealthy or make their money later in speeches and book deals. From what Harry heard, Temple's father was an honest public servant, and his son followed the same path. As in, neither ever used their positions to enrich themselves. In Temple's case, he was rendered unable to communicate shortly after he left office, which closed off the usual avenues of income generation for former presidents. Temple had enough for a comfortable retirement and no more. "All *my* money has been... everyone else's... think of it as getting all our bank accounts frozen. But we might have a lead."

"Tell me."

Harry gave her a brief rundown of the connection between Will Luce and James McCoy and the fact McCoy had been in Las Vegas the night of the murder. Also, he'd somehow avoided appearing on any of the surveillance tapes at the hotel.

She scratched her chin. "It won't be enough for the courts. You're going to need to prove this McCoy was in the apartment in

Brooklyn. Or at least somewhere around there to create reasonable doubt they got the wrong man."

"I *know*," Harry said, feeling bone weary. "But there are people—people with resources—who want to make sure I stay in Sing Sing until I die."

"And they want you to die fast," she said.

He nodded. "When I do, they'll go after Lilah."

"Lilah?" Officer Berra asked. "I remember seeing the name in the news about the network shit, but the CEO is a man... right?"

"He is," Harry admitted. "Lilah is his—" With a great deal of effort, he clamped hard on the spurt of envy. "Wife. She's his wife."

"Ah." There was a wealth of meaning in the one syllable.

They were together nearly three days. More than seventy hours with no food. The only water to be had came from the shower stalls. Screams from the prisoners and the nonstop siren reverberated inside Harry's skull. There was repeated pounding on the metal door to the outside. The peephole told them these were not rescuers. The corpse of the assassin bloated, changed colors. The stench of rotting flesh added to the dread.

Pain gnawed at Harry's belly. A hungry beast snarled in his brain. At one point, he stomped to the row of cells, intending to scream in the face of a fellow inmate to shut the hell up or else. Breathing heavily, Harry waited outside the bars for ten seconds. *Mind over body*, he told himself. A Navy SEAL could not fall victim to his own weaknesses. He could not give up control to pointless rage.

Pivoting away, he marched up and down the Box. Every so often, he stopped to do punishingly long sets of pushups and planks. Officer Berra did the same at the other end of the gallery. When she collapsed to rest, she kept eyeing Harry with a frowning expression but thankfully didn't revert to her earlier hostility.

Finally, finally... after what felt like an eternity, there was a bellow over a police horn. "Reggie!"

"Dad!" Officer Berra leaped up and ran to the peephole to confirm. She returned to the booth in excitement. "Give me the gun, Sheppard. And stay behind me."

As soon as they released the lever, officers rushed in, clad in metal helmets and bulletproof vests. Spotting Harry behind their colleague, their weapons swiveled in his direction.

"Stop," screamed Officer Berra. "Don't shoot."

Part XII

Chapter 31

Same time, March 1994

Upper East Side, New York City

The anniversary party for David and Grace Kingsley was in full swing at the Kingsley ballroom. In one corner, a live band played songs from the 'forties and 'fifties. The lavish buffet was exquisitely prepared by world-famous chefs. It seemed to Patrice the festivities never stopped since Steven managed to drive his cousins out. Every bigwig in New York City was present as though chaos were not reigning a few miles north in Ossining.

Behind the pillar, Patrice gulped dry wine, forcing the lobster-stuffed mushroom down her throat. Ever since she heard about the riot in Sing Sing, she hadn't been able to sleep or eat. There were reports of gunfire... explosions. Patrice had called Sabrina, but she was too hysterical with worry over Harry to give any details.

If something happened to him... Patrice's boys... she didn't even hear Grace Kingsley's words when the woman called on the phone with a reminder about the party.

Then, Mrs. Armor, the chauffeur's wife, approached Patrice. The guest list for the anniversary celebration included Steven's wife's sister, and rumor had it she'd zeroed in on Richard for Husband N° 4. Short, plump form bristling, Richard's adoptive mother insisted that even at almost forty-five, he could do much better than the bed-hopping socialite. There was a nice young lady Mrs. Armor had in mind for her boy... the daughter of a grocery store clerk Mr. Armor sometimes went fishing with. The girl now taught history to college students. Mrs. Armor asked if Patrice would make sure Richard didn't get tricked by the husband-hunting party girl into anything he'd later regret.

Normally, Patrice would've wholeheartedly agreed, but she couldn't bring herself to worry about Richard's love life at the moment. She was about to decline the invitation when the phone rang yet another time. Noah Andersen did not know much more about the riot than what was already in the papers, and he insisted—as he always did—that Patrice attend the party. His instructions were to stick close to Richard and listen for gossip.

Of course Andersen would blame Richard for the riot! Gritting her teeth, Patrice reminded herself the former attorney general was trying to help her sons. He was wrong about Richard, but she might pick up chatter relating to Steven which could prove helpful. Godwin, too.

Oh, Patrice remembered very well how the Kingsley patriarch tried to use her boys to make their father toe the line. She was confused when she heard about the interrogation in Cuba, when she heard how he argued against her sons and daughter-in-law. Even on the day they left on their exile, Brad, Victor, and Alex believed their grandfather was a saint, but Patrice wasn't sure what to think.

Like everyone else, she eventually assumed Godwin's hands were tied because of his position in Kingsley Corp. She assumed that he, too, wanted the five brothers to return safe and sound. Then, Andersen told her about Godwin's role in Richard's adoption and the first Kingsley-Sheppard alliance. It was him from the beginning, pulling all the strings. Her sons might not believe it, but she'd seen enough of the old man's machinations before, and Steven was cut from the same cloth. Richard believed Steven was his friend, but the Kingsley heir would throw the chauffeur's son under the bus to save his own skin.

So here was Patrice, toasting the forty-fifth wedding anniversary of Steven's parents. The Kingsleys never let anything slip in her presence, but she'd keep an ear out if only to tell Andersen there was once again nothing to suggest Richard was to blame for Steven's bad behavior. The Kingsleys couldn't be allowed to frame an innocent man for their crimes. At the very least, the husband-hunter would be packed off by the end of tonight's event.

Richard and Steven were at the open bar only ten feet to Patrice's right, Charles leaning sideways with his elbow on the counter. Keen on her pursuit, Steven's sister-in-law blatantly stalked Richard, her assets on display in the short, tight, red dress. Patrice craned her neck and peered at the catering staff. One of them—a sprightly young blonde working her way through college—nodded in Patrice's direction.

Holding a platter piled high with *hors d'oeuvres*, the waitress headed toward the men. Both she and the husband-hunter reached them at the same time.

The waitress's friend, a petite brunette with bouncy curls framing her smiling face, went to Charles with a tray of drinks. Charles leered at the girl and reached for a glass. There was a sudden scuffle. With a "Hey!" Charles tripped and fell straight onto the blonde's back.

The girl stumbled, the platter of appetizers wobbling in her hands. With a look of mild alarm, Richard reached for it.

Somehow, before his fingers touched the steel, all the contents were tipped on to the husband-hunter. She screamed, her red dress now decorated with creamy sauce. A shrimp sat in her hair, tail pointing straight up. The rest of the catering staff came running. So did some of the guests. One of the family's regular employees appeared with a bucket and a mop.

Richard turned away, his shoulders shaking with mirth. The predatory woman glared at his broad back, no trace of seduction left in her angry eyes.

Steven's face was red with laughter, which he quickly concealed behind a fist as his wife came sprinting to her sister's aid.

"He pinched my butt," snapped the brunette waitress, pointing at Charles.

"I didn't," Charles howled.

"Charlie," muttered Steven. "How could you? It's Mom and Dad's party."

"But I didn't," said the hapless Charles.

Setting her wine glass on the console next to the pillar, Patrice slipped out of the ballroom. Her work here was done.

#

Two days later

The Barnes & Noble bookstore on Fifth Avenue was the perfect place for a clandestine meeting with the two students from NYU. As she walked through the door with the rolled-up newspaper in one hand, Patrice thanked God for sparing Harry's life. The media was full of talk about the former SEAL who saved a correction officer and prevented the escape of the worst of the criminals in Sing Sing.

Chest heaving in a sigh of relief, Patrice paused a moment. There it was... the fiction section. Enjoying the smell of new books, she peeped into the rows one at a time. There were a few readers ambling between bookcases... a bearded young man in glasses, a pregnant girl perusing romance novels...

"Psst," came a voice. A hand beckoned Patrice from the Mystery aisle.

The English majors who worked for the catering company were waiting for the rest of the cash. "There's a thousand in each," Patrice said, handing the envelopes to the young ladies. She snapped her purse shut.

"Thanks," said the blonde, tucking the money into her tote. When Patrice took a step away, the blonde added, "Wait... don't go."

Patrice halted. Narrow-eyed, she studied the duo. Was she about to be blackmailed? It wouldn't work. She had her story ready. The bad blood between her and the other Kingsleys was enough to explain why Patrice arranged an "accident" with the food. She could do more harm to these silly girls with their employer if they chose to go the extortion route. "What do you want?" she barked.

Looking slightly taken aback, the blonde said, "You asked us to tell you whatever we heard them talking about."

"Ahh... yes... yes, I did." When Andersen called, Patrice could legitimately claim she tried every trick in the book to get intel on the Kingsleys.

"There was nothing about the man-crazy chick." The blonde glanced at her friend. "Business talk mostly... we think."

"We'll still get the extra cash, right?" the brunette asked, tone nervous. "I mean... it's not our fault they didn't talk about women. After you left, the blond man—you said his name's Richard—got a phone call. All of them were in a foul mood later. The Richard dude was going on about someone called Harry Sheppard and box and escaping. He wasn't happy."

A jolt of fear went through Patrice. Her thoughts stalled. "What?" she asked.

"We were talking about it," the brunette continued. "They couldn't be gay, right? Some kind of S and M thing? They were talking about business the rest of the time... oil business. The Kingsleys are in oil, right?"

"Yes," Patrice responded. "They're in oil." *What escape?*

The blonde asked, "So can we have the cash? I mean... it *was* probably about business. Anyway, we thought we should let you know just in case. It won't be cool to set them up with women if they're gay. One of them's already married. The poor wife!"

There was a numb feeling in Patrice's head. "Harry escaping? *Richard* said it?"

"Yes," said the brunette. "And—"

The blonde's hand shot out, grabbing her friend by the arm. "You can't let him know we outted him."

"I won't," Patrice said automatically.

Chapter 32

In the afternoon

Long Island, New York

From the French window of Sabrina's home, Patrice watched Michael and Gabriel toss a football around. "They're trampling the grass," she commented.

Honking into a tissue, Sabrina appeared next to her, still puffy-eyed and red-nosed. "This is their home… they're allowed to run where they want. For the last three days, we were worried to death about Harry. They need to work off some of that fear."

"Are you permitted to visit?" Patrice asked.

"Not until the cops are done investigating what happened," said Sabrina. "But they let us speak to him on the phone."

"Your parents?"

"Papa's still in the hospital. He's old. The doctor says it was no surprise he had a heart attack."

"Of course it was no surprise," Noah Andersen said from the door to the dining room. His bright-green eyes were pinned on Patrice. He was close to ninety, and his hair was completely silver, but the old fellow's voice was still as steely as she remembered. "You don't expect to bury a child, which is what Ryan thought he'd be doing."

With another sniffle, Sabrina wiped her eyes with her knuckles.

"Walk with me, Patrice?" asked Andersen. "I'm sure we could both use the fresh air. And this is your first time here if I'm not mistaken. You should see the garden. Trampled grass aside, it's quite pretty."

"Everything's Noah's doing," Sabrina said. "He hired the same people who did Temple's landscaping."

Leaving Sabrina in the house, they walked down the path to a little pond where pink lilies bobbed up and down. A pair of hummingbirds played fly-tag around the stone gnomes next to the water. Cool spring breeze ruffled Patrice's hair, and the sounds of her grandsons playing football echoed from across the backyard.

Vaguely, she noted that while the house and the yard were only a fraction of the size of the Kingsley castle in Panama, it was perfect for Sabrina, Michael, and Gabriel. There were even a couple of guestrooms and a home office, with space in the basement and the attic which could potentially be used by on-site security.

Pointing to a cast-iron bench, Andersen said, "Let's sit there."

"How big is the lot?" Patrice asked, making herself as comfortable as she possibly could on the metal seating.

"An acre or so," said Andersen. "What did you find out?"

Patrice started. "What makes you think... I'm just here to—"

"Cut it out," Andersen said. "We don't have time."

"Mr. Andersen," Patrice began, tone icy.

Eyes flinty, Andersen turned to her. "This is your first visit to this house in the four years since they moved here. Sabrina might have been born a Sheppard, but your grandsons are Kingsleys. They're *your* flesh and blood, but you still refused to visit. If you managed to get off your high horse and make your way here, it means something happened."

Her stomach churned at the thought of Richard being subjected to this man's scrutiny. Noah Andersen could well pick up the phone and report what she relayed to the FBI. What if the feds arrested Richard? *For trapping Harry wherever it was he escaped from. My God. Was Richard responsible for the riot in Sing Sing?* But if Patrice didn't say anything, any control she had over the situation would go up in smoke. "First, I need your promise you won't let anything happen to Richard."

Voice exasperated, Andersen said, "Listen—"

"You owe me," she insisted. "It was because of *you* that Brad started fighting with Lilah. *You* fed his insecurities until he snapped. And you wouldn't let me speak up."

Through clenched teeth, Andersen drew in a breath. "Fine. Unless it involves risking Harry's life or the lives of the rest of your family, I swear I won't do anything to Richard."

Words tumbling over each other, Patrice narrated what she heard from the students, including the reason they were near enough to overhear the conversation in the first place. Recounting Richard's dismay at Harry escaping, she petered off. There was none of the horror she expected on Andersen's face. "You knew?" she asked, confused.

With a huff, Andersen said, "Patrice, only you believed Richard had nothing to do with any of it. I hoped you were correct in thinking his involvement was limited to the role of military lawyer. I also wanted to keep him safe from Godwin... for your sake. But the last few years have shown me while Godwin's the mastermind behind Steven's moves, Richard has the brain and the willingness to do whatever it takes for Steven's success. Godwin wasn't the one who went on the jaunt to Bangkok, and he certainly wouldn't have taken the risk of getting caught arranging the murder of Will Luce. Even the attacks on Harry in Sing Sing have got to be Richard's doing. Can you imagine Godwin letting Steven deal with the likes of those prisoners?"

Tears filled Patrice's eyes. The garden turned into a green blur. "Richard's my son," she whispered.

"So are Brad, Victor, and Alex. The only mother-figure Neil and Scott have is you. Michael and Gabriel are your grandsons. Don't they have a right to your loyalty? And what about Harry? This is his fifth year in prison, Patrice. Prison! For trying to help *your* family. You brought up what I owe you. Think about what you owe Harry."

"Really?" she asked, feeling bitter to her core. "I owe Ryan Sheppard's son?" Limbs clumsy, she stood. "I shouldn't have... I'm going back home."

She hadn't taken two steps when Andersen's furious voice followed her. "Go home. And if you can, say a prayer for your daughter-in-law."

Patrice halted, her breathing heavy.

"Remember Lilah?" Andersen taunted. "Richard accused her of treason. She could've been killed for it. Richard was ready to have an innocent woman put to death to please his friend."

Patrice bit her lip, not wanting to respond.

Relentlessly, Andersen continued, "What's more, the only reason Brad's not rotting in prison today is that Lilah agreed to go on the exile with them. After what he did to her, she still chose to save his fool neck. Think about what your son—*all* your sons— did to her."

Desperately, Patrice searched her mind for a rebuttal.

She heard a creaky shuffle behind, then Andersen was next to her. "Yes, you were given a raw deal, but you're carrying your grudge too far. What you're willing to do to Lilah is a hundred times worse than anything you went through."

"No," Patrice whimpered.

"Yes," Andersen insisted. "You're ready to let Lilah die to satisfy your thirst for vengeance."

"I'm not," Patrice snapped. "I would never... I love Lilah like my own daughter."

Tone ruthless, Andersen said, "Richard and his friends are hunting your *daughter*, because as long as she's still alive, Steven can never be sure of his control of the empire. I believe the criminal— Jack Drummond—went to China to kill Lilah. You want to know what the grapevine in DC says about Drummond?"

Andersen's tone... terror quaked Patrice's insides.

"Beatings, burning, knives. Broken bones. Strangling."

"No," she gasped.

"Go home," Andersen mocked. "Play your little matchmaking games with Richard. So what if Harry burns to death in Sing Sing? So what if your grandsons never get to see their fathers? So what if Lilah is attacked by one more rapist? You'll have your vengeance on Ryan Sheppard. You'll still have the son you lost."

"Please stop," Patrice begged.

"You need to hear this," Andersen said. "Have you given a single thought to Lilah after you moved back into the Kingsley home? Do you think about what your other sons are going through? Do you ever wonder if they're still alive?"

"Don't do this," Patrice pleaded.

Andersen showed no sympathy. "You prefer living in your make-believe world, playing godmother to Richard. But this is not a fairytale, Patrice. There are lives at stake. The life of the woman you claim to love like a daughter. If you actually mean it, open your eyes and see Richard for what he is."

Sabrina's voice floated to the duo from the French window. Patrice jolted. No... Alex's wife was too far to have overhead anything. Clapping her hands, Sabrina asked the two boys to return inside. They were going to have an early dinner so Patrice could join them.

"Think hard about what I said." Not looking back, Noah shuffled off in the direction of the house. Patrice waited a few moments for her heart to slow down.

Temple was also at the dinner table. Relieved as they were at Harry's miraculous escape, there was a great deal of joking and laughing. When she was ready to leave, Patrice asked Andersen if she could again speak to him in private.

At the ornately carved front door, she batted back her tears. "What if I talk to Richard? If he knows everything—"

Letting out a breath, Andersen said, "I don't think it will work. For one, Richard's too far involved to quit at your say-so. Even if he does, what I told you before still stands. The Kingsleys will simply blame him for every crime and get away scot-free. It's one of the reasons I didn't insist you tell Harry everything right after Temple got shot."

"So what do I do?" Patrice asked, her tone sad and bitter. "Arrange for someone to kill my own child?"

"Patrice." Andersen halted and steepled his fingers before saying, "Brad and Lilah are well-hidden. Richard can't get to them. What he can do is get to Harry. If he does, Lilah and your sons will come flying back and get trapped. So we need to stay one step ahead of Richard. If we can keep Harry safe, Richard won't be able to lure Brad out. And once Brad gets pardoned, the company will be back in his hands... we hope. Steven will lose, and Richard will be..."

When Andersen didn't continue, Patrice whispered, "They won't forget, will they? Brad, Victor, Alex, Lilah, the twins... they won't forget what Richard did. Harry won't, either."

"Probably not," admitted Andersen. "Best-case scenario... you could come clean with all your sons. It's unlikely, but Richard *could* agree to switch sides. Your other boys *could* agree to forgive and forget. But what are you going to say to Lilah? I can't see her being naïve enough to buy any apologies from Richard. She'll know chances are he would use the info to help Steven."

"Then..."

Andersen sighed. "M'dear, the first step would be to talk to Harry. He's the most immediate threat to Richard. All the tricks from Steven's side thus far... Harry would see Richard as a major obstacle in the path to a pardon for Brad. It won't be easy, and I can't promise you anything, but you do need to talk to Harry."

No, it wasn't easy. In the back seat of the car, Patrice stared holes into the back of the chauffeur's nearly bald head, remembering the infant that had been torn from her arms to be given into his. The tow-headed toddler grew up playing in the Kingsley gardens. The same toddler watched from the servants' seating as she married Peter Kingsley. The serious little boy was invited to visit her newborn babies when she brought them home, one by one. A sulky pre-teen was left behind when she abandoned the Kingsley residence on the death of her husband.

She encountered an angry adolescent on her return. The cadet nodded at her when they crossed paths on one of his rare visits home from the military academy. The major challenged Alex at Godwin's party. A businessman showed up at Brad's board meeting. The lawyer who persecuted her sons on trumped-up charges of treason was also the criminal who ordered the brutal killing of Lilah.

Patrice closed her eyes and prayed for forgiveness for all these years of pretended ignorance. *Hide, Lilah,* Patrice whispered to her daughter-in-law. *Hide from the monster. Don't come out until he's gone.*

Then, she willed herself to crumple and die.

Part XIII

Chapter 33

Later in the week, April 1994

(eight months to go before parole)

The Box, Sing Sing Correctional Facility

Ossining, New York

"Made what up?" Harry asked, more confused than before.

Still blushing, Lilah glared from her chair. "Made up the story, you... you... you boy! I saw you going into the garage. And I wanted an excuse for being downstairs and seeing the light in here."

Warmth bloomed in the vicinity of Harry's heart. His arms ached to hold her close.

"Sheppard," shouted a male voice. Harry opened his eyes to darkness within his cell, but the harsh fluorescent lamps were still on next to the officer's booth. "Get off your ass, Pretty Boy," the same guard yelled, his face obscured by the shadows. The tone was pleasant.

After the rioters were subdued, the mattress in Harry's old cell was found charred. A Molotov cocktail, according to the cops on the crime scene. If Harry had been there, he would've burned to death.

As it was, there were no fatalities, but several correction officers were severely wounded before managing to lock themselves in various rooms. Among the injured parties was one of the A-block cats—the orange tabby called Tiger—who in fact took refuge in Harry's cell and lost his whiskers to the fire. Afterward, the feline had been too scared to get out and hunt for food. Since his rescue, Officer Tiger opted to retire from his rodent-control duties and was taken home by a human colleague.

Whether the culprit behind the bomb was the same guard who later showed up in the Box was anybody's guess. At this point, all they knew was the dead guard tried to get Harry to kill Officer Regina Berra, and Harry saved her life. Since no one could state with any degree of certainty if Harry was no longer in danger, the prison system decided the Box was the safest place for him. Warden Berra personally selected every guard allowed there.

Harry had been half afraid of Regina Berra's newfound affection, sure the remainder of the employees of Sing Sing would hate his guts for it. The officer wasn't exactly known for her warm and fuzzy personality, but it seemed the guards were grateful to him for saving the life of one of their own, no matter how obnoxious she was. Which explained the casual friendliness in the voice of the man who yanked Harry out of his memories.

With a sigh, Harry got to his feet. As he approached the bars, an inmate called out, *"As-salāmu alaykum,"* wishing the listener peace in Arabic.

"Wa alaykum as-salām," Harry responded, vaguely registering the fact that the other convict broke the rules of his religion by greeting a non-believer thusly. Harry didn't have time to ponder the mistake further. Behind the guard was a tall, bulky figure. The warden, a.k.a. the Bear.

When the guard marched off, Arthur Berra moved closer. "I was busy the last few days. Didn't have time for a one-to-one."

"I understand, sir."

"First of all, thank you," the warden said, tone steady but with an undercurrent of a father's fear.

Harry inclined his head, saying nothing.

"Quite a story you told my daughter," Arthur Berra mused.

"It's the truth," Harry insisted. "Not a story."

"The only way you're going to prove it is if you find evidence this McCoy was in or at least around the apartment where the corpse was discovered."

"Yes, but—"

The warden held up a hand. "I know. There are people who don't want you getting out, and they've made sure you don't have the finances to have it investigated. I'm planning to take a trip down to Brooklyn. I'll meet up with some friends in the police department. We'll go over the crime scene material and see if anything could've been missed."

Harry's plan was in place, ready to go the minute he was out on parole, and he wasn't about discuss it with law-abiding officials like the warden or his daughter. Still, the legit route was preferable. "You have my gratitude," said Harry. "My lawyer has been talking about DNA testing. He got me a paper on it."

In 1984, a British scientist developed a technique called genetic fingerprinting which was used in determining familial connections in immigration cases. A few years later, the same technology would be used to prove the innocence of a man arrested for the rape and murder of two teenage girls. The killer was eventually caught, also thanks to the genetic evidence he left behind. The use of it wasn't widespread yet, and there was never any argument in court of such evidence in Harry's case.

"DNA?" The warden frowned. "Yeah... plenty of noise about it among law enforcement these days. Problem is the crime scene will be useless for analysis after all these years... if we even get access to the place."

"It's what the lawyer says, too," Harry acknowledged. "Unfortunate timing. The technique wasn't widely used during the time the Luce murder was being investigated. Now... even if the apartment is not rented, it's certainly been contaminated. Other than the murder weapon and a pizza box with some used tissue, there wasn't much physical evidence available for the police to store."

"Still worth taking a look." Holding a finger up, the warden warned, "I'm not going to lie for you."

"I won't ask you to," Harry promised. "But I do have a request."

"What?"

"I'd like to have a couple of things from home. My saxophone... and there's a pendant."

#

The items were hand-delivered by Noah the next day. Temple and his entourage were of course with the former attorney general. There were also two people Harry wasn't expecting to see. He almost didn't recognize the woman—the short and skinny frame, the dark hair sprinkled with gray, the same refined voice uttering a greeting.

"Good to see you, too, Aunt Patrice," Harry responded, pulling a chair back to sit. "Aaron, what a surprise."

"I wasn't sure if you'd want me to visit." Aaron Kingsley—illegitimate son of the Kingsley clan and half-brother to David and Peter—was tall and dark-haired like his male relatives. There was something about his gray eyes... a gentleness which he surely got from his mother's side. "But Patrice... ahh... she asked if I would come along today."

"You can visit me any time, sir," said Harry. Aaron had been the only one of the family to show some semblance of support for Lilah at the military court in Cuba. Harry would forever be grateful to the man for the succor alone. Besides, Temple trusted Aaron despite his devotion to Godwin Kingsley, the patriarch. Clearly, so did Noah and Patrice. Nodding at the other two people in the group, Harry added, "Mr. Temple, Noah... it wasn't me who started the fight. I swear."

Aaron's worried face seemed to freeze in place for a second, and Patrice looked confused. The former president continued smiling. "Jeez, Harry," Noah muttered. "You joke about the damnedest—at least it means you're okay."

"Good," interjected Temple. Nodding, he repeated, "Good." One of the few words he seemed to have learned anew.

As could be expected when the former president showed up, the visiting room was empty of others. Stationed at strategic spots around the chamber were the four secret service officers. Sing Sing's own guards were also around.

Temple couldn't stay for very long without making life inconvenient for prison staff and the inmates. Schedules would have been cleared to accommodate his security needs. There would be no other visits until after he left the premises. Still, Noah would've wanted Temple to see his former protégé for himself if only for the reassurance. Who knew how much Temple understood about the happenings at Sing Sing? But Harry's picture in the nightly news... images of the chaos in the prison... Temple wouldn't have been able to relax until he saw Harry in one piece.

Alex's mother... when was the last time Harry talked to her? Patrice was around at his sentencing. She was probably as shaken as everyone else about what happened in the prison.

As shaken as Harry's own mother, Sophia Sheppard. She was taking Ryan home from the hospital today. Both had pleaded with Harry on the phone, asking to visit. But Ryan's doctors didn't think it was a good idea for him to be in a stressful situation like the prison this soon after a heart attack.

Harry's hand trembled. Heart attack... his parents were getting old. As was Patrice.

In the center of the table was Harry's saxophone, a small velvet pouch resting on it. The silver chain with the Eiffel Tower pendant would be inside. Grazing a knuckle across the fabric, Harry asked, "You doing all right, Aunt Patrice?"

Chair scraping the floor, Noah stood. "M'dear, Aaron and I will step out while you—"

Harry frowned in confusion.

"No," she said, an anxious look in her eyes. "I'd like you both to stay." Swallowing hard, Patrice addressed Harry. "Ahh... I asked Noah to bring me here. There's something I need to tell you... to explain about..."

Chapter 34

Forty-five years ago, Spring Break, 1949

Oyster Bay, New York

Patrice had found it strange that the Kingsleys would want to invite her—an absolute nobody—to the engagement party of their oldest boy. It was even harder to believe the family was going along with Ryan's plan to introduce her to the other eligible bachelor of the clan, Peter. Her! Sixteen-year-old Patrice Sheppard from Brooklyn! The girl with the perfectly average face and average figure and average everything else! It wasn't as if she were one of the rich Sheppards, either.

Ryan and his parents treated Patrice as part of the family, and they even paid for her education. It didn't mean she could act as though she were entitled to attend the same social events they did. Still, Peter Kingsley didn't seem to care Patrice was poor and rather... well... average. In fact, he cared so little that he hardly looked at her, having eyes only for the equally poor but blonde and gorgeous Madeleine Wheeler.

Patrice was left on her lonesome until a wicked voice said "Boo" in her ear, and she turned to see an utterly divine man. The Greek aristocrat was called Kyriakos Phoebus Sabazios, but Patrice would always remember him as Apollo, the Sun God. Laughing, flirting... dancing in the art gallery in the mansion until Peter Kingsley came looking. He warned Apollo to behave himself with women and informed Patrice her family was looking for her. Oh, Patrice was so angry with Peter for insulting Apollo, but the Sun God merely laughed it off. He was heir to a shipping company called Helios and wasn't answerable to the Kingsleys.

A few minutes later, she left the mansion in the company of Ryan and his wife. All the way back to the shabby home she shared with her father, Patrice smiled dreamily. The blond hair and blue eyes, the warm grin on Apollo's handsome face... she cried into her pillow, longing to be rich and beautiful so the love of her life would adore her back. Desolate, she returned to the boarding school to a wonderful surprise. Waiting on her dresser was a letter from Apollo, asking when he might meet her again. From the depths of despair, her heart leaped into the joy of romance. He wrote every week, grumbling about not being allowed to visit her at the school, and she primly told him to wait for spring break.

For the first time since she was quasi-adopted by the Sheppard family, Patrice informed them she would be spending her days off with her father. She had a sneaking suspicion Ryan wouldn't approve of her budding relationship with Apollo, but her father could always be depended on to ignore his only child. Lying to him about visiting a non-existent friend, she left around mid-morning. Apollo picked her up at the bus stop in a gorgeous car he called a Jaguar, and they drove to his cousin's vacation home in Oyster Bay.

The house was right on the beach, but everyone remained inside the walled compound. There was a pool party going on, full of absolutely stunning girls and handsome men swinging to "Buttons and Bows" from *The Paleface*. Their host greeted Apollo by his real name.

Apollo's cousin—the owner of the beautiful home they were in—pointed Patrice to the changing room where she could pick a bathing suit. The girls at school had drooled over the new two-piece swimwear called the bikini, but Patrice never imagined *she'd* be wearing one. Fingering through the selections, she tried to find something she'd feel comfortable in. The best she could come up with was this item, the striped halter-top and matching panties. The bra was tiny, but then, so were her boobs. The bottom... she tugged at the edge, wishing it would cover more of her buttocks.

When she padded her way to the pool, Apollo was already in the water, cutting across with clean strokes. His golden hair glinted under the bright sun. His smile flashed brightly. "C'mon in, darling," he shouted, sending splashes in her direction. A drop landed right in her non-existent cleavage, tickling her.

Heads swung in her direction, the feminine ones wearing frowns. They were all wondering what this wealthy prince was doing with a perfectly ordinary girl from Brooklyn. Patrice couldn't help herself. She preened. "Look all you want, ladies," she muttered under her breath, "but he's mine." Patrice Sheppard was the chosen consort of the Sun God. At least for this one afternoon.

Wet fingers closed around her ankle. She yelped and looked down to see Apollo at the edge of the pool. Before she could utter a word, she was flying, heading face-first into the deep end. A good bit of water went into her open mouth. She beat around wildly, struggling to surface. A tug on her arm, and she broke through, gasping.

Dripping hair plastered to the scalp, she panted, "What did you do that for?"

Apollo grinned. "Teasing. I want to make sure you have fun."

So he did. He insisted they play catch in the pool, his hands brushing against unmentionable places under the cover of the choppy surface. The reproving looks she tried went no place. For one, he simply winked and touched her somewhere even more outrageous. For another, she couldn't stop laughing.

Later in the evening, they clambered out to sample the delicious dishes on the buffet table. Patrice bit into a juicy, greasy hot dog and watched the fiery sun shimmer and dissipate, bathing the sky in ravishing reds and pinks and oranges. Stars soon spilled across the night like diamonds on black silk, and the moon was large and bright.

"We're going to do the Balboa," announced Apollo, setting his plate back on the table. "Your brother's not around to disapprove."

"I was afraid Peter and Maddie would be here," Patrice admitted. The other couple was young enough not to care about the sexy dance, but at her one and only encounter with them, it seemed they didn't approve of Apollo, either.

"Kingsley's a snob," Apollo said.

Patrice hid a frown. If Peter Kingsley were a snob, he wouldn't have been courting Madeleine Wheeler who was just as working class as Patrice. Also, at the Kingsley engagement party, the Greek prince dismissed Peter as a mongrel.

Apollo tugged her close. "Forget them."

His arm around her waist, her breasts crushed against his chest, they jitterbugged around the tiled space. Patrice heard the claps, the hoots, the whistles. She was vaguely aware of the other couples attempting the same. But she couldn't take her eyes off Apollo. Couldn't look away from his wicked grin.

To her dismay, he released her. "Did I step on your foot?" she asked anxiously.

"Come," he said and tugged at her arm.

Through the double doors to the house, up the stairs, and into a large bedroom they went. The brocade curtains were drawn, but the chandelier was lit, revealing the large bed. Apollo closed the door, cocooning them in the luxurious chamber. The music from the party was only a distant echo.

They stood still for a few seconds, their breaths heavy and loud. Apollo's gaze swept from her face, down to her breasts and hips before returning to her mouth. She so badly wanted him to kiss her. Patrice trembled. Her eyes dropped to her feet.

"We're getting the carpet wet," she whispered, eyeing the dark patches. "Your cousin's not going to be happy."

Apollo laughed softly. "You worry about such silly things, Patrice. No, he won't mind. This is the room he's given us."

"Us? But we're not staying."

"Cute. Who's talking about staying?"

Patrice smiled shyly when he yanked her closer. His hand stroked her back, fingers slipping under the strap of her bikini top. His head dipped, kissing her ear.

She giggled. "It tickles."

The frown on his face disappeared as quickly as it came. Brushing her wet hair aside, he touched his lips to her neck, the fingers under the bikini strap pushing it up. His warm hand closed around her breast.

"Apollo," she gasped and shoved herself away.

"What?" he asked.

"I don't think... just kissing for now, okay?"

"Come on, girl." He smiled, reaching for her again. "You don't mean it. Didn't you like me touching you?" Patrice smiled back, uncertain. She did but wasn't sure of going there yet. "I waited weeks to get you to myself," he complained. "If my friends knew, they'd laugh." Tilting her head, she looked at him with a frown. "I'm a god back in Athens," he explained, lip curling. "Girls wait for *me.*"

She'd called him a god, too, but that was different. The arrogance and entitlement of what Apollo said... Patrice was about to ask him to take her home when he waggled his brows. She laughed. A joke, she told herself. That was it.

"I want some time with my girl," he cajoled. "What's so bad about it?"

Nothing, she thought dazedly. Not when she was his girl.

When he drew her back into his embrace, she didn't object. When he stripped off her bra, she didn't resist. If there was a little pain when he bit her shoulder, she didn't complain. Patrice felt his hand on her inner thigh. She drew back once more, mewling a protest.

"What's the matter this time?" He did not sound happy.

"I don't know, Apollo. I'm only sixteen."

"So? You were old enough to decide to come here with me. Why are you acting coy now?"

"Don't be mad at me," she begged.

"Who should I get mad at? Your father? I could make a phone call, and he'd lose his job."

"No!"

"Just a joke," he crooned. "Come here. Everything will be okay. I promise."

Apollo turned gentle with her, even teasing her about her ineptness. When he stripped off his swimming trunks and joined her in bed, her mouth dropped open. All the paintings and all the sculptures never prepared her for the reality of the male body.

When she voiced her shock, Apollo laughed, but she couldn't help it. There had been no mother to tell Patrice how all the parts worked. Her schoolmates seemed so sophisticated that she'd been too embarrassed to ask them anything about sex.

By the time she figured out what went where, Apollo was already done. In fact, if it weren't for the sudden sharp pain, she might have even believed it to be a strange dream. She wasn't sure she wanted to go through anything like it again, but if the comical contortions on his face were anything to go by, Apollo seemed to have liked it well enough.

They repeated the pattern the next day. Well, almost. Patrice lied to her father and left the house, and Apollo drove them to his cousin's place, but there was no party. They spent the entire day in bed with very little talking.

On the third day, Patrice left Apollo face-down on the mattress and went to the large windows overlooking the Atlantic. Pushing them open, she let the cool breeze wash away the musky odor of sex. Froth bubbled on top of the blue-gray waves. On the sand, a little girl chased her big brother, threatening him with a plastic spade. Patrice giggled. "Let's go to the beach," she suggested.

"I can go to the beach any time I want back home," said Apollo. "Why would I come all the way here for it?"

"But I—"

"Get back in bed," he commanded. "I don't want to waste any time. It's bad enough I have to drive up and down every day just so you can pretend to your family you're still a virgin." Stricken, Patrice stared. "What are you waiting for?" he barked.

Like an automaton, she obeyed his order. When he was done, she curled up on her side, staring at the skies through the window.

An hour later, he parked his car at the bus stop in Brooklyn. "I'm sorry," said Apollo.

When Patrice didn't respond, he tugged her into his arms, saying, "It was only because I wanted your attention all to myself." He kissed her on her ear, using his tongue to tickle her until she erupted into helpless giggles. "Pick you up in the morning?" he asked, voice hoarse.

Shyly, she nodded.

On the last day of spring break, Apollo told her he was returning to Athens. "Just for a couple of months. I'll be back before your summer vacation starts."

#

Back in April 1994

Sing Sing Correctional Facility

Ossining, New York

Keeping his face expressionless, Harry eyed the woman across the table. Patrice had said she wanted to explain her animosity toward Ryan Sheppard. Harry already knew the Sheppards and the Kingsleys tried to unite the families through marriage, exactly as they did later with Lilah. What he didn't realize was young Patrice also had someone else in mind, just as Lilah did. Harry's father somehow forced the sixteen-year-old girl to give up her Sun God to marry the Kingsley heir.

The flush on Patrice's face, the shifting gaze... she was clearly uncomfortable sharing even the bare bones with Harry. Or she'd never been comfortable with the "liaison" she described in clipped tones. Contaminating the loss of her romantic dreams were the shame and guilt of having gone against the social norms of her generation. The Greek man on the other hand...

"How old was this Apollo?" Harry asked.

"He was done with university," said Patrice. "When we met, he'd been working with his family's company for a year or so. Twenty-two or twenty-three, I guess."

An adult to her child. The son of a bitch would've first seen the innocent Patrice as a fun way to pass his time at the Kingsley engagement party. After the warning issued by Peter Kingsley, Apollo would've seen her as a challenge.

Callous bastards like him rarely offered marriage to young women who brought neither looks nor wealth with them. The world of the 'forties condemned girls who were naïve enough to trust the wrong men. The illicit affair with Apollo would've ended any chance Patrice had at a decent life. Her marriage to Peter Kingsley was arranged to meet the political needs of the two families, but whatever the actual intentions, the Sheppards were right to call a halt to her romance with Apollo.

Reaching across the table, Harry took Patrice's right hand in both of his. Her fingers were cold—almost freezing—despite the pleasant temperature in the prison visiting room. "Aunt Patrice,

Apollo could've insisted... *you* could've waited until you turned twenty-one."

"It wasn't so simple," she whispered.

#

Forty-five years ago, Late May 1949

Brooklyn, New York

After the housekeeper at the school caught Patrice vomiting into the toilet several days in a row, the grim-faced nurse summoned a doctor. Within the week, a telegram went out to Ryan Sheppard, but he'd moved to the Middle East and couldn't be expected to pick her up. The next call the principal made was to Patrice's father. Pa apparently told the lady he couldn't afford the fare to Hartford to collect his wayward daughter, so one of the junior teachers took Patrice to the terminal and put her on a bus bound for New York City. She was told the rest of her belongings would soon be shipped home. It took Patrice two more buses and twenty cents to get to Brooklyn.

Clutching her valise, Patrice trudged up the steps to the top-floor apartment. It was only a rental, but she and her father lived there since she was an infant. Her tummy rumbled. She desperately hoped Pa would at least have bread. Or cereal and milk. At the moment, she was simply too tired to shop for groceries.

Within moments of stepping through the front door, she learned she'd not only have no food, she could expect not to be allowed peace, either. Her normally distant father had finally found something that outraged him enough to look at his daughter. His first words were, "Is it Kingsley's brat?"

"No," muttered Patrice, flushing. "I haven't met him after the party."

Pa didn't stop screaming for an hour. "Do you know what they call girls like you?" he berated her, spit spewing from the corner of his mouth. He was a perfectly mediocre-looking man, with average height and bland looks. Just like her. But looming over her as she cowered on the old couch, he was scary. "You've ruined everything!"

Wearily, she thought about walking out of the apartment, but where would she go? Ryan and Sophia were not in the country, and Patrice didn't know how the senior Sheppards would react to the news.

"So many plans... all down the drain because one stupid girl couldn't keep her legs together," continued Pa. She cringed at the crudity. It wasn't like that. Apollo loved her. "The money involved!" her father fumed. "God, I hope I don't have to give it back."

She frowned. What money was he talking about? They didn't have any. When Ryan's family offered to pay for her education, Pa had only been too happy. Did he think they would want the tuition returned?

"The school already contacted Ryan," Pa announced. "You hear me? He already knows." Hand to his forehead, Pa paced the threadbare carpet. "What am I going to do?"

"Ryan will find a way," Patrice muttered, voice timid. He would, too. Oh, he'd be angry, but he'd track down Apollo for her. In a matter of weeks, she'd be a married woman. A June wedding, she daydreamed.

"Go to your room. Now! I don't want you around when they get here. Maybe we can still salvage something."

When *who* got there? A loud thumping at the main door downstairs interrupted the screaming. Pa stalked out, giving Patrice a few minutes of reprieve. Adjusting herself on the lumpy pillows, she mentally counted the coins in her purse. Phone calls to Athens were bound to be expensive. She'd already written three letters to Apollo. He hadn't responded yet, and she could no longer afford to wait. Ryan would call Apollo for her, but this was not the kind of news a man wanted to hear from a future brother-in-law.

Raised voices echoed up the stairway. "The idiot! All the things we did for the stupid bitch! Everything destroyed!"

No, she thought dazedly. *That can't be Ryan.* He was in the Middle East.

A third voice intruded, the measured tones asking the angry men to cool down. Taking care not to make a sound, she went to the front door. Through the crack, she saw Ryan and Pa arguing in the vestibule at the bottom of the stairs. A man of average height stood behind Ryan, urging calm. He shifted, and their gazes collided.

He smiled. "Hello, Patrice," he said and jogged up the stairs. Kindly blue eyes crinkled in genuine warmth. "You remember me, right? I'm Temple."

Half hour later, she learned Sophia was not faring well in her pregnancy, and Ryan brought her back to the country so she could have their first child in comfort. Leaving her at her parents' home, he'd been preparing to return to his business when Patrice's father called him with the news. He didn't even know about the telegram the school sent to his overseas address.

Her vision blurry with tears, Patrice watched Ryan discuss options with her father. She didn't understand why they needed to consider alternatives. Not when the baby's father would happily marry her.

"Mount Sinai Hospital," Ryan said. "I know a doctor there who does abortions."

From the couch, she said, "I don't want to."

Beyond flicking a glance in her direction, Ryan didn't respond to the objection. "I'll get someone to take her there in the morning," he said to her father.

"I'm not going," said Patrice, clutching a pillow against her tummy.

"Yes, you are," shouted Pa.

Senator Temple was in the chair at the small dining table, rubbing his chin with a finger.

"She will," Ryan assured Patrice's father. "Even if I have to drag her there myself."

Bravely, Patrice said, "I'll tell the doctor I don't want an abortion."

Ryan wheeled around. "You don't want to?" he bit out. "Do you realize how much money is riding on this?"

"I don't care," said Patrice, beyond giving any thought to how there could be money riding on her pregnancy. "I'm not letting anyone kill my baby."

Nostrils flaring, Ryan promised, "You're going to. And you're going to marry Peter Kingsley."

"I will not," Patrice said doggedly. "He doesn't want to marry me, and I don't want to marry him."

Right arm flung up, Ryan took a step toward the couch. Patrice's heart flew to her mouth. Whimpering in shock and fear, she scooted back.

"Ryan," bellowed Temple. In two bounds, he was between them. "Let me talk to her." He sat and took one of her hands in his. "Patrice, my dear. How do you think you're going to take care of this baby? A single woman—"

"I won't be single for long," she said. "The baby's father will marry me."

Temple huffed out a sigh. Then, a look of puzzlement came over his face. "Who *is* the baby's father?"

A day later

The staff at the shipping company's New York office refused to give Patrice the phone number, but Senator Temple obtained it. He even allowed her to make the call from his office in New Jersey. Unfortunately, Patrice was still forced to contend with the secretary at the other end. It took three attempts and an intervention by the senator to get Apollo on the phone. She was left alone in Temple's office, sitting in his chair with the phone clutched to her ear. Papers were piled high on the desk. A few feet from her was the closed door. The senator would be right outside, waiting to learn the outcome of the conversation.

"Listen to your brother," said Apollo, without even letting Patrice complete her tale of woes. "They're willing to pay for the abortion, aren't they? And marry Kingsley. Your brother will get his business alliance, and you'll be rich. If you want, we could still meet."

"Apollo," Patrice shrieked into the phone. "This is no time for jokes. We need to get married fast."

"Don't be stupid," he said. "I can't marry you. I already have a fiancée."

There was a buzzing sound in Patrice's brain. A tremulousness to her limbs. "Please... Apollo," she begged. "Don't tease me like this."

With an irritated sigh, he said, "I am not teasing. If you don't want an abortion, give the child away. I don't care."

A sob erupted from her mouth. There was a muttered exclamation from the other end. The high-pitched tone that followed told Patrice he'd hung up.

She didn't know how long she stayed in the chair, phone in her hand. When the door squeaked open, letting Temple in, she stared at him without saying a word. He took the receiver from her numb fingers and set it back on the cradle. He didn't ask any questions. Didn't even speak. The politician simply sat in the other chair, a silent presence waiting at the periphery of her misery.

After a while, she whispered, "You knew what he was going to say, didn't you?"

"I had some idea," Temple admitted. "I've seen enough of his kind."

Tears trickling down her cheeks, Patrice went over the past few months. Her unexpected meeting with Apollo at the Kingsley party, the impromptu dance amid the artwork, the interruption by Peter Kingsley, Apollo later claiming Peter was a mongrel. If the Sun God thought the American aristocrat a mongrel, what did he think of Patrice? With her knuckles, she wiped the wetness from her cheeks. "I've been such a fool."

About everything, not just Apollo. With him, she at least walked into her own downfall. Ryan and his family had strung her along for years, using her longing for love. She hadn't known it until now, but they'd promised her father a cartload of money so he would let them adopt her. She'd be given a few shares in the family business, but the stock would always be controlled by Ryan and his legal agents. When she married a Kingsley, they'd have a business alliance under the guise of marriage.

All the love, all the warmth... it had been a lie. A colossal lie, erected to gain her trust and compliance. Patrice had no one. Not her father, not Ryan, not Apollo. The moment she refused to toe the line, she turned from "little sister" to "stupid bitch."

"No more foolishness," she said, tone hard. "But I'm not getting an abortion." The baby was a part of her. Even if no one else gave a damn about what happened to Patrice, her baby would. And she'd protect it from the cruel and unfeeling world. Somehow.

"I have a suggestion," said Temple.

#

Back in April 1994

Sing Sing Correctional Facility

Ossining, New York

At the door to the prison visiting room, the guards continued to chat. They were too far to overhear what was being said, as were the secret service officers. The people seated around the single occupied table were buried in dark memories. Except for

Temple. He was staring hard at a Rubik's Cube, working on getting the squares into place.

Harry wasn't terribly shocked by Patrice's tale. He already knew what his family did to Lilah, how they refused to even acknowledge her existence, let alone show gratitude for her assistance. What Lilah didn't have to deal with was a pregnancy. She didn't know it at the time, but the brutal assault on her in Libya when she was sixteen ended her chances at motherhood.

What would've happened if the attack resulted in a child, instead? The *Roe v. Wade* decision legalizing abortion in the U.S. was announced earlier the same year, but would Lilah have agreed to terminate a pregnancy? If she didn't, the Barronses would not have continued to support her.

I *would have*. Whatever her choice, Harry knew he would've stood by her. The baby would've been as much his as hers. If she decided to end the pregnancy, he'd have held her hand through it.

Patrice had no one to turn to for help. In the 'forties, single mothers didn't fare well. The only other suggestion the then-senator could've made was adoption.

#

Forty-five years ago, December 1949

The Sacred Heart Home for Unwed Mothers

New Orleans, Louisiana

Patrice whimpered. Her breasts were painfully tight, milk gluing the cotton fabric to her nipple.

"Feed him," ordered the nurse, placing the baby boy in Patrice's arms.

She sat in the rocking chair, singing "Hush, Little Baby" while the infant latched on. Three weeks since she'd gone into premature labor—that was all the time she'd be allowed with him. This would be the last time she held his warmth against her heart, the last time he would feel her fingers stroke the blond fuzz on his head.

Her vision blurred. Batting back tears, Patrice told herself she was doing the right thing. She'd given him life, but there was little else she could offer her boy. If she chose to keep him, all he would see were poverty and misery. All he would hear were taunts. This was the best option for both of them.

Fifteen minutes later, she carried him in her arms all the way to where the home's backyard ended at the Mississippi River. The nurse accompanied her, hauling the empty basket. A boat waited, drifting gently on the water. On the deck stood Senator Temple and another man. As soon as they saw the women and the child, they jumped to the bank and strode forward, the second man beating the senator by a few seconds.

The stranger was a slender individual of average height, his thinning blond hair combed over his scalp. His gray eyes were kindly. "Miss Patrice," he said. "My name's Armor."

She'd promised herself there would be no more tears, but there were. She cried when the nurse took her son from her arms and handed him to the man. She cried when the baby whimpered, opening his blue eyes in puzzled protest at being torn from the familiar warmth. She sobbed out loud when the baby was placed in the basket.

"Was he christened?" Armor asked, tone gruff.

The nurse spoke, "Adoptive parents like to pick their own names, so no."

"Do you have a name you like, Miss?" asked Armor.

Between her sobs, Patrice whispered, "Richard." The Lionheart. He would need to be one to survive in this cruel world.

"Richard's what the missus and I will call him," Armor promised. "So he'll always have something from the woman who birthed him."

Temple interjected, "He's going to have something from the man responsible, too. I contacted his father's family in Athens. They've put some money into a trust for him. With a non-disclosure clause attached, obviously. And neither Patrice nor the child can ever claim any part of the family property."

As if she'd ever want to.

"There's also a chunk of cash set aside for you, my dear," said the senator.

As though she'd ever touch a penny of it. "Keep it all for the baby," she said. "He has a right to it."

#

Back in April 1994

Sing Sing Correctional Facility

Ossining, New York

Harry pinched the base of his nose with a thumb and forefinger, trying to sort his turbulent thoughts. "Major Armor," he muttered. "He's your son." The corrupt prosecutor who'd threatened to drag Lilah naked to the courtroom, the criminal who arranged every attack on her, was Alex's half-brother. According to news reports, a contractor associated with Armor Drilling Co. was even under investigation for the trafficking of minors.

Patrice nodded, the blue-lined hand on the table trembling.

"How did you end up married to Peter Kingsley?"

#

Forty-four years ago, July 1950

Upper East Side, New York City

Patrice stood at the arched doorway, her eyes darting around the grand dining room. The polished wood floor gleamed under the discreet lighting. The red velvet upholstery on the chairs, matching drapery at the large windows, the crystal fruit dish in the center of the table... all spoke of money. Peter Kingsley might not have a title, but he was royalty just the same.

She wasn't here to admire the luxury, though. The house's architecture being what it was, she'd have a good view of the garage from multiple windows, but this one was closest.

The garage had an apartment over it for the chauffeur and his wife. Behind the structure was a small yard. Amid the potted plants stood a short, plump woman, enjoying the sun with a baby on her shoulder. If Patrice married Peter Kingsley, she'd get to see her child every day. She'd watch him grow into manhood.

"Is it him?" asked a voice from behind Patrice. When she turned, her eyes landed squarely on a button in the middle of a vast chest. Peter's curly, brown hair and blue eyes belonged on a pedigreed kitty-cat, but he possessed a lumberjack's build. "Of course it's him," Peter muttered. "What a stupid question to ask." Pushing his glasses up his nose, he joined her at the window.

"We promised each other honesty," Patrice said. "You know my reason. What's yours?"

Almost tonelessly, Peter recited, "Grandfather gave me two options. I can marry Maddie and lose my position in the business, or I can marry you and eventually become CEO."

When he didn't elaborate, Patrice said, "The whole truth, Peter. I don't believe you're that mercenary."

With a reluctant sigh, he added, "I could never return home. I could never contact either of my brothers. And Maddie... she was told her brother would lose his job. The Kingsleys would make sure he never found work again. She and I mutually decided it would be best if we—"

#

Back in June 1994

Sing Sing Correctional Facility

Ossining, New York

"Threats?" Harry asked incredulously.

"The times were different," Aaron Kingsley tried to explain. "All three of us—David, Peter, and I—were expected to do what was good for the family. Our father got the last say on what was good and what was not." He was referring to Godwin as the father, not the alcoholic who sired the three men.

"The family's what's important to Godwin," Noah said. "The Kingsleys as a whole... not necessarily the individuals."

Aaron nodded. "Don't get me wrong... I love my father. You haven't seen the side of him that I... he didn't owe me anything, not even love, but he made sure I knew I had it. I also heard what he said to Peter back then. I was in Cuba with everyone else when Brad and his brothers got arrested. I saw what happened. I still don't understand how Father could do what he did, but I saw it with my own eyes."

"Godwin was promising to rip away everything Peter ever knew," Noah added. "He might have risked it, but Miss Wheeler couldn't ask her brother and family to starve for her sake. Godwin would've made sure they suffered for her disobedience. The Kingsleys were more powerful back in the 'forties than they are now."

Loud laughter came from somewhere in the distance, startling Harry. The prison guards called out a crass joke to their comrade who was doing the laughing, then returned to chatting among themselves.

Harry shook his head. It was hard to believe it was still the same day. The room was still bright. Patrice was still across the table from Harry. Next to Noah, Temple still worked on his Rubik's Cube.

"I never even realized Godwin knew about Richard until Noah told me," Patrice mumbled. "I thought other than my father and Ryan, only Mr. Temple knew." Apollo, too, obviously. And Peter Kingsley.

Harry raised a questioning eyebrow at Aaron Kingsley.

"I heard Patrice's side of things only last week," admitted Aaron. "She told me. She... ahh... felt in need of some support during this visit. Right before Mr. Temple got shot, he'd asked me to keep him updated on any developments. Harry, I'm not sure if you'll believe me, but I would've done whatever I could to help Mr. Temple bring Brad back home. What happened to the five of them... it wasn't good. Short of causing harm to my father, I would've helped you and Noah and Mr. Temple. Well... I work for

Kingsley Corp, but the network... Steven's plans... I'm not in the loop. Patrice's story is pretty much the only development I've been privy to. Damn hard to believe at first, but it does explain many things I didn't quite understand at the time. Peter... what he did to Helios..."

According to both Aaron and Patrice, Peter had been a brilliant executive, ruthlessness giving him an edge. After the wedding and his installation as the main Kingsley heir, Peter went after Helios Shipping Corporation with a vengeance and advised all of Kingsley Corp's associates they could not expect to do business with him *and* the shipping company. Word spread. Wild rumors circulated about the incompetence of the Greek businessmen, about irregularities in their books. When news of the bankruptcy filing reached the couple in the third year of their marriage, they toasted it with the finest champagne. The next week, Apollo died in a car crash. Patrice examined her heart for regrets but found only satisfaction. A few months later, her father passed.

After a second or two, Harry asked, "Did Peter ever offer to adopt Richard?"

With a sad smile, Patrice said, "Peter was a nice man, but he was very much a man of his times. He didn't offer, and I have to say it didn't even occur to me to ask. The Armors had already adopted Richard. Mr. Armor knew I was the boy's biological mother, but Mrs. Armor didn't. She still doesn't. They worked for Godwin Kingsley. If I tried to take the baby back, their lives would've been turned upside down. Richard's, too."

"But the man of his times eventually left his wife and children," Harry pointed out. "He would've known what it would be like for you and your sons."

"The heart wants what it wants," Patrice said. "Maddie left New York before Peter and I got married. She went to college and returned with a business degree. I was pregnant with Alex at the time. She later told me she didn't know what prompted her to attend a Kingsley event with her brother... some desire to twist the knife in herself, I guess. We all have those moments. Anyway, Peter and Maddie met again. This time, they didn't care what happened to anyone else."

For the sake of her children and the life she'd built for herself, Patrice tried her best to hold things together, going to the extent of naming her youngest son after his father. Alex had been christened Alexander Peter Kingsley. She went to Godwin for support only to be told wealthy men always kept mistresses. Finally, after a few years of seeing the couple together, she stopped wanting to fight it. Peter was happy with Maddie in a way he'd never be with his wife.

On his part, Peter not only stopped caring about his marriage, he no longer gave a damn about the business alliance between the two families. Still, he did one last favor for the woman who continued to wear his ring. He couldn't go after the Sheppards the way he did with Apollo's family because of what Temple might have said. But Ryan Sheppard was no great executive to begin with, and Kingsley Corp's refusal to help at crucial junctures was enough to bring Genesis—the Sheppards' old company—to its knees. Around the time Alex was two, Peter and Patrice celebrated the prospect of Genesis filing for bankruptcy.

Unknown to them, Ryan had approached a distant cousin for help—the former U.S. Ambassador to India who'd just returned home to Brooklyn with a heavily pregnant wife. The men hit it off. And why not? Ryan Sheppard was quite capable of putting up the façade of being a perfect gentleman. Ambassador Nicholas Sheppard invested money in the sinking company.

Ryan and Sophia Sheppard's first-born was six at the time, and she'd just delivered their second son, Harry. Financial situation being precarious, the couple left Harry in the care of Nicholas and his Indian wife, Yashoda, before returning to the oil fields. When Ambassador Sheppard was appointed Special Envoy to the Middle East, Harry moved with the couple and their newborn twins to Tel Aviv.

Two years later, Peter Kingsley abandoned his family, and Patrice and her sons walked out of the Kingsley home. While the lives of four-year-old Alex and his brothers were collapsing around them, Harry was living with his foster family, secure in the warmth of their love. He'd have been eight and long reunited with his own parents in Tripoli when Peter died, and Patrice returned to the Kingsley mansion.

By then, a strange understanding had developed between the three people—Peter, Patrice, and Maddie. On his deathbed, Peter asked his wife to keep an eye on his mistress and their twin sons, and Patrice unhesitatingly agreed. Maddie soon passed as well. Patrice didn't dare tell her own sons the whole story, but she never let them disrespect their father in her hearing. On her insistence, they'd even name their business empire after the man.

When Patrice and her boys returned to the Kingsley mansion, young Richard was already Steven Kingsley's best friend and quite literally, his partner in crime.

If Peter Kingsley had thought slightly differently, if he took the trouble to imagine what life would be like for the boy growing up as a servant of the Kingsleys, destiny would've taken a different course. Not only for Richard, but for Brad, Victor, Alex, Neil, and

Scott. Perhaps even for Lilah and Harry. But the future of his wife's illegitimate child wasn't important to Peter Kingsley. Nor were his own sons with Patrice even until the moment of his death.

As for Patrice, her fury at the Sheppards continued to the point she ignored the pleas for help when they were arrested by Gaddafi's goons. Angry at her callousness and grateful for Steven's offer of his grandfather's assistance, Hector Sheppard directed his loyalties toward people who'd eventually become Harry's enemies. And Lilah's. It didn't matter to Hector that *Lilah* had helped and paid dearly for it, that she sacrificed her dreams to save the Sheppards' livelihood for them.

"What a mess," Harry muttered. "I assume the major is not aware of all this?"

"No," Noah interrupted. "Richard's too involved with Steven. Even if we tell him, he can't get out now, or Godwin will put all the blame on him. The Kingsleys will again get away scot-free. It's why I didn't insist on Patrice talking to you about this before."

Harry threw a glance at Noah. The old lawyer was too sharp not to know that far from wanting to get out, Armor was likely to use the information to his advantage. The sex-trafficking investigation involving his drilling company... the major might not have had an active hand in the actual crime, but he would have to be blind, deaf, and dumb not to realize something was up with the contractor. The company would've gone under a long time ago if Major Armor were so clueless.

If Armor were not above purposefully using the innocent to further his own selfish interests, he wouldn't be above using men he'd grown up hating even if they turned out to be his flesh and blood.

"Noah advised me to tell you everything," said Patrice. "Before you blame Richard for whatever happened, please remember he's my son."

Harry sat up. "What about your other children—Alex and Victor and Brad? Your grandchildren?"

Voice wet with tears, Patrice accused, "You want me to pick between them and Richard. I can't! I know what it looks like... that I don't care enough about my sons with Peter. It's not true. I'd die for any of my boys. But Brad, Victor, and Alex grew up as Kingsleys. They got advantages that Richard didn't. Even now, they have you and Andersen and Mr. Temple to help. Who does Richard have? A criminal like Steven? I can't stand by and... Harry, your father wanted me to abort Richard, and you want to send him to prison. Will Luce's murder... Governor Pataki has brought back the death penalty. What if Richard gets hanged?"

Emotional blackmail, said Harry's mind. *A woman wronged,* whispered his conscience. One who was treated shamefully by the Sheppards.

"Don't do anything to hurt my son," Patrice begged. "Save my children... all of them."

Chapter 35

A few weeks later, May 1994

(4 ½ years after Harry's arrest and 5 ½ after the exile began)

Sing Sing Correctional Facility

Ossining, New York

Residents of the Box were not usually allowed to attend services at the prison chapel, but Harry showed up with the warden's special permission. There was a bigger crowd than he expected for Memorial Day worship. The tan brick building didn't have any of the grand paintings or statues normally associated with churches, but there were the gentle souls from the external world volunteering at the service and the priest leading the mass. Amid the sea of grim faces on the wooden benches, these outsiders were pinpricks of light and hope. Harry needed to see them today.

He needed reconciliation for what he was about to do... with the universe and with the people who were relying on him to bring about closure for the wrongs they suffered. Four weeks of discarding idea after idea, and a thought had occurred. Except it would take considerable time and effort to put into action, which meant deferred justice for the Luce siblings and delayed return of the exiles. There would also be considerable uncertainty in any strategy which relied on the opponent's reactions.

A shuffling sound in the aisle caught Harry's attention. When he looked up, Regina Berra was standing there, gesturing at him to move over. "Fraternizing with prisoners?" Harry teased, picking up the hymn book as the officer slipped into place next to him. "More protocol breaches... what would the warden say?"

"There *is* a higher power," she mumbled. "I've squared it with him."

Harry glanced at her in surprise. "You're religious?"

"Huh?" She frowned. "I meant the commissioner of the New York State Department of Corrections."

"Oh, for the love of—"

"You sent a message you want to talk to me."

"So you tracked me down *here?*" Harry shook his head in mock-exasperation. "Why don't you sit through the mass? Might be good for your soul."

At her pithy curse, Harry chuckled and turned his attention to the booklet in his hands. Regina apparently decided to take his advice and participated in the proceedings with gusto, but he hardly heard anything.

In seven more months—toward the end of December—Harry would've completed his five years as New York State's guest. He would be eligible to apply for conditional release. The plans he put in place for Major Richard Armor... the computer virus designed by Sabrina... all the preparations done by Shawn and Liam... Armor's bank transactions would've shown he did connect with James McCoy. The major was the only one whose alibi for the time of the murder was weak enough for him to be caught in Harry's trap. Even if Armor's loyalty ran deep enough not to implicate Steven Kingsley as well, questions would be raised about Harry's guilt and right when he was out on parole. He would be free to move about while the defense lawyer approached the courts with the new information. There would be no need to wait for the appeals process to wind through the legal system before Harry requested personal meetings with certain lawmakers.

He would once again be in a position to use the information obtained through Lupe's angels. The politicians wouldn't be able to ignore the former SEAL, one who was wrongly convicted of murder. With Harry free, they wouldn't get the time or the opportunity to find ways around the threat he posed. Which was why it was critical to wait until parole was approved before the operation commenced. The representatives of the people would see the wisdom in supporting a pardon for Brad Kingsley, especially with Steven and Richard's roles in the whole saga becoming suspect.

Of course Armor would've made plans in case Harry managed to stay alive until getting parole. But the suggestion of the Kingsleys' guilt in the Luce murder would have been enough to make sure neither they nor Armor tried more tricks with Harry while the investigation was going on. It would also be enough grounds to take the Peter Kingsley Network's board to court, demanding Steven's ouster from his current position as chairman and CEO and the restoration of the chairman title to Harry. Lilah would've returned, her plan to dismantle the network back on track. Liam and Verity would've found some semblance of justice for the loss they suffered. Lupe's soul would've found peace. But now...

Harry glanced at the Eiffel Tower pendant dangling from the silver chain wrapped around his wrist. *Don't kill me, habibti,* he muttered in his mind. *It's for Patrice. I've got to do it for her. You'd agree if you knew.*

If destiny didn't decree Lilah would remain childless, her story would've been the same as Patrice's. No, not quite true. They were different women, who would've made different choices. Even if Harry weren't around to help Lilah, she would not have been powerless.

Still, young Patrice was coerced into helping build the first alliance against Sanders. No one intended to put her in harm's way, but she was harmed, nevertheless. Richard Armor was no longer the innocent infant who was yet another victim of what was meant to be a righteous war, but ignoring his mother's plea was not possible when she never volunteered to sacrifice herself in the first place. The deepest regrets in Harry's life all came about from his ignorance of the true meaning of sacrifice. If he repeated the mistakes, the war declared anew by Lilah would become amoral.

At the end of the service, the inmates in the little chapel rose. Under the cover of their mostly tuneless singing, Harry whispered to Regina, "Don't forget... I need a few minutes to discuss something."

"I gotta see someone about a schedule change," she said. "You go ahead to the Box, and we'll talk there."

The prisoners weren't allowed to dally at all before returning to the cells. When Harry walked into the Box, two of the officers were waiting to speak to him about the planned poker game. The girlfriend of one had insisted on him joining her family for dinner, so the game would need to be rescheduled.

"I'm not going anywhere," Harry promised, drawing groans from the officers.

On entering his cell, he found the sax exactly where he'd placed it on the mattress. Next to the instrument was something that hadn't been there when he left for church. A book he requested from the prison library—the Indian epic, *Mahabharata*. At the clang of the door closing, he looked up to see Officer Berra again, standing in the faint light. Tone gruff, she stated, "It's not from the library. The lawyer fellow sent it... Andersen. What's it about?"

"Dharmayuddha," said Harry.

"Heh?"

"Just war," he translated.

She eyed the pile of tomes on the small desk—one of the special privileges afforded Harry thanks to the Berras and the other staff at Sing Sing. He'd taken full advantage of the concessions and requested every title he could think of from the library... paperbacks to poetry to religion and philosophy. Unlike the library books, Noah's gifts stayed in the cell. The *Mahabharata* would now be added to the collection of Vedic texts and the Bible and Jewish works as well as Greek and Chinese philosophy. Noah also made arrangements for newspapers from around the world to be delivered weekly. There were textbooks and research papers on the oil trade, along with a few dossiers full of print clippings Harry considered important. On top of the pile of folders was a crystal paperweight with a peacock feather embedded in it. The plume had been a childhood gift from Lilah. Sabrina's son once spotted it in Harry's old office in Gateway, and she got the weight made. The light from the hallway outside the cell spilled through the crystal, casting an elongated shadow of the feather on the wall.

"What kind of stuff *do* you read?" Regina Berra shook her head. "You're a weirdo, Sheppard."

"True," he acknowledged. "You might relate to this book. There's plenty about doing your duty without looking left or right. Duty without desire... for reward, I mean."

She preened, then frowned. "You said you wanted to talk to me. Whatever it is, I'm probably going to get into trouble, or you wouldn't be buttering me up."

Harry held up a hand. "Only reminding myself there's work to finish. And I can't do it until I find a way out of here."

"Don't pull any dumb tricks," the officer warned. "You don't want to be here for real reasons. The warden's been talking to his friends in Brooklyn. Until they finish—"

"I know he's trying to help."

No, the Berras wouldn't be told about Harry's plan, but he let them pursue the legal route. If they managed to find some way... some proof inadvertently left behind by the real perpetrator...

Warden Berra possessed enough insider contacts to force a thorough review of available evidence, but there didn't seem to be much material to analyze. The apartment where Luce was found was not new, but only two sets of fingerprints were discovered—Harry's and the deceased's. The prosecution argued it was because the place was cleaned the day prior to the victim renting it. Still, there should've been something. Except for a pizza box and a dirty paper napkin, there was nothing. No fingerprints on the box, either. Arthur Berra was talking to higher-ups about DNA evidence also, but there wasn't much hope of finding any after all these years.

Despite it, Liam and Harry were convinced James McCoy was the one who stuck the knife into Luce, Sr.'s back. The timing of McCoy's post-conviction bail was too damned convenient to be ignored. He was Will Luce's accomplice in the embezzlement, and Harry had a major role in exposing the crime. McCoy possessed more than enough motive to want to see Harry jailed. So did the Kingsleys. Then, the criminal got permanently out of prison with some fancy legal maneuvering.

A connection surely existed between McCoy and the Kingsleys, facilitated by the lawyer in the group—Richard Armor. There was also Rickie Brennan, the mechanic who stayed in a Las Vegas hotel while Harry was being framed for Will Luce's murder in Brooklyn. Brennan picked the same hotel as McCoy for the same days, and McCoy wasn't seen on the surveillance tapes. Brennan was also the only remaining guest in the same time frame

Liam hadn't been able to track down, the time during which Armor supposedly stayed home all alone because of a bad cold.

The same name popped up on the visitor's list at Rikers where McCoy had been kept. Warden Berra brought the info to Harry, acknowledging again that it wouldn't be enough evidence to even have McCoy interrogated. Brennan had claimed to be a friend of McCoy's, so why wouldn't both men visit Vegas together? And why would McCoy have to know where Brennan was at the moment? There could've been a falling out... drifting apart... any damned excuse for Brennan being impossible to find. Any reason other than Rickie Brennan being the same man as Richard Armor.

Oh, yeah. McCoy's might have been the hand wielding the knife, but Steven Kingsley's best buddy masterminded the killing. Major Richard Armor committed cold-blooded murder and walked away, making sure Harry took the blame.

But knowing something and proving it were two different matters. The last five years of many people's lives had been spent planning for the moment the world saw Armor implicated in the same crime he trapped Harry in. Now... after what Patrice said...

"What I need is a new opening," said Harry. "A chance to take the fight to the enemy without..." Without inflicting more hurt on a woman who'd already suffered enough.

Harry spent the last five years studying the Kingsleys and their supporters. Godwin, Steven, Richard, Charles, Potts, Potts, Sr. As the alliance once did with Sanders, Harry would use the enemy's own nature against them, but any scheme which depended on the opponent's responses carried a significant risk of failure. A card played a little too soon could potentially lead to disaster.

He grinned at Officer Berra. "Before you start again, my request to talk wasn't about the Kingsleys. Not exactly."

"So what *did* you want?" the officer asked. "Spit it out, Sheppard. I don't have the time. The sisters are waiting for me to return home." Warden Berra—the big bear of a man—had somehow convinced three supermodels—all of them black—to marry him, producing five daughters in total. The warden ditched the wives as soon as they crossed the magical age of thirty-five, but he kept his progeny. Regina—his first-born—had once said the warden was a lousy husband but a great father. Unfortunately, his ex-wives weren't willing to tolerate his company even for the sake of the girls. Regina ended up as the mother-figure to her siblings.

Setting the book aside, Harry went to the bars. "Your father's looking into DNA testing."

"Yeah?"

"I... uhh... would like to give it as much publicity as possible. You think the cops might agree to put out a press release? And..." Harry hesitated.

"And?" prompted the officer.

"I need some info from the FBI. My former sources in the agency are not likely to be as open with me as before. I'm hoping you can persuade them to share a few details about an ongoing investigation... a case involving sex trafficking of immigrant women and children in Corpus Christi, Texas. Noah got me whatever is available officially, but I need more. There are always details the cops don't bother to record... their impressions of the various players... what incentives might make the victims talk... so on and so forth."

"Corpus Christi?" Regina frowned. "I've never been there, but it shouldn't be too difficult to find someone in their corrections department who can connect me with local agents."

"Thank you," said Harry. "One last thing. Could you call my friend Liam? I need to talk to him face to face. I... uhh... need to let him and a few other people know I won't be applying for parole."

Part XIV

Chapter 36

Four months later, September 1994

(nearly 5 years after Harry's arrest and 6 after the exile began)

World Trade Center, New York City

"No way," Steven said to Richard, glancing back from the ringside chair toward where his heavily pregnant wife was chatting excitedly with one of the instructors. Steven made it a point to train at least two days a week, and his wife picked him up after the sessions. Shouted directions from coaches, grunts and roars from the boxers, the healthy sweat of a good workout... this was where he found peace. Hector Sheppard's gym was also where Steven met the professional wrestler whom he would marry, and she now wanted to invite the staff to the baby's christening.

The entire family was excited about the impending arrival of the newest Kingsley. In the current generation, only Alex and Victor had children. Now, Steven would also have a son... or a daughter. He quite liked the thought of it.

Richard's personal life was also headed toward domestic bliss... sort of. Mrs. Armor—Richard's mother—had dragged him along to meet some history teacher. *"Nice enough,"* he said when Steven asked about it later. Richard expected to propose to the lady at some point soon. His parents wanted to see him married, and he'd do anything to keep them happy.

Inviting danger into their midst right when Richard found a woman he was comfortable with... right when Steven was about to be a dad... not the best idea.

"Friend," Steven called, stripping off his gloves before grabbing a towel from the rack next to the chair. Richard was also in workout clothes, but he didn't care much for boxing. Wiping the sweat from face and neck, Steven took a quick look around. There was no one close enough to overhear. "Don't jump into anything stupid just because you're pissed about what happened with Harry."

Keeping his tone low, Richard cursed. "Don't worry about me being pissed, Steven. Worry about your grandfather."

Godwin's mood had remained foul since the night of Harry's escape from the latest trap. A prison riot... how the hell did he manage to... sheer bad luck for the Kingsleys that Officer Berra showed up. There was only one remaining option.

In three months, Harry would again be out on the streets. The Kingsleys didn't have any standing to raise objections to a parole, but even if they did, no one would say a word. Given how the public simply didn't have attention span enough for the press to bother with five-year-old news, Harry would get the breathing room he didn't have before. Also, whatever media coverage there was this time would be positive.

"The medal—" Richard stopped to curse again. New York State Corrections Department had put out a press statement about the extraordinary step they took of nominating one of the inmates of Sing Sing for a Medal of Freedom. It would be Harry Sheppard's second award for exceptional bravery—as a civilian, this time.

There were the rumors about DNA testing. Damn McCoy and his pizza. At least nothing had popped up thus far, and the criminal insisted to "Brennan" he'd been careful not to leave any evidence.

Still, a two-time hero... the info Harry might have in hand from his time as the strip club owner's lover... the pardon could happen. And God only knew what he planned to do to the Kingsleys to clear Brad's path back to the throne of the oil empire.

But Harry would also need to make sure the authorities didn't look too closely into his activities. Richard and Steven had come up with a new plan. According to gossip, the second Sheppard son forfeited many things for his family, including a college education. He would make one last sacrifice for them. This time, it would be in full view of the media and the cops. He would be marched back to Sing Sing in handcuffs in a matter of weeks.

Except...

"I don't get what he's doing," Steven griped. He inclined his head toward the inner door where the owner of the gym—Hector Sheppard—stood talking to the manager. Hector opened the gym before his parents set up Gateway, and he now ran both places. The New York office of the Sheppard family business was located on the floor above. The offices of Barrons O & G and the Peter Kingsley Company were also in the South Tower. Steven had left Brad's staff in their old place, managing them and the original family business from the Kingsley Corp digs on Corporate Row. Godwin had been quite certain he didn't want the Kingsleys to follow other businessmen to the World Trade Center, so they didn't. "Hector was saying his parents are upset. I mean... the father had a heart attack. Harry calls home every chance he gets to check on the old man. Clearly, he hasn't given up on the family. So why the hell isn't he asking to visit at least for a couple of days?"

Richard snorted. "Trust me... he's got some other trick in mind. Before he manages to pull it off, we need to get our act together. Steven, we need a way out of this mess. The prison's like Sheppard's personal cave now. The warden's daughter has made sure no one can get to her pet inmate. Any *accident* we try to arrange for Arthur Berra or his brat will have the corrections department and the cops in an uproar. The Berras have deep roots in law enforcement."

"We can't risk it," agreed Steven.

A shout went up from the ring, and there was a smattering of applause. Clapping along, Steven craned his neck to check what happened, but there were a few people obstructing his view.

"But..." continued Richard, also clapping a couple of times. He nodded at an instructor walking briskly by. "If we manage to find Mrs. Kingsley and the rest of the group, Sheppard will come out on his own. We'll revert to our original plan. Your cousins and Mrs. Kingsley first, followed by Sheppard when he tries to retaliate... which is where Prince can help."

"Which is where I again tell you we shouldn't trust Prince," said Steven. "Not after what happened last time." The three of them—Steven and Charles and Richard—went to Thailand to meet the drug lord, but Prince arranged a little kidnapping. Who knew what he wanted from Brad and his brothers in exchange for Steven and Charles? Didn't matter. The exiles would've had no choice but to rescue the hated cousins if they didn't want to be suspected of being complicit in the abduction. Not knowing the truth, the media painted it as a wild bachelor party, and Steven was forced to grovel for a good couple of months before his then-fiancée agreed to take him back.

"One mistake is usually enough to teach me my lesson," said Richard. "But the offer presents possibilities... we can't ignore them. We're at a dead end where Sheppard's concerned. Phillip contracted the Russian mafia back when Sheppard was first arrested... before his trial even happened. It's been five years, and we have nothing to show for it. Prince has deeper connections all over Asia. We'd be fools to refuse."

"How did he reach you?" Steven asked.

"The Russians were asking questions on his turf. He tracked it back to Phillip." The CID officer's cover was he did it to make up for his father's failure to get the treasonous exiles. "Prince is a shrewd guy," Richard mused. "We'd already contacted him once about finding your cousins, and he knows Phillip's connected to us. There was a message at the CID HQ... Prince didn't beat around the bush. He told Phillip he wants to talk to me and you about teaming up."

"Which is what *we* wanted when we went to him," Steven groused. "How do we avoid getting tricked again?"

"For one, there will be no in-person involvement, especially not from you. For another, we have our own men on the ground this time."

"The Russians," muttered Steven.

"Right." Richard nodded. "Asia might be Prince's turf, but he won't be fool enough to double cross the Russians and start a mafia war when many of the governments are also keeping an eye out for him."

"True," said Steven. "But what does he want from us in return for his help?"

"Our cash and manpower with his connections... it could work. My bet is he does want revenge this time around. Alex and Victor whupped Prince's ass bad a couple of times. Men like him can't afford to fail more than once or twice... word gets around... rivals start thinking he's losing his touch... coup attempts and so on. He hasn't found Brad and the rest, or he wouldn't be talking to us. What he's trying to do is make sure we let him have at your cousins if we get to them first."

"And if he gets to them first?"

Richard shrugged. "Do we care as long as they end up dead? In either case, Prince is ready, willing, and able to take the blame." When Steven remained silent, Richard added, "If we don't do something now, we could lose."

"I get it." Steven glanced toward his wife again. She was making her way across to the inner door to talk to Hector, her hands linked over her pregnant belly. "How the hell do I take a chance right when—"

"Hire extra security for your wife and your parents," said Richard. "What we can't do is waste more time where your cousins are concerned."

"It's not only about me," Steven said. "You can't afford trouble at the moment, either."

"What do you mean?"

"The history teacher? Also, the FBI case? The illegal immigrants?"

"The... er... teacher..." Richard shrugged. "She'll be okay. I'm not rich enough for Prince to notice my family or... uhh... my friends. As for the case... it's going nowhere. There's no proof against me. Besides, I have plans. If there's anything I learned from my experience with the network, it's how public perception works. Trust me... I'm going to make it work for me on the immigrant issue. In fact, we need to lay PR groundwork for the possibility of your cousins' return. I have a few ideas."

"But you still don't want to be linked to the likes of Prince right when the feds are looking into your business," argued Steven.

"Which is why we won't deal with him personally," Richard said. Eyes softening, he added, "I thank you for the concern, but you really don't need to be. The contractor who hired the immigrants will pay for his own stupidity, not me."

Chapter 37

Six months later, March 1995

Goa, India

The room right next to the gym where guests took dance lessons stood empty of its students. If Tara were to look through the row of windows on the left, she would see tourists on the beach. They were celebrating Shigmo, the festival of colors that Indians outside Goa called Holi. Yellow, green, purple, red... smoke of many hues swirled in the air as the crowds sang and danced to Bollywood music. A group of paint-soaked men tossed a laughing young woman in the air as though she were bouncing on a trampoline. Except for the flying powder and paint sprays and smoke canisters, the scene on the sands was exactly the same as any other afternoon.

How? Tara wondered, thoughts foggy. How could everything possibly look the same when one of the two people she loved the most in the world—her mother—passed one week ago?

The gleaming mosaic on the cool floor beneath Tara's feet didn't change at all in the seven days since Mama's cremation. Nor did the tape player on the table. The narrow chairs lined along the right wall were also the same, one of which was occupied by Maestro, clad in the usual printed saffron tunic and sarong, long hair tied back with a leather band. The same garland of *rudraksha* beads hung around his neck.

Yet everything *was* different. There was no need for Tara to whine about her lessons. There was no Mama to push and prod Tara into practicing. Instead, Krishna was in the room, standing next to the table with the cassette player. So was Dev, one of the other members of the group.

A foot on a chair, Tara strapped the *ghungru* around her ankle. The dance bells were handcrafted by the local jewelry shop and cost a pretty penny. Mama had proclaimed her baby was worth it.

"You don't have to do this," said Maestro.

"Yes, I do," Tara said, tone stony as she set her foot back on the floor. "I always practice *mohiniyattam* on Saturdays." The dance of the enchantress. *Mama,* she whimpered in her mind. Tara would dance... act... do more ads... *any*thing to bring her mother back. The old agency still called the resort now and then, offering work to the child model despite Tara proclaiming the two she already did were enough, thank you very much.

"Let her do what she wants," said Krishna, her husky voice thicker still. "Sew clothes or dance or climb mountains. When my parents died—" She broke off.

"The day after my mother was buried, I played the violin for hours," said Dev. He'd brought it along today on Tara's request.

Of all Maestro's and Krishna's friends from Goa, Dev was Tara's favorite. He worked for one of the local bars on weekdays and played for the church choir on Sundays. Dev also gave lessons to the kids in the parish. If Maestro couldn't find an appropriate song for one of their dance sessions, Dev was the one they turned to for help. He'd play while Tara twirled around with Maestro. Sometimes, he'd stay late, telling Tara all about the stars in the skies while they waited for dinner. When she was a child, she'd dozed off on his shoulder a few times, lulled to sleep by colorful words like nebula and white dwarf and celestial sphere.

In the years he'd been in Goa, Dev had become fluent in the local language, down to the sing-song accent of the locals. He still dressed in the same uptight clothes he first appeared in... the same kind of dull, buttoned-up shirts and poorly cut pants. In style as well as in appearance, Dev was very similar to Raj, Maestro's other friend. Apparently, they were cousins. Family they might be, but how different in demeanor! The happy contentment on Dev's face was very appealing.

Tara had an entire sketchbook devoted to him, featuring him wearing white dress shirts and pleated-front pants with red suspenders. Plus, a bow tie. She'd kept his curly, brown hair the same. The rounded glasses, too. The neat beard was replaced by a five o'clock shadow. In the sketches, Dev oozed old-world charm. Even her friends at school sighed over the images.

"I need to go to the bank and talk to the manager," said Tara's papa, walking in.

"We'll stay with Tara," said Maestro. Their lessons involved only western dance forms, but Maestro turned up to watch Tara perform whenever he got free time from accompanying Krishna.

She, Tara reminded herself for the zillionth time. *Not he.* Maestro was a woman. Normally, Tara would berate herself for not being able to remember it even after these many years, but today, she simply lacked the will.

"Thanks," said Papa, his eyes still red-rimmed. The gray in his hair seemed to have doubled over the past week. He was already a thin man, and the added stress turned him scrawny.

With Ma passing unexpectedly from the car crash, the loan people wanted updates on the financial situation of the resort which now had a minor girl as the co-owner. Especially with said minor acquiring a cousin of her mother's as legal representative for her share.

Tara wished Mama hadn't pulled such a dirty trick. She loved her husband, *and* she loved her family, but didn't Papa have a right to know what she put in her will? Maybe she thought he'd never find out. The forty-eight-year-old woman certainly hadn't been expecting to die before her teenaged daughter reached adulthood.

Now, this cousin called Prince was expected to send his men to look into things. Papa still owed money to both Prince and the bank on the resort. Problem was Prince was not the sort the bank would be happy to deal with. If they realized Papa took a second loan from the fellow, they might look too closely into the happenings at The Mermaid. They might realize Prince used the resort as a meeting place for his associates. The man couldn't enter

India himself because of arrest warrants, but his friends could. Prince possessed enough clout with the local cops to have them look away... but an international bank?

Papa was going out of his mind with worry. Everyone who knew worried about the situation, including Maestro and Krishna and Chef Vikram. *Did* they know about Prince and his connection to Tara's mother? Many of the employees did, and nobody dared say a word to the cops.

"I hope you're ready for him," said Papa.

Impatiently brushing the wetness from her lashes, Tara asked, "Ready for who?"

"I was talking to—" His eyes skittered.

"Ready for Dev to start the music," Krishna interjected smoothly.

Violin to his chin, Dev said, "Say when."

Chapter 38

Six months later, October 1995

(nearly 6 years after Harry's arrest and 7 after the exile began)

Goa, India

Sneakers squishing wet mud, Lilah jogged across the moonlit beach. It was more like running an obstacle course... winding her way around partiers snorting, smoking, and shooting up while they jumped every which way to psychedelic music. Even with all the fluorescent lamps lighting the nighttime shore, the crowd gave her the invisibility she needed. Still, the tinted glasses were on her nose, and her eye color was hidden by brown contacts. At Lilah's side was Victor, alert gaze on the surroundings as he ran. The shaved head he adopted as disguise should've made his gigantic size seem even more intimidating, but there was an easiness in his general attitude which was very appealing. The women who worked in the salon sure thought so.

Past a group of teenagers selling chai and samosas was a shadowed shack. Over the last six years, Lilah had learned from the tourists who showed up at the salon that some of the boys also peddled something special to customers. Hash, cocaine, LSD... there was a relatively new entrant in the market called Ecstasy. The chemicals explained the glassy-eyed look on the men and women chilling next to the ramshackle hut. Eight-finger Eddie—the hippie who started the global trek to Goa back in the 'sixties—was with them. The gaunt fellow was frequently sighted on Vagator Beach.

Nothing could disturb the group's zen, not the noise from the party, not the helicopter hovering over the scene. The chopper was not a tour company vehicle... it was flying low enough for Lilah to see the word NAVY emblazoned in large white letters on the tail. Military aircraft were regularly seen flying the skies over Goa, but the sailors working at the base didn't seem to intervene in the shenanigans going on outside its walls. Turning around, the chopper flew off into the darkness.

A sharp pang went through Lilah's heart. Squashing it, she told herself to keep believing. Harry was surely working on freeing himself. The exiles hadn't heard about any parole application, but that kind of info rarely appeared in the papers. If the board already decided, Grayson would've made sure the news did get to the print media somehow, thus ensuring Lilah heard. Which meant the process was still ongoing. Perhaps even in a matter of weeks, the former SEAL and helicopter pilot would be allowed outside. The exiles would get to return home. Then, she would demand an explanation for some of his antics. Then, she might understand why Lupe Valdez chose to sacrifice herself. Then, Lilah might get back some of her faith in the principles which always guided her actions.

Skirting the group in front of the beach shack, Victor and Lilah got to their usual spot at the far end of the shore, behind the crumbling building. This had become their predawn ritual in the six years they spent in Goa—a run across the sands, followed by a little training session for Lilah. She hardly slept more than four or five hours at a stretch, anyway, and the workout at least kept her mind occupied for a short while.

"Ahh..." she screamed, throwing a kick which Victor blocked. Her voice was drowned out by the bass notes booming through speakers set all around the beach. Punching, pivoting, kicking again... Lilah landed a few blows with enough force to make him stagger, and he shouted encouragement. Thanks to the workouts and the protein shakes delivered from the resort's kitchen to the salon courtesy of Chef Vikram, she'd regained the weight and the muscle lost during the first year of their exile.

Poor Victor... training with her couldn't be doing much for him. There was a boxing gym not far from the resort, but he couldn't go. Sparring with other serious boxers wasn't possible with the ongoing worry of somehow giving himself away. Victor used The Mermaid's facilities for regular exercise—only during slow hours, of course. The other brothers also took care to keep themselves fit and ready for anything which might come their way.

When the session was done, Lilah untied the scarf from around her hips and wiped her steamed-up glasses before wrapping her sweaty hair with the saffron fabric. Her tank top and capris were soaked in sweat, too. Victor didn't look any better in his tee and shorts, his limbs dusted with sand.

On their way back to The Mermaid, Victor frowned heavily at the teenaged chai vendors/drug dealers. "Idiots! I wish I could knock their heads together. Barely older than Gabe and—" He fell abruptly silent.

Lilah didn't ask. Victor hadn't exactly been a hands-on father to Gabriel before the exile started. Who knew what their relationship would've been like if things were different? Still, the boy would be thirteen now, and his father hadn't seen him since he was six. Victor never spoke much about his wife, not in Lilah's hearing, but he never responded to any of the obvious invitations thrown his way by the female employees at the resort.

Alex, too, would lapse into silence at times, especially when he spotted a father-son duo around the resort. He stared at his wedding ring for hours on end while he waited in the salon, a painful longing in his eyes.

He and Victor at least had families to return to someday. The twins... there was a Goan nurse Neil occasionally met for dinner, but she broke it off with him when he wouldn't commit. How could he when he didn't even dare divulge his real identity? According to Victor, Scott took up a tourist or two on invitations to spend the night, and that was the extent of his love life. Hema never got a chance to experience the thrill of romance. Her life came to a standstill the day she decided to join Lilah in her exile.

They had all been counting down days until Harry could apply for parole. Now... Lilah didn't get the delay.

Another problem loomed. The seven-year-mark of their exile was coming up. Steven could well ask the American government to declare the fugitives officially dead. Grayson would of course argue that the very fact they were on the run from the law was enough reason not to presume death. As evidence, he could show transactions at the Swiss bank where Lilah kept an account. Those managers guarded the privacy of their clients, but the lawyer to said client could at least request confirmation of activity. The latest withdrawal from the account happened not long before the events in Beijing... which was more than six years ago.

Lilah planned to send a photograph of hers—without her current disguise—holding the latest copy of *The New York Times* to Rekha in Bombay. The woman could use some faxing service to send the picture to the Swiss bank, and the government there wouldn't disclose where the transmission originated. They likely wouldn't even reveal how they knew Lilah was alive... simply that she was. If the bank was somehow compelled to talk, India was a huge country, and Bombay was a big city. Chances of anyone zeroing in on Rekha were nearly nil. Also, Goa would be way down on the feds' list on account of Prince's connection to the place.

Lilah shook her head. How much time could she buy with such tactics? The not-knowing was the worst part of it, the uncertainty.

There it was again... uncertainty... it simply wouldn't leave her. War loomed, a war which was needed unless she was prepared to abandon the world to Kingsley tyranny. Yet Lilah couldn't stop worrying about the aftermath. From the day she escaped the attack in China, she never stopped thinking about the price she would pay for her refusal to yield, the price others would pay. About the blood which would be shed. About who'd be left standing at the end of it all.

By the time Lilah and Victor jogged back to The Mermaid, the partiers had—as usual—extended their revelry to the pool and the gardens of the resort. Guests were sauntering in and out of the neon-lit casino at the far end of the compound. Brad's part-time work there didn't involve actual gaming, thank God. He merely did the books, which also meant he was unlikely to be seen by any of the tourists. Brad's brothers didn't share Lilah's concern over his gambling problem. They simply didn't see what he did with the family business as an extension of his propensity to take foolish chances.

None of the other exiles who worked in the resort ever went near the casino. They couldn't take the risk of being spotted together, especially since regulars to Goa had begun recognizing them.

Even now, a guest or two waved at Lilah, glancing curiously at Victor. One woman stopped the duo to ask Lilah when the salon would open. Inwardly sighing, she answered. Questions from guests was not an uncommon experience for any resort employee, but she still started at each shouted call, at every shadowed form crossing her path.

Rounding the main building, Victor and Lilah were on their way to the staff quarters in the back, and a bikini-clad female popped up before them. "Oops," said a girlish voice, followed by a drunken giggle. Fumes of feni—the local hooch brewed from cashew fruit—wafted around her. "You're so big!" An Indian woman craned her neck and blinked at Victor, completely ignoring Lilah's presence.

Jet-black curls held high in a ponytail, kohl-lined eyes, full red lips... and the figure... bomb was the first word which came to Lilah's mind. A couple of guards stood right behind the lady.

There was a sudden gulp from Victor, quickly smothered. Lilah glanced up at the boxer.

The bomb frowned. "H-have we met? You seem..."

"Nah," Victor said quickly. Too quickly. "I would've remembered you."

With another slurry giggle, the woman said, "Of course! I used to be a movie star... then, I came back. Everybody still remembers!"

"Uhh..." said Victor. "Okay... good." Voice suddenly thickening as though with drink, he added, "Ex... excuse me... I need to piss real bad."

With a hand on Lilah's shoulder, he urged her to walk around the obstacles in their path. Victor wobbled a couple of times but never fell. The fingers around her upper arm never tightened in any effort to regain balance. Through it all, neither he nor Lilah looked behind. Neither said a word until they got to the door of the ladies' hostel.

Victor threw a casual glance around. A few of the employees were walking back and forth between the staff buildings and the resort proper—change of shift time—but there was no one close enough to overhear. "Could you get Alex down here?" Victor asked, his tone low. He couldn't go in to visit. Men weren't allowed, no exceptions. "Tell him it's an emergency."

It took Alex a few minutes to get ready. The long hair and smoothly shaven cheeks weren't enough for him to pass as a trans woman. Eyeliner, a little rouge, wild red lip color... stoically donning war paint, he followed Lilah to the front door as a sleepy Hema stumbled along. "What's up?" Alex asked, keeping his voice hushed.

"Bro, Priya's here," said Victor. "Prince's girlfriend. She saw me."

Chapter 39

Tall bushes shielded the service entrance in the back of the resort from guests' eyes. Following Victor to a shadowy corner, Lilah kept her face averted from the employees unloading sacks of vegetables off delivery trucks. The sky appeared to be lightening slightly. Dawn was on its way, putting an end to the party on the beach. Calls to room service would start any moment, and exhausted tourists would stagger into restaurants. Once brunch hour was also past, there would be relative respite for the resort staff until late afternoon. All tourist sections in town slowed down slightly—*very* slightly—while visitors caught up on sleep.

"Priya didn't recognize me," Victor insisted yet again. "She was wasted. Besides, she saw me only for a few minutes in Macau." When he and Alex went to Prince's boat to rescue their abducted cousins, Steven and Charles, Priya had been present. "And she was trying to get Alex to kiss her the entire time."

"Dude!" Alex snapped. "Do you mind?" Turning hastily to Lilah, he explained, "*She* was trying to kiss *me*, not the other way around."

Hema's mouth dropped open, but she didn't say a word.

"I don't care who was kissing whom," ground out Lilah. "Point is, Victor, she saw you here tonight. Trust me... you're not an easily forgettable guy. Yeah, she was drunk, but she might think back and remember. In fact, we must operate under the assumption she will."

"First thing she will do is call Prince," Alex said, nodding. "Any element of surprise we have will be gone."

The idea was to hang on until the pardon came through or Prince found a way to skirt arrest warrants and showed up at The Mermaid. If the exiles got to return home before, they could access enough cash to pay off the owner's loan for him in return for the sanctuary he provided. If not, Prince would meet an unexpected end at the hands of the Kingsley brothers. Now...

"Do we trigger plan C?" asked Alex.

The seven exiles had thus far made sure not to be spotted together, and their after-hours meetings at Neil's alternative medicine clinic were witnessed only by Tara and that, too, only in the initial years. Now, they limited any talk involving their real lives to times they were truly alone. The discussions were scheduled specifically when the other shops on the street shuttered for the day or were too busy to pay attention.

The clinic was also relatively hidden within a maze of side streets and served as the designated gathering place for potential emergencies. It was the reason they rented the tiny, single-story building full-time though it was open for business only a few days a week. There was a steel vault inside where a set of weapons were stored, and the heavy-duty front door was always secured. The vault also held a couple items which most Indians wouldn't think to keep under lock and key—color bombs they used to celebrate Holi, which could double as smoke grenades for the exiles. The second-hand van they purchased soon after getting to Goa remained parked in the clinic's tiny yard.

A couple of phone calls, and they would all gather in the building. Or rather, they would wait in assigned hiding spots— mostly behind walls or the tall coconut palms—from where the gates to the yard *and* the front door could be seen. Thirty minutes had to pass before determining it was safe to approach their escape vehicle. If any of the group was running behind, they'd know the city the van was headed to and were expected to catch up by either rail or bus. Each carried loose cash for the purpose and their own weapons. And yeah, at no point were Lilah and Hema to be left to fend for themselves.

"We need to talk to Mathur," Victor said, referring to the owner/manager of the resort.

"I'll contact the rest," said Alex. "We should leave Goa... pronto. Mathur's gonna be upset."

Hema's head bobbed in vigorous agreement, but she continued to stay silent.

"You have the lilies?" Lilah asked Victor.

He nodded. "At the apartment with Brad." Lily was the code they used for the rocks stolen from the Afghani terrorists. Only two of the gems remained, and they would do as temporary recompense for Mathur. The jewels would be difficult to dispose of for cash without raising questions. Still, better than nothing. Once the exiles returned home, they could send actual cash to pay off Mathur's debt.

If Prince asked about the exiles, Mathur planned to pretend he didn't know anything. The four people who worked for him were recommended by the drag show artists. The queer community in Goa couldn't offer any details, either, except that Rekha, who used to be one of them until she moved to Bombay, called about some American friends of hers who needed jobs.

Rekha would be notified to contact Lilah's cousin Shankar for help. Lieutenant General Shivshankar Mittal was the director of intelligence for the Indian military. He'd been part of the sting which snared Prince as well as some high-profile politicians in a drug-smuggling scheme, and Rekha knew him.

She'd claim zero knowledge of the exiles' legal problems. Yeah, she worked for Gateway as a guard, but it didn't mean she actually paid attention to what happened to the bigwigs of the company. She didn't read the news... watch TV... whatever. She didn't know she was supposed to contact the police if she heard from the exiles. And no, she didn't think it funny they needed regular jobs. Rekha assumed they went bankrupt. It was not an unusual occurrence in business.

Shankar would of course understand in a nanosecond that the whole story was a lie, and he'd be forced to give the woman a mild rap on the knuckles. Nothing else would happen to Rekha because Shankar Mittal would be as anxious as anyone else to keep Lilah safe though his official position prevented him from doing anything overt to help.

"I can get the gems to Mathur and be at the clinic in under thirty with Brad," said Victor. "But—"

"No buts," said Alex. "We don't have the time."

"Right," said Lilah. "Alex, you call Neil and Scott from the hostel while Hema and I get our stuff."

"Wait," Victor said, holding up both hands. "Just... both of you... wait a damn moment."

"What?" asked Hema, finally speaking up.

Victor huffed out a breath. "Look... maybe Priya will manage to work out who I am on her own... but she was too drunk to do it tonight. What if she asks around about me in the morning? If someone in the staff tells her I left in a hurry, she'll immediately decide we *have* met, and I don't want it to dawn on her when and where. If Prince realizes we were in India all this while, he's going to have his men watching every exit point. Not the best idea. I mean... we managed to escape him in China, but many things could've gone wrong at any given step. Play it cool for a few days, and we might possibly avoid getting made. Then, we could get out of India without playing risky games with terrorists."

"'Play it cool'?" A finger to her brow, Lilah said, "The more times Priya sees you, the more likely it is she *will* remember."

"We'll get Mathur to keep an eye on what she does," elaborated Victor. "You know... to alert us if she contacts Prince. In which case, we'll have no choice but to leave right away. If not... I'll make sure she doesn't see me, and we can skip town after a reasonable period of time without raising suspicions. All four of us will come up with some excuse for giving notice. Lilah can claim a family emergency. You and Alex are supposed to be related, so the same emergency will apply. Hema was always Lilah's assistant, and she'll continue in the same position. As for me... dunno..."

Hema giggled. "The salon ladies think Chef Vikram and Krishna are having an affair. Tell them you're going to get married."

Alex snort-laughed.

"Not a bad thought, actually," said Victor. "And I can be sick or something for the entire notice period... come down with something contagious... I don't know... chicken pox? It will stop Priya from looking for me. She wouldn't want to catch anything and end up with scars on her face, I'm sure. Then, we'll leave."

Alex's mirth got more intense, causing him to double up with muted guffaws.

Lilah looked heavenward for a second. "Of all the hare-brained—"

"Well," said Victor. "Do you have a better idea?" When she remained silent, he added, "We've been waiting so many damn years. Harry is probably on his way to getting parole, *and* he has his new medal. Hell, you and Alex keep claiming Harry would have a plan. Don't mess things up when we're this close is all I'm saying."

Chapter 40

"Thirteen days," Lilah said to the supervisor of the salon. None of them slept the few hours between their meeting and the start of the morning shift in the resort. Packing, contacting Brad, Neil, and Scott, making sure the second-hand van was ready to drive out of Goa at a moment's notice... Victor and Brad were on their way to Mathur's office with the gems.

"I didn't expect this of you, Krishna," the supervisor said, frowning. "It's not professional to leave us right when tourist season is about to heat up. And all three of you all at once? Vikram, too, obviously."

"I'm sorry," said Lilah. "I... umm... didn't plan on having the wedding for a few more months, but... umm... life's unpredictable. None of us expected my grandmother to fall ill. She was healthy as a horse... the old lady. She wants to see me married before she dies. Arjun and Hema don't want to miss my wedding. Afterward, we're planning to set up our own salon back home."

The supervisor shook her head and stalked to her little office, mumbling something about tight schedules. Hema was busy with a guest's hair, but she glanced toward the supervisor's disappearing form. Alex—makeup on his face and long hair tied back under a saffron bandana—was only a couple of feet away, slouched against the wall near the glass doors. He had on his usual combo of long-sleeved orange tunic and matching sarong and sandals.

Lilah tucked her hands into the pockets of her uniform—a lab coat with the resort's logo emblazoned on the lapel. Under the coat was her customary disguise, and the *rudraksha* beads were her only jewelry. "What are you going to tell Tara?" she asked Alex.

"Same story." Mumbling a curse, he looked away. "Poor kid. It's going to be hard on her. Losing her mother... now this."

Since their arrival in Goa almost six years ago, "Maestro Arjun" had been Tara's constant companion. Another father-figure... mother-figure... however she saw him.

"Once we return home," Alex continued, "I'm going to ask if she wants to study fashion in the States. Mathur won't like it, but the girl should get a chance to live her own life. Hell, in New York, she'll actually have people who care about her. Unlike her parents, I'm not going to saddle her with a drug lord for a guardian."

"You're going to miss her, too," Lilah said, smiling slightly. "Mikey's only a year younger."

"Yeah." Gritting his teeth, Alex added, "Dammit... six years! He'll be thirteen next February. God knows if he even remembers me."

Lilah didn't say anything in response. What *could* she say?

"Krishna," called the supervisor, tone peremptory. She was standing at the door to her office inside the salon, a bottle in her hands. "A VIP guest needs help in her room. She partied a little too hard last night and has an event to attend this morning. A friend of hers recommended you, apparently. Get your kit and go."

"Yes, of course," Lilah said. "Which room?"

"A celebrity, so treat her with extra care," cautioned the supervisor. She handed the bottle she was holding to Lilah. "Complimentary champagne. A little wine always makes them happy. This one used to be... is still a huge movie star... Priya."

#

The service elevator doors swished shut on Lilah, cutting off her sight of an anxious Hema.

"I don't like this," Alex muttered for the millionth time, shifting the large makeup box to his left hand. At least there was no other staff along for the ride to overhear their conversation. Nor would there be any other guests on the top floor. The two penthouse suites occupied almost the entire area, and only one was rented out currently.

"We don't have an option," said Lilah. She forced her grip around the neck of the champagne bottle to relax before the glass shattered. "The supervisor saw me hale and hearty. If I fake something, it might get back to this Priya. Our only choice is to play along. Besides, she's never seen *me* without the disguise, and you'll be right outside the suite." He couldn't go in and risk Priya recognizing him, but Lilah never met Prince or his sidekicks before with the exception of an Indian union leader called Hoda.

"Just make sure no one locks the door behind you," warned Alex.

When they exited onto the penthouse floor, there was a shouted "Hey!" from the other end of the hallway, where the guest elevators would be.

"Tara?" exclaimed Alex. "What are you doing here? You're supposed to be in school."

Lilah eyed the child up and down. She was in jeans and a tee with sneakers on her feet, not her school uniform. The usually messy black curls were brushed, prettily framing her oval face. "And just how did you sneak into the VIP elevator?" Lilah asked.

The girl snickered, the glumness and the near-constant worry of the last six months dissipating from her face for a moment. The familiar mischievous glint returned to the black irises as she held up the keycard she most certainly filched from her father's office. "I skipped classes for the morning. Papa thinks I have an upset tummy, but I want to meet Priya. Maybe she'll let me take a picture with her. Do you think she'll mind? All my friends will be so jealous!"

"Meet—" Alex's hand went to his bandana before falling back. "Tara, return to your house before your father figures out you lied to him. Also, Priya is a guest at the resort. You shouldn't be bothering her. In fact, she called the salon and asked for help, which means she's busy."

"Perfect excuse," retorted Tara, the angles of her eyebrows sharpening until she looked positively devilish. She tucked the keycard into the pocket of her jeans. "Krishna can just say I'm there to assist her." Before anyone could object further, Tara knocked on the door.

"But—" started Alex.

"Are you Krishna from the salon?" a voice asked from the door.

"Umm... yes," Lilah said to the beefy man dressed in a white Polo shirt and black pants. A guard?

"Come in, then," said the man. "Priya Madam is waiting."

The muscles in her tummy tightening, Lilah nodded. She took the makeup box from Alex and put a foot forward. Before she could go farther, Tara slipped by her side and sailed in. Behind Lilah, Alex mumbled something under his breath. "I'll be here," he reminded her.

Straightening her shoulders, Lilah stepped through the entrance. Tara was right inside, hopping from foot to foot in excitement. The guard shut the door. Before he could click the lock, Lilah said, "The resort has a policy. No locked doors when employees are in rooms with guests present. It's for protection of both the guests and the staff."

"Is it so?" inquired a voice from one of the chairs by the window. "Hello, Mrs. Kingsley. We finally meet."

Lilah's entire body stiffened. "Prince," she whispered in dismay.

Part XV

Chapter 41

A white fluorescent lamp flickered, buzzing in its effort to remain lit. Seated near the window was the man Lilah hoped she'd never meet. The man she'd avoided being face-to-face with in all their encounters. Prince, the drug lord from Myanmar. Even dressed in khaki shirt and pants, the build of a pugilist was obvious. The typical Southeast Asian face she'd seen in newspaper articles now carried the deep lines of approaching old age. Two local men—bodyguards, presumably—flanked him.

Sweat trickled between Lilah's shoulder blades. Tara moved close to Lilah, the girl clearly having picked up on the woman's unease.

"Leave, Tara," Lilah muttered.

"Oh, no," said Prince. "She's my niece. Why should she go anywhere? Besides, her presence might ensure your good behavior." He heaved himself off the chair and took measured steps toward them.

For a single incoherent moment, Lilah considered grabbing Tara's hand and running. They wouldn't make it. Not before the thugs with Prince shot them. The men were most certainly armed. If she were alone, she might have risked it. Now, all she could do was keep the drug lord talking until Alex figured out something was wrong and forced his way in.

Prince halted with only a couple feet between him and Lilah. With one quick move of his hand, he ripped off her tinted glasses.

Lilah just about held back a gasp. Tara whimpered in terror, but Prince paid her no mind. His bright-black eyes were pinned on the woman.

For a few moments, he simply stared unblinkingly. "No wonder," he murmured. "You were never around when I visited my old friend, Noriega. I should've known why the Kingsleys were keeping their queen away from me."

Lilah clenched her teeth, stifling the retort. Her left hand tightened its hold on the handle of the makeup box, the right still gripping the champagne bottle.

"The first time around in India, I could understand," Prince continued. "You were in disguise."

Tossing the glasses to the side, he raised his knuckles to graze her jaw. Lilah took an involuntary step to the rear. Tara's frightened sobs were getting louder and louder, but Lilah didn't dare turn her attention. She didn't dare look away from the enemy.

"Even in Macau, you chose not to show up," he complained.

"What do you want?" Lilah snapped, her heart pounding in fear and anger.

Throwing his head back, Prince laughed. "So eager to get down to business. A woman like you shouldn't be bothered by mundane things like work. What kind of work did they have you do, anyway?"

He didn't know? Confused, she said, "What? I'm... I was..."

"The CFO?" Prince asked. "I know about your title, but what did you actually do?" His eyes widened. "Ahh. I understand. The Kingsleys needed to keep your father happy."

"My father?" She'd utterly lost the drug lord's train of thoughts. Poor Papa died a long time before his darling daughter ever heard of the Kingsley brothers.

"They did need the alliance with him," Prince said reasonably.

Alliance with h—Andrew?

"With Andrew Barrons's help, Brad Kingsley got one half of his family company, and your title gave Barrons a say in the business," Prince mused. "You were thrown into the mix to keep everything legal. Not a bad deal."

Which was more or less what happened. Except the Sheppards had also been involved. Everyone concerned believed precisely what Prince seemed to be thinking... that Lilah would be a pawn. Her refusal to be one was what got them to this point.

"And the five brothers got the pleasure of your company." Prince's hand once again came up to her face, cupping her cheek.

With a hiss, Lilah dropped the makeup box and scrambled back, spreading her arms to either side to push Tara behind her. The wall stopped them. The door... *was* it locked? Would Alex be able to come in? The champagne bottle could be a weapon, and there was the pistol tucked into her pants, but she wouldn't win a shootout. Tara... no, Lilah simply couldn't risk it.

Prince tut-tutted. "You don't need to be scared of me. Why would I hurt someone as beautiful as you? In fact, if we met in Macau, I'd have offered to hide you in my village. You *and* the worthless lot you hang around with. For you, I'd have put up with them, too."

Wha— "You're crazy."

"*Very* crazy," he agreed, eyes glittering. "Your loveliness is enough to drive a monk mad."

"You came all the way to Goa to make a pass at me? At a married woman?"

"Where *is* this old married hag?" he asked, the teasing note in the words sending revulsion snaking down her spine. "All *I* see is a stunning woman." Once again, his fingers came up.

"Didn't you hear me?" Lilah asked. "I'm *married.*"

"To five men," Prince said, sounding completely serious. "Can't even blame them. How can one brother be allowed to keep you all to himself? *I* don't have any brothers."

Bizarre. Out loud, Lilah said, "Doesn't make a difference to me. I'll stick with the ones I already have."

Cocking his head to one side, Prince observed, "Your loyalty to the fools is endearing... but don't you see? They don't deserve you. With me, you'd live like an actual queen. You wouldn't have to dye your hair... unless you wanted to. Silks, satins, gold, whatever you want. Servants to cater to your every whim. Hell, if you agree to be my wife, I'd wait on you myself."

"Ahh." Lilah nodded in mock understanding. "So you traveled thousands of miles to *propose* to a woman you never met. Makes perfect sense."

Nostrils flaring, Prince confessed, "I'd only seen pictures of you. You looked lovely, of course. But God! I thought you were the actual CFO of their company. But you... you... you're no CFO. You're made for other things. And look how they're treating you! This resort and your miserable little job. No staff, no servants. These clothes..."

His fingers reached for the lapel on Lilah's lab coat.

"No," Tara cried.

Red... the room took on a red hue. A snarl spewed from Lilah's lips. With every bit of strength she possessed, she shoved hard. On a surprised grunt, Prince teetered, falling backward.

"Run," she yelled to Tara.

Guns drawn, the bodyguards bounded to Lilah.

"Run," she screeched again, throwing herself between Tara and the gunmen. The champagne bottle was held aloft. "Get Alex!"

"Who?" Tara asked.

Not responding, Lilah swung the bottle at the head of one of the goons, trying to buy the girl as much time as possible.

Glass shattered, followed by a furious howl. A rough hand landed on Lilah's shoulder. Her *rudraksha* garland snapped, beads scattering. Seconds later, a knee slammed into her hip bone. Crushing pain radiated all the way to her spine. The broken bottle dropped from her nerveless fingers. Her breath stopped. Her chest was tight, ready to explode. Eyes wide, Lilah opened her mouth to scream, but no sounds came out. The room darkened... swam.

A new sound joined the racket, a masculine bellow of rage. But Lilah could barely see. She doubled over. Legs moved around in her visual field. There was an angry shout as someone crashed into the coffee table. Then came the familiar voice of Alex, sounding disembodied to Lilah's ears as though an invisible demon had shown up to protect her. "Touch her again, and I'll kill you!" Alex roared.

Chapter 42

"Tara," Lilah wheezed, stumbling up. Through the pain-induced haze, she saw Alex holding his gun on Prince, the weapons of the drug lord's henchmen pointed at the newcomer. The child was still in the room, sobbing audibly by the open door. She had to be the one who let Alex in. "Get out of here," Lilah said to the girl.

"Both of you," snapped Alex. "Out! Now!"

Lilah didn't wait to argue. The pistol remained tucked into her waistband, but her vision was too blurry to aim the weapon. Alex could handle things better if he didn't have to worry about her and Tara.

Biting down against the intense ache on her hip, Lilah grabbed Tara's hand and ran. Thank God, the VIP elevator was still on the penthouse floor. When the doors swished shut, Tara said, "Papa will call the police."

Lilah nodded. "We're going straight to your father's office." Brad and Victor would be with Mathur, handing over the lilies— the jewels. Victor needed to run to the VIP room and help Alex. Then, the exiles would somehow evade Prince and his goons and get out of Goa.

Stalking through the noisy casino, Lilah got to the strictly utilitarian clerical section of the resort. Curious glances were thrown her way from the rows of desks. Likely because Tara was also present, no one stopped Lilah's march to the manager's suite.

She didn't knock or ask for permission. Slamming the heel of her hand into the swing door, Lilah strode in, Tara following closely behind. The three men at the desk looked up, all their faces white.

"Victor!" Lilah said on a hard breath. "Go to the penthouse right now! Alex is up there... with Prince."

Shoving his chair back, Victor stood. "With—"

"You!" said Lilah, pointing her finger at Mathur. "You knew he was here!" Mathur had to know. Yet the exiles got no warning.

"He was just telling us—" started Brad.

"He let me walk straight into Prince's room," Lilah accused. When Victor growled, she pivoted to him. "I'll deal with Mathur. You go to Alex. Right now!"

"No need, Mrs. Kingsley," said Prince's voice from behind.

When Lilah whirled around, Alex was at the door, the drug lord next to him. At Lilah's side, Tara gasped.

"Papa, what's going on?" the girl asked in a small voice, but her father didn't respond. Mathur remained in his chair as did Brad, neither man saying a word.

Prince inclined his head. "Your boyfriend agreed it would be wiser to gather here for a discussion instead of indulging in a shootout which wouldn't end well for either party."

Snarling like an animal, Lilah took two steps rearward. "Wiser? You kicked me!"

"Kicked you?" Victor echoed, tone outraged. With another growl, he lunged.

"Sit down!" shouted Brad. "Now!" Victor stumbled to a stop. Getting to his feet, Brad turned to Lilah. Beads of sweat dotted his forehead. "As for you... there are employees outside. They can hear us. The way you're screaming, so can the guests in the casino. They're here to have fun, not... stop making a scene for God's sake."

"He kicked me," Lilah repeated wildly. "And you're worried about me making a scene?" She turned to Mathur. "What about you? Is this how you run your business? Are you seriously going to look the other way while your brother-in-law attacks your female employees?"

Mathur gulped. "I... ahh... I didn't see what happened. So how can I—"

"Papa?" Tara whispered, tone disbelieving.

Angry eyes on Lilah, Brad asked, "Will you stop prancing around? Please! Let's hear what Prince has to say."

Neither Alex nor Victor opened their mouths to object. Neil and Scott wouldn't have, either, if they'd been present. Breathing heavily, Lilah glared at each of the Kingsley brothers. "Cowards," she finally ground out. "The whole lot of you. You sit here and negotiate with someone who... I'm leaving."

"Oh, but you shouldn't, Mrs. Kingsley," said Prince. "What I have to suggest involves you."

#

"What do you want?" Lilah asked the moment everyone concerned seated themselves around the conference table.

"So business-like," Prince reproved. "Don't you want to know about my long search for you?"

The drug lord had once again gotten into a deal with Steven and gang. None of them dreamed the exiles would pick Prince's backyard to hide in. But with Mrs. Mathur's passing, Prince got it into his head to check on the child. Coincidentally, the Indian government had recently completed its investigation of Priya and concluded she was simply an idiot who hung out with the wrong crowd. The arrest warrant on her was withdrawn, and the actress decided to make a triumphant reentry into her homeland.

Prince's boat—*The Olympus*—was anchored in the Arabian Sea, just outside of India's jurisdiction. The plan was for Priya to present her sexy self to an adoring public in the setting of Goa's golden beaches and blue ocean. Mathur would be asked to bring Tara to the yacht to visit her mother's cousin.

The actress's surprise arrival happened at night, and Mathur believed the morning was soon enough to contact the exiles. The resort owner didn't realize two of his American employees had run into Priya before as her name never came up in any of their initial discussions. Besides, Prince was still quite far away and not expected to make it ashore. Prior to his troubles with the Indian government, he always sent word about impending visits to the resort to meet his partners. Such meetings were attended by his underlings in the years since the sting operation by Alex which got Prince into said trouble.

Then came Priya's encounter with Victor. No, she didn't remember him, but her bodyguard called his boss about running into a giant of a man whom the actress thought looked familiar. The guard also said something about the sexy broad who was with the giant.

It was enough for Prince. While the exiles were making arrangements, the drug lord contacted the people he knew in local law enforcement. For a short period of two or three days, they could make sure the police stayed away from The Mermaid. Under cover of the dark night, Prince arrived at the resort. One look at Mathur's face, and the drug lord confirmed his suspicions. The owner/manager of the resort was told to keep his mouth shut about Prince's presence. Mathur didn't dare contact the exiles.

All the preparation that went into their plans to do away with the drug lord, all the escape routes they sketched out... everything involved Mathur's cooperation or at least silence on their behalf. Instead, he let his brother-in-law lay a trap for Lilah and Alex, daring to speak only when Brad and Victor showed up with the gemstones.

"I have a deal for you," Prince said to the five Kingsley brothers. They were on one side of the table in the conference room attached to Mathur's office. Neil and Scott had been called in some time ago. Tara was in the salon with Hema, but her father was permitted to listen in on the negotiations. "Nothing to do with your business or mine." The drug lord threw a glance at the foot of the table where Lilah was seated. "Mrs. Kingsley... she will accompany me to Burma... Myanmar."

Now that the drug lord saw Lilah in person, he decided she would do quite well as his next paramour.

Lilah laughed without amusement. "Are you a child?" she mocked. "Asking for the moon!"

Prince wanted payback for his defeats at Victor and Alex's hands. Steven Kingsley wanted all the exiles dead. The drug lord could make Steven happy. "The alternative..." continued Prince.

Parading Mrs. Brad Kingsley as his mistress for the whole world to see would be sweeter revenge. He was also prepared to marry her if she so wished. Either way, it would be a public black eye for the Kingsley brothers. As bride price, he would let the brothers leave. They could even continue at The Mermaid. The role of Lilah as concubine in the court of the opium king would not be made public until the pardon came through. Steven would be told nothing. Nor would the Russian mafia he contracted to find the exiles. Once Brad was back in charge of the network, Steven would be too busy running from his past crimes to worry about Prince's double cross. Without someone writing them a paycheck, the Russians wouldn't care, either. Even if the Kingsley brothers then used their returned clout to force Prince to surrender Lilah, they would still have to live with the knowledge she'd been in the drug lord's keeping. Everyone who saw her with any of the Kingsley men would remember what happened and know not to cross Prince.

"Don't try any of your usual tricks," he warned. "Mrs. Kingsley cannot set foot out of this resort unless it's in my company. If any of you feel tempted to spirit her away, remember the Bratva."

The Russians didn't know yet Prince was at the resort, and even if they did, they'd assume it was a visit to his brother-in-law. Nothing to do with the missing exiles. One wrong move, and the exiles would find it impossible to hide anywhere in India. They'd be on the run not only from the authorities but also from the Bratva and their allies. Not to mention Prince's men.

"What makes you think I'll agree?" Lilah asked. "One phone call, and I'd be back in the U.S." Brad would be arrested, but she'd be all right... eventually.

Prince laughed. "Ask your men why it would be a bad idea. They'll confirm every call you make from here on out will be monitored by my people. No matter where you go even within the resort, you'll be watched. The moment you contact the American consulate... you... all of you will be dead before the cops show up." He nodded at the Kingsley brothers. "I imagine you'll need a few minutes to convince her to go without kicking up unnecessary fuss. You have until dinner. I need to leave tonight. My friends in the police have given me a couple of days, but I don't want to take unnecessary chances."

Lilah couldn't help it. She snarled.

"This is not the right time for anger," snapped Brad. "We're this close to a pardon."

"Not the time for..." Lilah shook her head. "You're still gambling with my life." She stared hard at the four younger Kingsley men. "And the rest of you are letting him do it. Again!"

"*You're* unwilling to look beyond your convenience," said Brad. "I would've hoped my wife gave a thought or two to my safety. Then, I would also have done whatever it took to make her happy." He turned to his brothers, index finger stabbing the air. "*I am going to make the call on what needs to be done. Not one of you will go against my orders. Got it?*"

Prince smiled. "As a matter of fact, Mrs. Kingsley, why don't you join me in my room for dinner? I don't believe you'll have a pleasant time with your former..." He glanced at the Kingsley brothers. "...with any of your former partners." The drug lord took something out of his pocket and slid it across the table. "Your glasses... you might need them."

Mind full of savage misery, Lilah marched to the salon in search of Hema and Tara. Talking logic with the Kingsley men would not be enough to save her skin when big brother's life and freedom were at stake. They might have flouted his orders once or twice as long as it was clear that helping her would not harm him. When it came to a zero-sum game, she would always lose to their fraternal solidarity. She'd seen enough evidence of it over the last seven years, starting with Brad's insane wager with their company. Well... seven years ago, she didn't know how to breach the wall built by the brothers. Today, she did. Today, she was willing to use every weapon in her arsenal.

It was time once again for the Indian Defense. While Prince reveled in the anticipation of victory, Lilah would assemble her army. She would mount a devious defense, moving in for the kill right when the enemy believed he won. There would be no mercy shown, no opportunity for the drug lord to escape.

Chapter 43

An hour later

The sun was high in the sky, and the beach was already filling with tourists, but it wasn't crazy-packed like it got in the evenings. There was music coming from somewhere and the sound of barking stray dogs. Running wildly down the shore, Tara bumped against a couple of men, prompting a blond chap with an Aussie accent to exclaim, "Watch it, kid!" A few feet farther, she tripped over an icebox, flying face-first into the sand.

Ignoring the shouted questions of concern, Tara scrambled up and continued running. *Papa,* she murmured in her mind. *How could you?*

The fellow called Prince turned out to be worse than what her father claimed. But Papa... his reaction...

With a brusque hand, she wiped the tears which spilled. Crying made her look even younger than her thirteen years, which wouldn't do. Tara squinted. There... seated on a rock with his bare, twiggy legs stretched in front was Eight-finger Eddie. The usual admiring crowd surrounded him, all trying to learn how to achieve *nirvana*. They usually ended up finding enlightenment and transcendental bliss with the aid of magical chemicals. Which meant drug peddlers hung around the group, mostly boys who were in their mid to late teens. Papa had been clear with her what they did, how they made their money, and what the drugs they sold did to a person's mind and body.

Papa, she thought bitterly. Tara never believed her mama when she asked him why he'd been weak-willed enough to take money from a drug lord if he were so offended by the business. Today, Papa practically shrank into his chair when Krishna/Lilah demanded protection from Prince. The same Krishna had thrown herself between Tara and the drug dealer's goons. The idiot, Prince, had been practically slobbering over Krishna, and her first thought was to save the kid of the same fellow who turned out to be too scared to help her.

Gritting her teeth, Tara jogged the last few feet to the group around Eddie. A brown-haired woman wearing only bikini bottoms was rocking in time with the music from the loudspeakers, taking occasional puffs from the joint in her hand. She looked about seventeen, eighteen. Not older than early twenties, for sure.

Worrying she made a mistake by not exchanging her jeans for a pair of shorts, Tara collapsed onto the sand. The more she stood out amid this crowd, the better they would remember her, but there was no helping it now. "Hi," she said to the brown-haired girl. Tara also started swaying to the music and didn't say anything else for a few minutes. She couldn't! The smell of weed and unwashed human bodies almost made her gag. Running the tip of her tongue over her upper lip, Tara prepared to blurt the question. No, not blurt... she needed to do it exactly as Krishna said, or they could all get into trouble. The dollar notes Krishna gave were safe in Tara's pocket.

Before she could open her mouth, the brown-haired girl held out the joint. "Want a hit?"

An hour later, when Tara walked through the gates of the resort, she went straight to the main building. Less than ten steps in, there was a shouted "She's here!" A chorus of where-have-you-beens and your-father's-looking-for-yous and young-lady-you're-in-troubles echoed around. Ignoring them, Tara stalked to the salon.

A skinny form materialized in front, blocking her path. "Tara!" said Papa. Holding her by the shoulders, he gasped. "Oh, my God... you're okay. Thank God... you're okay."

She stared stonily at him, saying nothing.

He flushed. "There isn't much I can... you won't understand until you grow up."

Tara shrugged. "Excuse me," she said, stepping around him to walk into the salon. Hema was watching from behind glass doors. Walking straight to the Nepali woman, Tara gave her a hug. Over Hema's shoulder, Tara stared at the blowup picture of herself on the wall, grinning widely for the camera.

No one saw the child dropping four small packets of white powder into the pocket of Hema's lab coat.

Chapter 44

An hour later

The door to the dance studio stayed shut, but sounds from the main gym still filtered in—overhead music, metallic clangs, grunts, shouts of encouragement. Lessons in *corredinho,* the Portuguese dance, and freestyle Bollywood had been canceled on Lilah's request. Who knew what the other employees thought of a mere salon worker being given use of the room for the day? But Mathur was the owner, and if he said she could... well... she could. After all, Prince had decreed Lilah couldn't leave The Mermaid unless it was to follow him to his boat. She would not be allowed the chance to seek help from the external world, which meant the Kingsley brothers needed to use the premises of the resort to persuade her to cooperate. And of course, she would bid goodbye to them in this chamber.

But Lilah couldn't find anything to say to the two men with her. What demand—what plea for help—could she make that they'd agree to?

She remained silent in her chair, eyes fixed on the blue ocean visible through the row of windows on the opposite wall. Neil and Scott occupied seats along the same row.

"Damn it all!" Neil finally muttered, voice breaking on the last syllable. He yanked the bandana from his blond head and tossed it to the floor. "Lilah..."

She held up a hand, taking a couple of deep breaths to compose herself. There was a clatter, a movement. Neil was suddenly in the chair on her right side, wrapping his arm around her shoulders. Scott took Lilah's left hand in his. "Whatever you decide," said the astrophysics professor-turned-violin teacher, "I'm with you."

"Thank you," she whispered.

When the twins left, she glanced at the wall clock over the door. The person she needed to show up—

There was a shuffling sound at the entrance. Hema was at the door, mouthing *Now?* With an infinitesimal shake of her head, Lilah said, "Please let Brad know I'm waiting to talk to him."

It took only a couple of minutes for the eldest of the Kingsley brothers to present himself. Shutting the door behind him, Brad remained standing. Same as the twins, it seemed he couldn't find anything to say to the woman he was trading for his safety.

Hands in his pockets, he eventually offered, "We'll get you out later. It's only a matter of time."

Lilah stilled. "Prince kicked me," she reminded the man who'd married her.

Flushing, Brad asked, "You want revenge? Will it make you happy? Fine. We'll make sure you get it."

Gritting her teeth hard, Lilah stood.

"Krishna," called a female voice, followed by a loud knock. Hema, again. Barging in, she said, "Tara and I want time with you, too."

Brad muttered something under his breath before striding out.

"Thank you," Lilah said to Hema.

"There really isn't much time left," said Hema. *"Now,* Lilah?"

Lilah's hand went to the pocket of her lab coat. Four little sachets were in there, two of each as she instructed Tara. The young girl was also coached on what else to do. All that remained was for Lilah to convince the one man who could help her. The Kingsley brother who'd been on a nonstop guilt trip since the exile started.

#

The lab coat was draped carefully over the chair on Lilah's left. The gun, which was normally tucked into her pants, lay on top of the coat. She couldn't take the weapon with her, of course. The drug lord wouldn't allow it. The weapons carried by the Kingsley brothers were already confiscated.

Victor was in the chair to her right, his torso twisted to face her, his hands clasping hers. He was still in the shorts and tee from their nightly exercise routine. Observing his red-rimmed eyes, Lilah asked, "Were you taking a nap?"

"Nap?" Victor blinked. "I don't underst—"

Lilah shrugged. "You look like you were. I mean... how does it matter to you, right? That drug dealer *kicked* me, but it's not important. Not to you, not to Brad, not to *any*one."

There was shocked silence for a second or two. "How can you say—" Victor started. "You know I—"

He hadn't shifted his hold on her even an inch, but she winced. "Careful. I'm still hurting."

Abruptly, Victor released her hands. "I'm sorry. Did you get Neil to check it out?" He flushed. "Of course not." They didn't have the chance. "Lemme call him and—"

With a sad laugh, Lilah murmured, "What would be the point? It's not as if Prince will let any of you go to the clinic and bring me pain pills." And she certainly wasn't asking him to have his lackeys fetch her anything. Gingerly, she placed her fingers on her hip.

Victor's eyes went automatically to her midriff. The tips of her nails brushed against the slit in the side of the tunic, shifting the fabric ever so slightly to reveal the injured skin.

"I'm black and blue," she whispered.

His breath came in angry puffs. "The bastard," he ground out.

"What else can you expect from a drug lord?" Lilah sighed. "Victor, you know I... you've seen me in the corporate world. I can argue constitutional law. I can play my part in your plans. This is the first time I... I'm going to be alone, Victor. With Prince! Do you understand what he expects me to do? Do you understand what will happen if I dare to say no?" She glanced down toward the bruise on her lower belly. "I am afraid. It's... God, I'm so afraid."

In an instant, Victor was holding her hands again. "Nothing's going to happen," he soothed.

"And your brother... more than a decade of marriage, and this is what I get from him?" A couple of awkward pats landed on the back of her head. "Prince *kicked* me, and all Brad can say is—"

"I swear to God I will..." With an indistinct mutter, Victor wrapped an arm around her shoulders. "*I* will make sure Prince pays for it."

"How?" Lilah asked, her tone bitter. She rested her cheek against his chest. "You're not going to be around in Burma. Am I supposed to handle it myself?"

"Tell me what you want me to do," he said, his deep voice rumbling through her skull.

"What about your brother?" she asked. "Family first, right? I'm not family."

"Who says?" Victor exclaimed. "You're as much family as Brad. He thinks you'll find a way. I mean... you always do. But you've made it clear you need help this time. I'll talk to Brad."

"Will you? You agreed when he asked you to sacrifice your whole life for him. How long were you and Luisa married when you decided to go on this exile with your brother? A few months? And remember Gabriel. Brad asked you to sacrifice your *wife* for him. Your child, too. You agreed."

Releasing her, Victor said, "But *you're* in danger. Luisa and Gabe weren't."

"Brad doesn't care whether I live or die. Remember what happened with the congressman... Helen's husband. Brad let the rapist go." Lilah sat up. Eyes swimming with tears, she lamented, "And all of you agreed. None of you cared what could've happened to me."

"C'mon, Lilah," Victor admonished. "*I* care."

"Only until Brad talks you out of it."

Victor protested, "Not true."

"Oh?" Lilah asked. "Look around... look at all of us. Scott should be in a lab somewhere, charting stars. Instead, he's... Neil's working as a quack! And Alex. My God! Because of Brad, Alex turned himself into a woman. You... you lost your wife and your only child."

"Lilah—"

A sob escaped, quickly stifled. "I begged you not to let Brad get himself mixed up in Steven's plans. You and Alex told me you didn't have any option but to follow orders because Brad wasn't merely your big brother. He was your boss. Look where following him got us. Gabe is what... thirteen now? Would you recognize him if you saw him on the street? Even after all this, you continue to blindly follow your brother's orders. So how can I possibly expect you to help me with Prince? What difference will it make to you if I get killed?"

"It's different," Victor swore. "Of course it's different. I won't let you face Prince on your own no matter what Brad has to say about it."

"He'll have plenty to say. I'm so tired. I simply can't bear another fight." She stood, stumbling a little. "I... I should go. I don't know why I thought you'd—"

"Please don't go," Victor said, his fingers closing around her wrist. "We won't tell Brad. You and I will find a way to get us all out of this mess."

More soft sobs... husky voice low, she said, "Don't say it if you don't... do you really mean it, Victor? Because there might be one way."

In a few minutes, she watched as Victor marched out, shutting the door behind him. Lilah willed her muscles to relax. Survival was the name of the game now, and her moves were merely intended to ensure the allegiance of every piece on the chessboard.

Chapter 45

7 PM

Penthouse floor, The Mermaid

Outside on the beach, the rave party started. Electric guitars, drums, the roar of the crowd... only the faint reverberation of the sound-proofed walls would've alerted the occupants of the top floor to the wild celebration going on by the ocean.

Lilah took a cautious step out of the elevator. The hallway was empty except for her and the two men standing guard at the door to the suite.

"Weapons?" one of them asked, holding out a hand. The tone was impersonal as though he were simply asking someone to surrender contraband at the airport check-in line.

"None." All the exiles got their guns confiscated. Except of course for Alex's sniper rifle and submachine gun, both of which were safely concealed below the false bottom of his suitcase. Prince's security weren't aware of the spare weapons in the clinic, either, but they would still check anyone getting near their boss.

With a short nod, the guard said something into a two-way radio. In a few seconds, the door opened, and a sari-clad woman stepped out. A quick pat down later, the female guard said, "She can go in."

The tightness around Lilah's chest loosened a little. *Step 1, cleared.* The packets tucked into her bra remained undiscovered.

When she entered the suite, it was to dimmed lights and the smell of roses. Soft music was coming from somewhere. The broken furniture from earlier in the day had been replaced by a little dining table. On top was an ice bucket and wine glasses. Dressed in a dinner jacket and pants, Prince stood from his chair. He frowned. Eyeing her up and down, the drug lord said, "You haven't changed. My own fault, I suppose. Since you were stuck inside the building, I should've asked one of the local shops to deliver."

"I... umm... I..."

"Never mind. I know you've come down in the world. Wait until we get home to Burma, and you can shop to your heart's content. London, Paris, Milan, wherever..." Wicked look coming into his eyes, Prince mused, "Or maybe I won't let you buy *any* clothes for a few months. You're not going to need them."

Lilah just about stopped herself from gagging. Telling herself to focus, she darted a glance around the room. There was another table to the right, near the window, holding covered dishes. No serving staff seemed to be present and no other guards.

"No one else is here," Prince said, startling her. "I'm not an exhibitionist. Priya moved into one of the regular VIP rooms. But the guards outside will remain to make sure there's no funny stuff from your side."

Two male guards and one female. The drug lord had claimed Lilah would be constantly watched, yet she didn't notice any special security around the elevator doors on the ground floor or the emergency stairwell. He couldn't afford to attract attention by bringing a large enough entourage on shore to man all entry points. Even his buddies in the local police force could be compelled to react if it became public knowledge Prince was at The Mermaid. Not to mention the fact the Russian mafia couldn't be allowed to know the real purpose of his visit to the resort.

The vise around Lilah's ribcage loosened further.

#

7:10 PM

The hallway

"Hey," shouted Tara, marching out of the service elevators. The two stupid men she remembered from before were still hulking around the suite entrance. A woman, too, dressed in a sari. All three pivoted at her call, weapons drawn.

"Tara, stop!" yelled Hema, scurrying out from the elevator behind Tara. The Nepali woman shrieked. "Guns! Oh, my God. Tara, they have—"

Ignoring the sudden churning in her tummy, Tara clomped toward the bad guys—Prince juniors. "Where's Krishna? I want to see her."

Krishna wouldn't hear Tara calling. The sound-proofing on this floor was excellent. None of the noise from the hallway would be heard by guests in the two suites. Only one of them was occupied currently, anyway.

"Tara!" A hand on the girl's elbow, Hema tugged. "Let's go back."

Shaking off the hold, Tara insisted, "I want to see Krishna. I'm not letting her go anywhere." Her voice quavered, but Tara kept her eyes on the baddies. Her skin was so hot. Super hot like she'd once again been running outside.

"The boss's niece," one of the villains murmured.

"How did you get up here?" the female baddie inquired, tone sharp. The VIP elevator was off-limits to anyone but the Very

Important People and their staff, and access to the service lift was also strictly controlled.

"Papa gave me a keycard for my birthday," Tara snapped back. They would at least suspect the claim was a lie, but it didn't matter.

Waving down her partners, the evil chick tucked her gun into a belt of some kind. "Take her back to the salon," she instructed Hema.

"I'm trying!" said Hema, tugging again at Tara's arm.

"Tara!" boomed a voice from the stairwell. Chef Vikram—Victor—bounded toward the group outside the suite door, his shaved head shining under the lights. At the sight of the weapons pointing in his direction, Vikram screeched to a halt, his hands up in the air. "Sorry... I'm only here to take the kid back down. She shouldn't see any of this."

"So take her and leave," ground out the female baddie.

Hema once again tugged at Tara, this time by her tee.

"No!" shrieked Tara, stomping a foot.

The evil woman's gun remained tucked into her holster, but the men kept their weapons trained on Vikram. Dammit. Tara was supposed to leave once the chef came on scene, but...

With an ear-splitting wail, Tara threw herself against the evil female. The chick staggered to the rear, but Tara wouldn't let go. Her nose was smushed against the fabric of the baddie's sari, and she couldn't see what else was happening around her, but the girl clung hard. "I'm not going."

"For God's sake!" Hema's fingers closed around Tara's wrist, trying to pry her away.

"What the hell now?" one of the male guards asked.

"Tara, go!" yelled Vikram.

A thud, a groan, a shout cut short. A soft weight landed on Tara's back, sending her and the evil chick lurching. Hema... reaching around Tara, the Nepali woman grabbed the pistol from the female villain's holster. In the few seconds it took for Hema to step back and Tara to release her hold on the baddie, Vikram had the two male guards in headlocks, one of them limp and the other waving his gun uselessly around.

Hema pointed her newly acquired weapon at the evil woman. "Don't move. I know how to shoot." Voice trembling, she added, "Leave, Tara."

She wanted to! Tara tried to make her legs move, but they somehow wouldn't obey her commands fast enough.

"Dammit," muttered Vikram. "This one has a hard head." He rammed the skull of the still-conscious guard into the wall.

A muffled report... the disarmed female screamed. Tara didn't realize the gun in the hands of one of the male guards went off until a hole appeared in the door to the suite.

#

7:20 PM

Inside the penthouse suite

Lilah kept her gaze pinned on the wine glass, still refusing to say a word. The muscles in her shoulders were knotting harder by the second. Her back was toward the door, and she didn't dare glance at her watch. How long had it been? The view through the window didn't help at all. Night had arrived before she walked in.

The lack of noise from the hallway was expected... no, it was critical to their plans but still nerve-racking. Prince's idea of romantic lighting was adding to her dread.

The drug lord had progressed from arrogant amusement to cajoling to outright threats. "Giving me the silent treatment is only going to make—"

A sudden whoosh, a crack... Lilah froze.

Eyes snapping wide, Prince twisted around in his seat. On the wall behind, a painting shuddered, then toppled to the floor.

Lilah leaped from her chair and ran to the door.

"Stop!" bellowed Prince. "I'll shoot."

Lilah wheeled around and lurched backward as she saw the gun in the drug lord's hands. The door shook, clicked open. "Down, Victor!" she shouted. Gunfire, screams, the sound of running feet... Lilah saw the two male guards lying unconscious in the hallway, their female partner sprinting to safety. Hema and Tara were stumbling around in confusion.

Why was the child still there? She was supposed to have distracted the guards and fled the moment Victor showed up. It was the only way to shield her from Prince's wrath if the plan failed. The girl could claim she really was trying to see Lilah and didn't know Victor and Hema prompted her to do it for their own purposes. Even the role Tara played in acquiring the little packets of white power could be explained away as being duped.

"Go to Alex," Lilah screamed, adding, "Maestro."

Victor's roar yanked her attention back to the situation in the room. The boxer/chef had rolled across the floor all the way to the dining table. Prince fired a couple of times, then stopped.

Thanks to the poor lighting and the furniture, he wasn't getting a good lock on the intruder, and the drug lord wouldn't dare waste the limited number of rounds in his revolver. Not when stopping to reload would give Victor time to launch an attack. But Victor couldn't stand, either, without giving the enemy the clear shot he needed.

Lilah snapped the door shut. It would take Alex a few extra seconds to get in with Tara's keycard, but any help fetched by the female guard would also not find it easy to barge in. Nor would the sounds of the fight escape the room.

Something, something... Lilah's eyes darted around the room. The vase on the side table next to the couch... the roses were tossed out. Hollering, "Prince!" she heaved the crystal jug at the drug lord.

One second, two seconds, three... Prince's eyes shifted. It was enough for Victor. Rising to his feet, he hefted a chair and threw it at the enemy.

Afterward, Lilah barely saw Victor move. The dining table toppled, spilling food and wine. Glass shattered. Somehow, the drug lord's gun was also on the floor, and both men were grappling, grunting.

Victor seemed to stumble. With another roar, he regained his footing. Windowpanes shuddered as the combatants slammed sideways into a wall. Running to where the weapon lay discarded, Lilah grabbed it.

Victor got Prince in a headlock, but with a jab to Victor's jaw, Prince broke loose. Before he could move away, Victor yanked him back by the elbow into a macabre embrace. Arms wrapped around each other's necks, they struggled.

"I have the pistol," Lilah shouted, but neither man seemed to hear. The air stank of angry sweat, but neither showed signs of tiring. Gunfire was supposed to be only the last resort in dealing with Prince, but she couldn't fire in any case. There was no way to make certain she wouldn't accidentally hit Victor, instead.

Sweat-slick fingers on the butt of the weapon, she watched for an opening. *Oh, God.* How long now? She never expected the fight to go on for more than a minute. She never expected Prince to *put up* much of a fight. He was some years older than Victor. Plus, while the drug lord was not a slender man, Victor was huge, and she'd seen him finish off the criminals in Ecuador in ten seconds flat. Not to mention the Pathan on the Pamirs. If the same Victor lost today...

Alex... where the heck was he? Tara would've told him by now what was going on, so why wasn't he here, helping Victor?

Victor stumbled again... and lost his grip on Prince's neck. The drug lord used the opportunity to throw his enemy to the floor. With a howl of outrage, Victor rolled with the fall and leaped to his feet.

Pivoting to the door, Lilah yelled, "Alex!"

"Wha—" The drug lord's head swiveled between the Victor and the door.

Before he could complete his exclamation, Victor once again grabbed Prince in a stranglehold. In seconds, the drug lord was on the ground, arms wrenched behind and Victor's knee on his upper back.

With Lilah holding the gun to Prince's nape, Victor used the enemy's own belt to fasten his wrists behind him. Then, the drug lord was in a chair, his mouth forced open by yet another tight grip on his throat.

Not waiting for an order from Victor, Lilah tugged out the four small packets hidden in her bra. One, two, three, four... Prince's eyes darted around wildly as she poured the contents of the packets into his mouth.

"Heroin," she informed him. "And MDMA."

The drug lord tried to spit out the white powder, but Victor kept up the tight squeeze on his victim's larynx, forcing the fellow to gulp air through his mouth. Lilah drew the curtains and flipped on every light switch she could find. The chamber flooded with brightness. While she settled herself in the chair straight across from Prince, Victor's firm hands on the drug lord's shoulders pinned him to his seat.

The noise outside was not supposed to penetrate the sound-proofed walls, but the air vibrated in time with the faint echo of guitar twangs from the beach. Seconds turned to minutes, which seemed to stretch into eons. Prince's color began to change, grow ruddy. Sweat visibly pouring down his body, he retched.

"We're ready," Victor said. "You don't need to stay."

"Yes, I do," said Lilah.

Elbows on the armrests of the chair, she sat straight and crossed her legs. Lilah watched unblinkingly as Victor simulated a fall from the seat for the drug lord. His head struck ground at an awkward angle. One gurgle, and it was done.

The twitching body turned abruptly flaccid. Jùn Wángzǐ, a.k.a. Prince, the drug lord from Myanmar, was quite dead.

Chapter 46

Out in the hallway was the female guard, Priya behind her. The actress's security flanked the women. Alex was holding guns on them, one weapon in each hand. The two semiconscious men on the floor—Prince's security—were groaning. Their revolvers appeared to be missing, presumably the ones currently in Alex's possession. Tara stood next to the elevator.

When Lilah exited, there were multiple gasps, some of relief, some of disbelief. Victor was still in the suite, hidden from view by the door.

Lilah nodded. "Yes, your boss is dead. Yes, I got him killed. And no, none of you is going to say a word." Smiling nastily at the actress, Lilah asked, "Do you seriously want to start another inquiry into your involvement in your lover's activities? You saw nothing; the people who work for you saw nothing. The cops will make sure Prince's presence in Goa is kept secret. They have plenty to lose, too, if it comes out he was here with their blessing. The autopsy is going to show a random tourist died of a broken neck... an unfortunate fall resulting from a drug overdose."

Now that Prince was out of the picture, Mathur could grease enough palms. The cops would agree such accidents were not unusual in drug users, especially when they mixed chemicals. The authorities wouldn't want to look further and start trouble for themselves. The corpse would be tagged with the name in whatever fake passport Prince carried.

"Go home," Lilah instructed the guards. "If you play it right, you can live off your boss's wealth for a good long while." Until other gang members realized Prince was no longer around.

Twirling on her heel, Priya stalked off. The guards dragged their still-groaning colleagues—Prince juniors as Tara called them—along.

Scurrying to Lilah's side, Tara asked, "Is he really..." She made a face, her expression a mixture of horror and curiosity.

"Yes," said Lilah, biting down the urge to reprimand Tara for not scuttling as soon as Victor showed up. A thirteen-year-old girl had no business... she could've ended up in Prince's crosshairs. A child could've died tonight as collateral damage in Lilah's war with the Kingsleys.

The elevator doors swished shut, and Alex finally lowered his gun. "What happened in there? I want to know."

"Why do you care?" Lilah taunted. "Live happily in the ladies' hostel until Brad's pardon comes through. Don't give a thought to what happens to me."

Alex's face blanched. "Not fair, Lilah. *You* decided not to tell me anything about what was going on."

"Fair?" she snapped. "Fair would've been you telling your brother enough was enough. Fair would've been you showing up to help on time—"

"Krish—" Tara interjected. "I mean... Lilah... that Priya woman and the rest turned up the same time as us. Maestro was holding them off."

"I was trying to..." Alex started. "We're lucky she and her goons didn't get here before me."

Lilah knew quite well the actress was supposed to be the star attraction at tonight's beach party. The flyers announcing her presence were all over the lobby. The hope had been Prince would already be dead by the time his mistress and her guards could attempt a rescue.

"You didn't bother telling me about your plan," ground out Alex. "And you never asked me... Lilah, I was trying to... you don't have a clue what I was thinking, what was going on in my mind." Raking his hair with his fingers, he added, "So don't... just don't, all right?"

Lilah laughed bitterly. "Yeah... you were trying. Too bad we'll never know what you might have done."

Inclining his head, Alex echoed, "Too bad."

"Let's get out of here," said Victor, limping to the door of the suite. "Mathur can handle the police. We need to figure out a way to keep the news of Prince's death from the Russians."

Glancing away from Lilah, Alex said, "He didn't get a chance to snitch to his commie buddies about us, and Prince juniors ain't gonna talk after what Lilah said to them. Also, Harry should be out on parole any day now. The pardon... a few more months... we should be safe from the Bratva until then. Worry about making peace with Brad over this."

"Nah," dismissed Victor. "He'll be happy Prince is gone. No harm done to any of us, including Lilah. Our immediate worry is finding a hospital."

"Hospital?" Lilah asked.

Leaning against the doorjamb, Victor groaned. For the first time, Lilah noticed the faint glaze of pain in his blue eyes. "I did something to my foot. It might be broken."

Lilah's eyes went to his lower leg. The right ankle was already swollen. Victor had continued fighting even with a fractured limb, refusing to stop until he killed the drug lord.

Part XVI

Chapter 47

Three months later, January 1996

Long Island, New York

The cast of *Friends* leaped around on the television screen as Michael nodded along to the title song.

Phone cradled on her shoulder, his ma ignored the show and walked up and down the basement. "Thank you," she said, tone grateful.

On the couch, Michael and Gabriel exchanged glances over the head of their female schoolmate. "The bitch," mouthed Gabriel. He meant the woman on the phone, not Sasha, the middle school hottie sitting between them. For the Kingsley boys, Officer Berra would forever be "the bitch."

For the last two years, she'd been acting like she was Ma's best friend. Ma never personally encountered "Reggie" when she'd been busy getting her kicks from humiliating Uncle Harry. What Michael and Gabriel didn't understand was why *Harry* was letting the officer worm her way into their family. He knew what she was like.

But neither boy could deny there was peace in knowing Harry was all right. They weren't happy Harry couldn't come home on parole when it was clear the board would approve in a heartbeat, but Michael's ma kept asking them to be patient. Harry surely had something up his sleeve, something he couldn't talk about. Right now, *Michael* had an important matter to take care of.

Ma was finally making her way up the stairs, the phone still glued to her ear. Michael jerked his head to the side at Gabriel, asking him to remove his butt from the basement. Sasha's mom would soon be here, and the longer Gabriel stuck around, the less time Michael would have to bring up the one burning issue in his mind. With more comical swag than needed, Gabriel disappeared up the stairs. Giggling as she was at the antics of the characters on the show, Sasha didn't notice. Her darkish blonde hair swayed across her shoulders with every movement of her head.

Closer. Closer. Michael inched carefully toward Sasha until his thigh was almost touching hers. "Hey."

She looked up, a puzzled look in her gray-green irises. "Hey."

Play it cool, Mike. "So I was thinking. Do you wanna kiss or something?" *Smooth. Real smooth, Kingsley. Idiot.* At least his voice had changed from the babyish pitch of the year before.

Unblinkingly, she eyed him. Then, she shrugged. "Okay."

'Okay'? That was it?

"But I have braces," she warned.

"I don't mind," he said quickly. He'd seen them flash every time she smiled. She also had tiny boobs under her thin tee and long, skinny legs, now encased in pink leggings. Puckering his lips, he leaned forward and touched hers. Soft and warm. She didn't move away. Encouraged, he pressed.

"Oww."

He leaped back. "What happened?"

"You cut my lip," she complained.

Outraged, he said, "No, I didn't." His teeth had been firmly inside his mouth.

"I told you I have braces."

It took him a second to compute. "Oh. Sorry."

Adult voices sounded upstairs, followed by footsteps thundering down. Michael scooted to his side of the couch. His heart slammed painfully against his ribs. In silence, he waved goodbye as Sasha's parents collected her and left. At the top of the stairs, she turned and stuck her tongue out at him.

"Did you two argue?" Ma asked, turning off the TV.

"No," said Michael, keeping his eyes averted. He half expected a neon sign to flash on his forehead, announcing to the world he'd just kissed a girl for the first time.

He frowned on a sudden thought. They never made tongue contact. Did it still count?

#

Few weeks later, March 1996

"I'm done with girls," Michael announced, flinging himself onto the couch in Temple's library. School was going badly for this particular seventh-grader.

Seated in his customary chair, Noah Andersen was playing a jaunty tune on his mandolin and stopped mid-note. Next to him was the plump, gray-haired lady called Wilma who used to be Mr. Temple's secretary. She visited her former boss almost every month, and they watched old silent movies starring Temple's mother. Miss Wilma always brought candy for Michael and Gabriel. Her right eyebrow was now raised.

Even Temple looked up from the chessboard on the table by the window. He was playing himself, and his black was close to checkmating his white. The former president might not be able to speak anything more than a few words here and there, but he wiped the floor with Michael and Gabriel every time they challenged him to a game. The boys hadn't given up hope of winning, though. In the meantime, Temple had his puzzles and his models. Assembly puzzles, disassembly puzzles, interlocking puzzles, fold puzzles, lock puzzles... you name it. There were replicas of architectural marvels Temple carefully assembled himself, model cars, wooden clocks, airplanes, even ships in bottles. The special workshop built next to the garage was a boy's dream.

Gabriel sauntered in, a hand in his pocket. "Sasha dumped Michael," he announced to the room.

"The young lady who drew all the hearts in your notebook?" asked Miss Wilma. "What happened?"

Frustrated beyond endurance, Michael snarled at Gabriel. "Why don't *you* explain?"

Gabriel said, "She says she won't go with him to the middle school dance."

Andersen's face brightened. "Easily fixed. We can arrange lessons for you."

"I'm not Gabe," Michael said, shooting a malevolent look at his grinning cousin. "I don't break girls' toes."

Tone injured, Gabriel said, "Hey! It was just one time. I didn't know I stepped on her foot."

"She needed a cast for weeks!" Michael revealed. The pretty gymnast with Olympic hopes had since refused to talk to Gabe. Her irate coach called Ma at home, but she soon showed him who was the boss. For a little bitty thing, Ma sure had a set of lungs on her and an impressive vocabulary. Both Michael and Gabriel learned some new words that evening, words she made them swear never to repeat.

"*Both* of you need dance lessons," stated Andersen.

"Not the problem," Gabriel said, walking to Mr. Temple to stare at the pieces on the board. He was taller than the former president now. Almost six feet. "Sasha gave Mike a long list of things he needs to work on. He doesn't dress nice, he doesn't talk nice, he's not romantic..."

At least she hadn't said anything bad about the kisses they exchanged. They even used tongue the last few times.

Gabriel continued, "Also, she thinks Mike has no sense of humor."

Michael defended, "I do, too. She just wasn't very funny."

Nodding, Gabriel informed the rest, "He said that to her."

Miss Wilma clapped a hand over her mouth but not before everyone heard the startled squeak. Andersen let out a crack of laughter, stopping when he encountered Michael's glare. "Sorry, but in matters of the heart, you need to exercise finesse, young Mike."

"How do *you* know?" Michael asked. "You're not married."

"True," agreed Miss Wilma, nodding. "But Mr. Andersen's what we women call a silver fox."

Andersen set his mandolin on the coffee table and took a moment to smooth back his gray hair. "I'm a musician, Michael. The ladies love to hear me play. They're going to love you, too. What *you* need to do is add some polish to your approach." Eyeing Michael's jeans and the faded tee under the half-sleeved, plaid shirt, Andersen added, "Maybe some decent clothes."

"Noah!" Ma objected from the door. "What Mikey needs to do is be exactly who he is," she continued. "If some girl doesn't like him... well, she doesn't know what she's missing."

"Sasha's not missing any dances," Gabriel called out. "Only Mike is."

Gabe wasn't missing the dance, either. Michael directed another murderous stare toward his cousin. Gabriel was a football player and overall good guy, and everyone in school liked him. Even after the toe incident, he practically fell over girls waiting to talk to him at every corner.

Chewing her lip, Ma was silent for a few seconds. "Maybe Gabe can ask Sasha to dance with you."

There was a strangled sound from Andersen. Miss Wilma was red-faced and clearly trying not to laugh. Next to Temple, Gabriel clutched his belly and bent double, shrieking like a hyena.

"Why don't you just kill me now?" Michael demanded, glowering at his ma.

"Okay," she admitted. "Bad idea."

"I don't care, anyway," Michael muttered. "Sasha's dumb." Except she wasn't.

"Mikey!" Ma plunked herself into a chair. "Mike, a relationship involves two people. You need to respect Sasha's decisions. You're not going to get her back by being mean to her. What you can try is being honest about how you feel. Is it just a dance, or are we talking boyfriend and girlfriend?"

"Sabrina," exclaimed Andersen. Turning to Michael, Andersen explained, "Don't listen to her. There *is* something called subtlety."

"Don't listen to either of them, Mike," a voice said from the door. Liam stood grinning, and right behind him was the lawyer, Grayson Sheppard. Uncle Liam added, "I'll give you all the tips you'll ever need."

"Yay!" said Michael, fervently thanking God for bringing the duo to the house at exactly the right moment. "Let's go, Gabe. Mr. Andersen's probably not gonna have time for flute lessons."

"Hold on, young men," said Grayson Sheppard.

His face grave, he handed a newspaper to Andersen. Ma read over his shoulder. They exchanged glances, and then, Ma said, "She'd called me. We knew this was coming as soon as you contacted Lilah's bank about activity."

Grayson had been very worried the Kingsleys would try to declare the exiles dead. So he preempted them by requesting the bank in Switzerland to put out some kind of statement about Lilah being alive.

"She couldn't get him declared officially dead, so she..." Sabrina trailed off.

What the— Michael was beginning to get scared. His mother certainly wasn't talking about *Lilah* declaring anyone dead, so who was this new she?

Maybe it was something to do with Uncle Harry's parole? The ongoing appeal? Michael and Gabriel were told enough of the adults' plans to keep themselves out of trouble, but the details of the scheme to get Harry released for good was not something shared with the boys. Still, they understood Uncle Harry pulled the brakes on the original plot, as he was worried it would be too dangerous for the people involved. Liam made it clear he didn't like the delay. He told Uncle Harry the only reason he agreed was because he, too, had a sister. Which gave both lads pause... there was danger to Sabrina? If so, the boys were relieved their uncle decided against the idea. So who called her now with whatever this new trouble was?

"How long before she files?" Ma asked.

"A few weeks," said Grayson Sheppard. "Their pre-nup was quite specific about financial arrangements, so the proceedings shouldn't take long."

Ma gestured with her hand. "Gabe, come over here."

Gabriel's eyes were narrowed when he reached her.

"We... ahh... have some news," Ma said. "There's no good way to say this. Luisa... ahh... your stepmom... she's applying for divorce."

Gabriel stilled, his eyes suddenly blank. He was several inches taller than Sabrina and more than a few pounds heavier, but he was docile when she tugged him into an embrace.

#

Later in the night

Michael opened the door to Gabriel's room and peeked in. The lights were off, but the full moon outside the sash windows was enough to show the occupant sitting cross-legged in bed, clutching one of the figurines his foster mother sent. Gabriel held fast to all the supernatural beliefs of the couple who raised him until the age of eight. He once explained to Sabrina in incredible detail the powers of the Great Goddess, whose statue was currently in his hands. He wasn't saying anything at the moment, although he surely knew Michael was at the door. There was absolute silence, with even the music system Gabriel got for his last birthday staying mute.

"You all right?" Michael whispered.

"Yeah," Gabriel said. "Luisa was never my mom. I mean... I saw her only a couple of times after Dad left." Gabriel flew to California at least once a month to visit Mrs. Garcia who fostered him until he came to New York to live with Michael and his mother. The lady suffered some kind of chronic illness and couldn't keep Gabriel any longer, but she adored him. The entire Mexican-American community in San Diego seemed to know Gabriel Ramirez Kingsley. Luisa was the only one who never called to ask about him. "The notice said she doesn't expect my dad to return, so she wants to move on. I was thinking... are they ever gonna return?"

"Uncle Harry says he'll bring them back."

"What if... what if they really are dead or something?"

Too startled to be upset, Michael asked, "If they died, the bank wouldn't have done what Uncle Gray wanted, right? Also, the Kingsleys would've told the papers about it."

Gabriel tossed the goddess icon to the table by the bed and swung his legs out. "But they could've died without anyone knowing. Maybe the bank just... I don't know..."

"Don't you want them to return?" Michael asked, perplexed. His own feelings about his dad were mixed to say the least, but he wanted all of them to return. He wanted them to get their business back. He wanted the enemy punished.

"No! I mean, I don't want them to die. But—" Gabriel took a couple of deep breaths. "What if it was not just about them not returning? I'm sure Luisa didn't like all those things... you know, the rumors about Lilah being married to all of them. I mean, can you really blame Luisa? I don't know why Aunt Sabrina wants them back home. Also, look at all the new stories about the Armor fellow and Lilah. Can you believe... some of them even said things about Uncle Harry and her?"

"Weren't you with me when Uncle Harry said the major is planting stories on purpose to make Lilah look bad?"

The whole world now believed Armor was some kind of working-class hero. Self-made, the papers called him, held back only by the circumstances of his birth. He also implied he'd "met" Lilah before her wedding to Brad. Some silly tabloids claimed the exiled "empress" had a fling with the major when she was a mere princess, their romance thwarted by her ruthless ambition. A few so-called journalists even claimed to have shed tears over the doomed love affair.

Uncle Harry, on the other hand, almost puked his guts out laughing when he first saw the story in the paper. His mirth sputtered to a stop when he saw his own name linked to Lilah's in one or two out of the dozens of reports.

"None of the shit is true," Michael stated firmly. "Ma said so. Uncle Harry said so."

Nodding vigorously, Gabriel agreed, "I know what they said. But Mike, haven't you ever wondered? Don't you remember? Lilah was beautiful. Maybe they—"

"Ice cream," Michael said, a sudden memory tugging him back to the happy past. "Chocolate-flavored."

"Heh?"

The foggy image of a restaurant. The view of the blue ocean from the window. There were lots of kids, laughing, playing, fighting, but they sounded so far away. And across the table were two women: Mama and Lilah. Their faces were serious. Michael heard a few names—Godwin, Temple, Amber Barrons—but mostly, he let it all fly over his head.

Dipping his face into the cup, Michael swirled his tongue around the creamy chocolate sundae. He slurped, letting the ice cream slide down his throat. A thought struck. If he used his tongue to dig all the way to the bottom of the cup, would he be able to bring the whole thing out of the dish like ice lolly on a stick? Heroically ignoring the fierce cold, he set about his mission.

"Mikey," came Lilah's voice.

Uh oh.

"What are you doing, little man?"

Lifting his head off the cup, he muttered, "Makin' ice lolly."

His mouth was nearly frozen solid, but Mama understood what he was saying. She laughed. "Like this?" she asked and swirled her tongue around her dish, coming up with a glob at the tip.

"Sabrina!" exclaimed Lilah. "That's terrible." She picked up her cup and held it to her face. "This is how you do it." In ten seconds, she was balancing almost one whole scoop on her tongue.

Under Michael's impressed stare, the glob wobbled. Eyes comically crossed, Lilah tried to slurp it back, but it plopped onto the pretty tablecloth.

Michael chortled. Mama guffawed, high-fiving him. A hand shoved a bundle of paper napkins under Lilah's nose. Clearing her throat, she sat up. "Thank you," she said to the waiter, her prim tone marred by the chocolate ice cream dribbling from her chin.

"Lilah used to take me out for ice cream," Michael said. "She used to hang out with Ma and me a lot. Ma's the smartest person I know." Technically true since Michael couldn't count as the smartest person *he* knew. Not too many people could claim an IQ of 150-plus. If his ma weren't worried about his social development, the school would've moved him up several grades. "If she says Lilah was nothing like what they say, I believe her."

"Thank you, baby," came Sabrina's soft voice from behind Michael. She brushed past him and settled on the edge of the bed, right next to Gabriel. Following her, Michael climbed on the mattress and sat cross-legged on top of the covers. "Gabe, why don't you tell me what's really going on in your mind?" she asked.

Picking at the comforter, Gabe mumbled, "When my... umm... dad returns, I'll have to go with him."

Ma contemplated Gabriel for a few seconds. Then, she said, "Victor's either going to agree to let you live with us, or he's going to get beat up—by me."

Gabriel laughed a little. "You're a girl."

She wrapped her arms around both lads, gathering them close. "I'll fight anyone in the world for my babies." Releasing them, she admonished, "Don't believe the stupid stuff the Kingsleys say about our family."

After she left, Michael accused, "You're a schmuck. You don't want Uncle Victor to return, so you start blaming Lilah?"

"Bro, you don't understand." Choking down on a half-sob, Gabriel continued, "I've never—he never wanted to be my dad, so why should I go with him?"

"Whatever," Michael said, getting angrier with each passing second. "Ma might feel bad for you, but I don't. You called Lilah a... a... like all those papers. Just 'cause you're mad at Uncle Victor."

"Yeah? Like you're not mad at Uncle Alex. He hasn't seen you for seven years. You don't have a dad, either."

#

Two weeks later

Sing Sing Correctional Facility

Ossining, New York

Girls, Michael fumed. Nothing had gone right after Sasha dumped him. She'd sashayed by his lunch table and told him to make sure he dressed nice for the dance as though she never said she wouldn't go with him. By then, Michael had stupidly asked another classmate. Taking back *that* invitation made things worse. The new girl made sure the news reached Sasha, and two days after they made up, they broke up a second time. All of Michael's dumb friends were laughing at him. The entire school thought it was a damned comedy!

Then, Ma picked up on the cold vibes between him and Gabriel. When they refused to divulge the source of their rancor, she dragged them both to visit Uncle Harry. Michael kept his gaze fixed on top of the table while Officer Berra talked to Harry.

Gabriel sprawled in his chair, with Ma between him and Michael. There were new shadows around her eyes.

"Sheppard," hissed the officer. "They're minors. Leaving them alone with you is out of the question. It's against regulations."

In a soothing tone, Harry said, "They won't talk if Sabrina's around. Please... just this once."

Officer Berra looked skyward for a second. "I could lose my job. If your sister wants, she can wait with the guards. But *I'll* have to be here."

Gabriel snorted.

"Take it or leave it," the officer said.

"We'll take it," said Harry.

Ma stood. "Thanks, Reggie," she said before joining the guards as directed.

When Officer Berra plonked herself into a chair, Michael and Gabriel shot annoyed glances at each other. They might not have exchanged a word in two weeks, but both knew exactly what the other was thinking. Officer Berra was trying to sneak her way into their family, and neither Sabrina nor Harry could see it. It aggravated the hell out of the boys.

"Talk," said Harry, tone steady.

With a smirk, Gabriel jerked his head in the officer's direction. "I think she's got the hots for you."

Michael chortled. They'd discussed it before. It was the best explanation they could find. Maybe she was bi instead of gay as she claimed to Sabrina. The boys always hoped to say it to the officer's face at some point... humiliate her like she used to humiliate Uncle Harry.

A red stain appeared on Officer Berra's brown cheeks. Her chest heaved in an angry breath.

The pleasant expression on Harry's face faded. Sitting back, he said, "Sabrina will take you home, and I'll let Liam know what needs to be done."

Home? But— "You're not going to talk to us?" Michael asked.

Eyes narrowing, Harry smiled. Somehow, the smile sent a shiver down Michael's spine. "I heard all I need to," Harry said. "What *you* need is a butt-kicking. Liam will make the arrangements." Leaning forward, he added in a quieter, meaner tone, "You two privileged jackasses think you can get away with disrespecting me and someone I care about. If I weren't in here, I'd have beaten the crap out of you myself. Trust me, neither of you would worry about having 'the hots' for anyone the rest of your miserable lives."

Face red and sweaty, Gabriel straightened. "Sorry," he blurted. "Sorry," he repeated, nodding in the direction of the officer.

Harry turned his cold stare on Michael.

Neck muscles hurting from the effort not to look away, Michael slouched in his chair and hooked his right ankle over the other knee. "Me, too. We didn't know you really liked her."

Contempt flaring in his gaze, Harry took in his nephew's defiant posture. "Understand this, genius," he said. "My liking should have nothing to do with the respect you show her. It should have nothing to do with her age or gender or even her badge. It should come from within *you*. The way you treat her—or anyone else—says more about you than about the other person."

The man sitting across the table from Michael was not Uncle Harry. He was Petty Officer First Class Harry Sheppard, celebrated SEAL and Medal of Honor winner. The voice did not belong to Ma's brother. It was that of a commander dressing down a subordinate.

Perspiration soaked Michael's shirt, gluing it to his chest. His pulse thundered in his ears. He could still see Ma at the far end of the room, but she seemed so far away.

The commander asked, "Michael Kingsley, do you want to know what your behavior is saying about you right now?"

Suddenly, Michael felt about two inches tall. Uncrossing his legs, he sat up straight. "You don't have to tell me, sir. It was conduct unbecoming, and I'm sorry." He made himself meet Officer Berra's glare. "Sorry, ma'am."

"Not enough," said the commander. "At Officer Berra's convenience, you two are going to do whatever chore she sees fit to assign."

Face brightening, the officer said, "My garage could use a cleaning."

Michael and Gabriel said in unison, "We'll do it." How much work could it be?

"Now," said Harry, tone still tense. "Let's hear what happened."

Once again, Gabriel and Michael exchanged glances. "Just the same stupid shit from magazines," Gabriel admitted. "I said maybe the stuff about Lilah was true. My mistake. It won't happen again."

"Is it why you weren't talking?" Harry asked Michael. "Because Gabe insulted Lilah? But you found it funny when he said something similar about Officer Berra."

"I'm sorry." Michael said. He'd keep saying it until Harry relented. Until the pride Michael was used to seeing returned to his uncle's eyes. "We were trying to embarrass her, but we were wrong. It won't happen again."

Uncle Harry subjected Michael to a steady regard. It couldn't have lasted more than a few seconds, but when it ended in a slow nod, Michael felt like he won a marathon.

"We were thinking..." Michael continued. "It's been years since they... our... uhh... fathers... I mean, papers say dumb stuff all the time, but it's... it's..."

Harry winced. "Not easy, I know, but preparation is critical in any war. Mike, will you take my word for it when I say I'm not simply wasting my time?"

"I get it, sir," Michael said. "We're ready to wait."

"Won't be long," Harry promised. "In the meantime, we cannot have dissension in the ranks."

Gabriel turned to Michael. "Bro, I shouldn't have said the stupid stuff about you having no dad. None of them got any choice about leaving... not my dad, not Uncle Alex."

Didn't they? Michael wasn't so sure. But Gabriel was wrong, anyway. "I do have a dad," Michael said. "Uncle Harry." For the last seven years, Michael Kingsley had been Harry Sheppard's son. Holding his breath, Michael waited for Harry's response.

For a moment or two, Harry did nothing. Then, he reached over the table and grabbed both boys by the scruff, saying, "Don't let Sabrina hear you."

Michael grinned in relief, having seen the brightness in Uncle Harry's eyes.

Chapter 48

A few months later, June 1996

Ossining, New York

The brakes hissed as the train rumbled to a stop. Michael followed Gabriel out and spat the wad of gum into the trash can. They didn't have far to walk. The home Grandma Berra left the correction officer was close enough to the tracks to make the walls shake in sync with Metro-North's schedule.

"Why the hell did the old lady keep so much junk in there, anyway?" Gabriel complained.

The punishment for mouthing off wasn't as bad as they'd expected. It was much, much worse. Apparently, Officer Berra was so damned busy at her job she never got to clean out the garage in the time between her grandma's passing and her moving in. Stacks of old magazines and newspapers, boxes crammed with photographs and memorabilia, broken electronics, gasoline containers, power tools, stained rags, bricks, flowerpots, electrical fixtures... Gabriel even found a couple of dead rats. Piles of junk forced the officer to park outside.

Then, she discovered a puddle in her living room. Neither Michael nor Gabriel had any experience with such things, but climbing on the roof to fix the tiles was fun. So when they were asked to return to do more maintenance work, both agreed with alacrity. Gabriel's current protest was merely for show.

"She's *paying* us," Michael reminded his brother. Unlike Ma, who felt they should be doing chores for free, the officer promised minimum wage. Michael sure could use the money. Since he and Sasha got back together (again!), his expenses skyrocketed. Movie tickets cost a lot, as did snacks, but man... was she ever worth it! With her Rachel haircut and her long, toned legs, Sasha was the girl of every middle-schooler's dreams.

At least she let him get to second base. Michael nearly whimpered at the memory. He was still far, far behind Gabriel who'd already gotten a home run. Once he shot past six feet, Gabriel constantly had older chicks drooling all over him. Michael was not going to be left behind. He was doing his best to talk Sasha into *it*.

A couple of hours later, he used the broom to whack at a dried clump of... something on the garage floor. It looked red. Ketchup? Or maybe it was *blood*. Maybe a criminal was beaten up by the officer. She brought one of the inmates here to brutally torture him to death. Michael grinned to himself. He'd have to run the theory by Gabriel. At the moment, Gabriel was in the basement, moving boxes. The *air-conditioned* basement, while Michael was stuck in the garage.

Like his dad and uncles were stuck God only knew where, and Major Armor was chilling it in New York and making up stories about Michael's family. The major needed to pay for what he did. Michael would never forget the satisfaction on Armor's face when he ordered his subordinates to slam Alex Kingsley's face into the wall. Armor watched in glee as Charles Kingsley assaulted Lilah.

The major in fact instigated the attack. Someday, he would regret his role in it. Michael would make him.

A horn blasted through the relative silence. Michael jumped and followed it with every cuss word he knew. Another train. How did the Berra woman sleep in this house? And the heat... the shutter was left up, but bright daylight beat into every corner, turning everything blistering hot. Michael could barely look out into the street without the sun scalding his eyeballs. Perspiration trickled its way down between his shoulder blades. With a growl, he tugged his tee off and threw it to the side. Officer Berra could either install air-conditioning in her garage, or she could put up with the sight of Michael clad only in his khaki shorts and Birkenstocks.

"Chugga, chugga, chugga, chugga, choo, choo," he sang. The ground trembled as the locomotive rolled past.

"How old are you, four or something?" shouted a female voice.

Startled, Michael squinted in the direction of the open shutters. As the sounds of the engine faded, a silhouette detached itself from the blinding light and walked in. It was all Michael do to keep his jaw in place.

Dainty feet—clad in those stretchy sandals girls seemed to like—led to long, brown legs. Perfectly spherical buttocks were covered by a pair of Daisy Dukes so tiny they might have been a bandage. Her waist was so small Michael could've spanned it with one hand. Gorgeously rounded breasts strained against the ribbed fabric of her cropped tank. Tight, black curls tumbled to her mid back. Blue eyes, startlingly bright against dark coloring, stared back at Michael.

A throbbing started in his groin, radiating through his chest, his limbs, his brain. Blood pounded through his arteries, mimicking the chugging of the train. All thoughts of Richard Armor and the network and the war they were fighting faded from Michael's mind. He struggled to break free of the lust pulling him off-track.

The girl's upper teeth peeked out, tormenting the full, luscious, blood-red lip.

Michael lost the battle. His groin turned to granite. Voice hoarse, he said, "Fourteen." Under his breath, he added, "Almost."

Unfortunately, she didn't miss his amendment. "You don't look thirteen," she observed, eyes leisurely caressing his pecs and abs.

"I'm a wrestler," Michael said. "How old are *you*? Actually, *who* are you?"

"Sixteen," she said, sauntering to him. "I'm Erika." They were so close Michael could smell the gum on her breath, could feel the rise and fall of her chest with every breath. "Who are *you*, and what are you doing in my sister's garage?"

Part XVII

Chapter 49

A month later, July 1996

(6 ½ years after Harry's arrest and 7 ½ after the exile began)

New York, New York

Richard eyed the wall clock in his living room, his irritation mushrooming by the minute. Phone call after phone call after phone call from the customer's personal assistant had delayed the major almost to the point of missing the flight to Corpus Christi to meet with the *same damned customer.* If the gentleman had not been the youngest son of the monarch of a small but wealthy kingdom looking to purchase oil, Richard would've told them where to shove their anxieties.

To top it off, the cleaning service hadn't shown up yet. Richard forked out a good amount of cash every week to leave his apartment as neat as possible so when he returned, he could relax in peace. It looked like he wasn't going to get what he paid for this time.

"Right," he said on the phone to the royal fellow's assistant, barely managing to keep the impatience out of his voice. "But we can discuss this face-to-face. I'm on my way there. Or lemme get to the cab, and I can call you on my cell." The buzzer rang. *Finally!* It was the doorman's signal, letting Richard know the cleaning lady was on her way up. "Got to go," he said into the phone. "I promise we'll talk more when I get there."

It took another couple of minutes for the whiny idiot to hang up. Grabbing his blazer from the back of the La-Z-Boy, Richard strode out. When he jerked the door open, the person he'd expected was nowhere in sight. Wearing a cream-and-white housekeeper's uniform, a new maid waited. A petite blonde with bouncy curls.

She smiled, her lips curling seductively. "Hi," she said. "I'm Nikki. Your usual girl is out sick."

With a brisk nod, Richard said, "I don't have the time to wait until you're done. Call the doorman, and he'll give you a tip." The fellow would also make sure nothing went missing from the apartment.

#

Two weeks later

If Richard could turn the clock back, he'd have never left active military service. Armed with the hindsight of the last few years, he knew he could've eventually won against General Potts and the Kingsleys. Since Richard changed careers—first to law, then to business—he'd been successful, but he never found either enjoyable.

To add to months of playing cat-and-mouse games, the royal pain in the ass who wanted to buy oil from Armor Drilling Company drew out the final negotiations for days. At the last minute, he inexplicably changed his mind. A colossal disregard for other people's time, but what else could you expect from someone who never worked for a living?

If it weren't enough, Phillip Potts called with the news he simply couldn't get anything out of Prince except messages through his associates, claiming he was still searching for the missing exiles. There was also the gossip swirling about DNA evidence in the Luce case. Richard had studied the police records over and over. Warden Berra's cop friends could look all they wanted, but nothing would be found. Still, if Sheppard and his team started the rumors, there was most certainly some purpose to them. His refusal to apply for parole was yet another concern. Steven constantly brought up Ryan Sheppard's fragile health to Hector, marveling how Harry could stay away. Nope, no dice. The tricky bastard was up to something.

Needing to work off contained aggression, Richard ran up the stairs. Footsteps echoed, and warm air swirled around. He opened the emergency exit to his floor and frowned at the racket. His neighbors were a couple, the chief of surgery at one of the university hospitals and his trophy wife. They weren't usually the noisy sort.

He craned his neck. Looked like the open door was *his*. There was yellow tape across the space, two cops standing guard outside. "What the hell?" Richard demanded.

"Stand back," shouted a man in NYPD blue. "This is an FBI investigation."

"This is my home," said Richard. "If you got in without my permission, you'd better have a warrant." They did have a warrant. Cold and shaky, Richard watched as they carried his computer out, followed by the folders from his desk. "Your chief will hear from me," he promised the agent in charge.

#

A few days later

Pacing the living room, Richard shoved his fingers into his hair. Someone apparently called in a tip to the FBI, saying there was documentation of Richard directly profiting from child sex trade... with James McCoy working as his assistant. The caller provided enough evidence for the judge to issue a search warrant.

"How could you have been so stupid?" JD taunted from the couch. "Having McCoy work for your company."

Richard wheeled around, his fingers curled into tight fists. Only the awareness of the bastard's relationship with Steven stopped Richard from smashing the aristocratic nose into the worthless brain behind. "Get the hell out. And stay out."

Steven didn't say a word to stop the former congressman as he slunk away. Nor did the other two men in the room—Major Phillip Potts and Steven's maternal uncle, Stanley Gander. Richard was thankful Charles wasn't around to make the headache worse.

"I didn't hire McCoy for anything except the Luce episode," Richard said to his friends. In fact, he even considered arranging a little accident for the murderer afterward. Problem was the attention it might have invited from the authorities, especially with Sheppard claiming McCoy was involved in Will Luce's death. There was also the fact Richard would either have to take care of it himself or hire yet another killer to do the job. Besides, McCoy didn't connect Brennan with Major Armor. Richard was safe... or so he believed. Now, he'd be the prime suspect even if McCoy got killed by a random car. "And I had nothing to do with the contractor's side business."

"I believe you," said Phillip, leaning back in the recliner.

Steven nodded in agreement. "You're not an idiot."

"M-Major," stuttered Steven's uncle, his accent southern. Unlike Phillip who was only unnoticeable when he made himself so, Stanley Gander's slight form and quiet demeanor rendered him nearly invisible among the Kingsley crowd. Even Mrs. Gander—who raised their kids in Texas while her husband worked up north—was small and meek. The Gander role in the saga was limited to assisting Steven exactly once, but Stanley was routinely named among the villains by Noah Andersen. "How did..." Stanley shook his head. "I don't understand how anyone managed to sneak in here and plant evidence."

"The maid service," Richard said, continuing his march up and down the hardwood floor. He should've checked. As soon as he saw the strange face, he should've called to verify. Only, he'd been in a damned hurry thanks to the royal fool. Or perhaps Richard was the one played for a fool with deliberate delays intended to distract. "This supposed link between my business and McCoy... Warden Berra has been asking questions. It's connected, I'm sure."

With the heel of his hand, Steven wiped sweat from his forehead. "We have to do *something*. Maybe Grandfather can get this warden transferred."

"Justice Kingsley has already told us his criteria for dealing with corrupt officials," Richard pointed out. "Only someone with as much to lose as us... and also through multiple layers. Or the justice would need a compelling cover like he did with the trial in Cuba. What excuse will your grandfather give for wanting Warden Berra transferred? Moreover, what makes you think transferring him will do the trick?"

"If he's not around, the girlfriend won't be enough to protect Sheppard," Steven argued. "We can get him in prison."

"The minute we do, the warden will scream bloody murder." Literally.

Voice desperate, Steven suggested, "Let's kill *him* then. It will put an end to the investigation."

Richard snapped, "We already talked about this, Steven. If a high-level official like Berra ends up dead, even in an accident, the department will investigate. The union will raise a stink. Cops, correction officers... they don't let such things slide. Every prisoner in the state will be asked questions. Somewhere down the line, someone will blab, and *we'll* end up in prison. We'll need to leave the warden alone for now and figure out how to deal with the planted evidence. The papers can easily be disproved, but the computer—" Arrested by a sudden thought, Richard halted. "What we did in Panama," he muttered. They'd sneaked evidence into Lilah Kingsley's computer to trap her. Except it didn't work as intended.

Both Phillip and Steven sat up. Stanley Gander blinked rapidly, his mouth open. "Sheppard," Steven ground out.

Feeling dizzy, Richard said, "This was not simply an attack. It was a message." Sheppard *wanted* Richard to know who arranged it.

Chapter 50

The next day, July 1996

Sing Sing Correctional Facility

Ossining, New York

"Warden," Harry greeted the approaching man and slid the magazine to one side of the table in the visiting room. The May 6, 1996, edition of *Time* carried an old picture of John and Jackie Kennedy on the cover. Harry harbored no particular interest in the former president, but he'd asked Noah to bring a copy. Inside, there was an interview of the terrorist named Osama bin Laden, who was suspected to be behind the truck bombing in Riyadh which killed five Americans and two Indians. Something about the fellow... Harry had not been in touch with old contacts in the CIA since his arrest, and he hoped like hell Noah was wrong about the complacence of the intelligence brass after the end of the Cold War.

"Read later," said the warden, seating himself. "This is important. Noah, good you're here."

Harry raised an eyebrow. A correction officer or two always asked to stop by when Noah and the former president visited. The Temple Foundation's latest endeavor involved a jobs training program for disabled cops and prison guards and scholarships for the children of deceased law enforcement personnel. On Harry's recommendation, a legal aid division for prisoners was also started, as well as a rehab center for inmates who completed their sentences. With Temple unable to do the usual fundraising, cash was initially difficult to attract, but businesses soon began seeing PR opportunity in the plans. The foundation was fast getting to be the most prominent such organization in the country. Not charity... Noah called it social rebuilding. After submitting requests or expressing gratitude, the officers usually retreated to a spot a few paces away.

If Warden Berra himself showed up to talk to Harry's visitors, something was certainly cooking. Three minutes later, Harry exclaimed, "Hair?"

"My God," Noah marveled.

"Yup," said Arthur Berra, nodding.

With an exultant laugh, Harry sat back in his chair. "It's... are you sure?" he asked the warden.

"Positive," said the bear of a man. Two microscopic hairs were found on the tissue in the pizza box at the scene of the crime. "Facial samples from what the technician told me." DNA was only starting to get big around the time of Harry's arrest and trial. Once he was sentenced, the cops stopped being interested in looking for other evidence. If it weren't for Arthur Berra's persistence, the two hair follicles would've remained hidden for all eternity. "We have the victim's DNA already," continued the warden. *"You* will need to provide—"

"Done," Harry said, almost feeling ... surreal was the word he was looking for. "Are you sure?" he asked again.

"A hundred percent," said Berra, holding up a hand. "But it's not as simple as you might imagine."

Noah nodded. "We need to put the suspect in the scene of the crime, or it could be dismissed as any random person's hair. The cook who made the pie, the delivery boy if there was one... whoever. We'll need a reason to crosscheck McCoy's DNA."

"And McCoy's not going to volunteer," Harry brooded. "Damn... a warrant?"

"We can try," said Noah. "The court has to be convinced there's reasonable suspicion to compel McCoy to provide a sample."

"McCoy will counter with the same cooked-up evidence from before," Harry stated. "He wasn't anywhere near Brooklyn, so why should he subject himself to government intrusion?"

"Yes," Noah said. He, too, laughed a little, the sound a mixture of bemusement and relief and elation. "The hand of God... incredible!"

"Some cases boggle the mind," agreed Berra.

Pushing his chair back, Noah stumbled around the table to embrace Harry in a one-armed hug. Temple looked on attentively as his friend of many years returned to the seat beside him. The two senior men were both in their early nineties, but unlike Temple who now used a cane to walk, Noah remained active and agile. The former attorney general's green eyes were also as sharp as ever, but they glistened with moisture all of a sudden. The secret service officers and the prison guards threw curious glances in their direction.

DNA... it was starting to sink into Harry's brain. He was going to be free!

"McCoy can refuse all he wants," said Noah, "but we're not going to let it go. You bet we're not. Lemme talk to your lawyer, Harry. All these years, and we're finally catching a break. I can't wait to tell Sabrina and the boys. Liam's going to be—"

"Hold on." Leaning forward with his elbows on the table, Harry pinched the bridge of his nose. "If there's actual evidence to prove McCoy was the one who stabbed Will Luce..."

"You'll be out of here," Noah completed.

Out the legit way, no schemes or tricks needed. Zero chance of failure.

Noah wasn't told anything about the original plan to free Harry using fake bank transactions. As a former attorney general, the failure to report an impending crime would land him in legal hot water, and the exiles couldn't afford to have all their supporters locked up. But Noah surely knew there was a plan. He would also have realized the delay in applying for parole was because of Patrice and her firstborn. It took time to sketch out and execute a new strategy, especially without help from Harry's former contacts in certain government agencies.

Liam was actively involved in every aspect of the mission, but he didn't know Patrice's story. It would've been unfair to even ask him to understand her pain when it was her son who was behind the murders of Will Luce and Lupe Valdez. Increasing worry over potential legal repercussions for Sabrina was the excuse Harry came up with to explain the change of plans. Once again, Noah was left in the dark, but both he and Liam would know the DNA—if they could prove it as McCoy's—would get Harry out without involving Richard Armor, without any uncertain schemes.

"Sir," Harry addressed Warden Berra. "I need one more favor from you. Could you make sure word of the new evidence doesn't leak?"

"What do you mean?" the warden asked. "The police department put out a press release two years ago they were reviewing your case for any DNA. You *asked* me to prod them into giving it publicity."

"And I'm very thankful for it." A tabloid or two came up with some crazy theories afterward, including visiting aliens and chimps trained by the CIA. "Let the gossip continue. What I don't want is any official confirmation. The... uhh... wrong people should not hear of it before we want them to."

The warden shook his head. "Once the defense attorney brings it up in court, there will be no way to keep it from the public."

"Besides the investigation team, the only people who should know are those at this table," Harry requested. "Sabrina and Liam and the rest... I'll talk to them, but no one else should be told, including my lawyer. Not until the timing is right."

"Not your lawyer?" started Noah. His eyes widened. "You're planning to stay! What the hell, Harry? Why?"

Because there was no other way Harry could keep his promise to Patrice Kingsley *and* ensure the failure of whatever new trick Richard and Steven devised to do away with their enemies. To save all of Patrice's sons, Harry would need to stay in prison a little longer. Lilah and the Kingsley brothers would be forced to wander in the wilderness for some more time. The cards needed to be played at precisely the right moment, or all of them would lose.

Chapter 51

Six months later, January 1997

(7 years after Harry's arrest and 8 after the exile began)

Corpus Christi, Texas

Air-conditioning was on full power, but the heat behind Richard's eyeballs skyrocketed. His attorney had made a trip to Armor Drilling Company's offices to deliver the news in person. The other shoe just dropped.

Richard already knew the FBI was angling to charge him as accessory after the fact to sex trafficking, including a few minors. Still, for six months after the raid at his apartment, he managed to avoid being placed in the same room as McCoy, his supposed assistant. The army major and Brennan, the Irish mechanic, looked and behaved very differently from each other, but Richard didn't want to take the risk. He escaped being IDed as Rickie Brennan by McCoy, which would have set him up for lifelong blackmail.

The FBI continued to insist James McCoy was Richard's assistant, dating back from the time McCoy was let out from prison. According to the update brought by the attorney, one of the alleged meetings happened in Las Vegas, the date coinciding with the day of Will Luce's murder.

"They have receipts under your name," said the lawyer.

The room rented under James McCoy's name had Rickie Brennan's on the left. According to the evidence collected by the bureau, Richard occupied the suite to the right. All the records from the hotel were altered to make it appear so. The security camera footage didn't show Richard, but the film didn't show McCoy, either. The feds contended the two men found some way to stay out of sight of the cameras.

"We know they're fakes," continued the lawyer. "Your apartment building in New York also has security cameras. All you have to do is show footage from the time, and you can prove you went in the day before and didn't step outside for a couple of days because of a respiratory illness."

Richard gave the exact contrived story to the cops about his activities on the week of Will Luce's murder. "It's been years," Richard said, trying to find a way out. "I doubt the management keeps the tapes this long."

Even if they did, Richard didn't dare ask for the film. Because while Richard Armor never left the apartment building, Rickie Brennan did. Rickie would be on the tapes from the hotel in Las

Vegas, too. The feds would connect the dots, and Richard would be outed as the mastermind behind Will Luce's death.

The lawyer tapped his chin with the tip of his pen. "It's a pity you already have your whereabouts on record with the police. If not, we could've arranged proof you were in a completely different city. We do have another option. We can get *McCoy* to say he was someplace else."

Richard leaned back in the swivel chair and hooked an ankle over the other knee, seething.

To save his own skin, he would be forced to withdraw the bullet he fired so long ago. He'd have to show McCoy had *not* been in Las Vegas. If the man lied about his location on the night of the Luce murder, the cops would immediately ask why. Why the elaborate setup in Sin City? They would conclude McCoy might have been in Brooklyn with means, motive, and opportunity to kill Will Luce, Sr. and blame Harry Sheppard for it. Richard could either go to prison for a long time for sex trafficking, or he could turn snitch, blowing the whistle on all of Steven's schemes in return for a lesser sentence. The FBI would see getting the rich and powerful Kingsleys for murder as more critical and would agree to minimum punishment for Richard. Sheppard would then be free, and Brad Kingsley would get his pardon.

Faced with evidence of Steven's treachery, the network's board would turn to Sheppard, the chairman ousted through the same deceit. Petty Officer Sheppard was also the proud owner of a second medal for bravery now. He could well get Brad reinstated as CEO.

And what a carefully calculated move! No one at the bureau seemed to be actively involved, or it wouldn't have taken this long after Sheppard's arrest to set up the ambush. The investigators were merely baited by evidence planted for them to find. In a better frame of mind, Richard might have admired the patience and the painstaking strategy. Right now, the only urge he possessed was to beat the smirk off Sheppard's face.

It wouldn't have mattered if the Myanmarese drug lord did what he swore he would. More than a year went by since the fellow last talked to Phillip Potts. Prince simply wouldn't come on the line, sending his lieutenants instead. Given the double cross he did before, Richard was worried. If Brad and the rest couldn't be found before Sheppard's plan succeeded...

Straightening in his chair, Richard said, "Let me think about a couple of things." Major Armor wasn't about to let Sheppard win. Even if Richard went to prison for a long, long time, the petty trickster was not going to get he wanted. *Parole.* Somehow, they needed to get Sheppard to apply for parole.

Chapter 52

Ten months later, October 1997

(8 years after Harry's arrest and 9 after the exile began)

Sing Sing Correctional Facility

Ossining, New York

The color of the massive steel door between the prison and the outside world was almost the same green as Harry's recently discarded uniform. Unlike the day he walked in, the bulky guard who now escorted him had a friendly beam on his face. Helping Harry haul bags crammed with books, the officer said, "Gonna miss the poker games, Sheppard. Wish you'd tell me the secret behind your damn royal flushes."

Harry grinned and set the bags on the ground. "You'd better return before Officer Berra reports you for tardiness."

When the door clanged shut, Harry turned. Sunlight hit his face hard, blinding him for a second. A warm breeze drifted around. He took a deep breath, filling his lungs with the smell of dug-over earth and fresh mulch. The smell of freedom... parole for now but exoneration if everything went as planned.

"Uncle Harry," called someone.

Shading his eyes, Harry blinked.

Parked outside the thirty-foot-tall tan wall was a black car. Laughing uproariously, two young men raced along the grassy mud bordering the tarred road. They were dressed almost alike— sneakers, jeans, plain tees under flannel shirts left unbuttoned. Except Michael had his sleeves rolled up.

Gabriel—already taller than Harry by a couple of inches— lifted him off his feet in excitement. Michael shoved his cousin aside, shouting Harry's name and smothering him in an energetic embrace. Tangled in youthful exuberance, Harry staggered.

He kicked to the side, sending Gabriel's foot sliding. The fifteen-year-old tumbled to the ground with a surprised grunt. Harry turned to Michael and wrapped an arm around his neck. In one smooth move, Harry spun the boy around and thrust him face forward onto the mud.

"Ha!" said Harry. "You make it too easy—*both* of you."

Gabriel scrambled up, roaring. "Prepare to go down! Let's get him, Mike."

Michael spat a tuft of brownish-green grass to the side and stood. "Careful, Gabe. Uncle Harry's an old man. Not as strong as he used to be."

"I still have enough juice to take on two little boys." Leaning forward and gesturing to them with his hands, Harry said, "Come on, *kids.*"

An insulted second later, the young men rushed him. Momentum kept them going when Harry jumped to the side. Gabriel teetered, unable to right himself, and Harry pushed him to the asphalt and dropped to the ground, a knee on Gabriel's back. Before Michael could react, Harry grabbed his nephew's arm and tugged. Michael fell across Gabriel with a frustrated roar.

"When you don't have tactical advantage," Harry grunted, "your best bet is to run. Not to get provoked into an attack."

Michael complained, "Two against one. We did have tactical advantage, but you cheated."

Gabriel shoved an elbow into Michael's belly. "Get off me."

Harry laughed. "Barely a whole brain between both of you... expect the unexpected, boys."

Leaving the two on the road, Harry stood and strode to the grinning man by the car. "Took you long enough."

Liam was talking on the phone. "He just walked out the gate." Snapping the clamshell device shut, he tucked it into his pocket. "Noah," he explained to Harry. "He and Mr. Temple are expecting you at least an hour before the press conference. Your parents and Dante are with Sabrina in Long Island."

Temple was still avoiding meeting anyone outside the select list he'd given Noah. Ryan and Sophia Sheppard were not on it.

Nor were most of the Kingsleys and the Barronses, including Lilah's brothers. The former president would wait in his own home next to Sabrina's until Harry showed up. Dante was one of Gateway's executives and could not be part of any public events in which Harry might talk about the company.

With one last look at the enormous structure which housed him for the better part of a decade, Harry climbed into the car and slammed the door.

There you go, Aunt Patrice, he murmured in his mind. *I'm doing everything within my power. Let's hope your son doesn't know much about poker.* Because Harry was about to pull off the bluff of his life.

Part XVIII

Chapter 53

A few hours later

Long Island, New York

Déjà vu... it was as though Harry were once again walking into the library in Temple's home for the presser mere days after the exiles fled the country. Outside the large windows, an unseasonably warm sun shone in the clear sky as yellow and orange leaves flitted about the browning grass. A hummingbird dive-bombed with more flair than a fighter pilot, trying to convince the female perched atop a lawn chair how he was the strongest feathered fellow in town, the one with the reddest throat.

Inside, furniture had again been moved to make room for the rows of chairs meant for the media. Newspapers were arranged in a neat pile on the main table, some carrying pictures of the late Princess Diana of Britain more than a month after her unexpected death. As always, the thermostat was set to seventy-two, the air dry to protect the books lining the shelves. First editions and famous texts in original languages remained locked inside glass cases. There was a steel-doored locker hidden behind one of the shelves, the same one Noah spent futile hours looking through for any records on Amber Barrons.

The models arranged alongside the books were new. Architectural marvels, ships in bottles, tiny cars, airplanes, a miniature Harley Davidson motorbike... all put together by Temple. A half-finished replica of the Roman Colosseum sat on the table by the window.

Harry blinked. A paperback lay spine up on the chair just as it did at the press conference years ago. Instead of Tom Clancy, this time it appeared to be a children's book, the cover depicting a bespectacled boy gaping at a cartoon train.

"Harry," called Noah. "We should wait outside."

When Harry turned, Noah was already walking out, but the former president lingered, staring at the two oil paintings on the wall across the windows. The portraits were also new since Harry was last in the room. The gentleman in the frock coat and stiff collar bore a slight resemblance to Temple... his father, perhaps. Harry recognized the lady as Temple's mother, Sylvia Fontaine. The glamorous blonde who once ruled the silver screen would walk out on her politician lover and their infant son, eventually marrying Godwin Kingsley's widowed father.

"Sir," said one of Temple's security officers, tapping him on the shoulder.

Harry followed the duo to the small office across the hallway. Liam and Grayson were already there. Harry's attorney was out of town, but one of his colleagues was filling in. Vahagn "Falcon" Papazian's concern was not criminal defense, though. He interned for the then-Senator Temple and considered himself a student of the former politician. Falcon looked like Hollywood's idea of a corporate lawyer with slick hair and expensive clothes, but he came with an impressive repertoire of legal maneuvers which earned him his nickname. Noah thought well of Falcon's skills, which said a lot. Just as importantly, his specialty was antitrust law. He usually defended companies from the government, but on Harry's request,

Falcon spent the last few years studying the network. Nothing would be said today about Lilah's plans for her former empire, of course.

In another twenty minutes, Harry dawdled in the small chamber as the rest of the group filed into the library. The media personnel were already in their chairs, anxious for the event to start.

Harry waited until the others in the team seated themselves. "Gentlemen," he called from the door. The chatter in the large hall gave way to the clatter of chairs and excited mutters. "Ladies," Harry said, nodding to the women in the crowd.

Clicks, flashes... TV crews moved equipment around to capture Harry's casual saunter to the main table where the former president sat alongside Noah, Grayson, Liam, and Falcon Papazian. The dress shoes on Harry's feet gleamed with his every step. The new haircut was courtesy of the celebrity stylist hired by Sabrina for the event. A Rolex adorned his wrist.

Tugging down the cuffs of the tailored blazer, Harry settled into his chair and grinned at the new and old faces in the gathering. "Petty Officer First Class Harry Sheppard, formerly of Gateway."

#

A couple of hours later

Juvenile voices echoed from the dining room of Sabrina's home where Gabriel and Michael were bickering over something or other. The setting sun bathed the garden in a mellow glow, and the temperature was fast dipping, but the argument between Liam and Sabrina showed no signs of cooling down. The Barrons brothers stayed silent as did Harry.

Swallowing the last bit of sweet, flaky baklava, Harry glanced through the dining room windows. The two young lads were apparently done talking and were headed toward the group of adults standing on the lawn.

"Hey, Uncle Shawn," Michael called, sounding irate. "Could you please tell Gabe mp3s are gonna *destroy* the record business?"

Liam and Sabrina's spat came to a sputtering stop. Sabrina's computer skills were no secret to her boys, but Shawn Barrons owned Game Changer Consulting, which made him a celebrity in technology circles. And apparently an expert in predicting the destiny of the music industry.

Shawn laughed and nodded. "Movies, too."

"Keep your records, Gabe," suggested Dan, also laughing. "In a few years, they'll be in demand as vintage items."

Singing some song Harry never heard before, the boys leaped and reeled their way to the basement stairs. Bemused, Harry shook his head.

There was the feeling again... *déjà vu.* Unlike Gabriel's buzz-cut hair, Michael's brushed his collar like Harry's did at the same age. Many commented on their resemblance, but Harry never saw it this clearly until now. The stride, the build, even the features. Except for the eye color which Michael got from his father, it was like looking into the past for Harry.

As soon as the lads disappeared, Sabrina demanded, "Say something, Harry!"

"What's he gonna say?" snapped Liam. "He saw the printouts Shawn brought us." Bank activity... showing transfer of money from Gateway to James McCoy's lawyer through a web of fake accounts. Jabbing the air with his finger, Liam continued, "How the hell can someone simply take a couple of million from the general expense account without Hector knowing? It's him. No question it's him."

"Are you *crazy?*" Sabrina ground out, nearly hopping around in her anger. "You think my family paid this McCoy character to kill your father, then got Harry framed?"

"How can you support Hector after everything he's done?" Liam asked. "He wouldn't release the cash for Harry's bail. Hector was behind Gateway's little trick with Harry's stock dividends." The company refused to release payments under the pretext of some internal review of the events which led to Luce, Sr.'s embezzlement and the murder. "Steven did nothing wrong according to what Hector says. Your *husband's* still out there somewhere because of Hector's buddies."

Tears thickening her voice, Sabrina asked, "Hector's an idiot, but he's still my brother. He's not going to... is this is your twisted idea of revenge, Liam? You must hate all of us. Your family's stock, the divorce, your father—"

Shawn murmured in distress. "Sabrina," called Dan, placing a pacifying hand on her shoulder.

"Revenge?" shouted Liam, clutching at his hair with both hands. "After I spent all this time... how can you..."

"Stop," said Harry. "Both of you. Right now. And think for a minute."

"About what?" snapped Sabrina.

"About how much Liam has done for us," Harry said, keeping his tone steady. "He lost his job with Gateway because of me. The board still hasn't released his father's stock, so he's working for Shawn. Liam went from being an oil broker to working as a clerk in a tech company. Thankfully, Gateway can't touch Verity's alimony payments. Now, we hear our family might have been behind his father's death. Runt, I love you, and I know you love me and Hector, but please make an effort to understand where Liam's coming from."

"I'm sorry, Liam," said Sabrina. "I do know how much you've done for Harry and Alex. But—"

"And you, Liam," continued Harry. "Wait a damn moment and remember we were expecting tricks from the Kingsleys. For God's sake... we *wanted* them to show their cards. So consider the timing of this new info. Eight years after your father's death, and you couldn't find anything except that McCoy couldn't possibly have been in Las Vegas. All of a sudden, just when it's looking like we'll force a confession from Major Armor, McCoy's lawyer gets money wired into his personal bank account? From an account being monitored by Shawn? And presto! On the first day of my parole, we find Gateway paid for McCoy's defense. It's the same trick we were going to pull on them, except in a roundabout way."

There was silence for a few seconds. "Elaborate," said Liam.

Harry inclined his head. "Chances are Armor and the Kingsleys are behind this. If they meant for me to think Hector is responsible, they'd have made damn sure his name was on the account. They don't believe I'll do anything for him, so they want me to consider other names. They want me to worry who else could be trapped. My elderly father, perhaps?" This was Richard Armor's answer to Harry's bluff. Voice lowering to a murmur, Harry added, "Game on, Major."

Chapter 54

Later in the week

New York, New York

Silence. There was absolute silence in Harry's fifth-floor apartment, but the stillness was nearly as overwhelming as the sounds of boredom and anger ricocheting off the walls of the Box. The gloom of night was almost as oppressive as the harsh fluorescent lighting in Sing Sing. Not even a roach showed up to give him company.

Sabrina and the boys had offered Harry the use of their guest room, but he declined, savoring the idea of being alone for the first time in years. Well... somewhat alone, given how Liam crashed in the apartment whenever he was in New York City. He was right now in the other room, presumably fast asleep.

Perhaps Harry should've taken up his old friend Saeed's offer to visit for a few days. As a small oilman with some peripheral involvement in the network, his vote could come in handy in any later tussle with the Kingsleys. It was imperative he not be implicated in any wrongdoing should Harry's latest plan go off the rails. Saeed was firmly told to stay out of it. Even the financial assistance he gave Liam during the investigation into the Luce case would've made him a target in Steven's eyes.

No old buddies, no former schoolmates... those whose help wasn't absolutely needed couldn't be allowed to risk themselves by associating with Harry, but he never anticipated the solitude would get to him.

Clad in comfortable drawstring pants, he stood next to the living room window and played a few notes on the saxophone. A loud buzz interrupted the familiar tune. Startled, Harry stopped and glanced toward the slightly ajar front door. The intercom from the main entrance... it was a new addition since his arrest.

In five minutes, Harry was staring into a face he hadn't laid eyes on in eight long years. Hector never bothered to visit his brother in prison, routing all communication through the defense attorney.

Harry scanned his brother's form for changes. Nothing in Hector Sheppard's blue irises suggested softening toward his sibling. There was gray in the blond hair, but neither the face nor the pugilist's body had lost any of the toughness.

"Are you crazy?" Hector asked, tone irritated. "You left your front door open."

"I got used to the service at Sing Sing. There was always someone to lock the door behind me."

Hector didn't laugh. He took two quick strides to Harry's side and enveloped him in a bear hug. "It's good to see you again." Drawing back, Hector swept his gaze up and down his brother, squinting for a moment at the small white patch of hair on Harry's left chest.

The strands marked the gunshot wound from nine years ago, the one he acquired at the first ever board meeting of the Peter Kingsley Network. A constant reminder of his and Lilah's story thus far... as if Harry needed one.

"It's good to see you, too," he said to Hector. "We have plans to make."

#

Almost a month later, the day before Thanksgiving 1997

When Hector called on Harry again, it was with the information Steven Kingsley wanted to negotiate.

"Half the network?" Harry asked, pouring fine bourbon into glasses.

"It's not a bad idea," said Hector, accepting the drink. "If Brad and Steven agree to take half each and cooperate to run them as one entity, we'll finally be done with this mess." Taking a sip, Hector added, "C'mon, Harry. How long can everyone keep going back and forth like this? You do want Lilah and the rest to return, don't you?" Hector paused, then continued, "All this time, and no one's spotted them. Even the false alarms stopped after the first couple of years."

Collapsing onto the couch with his own drink, Harry inclined his head. In the beginning, the tabloids averaged a story a week on sightings, mostly from India and Africa and the Middle East. "Lilah's bank said she's alive."

"Yeah, but who knows in what shape..." Hector downed a large gulp. "There were so many phone calls in the initial few months. First question would be about the reward for finding them. Thank God for secretaries who know how to... actually... let me take it back. Steven said there was one call last week. Someone from Bombay." Hector laughed. "The fellow had the audacity to demand his cell phone number."

"And?" asked Harry.

"And what?" returned Hector. "The secretary didn't give it to him, obviously. Crazy... he was mumbling something in broken English about transgenders and drag shows."

Transgenders? Harry narrowed his eyes. There *was* one transgender woman at least two of the exiles—Alex and Lilah—

knew well. *Rekha?* But if the group went to Bombay, they would've been found by now. Given Lilah's connection to the country, Bombay was not a city either the feds or the Kingsleys would ignore.

"My point is," Hector went on, "we can't keep battling each other like this. Alex and his brothers have spent nine years in hiding. You've been in prison for eight. Steven really would like to make peace. What's the harm in at least meeting him to talk about it?"

Of course Harry wouldn't refuse to meet. He couldn't. The fake bank records made sure there was no option for him but to show up and discuss terms. He would walk into the trap waiting for him.

"No harm at all," Harry agreed, nodding.

Hector heaved a sigh of relief. "Good. I wasn't sure you would... wait and see... it will be good for all of us."

One of the conditions was Harry needed to be personally present at the summit. Allowing himself a rueful grin, Harry consented, but with a condition of his own. All the Kingsleys had to show up, as well as Major Armor and General Potts. Phillip Potts, too.

Later, Harry shut the front door behind Hector and went to the phone. Despite it being the night before a holiday, everyone concerned agreed to convene at Sabrina's home.

"One more thing, Noah," Harry said at the end of the emergency conference. "Right before you leave for DC to talk to President Clinton, I want you to inform Godwin Kingsley."

"What?" exclaimed Dante. Whatever hair Harry's former boss had left was completely gray now. There were wrinkles, but Dante had wrinkles even ten years ago, long before Harry's imprisonment. The price he paid for being a worrywart. "Harry, are you—"

"When the Kingsley delegation arrives to negotiate, everyone present should be worried," said Harry. "Let Godwin know there's enough support in the Congress, but they're waiting to see if something comes up in the DNA investigation... you know, with all the rumors about possible new evidence. Once there's definite proof of my innocence, I can argue Brad was also framed. Let Godwin know I'm hopeful. By the time we get to Las Vegas for the meeting, I want him and Armor and the rest of the Kingsleys shitting bricks."

Chapter 55

In two days

Corpus Christi, Texas

Richard rocked in his chair, holding back the urge to get his hands around the FBI agent's throat. Steven was in the other chair, worry muddying his eyes, but he stayed silent. So did Richard's lawyer. Outside the office, fingers ran over keyboards, printers whirred, phones rang. The staff went about their business, but Richard knew they were all anxious about the future of the company what with the rumors swirling around about their CEO's involvement in the sex-trafficking case.

"Major Armor," repeated the agent. "Harry Sheppard is not an ordinary man. He's a former SEAL with a Medal of Honor and a

Medal of Freedom. Our chief trusts him. When he tells us McCoy was in Brooklyn the night he was supposed to be in Las Vegas, we have to investigate it."

As though any damned SEAL with a medal or two could order the FBI around! Besides, Sheppard had been saying the same thing for years. Except, his heroism during the prison riot transformed him back into a hero in the public eye. The press conference he did in Temple's home was mostly fluff, talking about his time in Sing Sing and the work he did through the Temple Foundation even while incarcerated. The issue of the exiles was of course discussed, but the talk was kept to generalities. Sheppard reiterated his determination to bring them home, stating Brad was blameless. A woman was assaulted while in custody, he reminded the journalists. Not one of the reporters challenged his assertions openly though support in the media was split more or less equally between the two sides. Political backing for Sheppard was also increasing, which meant the FBI now took his claims seriously.

Whereas Richard... oh, he had plenty of support, too. The charity division of his company donated money lavishly, and Major Armor was now a known name in philanthropy circles. His background, including the supposed heartbreak he suffered at the hands of Lilah Kingsley *née* Barrons was red meat for the tabloids. Unfortunately, the sympathy factor didn't prove enough to make the feds back off when the target of their investigation was the son of a mere chauffeur.

"Help us," continued the agent, "and it will also clear you of the sex-trafficking charges. Was McCoy in Vegas with you or not?"

"*I* was not in Vegas. I was in my apartment in New York."

"We have proof you were in Las Vegas."

"Your proof is bogus. My lawyer will convince the court of the fact."

The agent huffed in exasperation. "I don't get why you won't admit to it. I could understand the lie when we didn't know about the Brooklyn business. But now, you can come clean. If you were in Vegas, and McCoy was in Brooklyn, the case against you won't hold up. It will also help rectify the miscarriage of justice which happened in the Will Luce murder case. I could even help you work out a deal so the bureau won't prosecute you for lying. If not... Major, aren't you supposed to get married soon? You have the rest of your life ahead of you. Don't mess it up."

Richard stood. "My fiancée trusts me. She knows I was in New York. Alone... in my apartment. Now, I want you to leave."

As the door closed behind the agent and Richard's lawyer, Steven muttered, "Sheppard's setting the stage. I bet he's already told the bureau you arranged the murder."

"No question about it," Richard agreed, gulping cold water from a plastic bottle. "He hopes I'll crack and betray you. If I admit I was in Vegas faking McCoy's presence, they'll let me plead to some lesser charge. They want me to snitch on you, instead. It will be a big catch for them... Steven Kingsley, CEO of the network, going down for the same murder Sheppard went to jail for. Not gonna happen."

"If you don't turn snitch, Harry will make sure the agents are around to watch the grand meeting in Vegas. I'm sure he's tipped them off McCoy's likely to be there."

"If I don't confess, he wants them to hear McCoy identify me as Brennan."

"We should've killed McCoy before," said Steven. It wasn't considered necessary since the murderer didn't have reasonable cause to suspect Brennan and Armor were the same man. Nor was it thought prudent to do away with McCoy with Sheppard accusing the embezzler of killing Will Luce. Now, it was impossible to get rid of him without further scrutiny falling on Richard. "Or Sheppard... we should've tried harder to get the damn bastard. Because of him, you're in trouble."

"Petty Officer Sheppard is going to learn I don't give up easily. Even if I go to prison for sex trafficking, he's going to be back in Sing Sing for the murder of McCoy. So will Sheppard's father. Sheppard will regret tangling with me."

"Rich," exclaimed Steven.

"I'm not letting the son of a bitch win," Richard said, tone hard.

"I wish we never started this. I'd rather lose it all than see you in jail."

"You're not going to confess to anything stupid," Richard warned. "I'm not about to lose to someone like Harry Sheppard."

"What the hell, man?" Steven asked. "This is not a game. We're talking about prison. *Prison.*"

"Either way, I'll be in prison. I'd rather see Sheppard there with me than you."

Part XIX

Chapter 56

A week later, December 1997

Miami Beach, Florida

Timeshares were a fantastic business. Selling the same property several times over? Legally? One of McCoy's pals from his Hell's Kitchen days now owned a company managing such properties and offered him a cut if he could bring in so many customers a year. McCoy put to work his short, lean build, dark, curly hair, and blue eyes, charming marks into signing contracts. He once again had cash in his wallet. Also, the ability to stay at any of their apartments which were not occupied.

Looking around the one-bedroom maintained by his company, he grinned in satisfaction. Didn't matter if the décor was slightly shabby, if the blue paint was faded, or how the air smelled strongly of coconut. The place made him money. James McCoy was indeed a happy man.

James McCoy was also a smart man. He knew Rickie Brennan didn't drop out of the sky just to help ol' Jimmy out of jail. Brennan had a reason for wanting Harry Sheppard arrested. After the successful completion of the operation, McCoy kept his eyes and ears open to find out who profited the most. His money was on the Sheppards. The older brother, Hector, probably decided he had enough of the younger one's tendency to poke his nose in where it didn't belong. The other possibility was Steven Kingsley.

When the FBI first came knocking, McCoy was scared out of his mind. He'd actually thought it was about the death of Will Luce. Talk of the sex-trafficking ring confused McCoy until he figured out the Kingsley lawyer was the second person accused of involvement. The man was supposed to be Steven Kingsley's best buddy—at which point McCoy became sure the Kingsleys sent Brennan to Rikers. Harry Sheppard or someone close to him arranged this new problem to get the Kingsleys to confess McCoy had been in Brooklyn, killing Luce.

McCoy was content to let the Kingsley family fight the FBI. It wasn't like they could snitch on him without landing themselves in jail. McCoy might have been the one holding the knife, but it was Steven Kingsley who put it in his hands. Technically, it was Brennan, but the fag was surely a Kingsley agent.

Too bad McCoy hadn't been able to pin down Brennan or the Kingsleys could've been persuaded to part with some of their oil money. After Brennan's initial arrival at Rikers, everything was done over the phone or through McCoy's legal counsel. To top it all, even the lawyer never met Brennan. The poor excuse for a defense attorney collected the money and followed whatever orders were given via messages. McCoy tried tracking the source of the cash, but he encountered a web so complicated he kept going in circles.

This morning, there was a call from the attorney, asking McCoy to meet Steven Kingsley in Las Vegas in a week. There were only two possibilities McCoy could think of. The Kingsleys were going to bribe him into confessing to the Luce murder without involving their heir and the lawyer-best friend, followed by moving to some island where he could live like a king, safe from the hands of American law. Or they could try to kill him. But

McCoy's death wouldn't put him in Brooklyn at the time of Luce's murder so the sex-trafficking case against their lawyer wouldn't vanish into thin air. No, the Kingsleys needed McCoy's cooperation, not his corpse. All in all, James McCoy was quite confident he was going to stay alive at the end of the meeting. Also, come out much richer, perhaps by millions.

In the meantime, there was the other scheme he had going. Phone cards. Again, completely legal. McCoy chuckled. Things sure had changed in the world. These days, there were legitimate ways to fleece The Dumb and The Stupid. McCoy checked his watch. Time to meet his new business partners.

#

Later in the day

The pool at the Ritz Carlton was crowded, families with young children splashing around. Old broads in flamenco-pink swimsuits enjoyed the sun in their motorized wheelchairs. McCoy cast an irritated glance at all the nauseating domesticity before walking into the restaurant. Major hotels no longer entertained the kind of glamor popular back in his day.

A white-haired man brushed past McCoy. Under his arm was a busty redhead, wearing a slip dress which left the lower edges of her panties visible. There were some things even the hotel chains couldn't control. Thank God.

Peering at the redhead's bottom, McCoy almost didn't hear his name being shouted. His partner was already at the reserved table with the second-in-command in the other chair.

The first thing anyone noticed about Albert "Blade" Wayne— even before his considerable girth—was the broad X-shaped scar on his dark cheek. Like McCoy, Blade was dressed casually in a cotton shirt and khaki shorts, but the blue Hawaiian couldn't mask the dangerous vibes emanating from him. Blade removed the baseball cap, revealing the tattoo of the dagger curving over his shaved scalp, the handle behind one ear and the tip ending close to the brow. Blade had recently been released from Sing Sing, where he encountered Harry Sheppard.

The second-in-command was skinnier, but not by much. Despite the hot sun, he was dressed in shiny polyester pinstripes, a fedora covering his lanky blond hair. A regular fashion plate. He, too, had been in Sing Sing and used to be the second of the other major gang, the Rivals. The Rivals' chief was McCoy's old buddy, but he'd been charged with the murder of a correction officer and disappeared shortly after. The dead officer was the same one who'd been tasked with assassinating Harry Sheppard according to rumors picked up by Blade Wayne. *Stupid cops,* McCoy thought contemptuously. Anyone with half a brain could've figured out Sheppard killed the officer and framed the boss of the Rivals for it. The second rose to the position of chief, but he didn't really have the brains or the personality for it.

Since their release from prison, the two former gangsters joined hands and turned legit, dealing in new businesses. Technology helped change the world back into the Wild, Wild West, and there was money to be made for enterprising souls. Few months ago, the duo came looking for McCoy, having heard his name in connection with that of Sheppard's. Curiosity, they claimed, about the man who put Sheppard in jail. McCoy admitted to nothing even after learning the other two shared his hatred of Sheppard. Blade's ascension to the position of undisputed chief of A-block was partly because of Sheppard's meddling, but the gang leader didn't appreciate the preferential treatment given to the prison hero. The meeting with McCoy was the start of a beautiful business relationship.

"What's wrong?" McCoy asked, pulling out a chair. "I thought we got everything signed and sealed."

"Boss," said the second, "we're here about something else. There's a new opp-or-tunity."

Blade held up a hand. "Let me. Jimmy boy, have you heard of the World Wide Web?"

Who hadn't? Everyone was talking about something called Y2K. Apparently, all the computers on the planet would come to a standstill when the new millennium rolled around. "Go on."

"Internet gambling," said Blade. "Completely legal, and we get to keep a cut of the stakes."

"I want in," McCoy said without hesitation.

Blade smiled, showing teeth in an even row. The money from phone cards had been good enough for him to afford a trip to the dentist. "You can, but it's not why we're here. Our tech has a sideline in—what do they call it—hacking. Banks, especially. We found something funny in one of the Caribbean banks. Cash transfers under your name. From a Rickie Brennan."

Heart thundering, McCoy sat up. "Tell me."

#

A week later

To circumvent U.S. laws, The Lucky Blade's proprietors had set up shop in Belize, but they kept a small office—a windowless room in one of the high-rises—in Miami. Folders containing the names of their patrons, a couple of computers, and two phones on a desk completed the arrangement. Just one employee: the tech "guy," with a weakness for electronic bank robbery.

McCoy had pictured a nerd with glasses and a pale face. The glasses were there, but the nerd turned out to be a black broad with one of the best butts McCoy ever saw. Something about the way she moved was simply magnificent... almost like a dancer who knew exactly how to keep men's eyeballs riveted on her body. Unfortunately, the dark curls cut close to her scalp ruled her out as a bed warmer for him. McCoy preferred hair he could grip in his fist.

He'd been back and forth between his apartment and this office for the last one week. He was supposed to fly out to Las Vegas in a couple of hours and needed the info on Brennan before confronting the Kingsleys. It would help him squeeze more money from them. Unfortunately, the "tech guy" had yet to come up with answers, and McCoy was barely hanging on to the last threads of his patience.

Pacing the carpet, McCoy asked, "Did you find the location of the sender?"

Ursula Robinson spat the wad of gum straight into the trash can and leaned back insolently in her swivel chair. "If you think it's so easy, do it yourself."

Luscious backside aside, "Urse" was a Class A bitch. Too bad.

"You know," McCoy said, trying a different tack. "With a better attitude, you could make serious cash. I know a couple of businessmen up north who'd be happy to keep you around."

With a foul curse, Ursula said, "I'll do my own keeping, thank you."

Feminism! It infected every class, including the hitherto uncorrupted criminal class. There was a time when women of his acquaintance would've been thrilled by the offer.

With a sigh, McCoy tried again. "You have no idea how much money is riding on this one. Find Brennan for me, and I'll cut you in... ten percent?"

"Ten percent of zero is still zero. How much money are we talking about?"

"More than you'd ever make from your thievery. Hundreds of millions."

Ursula eyed him unblinkingly for a few seconds. "Make it fifteen, and I'll throw in a bonus."

Dumb bitch. "What kind of bonus?"

"I couldn't locate Brennan from the bank's computer, but I hacked into the computer of this man you and the bosses were talking about: Harry Sheppard. Well, his sister's computer." McCoy's eagerness had prompted Blade and his sidekick to ask if Brennan was connected to Harry Sheppard. All McCoy said was Brennan was someone else with a grudge against Sheppard.

Excitement churning, McCoy asked, "And?"

Urse swiveled the chair back to her computer and stroked a few keys, bringing up a screen. "Take a look. These are his emails... and his sister's. Sheppard's talking about DNA. *Your* DNA."

"What do you mean?"

Mouth curled in contempt, she explained, "Like body tissue. You left some evidence somewhere. The cops are trying to get a warrant to match it with yours."

Evidence? To what? To Will Luce's murder? McCoy's head swam. He'd been cautious. His gloves were on the entire time, even while chomping on the pie. Brennan sent a curt message about the stupidity of leaving the pizza box and soiled paper napkin in the apartment, but the cops never found anything. So what tissue was Sheppard talking about?

"Bad?" Ursula asked, tone mocking.

Bad?! McCoy's breath came faster. All these years of thinking he was safe... if the cops put him in the apartment on the night of the murder, he was going down for a very long time. He needed... he needed... the Kingsleys could— "No," exclaimed McCoy.

This was why Steven Kingsley asked for the meeting. The DNA would convincingly put McCoy at the site of the murder, thus disproving he ever met the Kingsley lawyer in Las Vegas. All the Kingsleys would have to do was make sure McCoy kept his lips zipped about Brennan. DNA could be obtained from corpses, too, and corpses didn't talk. The Kingsleys could still be trying to bribe McCoy into giving DNA and disappearing, but chances were James McCoy would not make it out alive from the conference.

"I need to find Brennan," McCoy said abruptly.

The fag could help. He would *have* to help. He would be the other one with his neck in the noose once McCoy's DNA was proved to have been at the murder scene. Maybe Brennan could help McCoy get out of the country or something. He pivoted and sprinted to the door, only to find the bitch blocking the exit.

"Hold on," she said. "Where are you running off to?"

Voice hoarse, he said, "Get out of my way. I need to call my attorney." The hacker couldn't find Brennan, but McCoy's lawyer was used to passing on messages at some foreign phone number for Brennan to see.

"I thought you wanted to find Brennan," said Ursula.

"It's why I'm going to the damn lawyer," McCoy shouted. "Get out of my way."

Tone puzzled, she said, "I already have Brennan."

"What? But you said you didn't—"

"Sheppard's IT guy located Brennan. Sort of. According to Sheppard's email, Brennan's supposed to be attending a meeting tonight at New York-New York."

"Huh? In Manhattan?"

"The hotel in Vegas."

The same hotel where McCoy was scheduled to meet the Kingsleys? What the hell was going on?

Urse continued, "Sheppard's meeting someone called Steven Kingsley. This Kingsley dude promised Sheppard he'll get both you and Brennan there. If you want to talk to Brennan, you'd better get going. Take one of my bosses with you for security. You can't really trust your lawyer. They're usually bigger crooks than us."

Chapter 57

Few hours later, December 19, 1997

10 AM

Las Vegas, Nevada

Harry shifted the flip phone to his left ear and paid the driver. As the cabbie drove off, Harry sketched the replica of Lady Liberty an irreverent salute. Flame held aloft, she guarded the entrance, resolutely unmindful of the screaming riders in the rollercoaster twisting around and between the towers of the newly built hotel. The Empire State Building, the Chrysler Building... they were all there in this recreation of the Manhattan skyline. Even the weather today was New York-like, with temperature in the fifties.

"Did you have any problems?" he asked into the phone.

"Nah," said Ursula. Nikki would've taken on this role, too, but her stripper pals shot down the idea. No way could she pass herself off as a computer nerd. Ursula volunteered. She owed Lupe. With no interest in school, no particular talent, and no parents who gave a damn about her, Ursula was going nowhere in life until she followed an older friend to an audition for Eden, the fancy strip club in DC. Lupe plucked Ursula out of the watching crowd. "I didn't even have to suggest Brennan could help with the DNA. McCoy thought of it all on his own. Man, but I was worried about the computer. If he asked how I managed to 'hack' your device, I'd have been in deep shit. We're lucky he didn't know anything more than me about the electronic stuff. Thank your friend. He taught me how to sound 'techy.' What's his name? Shawn?"

Shawn had not only been responsible for coaching Ursula on sounding "techy," he and Dan were tracking all their enemies' movements. Since Harry's release, Shawn knew where every Kingsley was on any given day. Where all their associates were. No doubt the enemy was doing the same to them.

"And he thanks you," Harry said. "Shawn and Dan, both. Lilah's their sister."

It was strange to think Lilah had once been too worried to ask Shawn about Amber Barrons. After all, Shawn's father was cousin to the dead girl. Dad and son might be estranged, but any suggestion of Andrew's involvement in Amber's tragic ending could send Shawn running back home with a warning. Eventually, Lilah did muster up the courage to ask—without bringing up Andrew's name—but Shawn simply shrugged and said he knew only as much as anyone else. Then, the exile happened. Andrew refused to help his adopted daughter, but Shawn had been as involved as Lilah's twin in trying to bring her back home.

Skirting the fake Elvis at the front door, Harry entered the casino floor. He walked past the jangling slot machines and the crowded blackjack tables, going toward the elevators. "Gotta talk later, Urse. I see the man I was waiting for."

Bald pate, hook nose, potbelly. Eugene Bishop, proprietor of *The Big Apple Reporter*, was both blessing and bane to Harry's existence. The tabloid was responsible for the most outlandish of stories about him, including the astronomical number of women he was supposed to have had sex with. The paper even speculated how Harry acquired his third "queen" at Sing Sing, a certain Officer Regina Berra. Thankfully for both of them, the officer was such a damned stickler for protocol that her every moment in the prison was witnessed, documented, and probably signed off in triplicate. The corrections department would find nothing untoward in her behavior despite Bishop's insinuations.

His was also the rag to have started the ludicrous rumor about Lilah being married to Brad and all his brothers. Bishop worked with her since then, but the sonuvabitch still didn't regret what he did one bit. He considered it his sacred duty to keep his readership entertained. Not surprisingly, Lilah's enemies were using the gossip to discredit her.

"Which man is waiting?" asked Ursula. "Is it Shawn? Cute guy."

Harry laughed. "I'm sure... he's also gay."

"Gay?" echoed Ursula. "I should've known. First Liam, now Shawn. Dammit... why can't I like a man who might like me back? Liam hasn't been interested in any girl since... since Lupe died. I guess he needs... what d'you call it? Closure. We all do."

Slipping the flip phone back into his shirt pocket, Harry hoped Liam would get his closure tonight. Everything depended on him. One wrong move, and the whole scheme would unravel.

Chapter 58

Same day, 5:45 PM

Henderson, Nevada

Liam could be forgiven for refusing to believe he was only sixteen miles from Sin City. With no glitter or color or garish lighting, the apartment complex could've been in any one of New York's outer suburbs. The Olympic-sized pool in front was empty, but there were children playing around it, their high-pitched voices raised in some squabble or the other. Beyond the buildings, the earth was deep red, reflecting the color of the twilight sky. The air smelled of cold, dry desert. Liam zipped up the black bomber jacket. The punk rocker wig kept his head warm.

Sunglasses on his nose, he counted from the left until he reached the building he wanted, the one with the second-floor apartment which currently housed his father's killer. He'd been waiting almost an hour before McCoy arrived there from the airport, accompanied by Blade Wayne. The murderer walked in only five minutes ago. Hands tucked into the pockets of his leather jacket, Liam made his way toward the entrance. With each step, he remembered the events which brought him to this moment.

Will Luce's greed and stupidity getting him into business with McCoy... the attempted murder of Dan and Neil which led Harry to McCoy... Steven Kingsley and Richard Armor needing to put Harry away... their deal with McCoy to kill Liam's father and blame it on Harry. Lupe died trying to prevent a murder. Harry was sent to prison for a crime he didn't commit. Unknown to Liam and Harry, Hector Sheppard's shadow hovered over it all for the last eight years. Whether or not he arranged the bank transfer to McCoy, the fact remained Hector refused to help his own brother and sister. Will Luce had been dead for eight long years without justice because of Hector.

Ignoring the elevator, Liam took the stairs. They were lit well, and the hallway with the two doors at each end was scrupulously clean. Very different from the dump his father's body had been found in. "2A," said golden lettering on the door. With his knuckles, he rapped on the wood panels.

A voice called out, "Who is it?"

At the faint quaver, Liam smiled. "Luce," he said. "William Luce."

Seconds of stunned silence later, there was a crash inside, followed by sounds of wild scrambling.

Liam didn't wait for Blade to open the door. Whistling under his breath, Liam jogged back down the stairs and out of the complex to the motorbike waiting by the gates. Sure enough, James McCoy's wiry form could be seen climbing out the window.

His rental car zoomed past Liam in less than five minutes. The bike vroomed.

Between the houses, along the two-lane road, under the darkening sky, went the off-white Hyundai. Cold wind hissed around Liam as his bike twisted its way between shadowed cars. Headlights and taillights blinked all around him. Neither the roar of vehicle engines nor the honks from irate drivers could drown out the pounding within Liam's skull. Vengeance... for his father, for Lupe... and for Harry whether he wanted it or not.

As to be expected on a Friday night, the Strip was packed with pedestrians. Drunk tourists and scantily clad prostitutes with impossibly big assets walked under flashing neon. Music blasted from the establishments on either side of the street.

Liam drove into the garage of the New York-New York right behind the Hyundai. He followed the car to Level Four and illegally parked two spots down. Incredibly, McCoy didn't seem to have realized the bike was following him.

Dusty from the ride, Liam threw his wig and dark glasses onto the seat of the bike before joining the stream of hotel guests walking toward the elevators. They were all laughing, singing, and generally making fools of themselves. Head pivoting left and right, McCoy kept to the middle of the chattering crowd.

"One more," said Liam, wedging his foot between the closing doors.

Thumbs hooked on the pockets of his jacket, he waited for McCoy to recognize him. The sudden, stark pallor wasn't long in coming. McCoy's eyes widened in horror. Liam clamped his fingers around McCoy's upper arm as he tried to squeeze out. The murderer blabbered.

"Excuse us," Liam said, keeping his tone pleasant. "My uncle could never hold his drink. I need to get him back to his wife before he loses all their money."

Ignoring the chorus of howls and hoots and shouted agreements, Liam forcibly escorted McCoy back into the garage.

"See the jacket?" Liam muttered straight into McCoy's ear. "It's been rigged to explode. Make one sound, and I'll set it off. We'll both die. You're looking at a man with nothing left to lose, Jimmy."

McCoy didn't utter a single peep afterward. Not a murmur was made about Liam using an emergency exit, the lock of which had already been disabled... the handiwork of a certain Blade Wayne. Two minutes later, the murderer was shoved into Liam's room at the hotel.

Locking the door, Liam dug into his pocket and brought out his phone. He dialed a number and waited for it to ring three times. He stopped... dialed again... it rang five times before he cut the call. Turning back to McCoy, Liam said, "Now... let's talk."

#

Sometime later

"I gave them everything," Liam railed, stomping up and down the room. "Eight years of running around for them... I lost my job, our stock... look at this room." The white light made it look even more spartan, and it was already one of the most basic the hotel had to offer with twin beds and only essential toiletries. The screams of those riding the roller coaster outside surged and ebbed every few minutes. "I have no life because of the Sheppards. All I wanted was justice for my father."

McCoy sat in the single chair by the drawn curtains, eyes wide and fixed on Liam. A sheen of sweat covered the murderer's face.

Turning to him, Liam raged, "I know you killed him, but you were merely the weapon. The Kingsleys are the main people responsible for my father's death. And Lupe... no, you couldn't have killed her from Brooklyn, but everything was planned by the Kingsleys. Until last month, Harry agreed with me. Now, he doesn't want to do anything about them. You know why? *You know why? Ask me why, dammit.*"

Throat working, McCoy croaked, "Why?"

"Because the Sheppards are also involved." Liam laughed, sounding unhinged even to his own ears. He tugged open the desk drawer and threw the printouts in McCoy's direction.

"Wh... what's this?" McCoy asked.

"Bank records," said Liam. "Hector Sheppard worked with Steven Kingsley to put his own brother in prison. The money Rickie Brennan paid you to kill my father came from Gateway. Harry's worried about *his* father taking the fall for it, so he doesn't want to do anything to any of them. Only to you... to get his acquittal. Which is where the DNA comes in. But you know what? It's not enough. They have to pay. They all have to pay. And you're going to help me make them pay."

"What's in it for me?" McCoy asked, animal cunning now threading through his fear.

Liam bared his teeth. "I'll tell you what's in it for you. You're going to escape the death penalty is what. I'll help you leave the country. Go to Belize where your business partners have their office. Live off the money from the phone cards." At the shock on McCoy's face, Liam added, "What do you think I was doing all these years? I could even tell you what you ate for breakfast this morning."

"Good enough," McCoy said quickly. "What do you want me to do?"

"Harry and Steven are working together now. They're planning to kill you and Brennan. If you're dead, there won't be any need for reasonable suspicion to test your DNA. The cops will prove you were in Brooklyn at the time Steven's lawyer supposedly met you in Vegas. Harry will be acquitted, and the sex-trafficking case will go down the drain. Everyone will be happy."

"Except me and Brennan," McCoy said on a bitter note.

"And me," said Liam. "There's no way in hell I'm going to let eight years of my life go to waste. The Kingsleys and the Sheppards are going to pay for what they did to my father."

"What do we do?"

"We need to get to Brennan before Steven gets to him," Liam said. "I can help you both leave town, but first, I want a confession from you and him on everything. With those and the bank records, I can take the Kingsleys *and* the Sheppards down."

"I'd already figured out Steven was trying to kill Brennan and me," McCoy said, tone eager. "I came here to talk to Brennan. He could help me leave the country."

"How?" Liam scoffed. "Once Steven gets to you, you're a dead man. You wouldn't even get close to Brennan. Hell, I bet you don't even know what he looks like under the disguise."

"Disguise?"

Mockingly, Liam asked, "Did you really think Brennan met you at Rikers looking like he usually does?"

Chapter 59

6:45 PM

Casino floor

The sweet smell of cigar smoke curled around slot machines. Spinning reels whirred. Music jangled. Oxygen tubing dangling from her nose, a white-haired lady in a wheelchair pumped her fists in the air before directing her cup to the coin dispenser.

Turning his attention from the winner, Steven craned his neck and tried to spot the tuxedoed man at the blackjack table—Harry Sheppard.

The negotiations were to kick off with an 8 PM dinner in the banquet hall. Sheppard had arrived with the proprietor of *The Big Apple Reporter* in tow and immediately decided to throw down some cash at the tables. He was making an exhibition of himself with drink after drink and the barely clad women hanging around him. Even now, his left hand was on the butt of the pink-haired woman leaning over his shoulder. Her strapless cocktail dress left almost all her leg exposed.

"He's not giving us an opening," Steven grumbled. "From the minute he landed in Las Vegas, he's been around people." Bishop had been clicking pictures all day. Apparently, Harry was doing another interview with the tabloid.

Voice just about audible over the clanking of the slot machines, Richard said, "We didn't really expect him to walk meekly into our trap. Are his parents here?"

"Yes," said Steven. "All we're waiting for is McCoy."

Harry agreed to the negotiation only as a pretext for identification of Richard as Brennan, McCoy's accomplice. No question. Once Sheppard figured out McCoy was going to meet his father, he would run to the rescue. He wouldn't want the FBI catching hints of any kind of association between Ryan Sheppard and James McCoy. This time, Harry would actually do the killing... in full sight of his own family.

"*If* McCoy shows up," Richard said grimly. "Where the hell *is* he? We can't just shove him in a room with Sheppard's parents. McCoy's going to need to see those bank papers and decide to do some blackmailing. If he doesn't get here soon—"

"I'll have Phillip check."

Quickly, Richard said, "No, don't. He needs to keep an eye on Charlie." Thanks to Sheppard's insistence, everyone was present for the meeting. If Charles ended up saying something stupid, they would all get caught. Phillip Potts was the designated minder for the evening. "*I'll* make the calls."

"Careful," warned Steven. "The minute McCoy steps through the door of the hotel, you need to hide. We can't afford to have him see you in person. Dammit, none of this would've been a problem if we got Sheppard before. I wish we ignored his press conference."

"We couldn't," Richard said. At the media event right after the assassination attempt on Temple, Harry blamed Steven for every misery befalling the exiles and their allies. "You know we couldn't... not at the time. You would've been the prime suspect if we ordered a direct hit on Sheppard."

"Instead, *you* are now looking at jail time," Steven said bitterly. "I don't even get why he's... my God! For Brad... *Brad!*"

In response, Richard raised a sardonic eyebrow.

"Yeah, Sheppard wants to bring whatshername back, but end result will be Cousin Brad on the CEO throne, won't it?" Steven asked. "How can any reasonable person believe the whiny idiot is better than me?"

"Sheppard's not going to get what he wants," Richard stated. "He'll go back to prison for killing McCoy. And no, McCoy's not going to make me. Even if he happens to see my face, Rickie Brennan didn't look anything like Major Richard Armor."

#

7 PM

Across the room

Onstage, the fake Elvis Presley flicked his wrist, and girls screeched hysterically. "Burning Love" belted forth in a fair imitation of the King's '72 hit.

At the blackjack table, Harry downed the amber liquid in his glass and let the grimace show. No matter how beautifully camouflaged, iced tea was never going to be whiskey. As soon as he returned home, he would bathe in a barrel of Scotch to wash off the sickening sweetness. Raising his hand to signal for more, he let his body wobble a bit.

A pair of slim arms twined around his chest. Soft breasts pressed against his back, sharp teeth nibbling on his earlobe.

Not paying attention to the flash from Bishop's camera, Harry murmured, "Careful, Nikki. You don't want the major recognizing you as the phony maid."

"Pink hair... he's not going to know it's me," she murmured. "Also, he already left."

The major was likely worried about McCoy's non-arrival. "Charles?" Harry asked. Steven's younger brother might recognize the girls who worked in Lupe's strip club.

"I made sure he didn't see me when he walked in," Nikki said. "He's off at the dice tables with the Potts guy. One of the girls is keeping an eye on them... on all of them as you asked."

"Good," said Harry. Charles would pay for what he tried to do with Lilah, for what he did to Lupe. Unfortunately, it wouldn't be tonight.

Nikki wound her way around and settled into Harry's lap, the short, strapless dress giving him a generous view of her breasts. Bright-pink curls bounced around her face.

Face bland, the dealer asked, "You, sir?"

"Hit it," said Harry. Twenty to the dealer's eighteen. The other players clapped. The dealer added chips to Harry's pile. Picking up a thousand-dollar token, Harry tucked it right into Nikki's cleavage.

Someone gasped. There was a laudatory "Oh, yeah!" and emphatic nods from the other men at the table. The waitress serving drinks muttered excitedly with one of her colleagues. Standing next to the slot machines, Steven continued his watch. On the stage, the fake Elvis continued singing. Eugene Bishop snapped yet another picture.

#

7:15 PM

Next to the stage

Puffing on a cigar, Dante stayed close to the stage and Hector Sheppard.

"Older and wiser," muttered the elder Sheppard son, tone displeased.

Dante laughed. "Harry? Well... older, certainly."

"The way he's acting..." Hector shook his head. "Sorry, Dante. I'd hoped... never mind. Is Virgil joining us?"

Dante's son was an aerospace engineer, working in California. Vegas was only a short drive away from where Virgil lived, and Dante had asked him— "Nah," said Dante. Virgil was good man, calling his father every week to check on him. He even helped Harry escape Kingsley assassins during the Cuban episode. But— "He has his own life. I suppose it's a good thing he's far removed from all the madness." Loneliness. Even to his own ears, Dante's words carried the ring of utter loneliness.

Between him and Hector was a bar table on which two glasses of whiskey rested. Grabbing his drink, Dante took a healthy gulp. At the end of Elvis's performance, both clapped politely but didn't talk further. When Dante joined the Sheppards' company as their father's secretary, Hector had already left home. They never developed the kind of rapport Dante had with Harry.

Hector was very different from his brother. Dante couldn't imagine the current boss of Gateway bantering with its COO by calling him "old man." Nor could Dante imagine having with Hector the kind of conversations he'd had with Harry—the sobs which followed Dante's wife's death, the unsolicited advice on Harry's love life, the regrets over the wrong decisions which got them to this point. If he took a million years, Dante still wouldn't understand how Hector could let his hatred of Patrice outweigh the gratitude he should've felt for Lilah.

The one thing in common with the brothers was the disregard they showed toward the women they married. In Harry's case, his obsession with the network got in the way. Not to mention Lilah. Hector... he was chummy with the Kingsleys to the point of going on vacations with the drunk of the family, Charles, and the politician brother-in-law. There was a story which recently popped up in the tabloids which Dante planned to check on. Something about it... the timing of events... Hector's wife finally walking out... they didn't have any children, but the lady hadn't filed for divorce as far as Dante could tell.

"What the hell is Harry doing?" Hector exclaimed, drawing Dante from his musings.

It wasn't simply one girl on the former SEAL's lap now. Two more had their arms around him. The angels of Eden were giving the performance of their lives.

"Cut your brother a little slack," Dante suggested, suppressing a grin. "He was in Sing Sing for eight years."

Hoots rose from the blackjack tables. Almost everyone in the casino was gawking at the tall man who had a pink-haired stripper sprawled across his thighs while shoving his tongue down the throat of a second girl. A third one rubbed herself against his back. As though hundreds of eyewitnesses were not enough, the proprietor of *The Big Apple Reporter* clicked away, creating incontrovertible proof of what Harry Sheppard was up to every second of the evening.

Hector swore. "Harry knows the Kingsleys are here, and they're watching. What kind of credibility is he gonna have after making a fool of... dammit, there's Godwin... and General Potts."

The two older men were joining Steven Kingsley. Major Armor was nowhere to be found. The general was a well-maintained seventy-something, but the former supreme court justice would be... ninety-two? Ninety-three? Around Temple's age, certainly. Temple was in reasonable health, but his advanced years showed in his gait and the necessity of a cane. Godwin, on the other hand, walked in without any assistance whatsoever. His hair was all white, but then, it had been so for decades, tied back with a leather thong since his time as a judge.

"Where are your parents?" Dante asked.

"With Steven's parents and his wife and kid," said Hector. "Rich's fiancée also showed up. Aaron—Steven's uncle—and that woman, Patrice, are watching one of the shows in the hotel. This really doesn't involve any of them, but Harry insisted on dragging everyone here. Steven agreed only so they can all see this conflict finally put to rest."

Hector, you fool. Steven's playing you like a cheap violin. Dante couldn't really blame Hector when he'd been taken in, too. No matter what Harry said, Dante couldn't forget his part in what happened to Lilah. When the Kingsleys were conspiring to trap her husband, she begged Dante to let her talk to Harry. Dante didn't believe her. Because of him, she was left alone to handle Brad's idiocy. If Harry had been around, he could've used his clout as chairman of the board to put a stop to Kingsley machinations. This was Dante's chance to make it up to her. Stubbing out the cigar on the ashtray on the bar table, he remarked, "Ryan and Sophia must be happy about the DNA."

"Huh? What DNA?"

"The cops found something in the Luce crime scene. Didn't you hear? In fact, I'm sure it's why Harry's celebrating."

When Dante got the news more than a year ago, he thought Harry was once again pulling one of his card tricks. Actual evidence? And right when Harry was going to bluff about it? Liam and Sabrina were also just as stunned. There was the fact Harry didn't want his lawyer involved yet, which made Dante even more suspicious. Only after Harry was out on parole did he deign to contact the criminal defense attorney. The legal team would take the info to court once this farce of a negotiation was over.

"DNA?" Hector asked, his tone as shocked as everyone else's when they first heard. "They found DNA? But I thought—"

"I know what you thought," Dante said, voice gentle. "Harry didn't do it, Hector. Your brother's not a murderer."

Face pale under the artificial lights, Hector opened and closed his mouth a few times.

Dante continued, "The cops think it might be McCoy's. Unfortunately for us, it won't be just Harry getting exonerated. Major Armor will escape charges, too."

"Rich? What does he have to do with it?"

Dante shrugged. "Nothing. But you do know the FBI is investigating the major for sex trafficking, right? He's supposed to have met McCoy in Vegas on the night of Will Luce's murder."

Hissing, Hector said, "But if McCoy was in Brooklyn the night of the murder, he couldn't have been Las Vegas, meeting Rich."

"Exactly," agreed Dante. "I was hoping he'd finally face justice for what he did to Lilah. But once again, Major Armor is going to escape."

#

7:35 PM

"What in God's name?" Richard muttered, striding back toward Steven. Godwin Kingsley and General Potts were there with Steven. All of them were staring at the stage where Harry Sheppard was dancing in the middle of the cabaret troupe. The crowd gathered around was laughing and clapping.

One of the showgirls handed Sheppard a saxophone. He took the instrument, and the other arm sliding around her waist, he plastered her body against his in wild kiss. The air rang with cheers and whistles.

Potts saw Richard and called his companions' attention back. One eye on Sheppard's antics, Richard reported, "Except for his business partners—those ex-cons—McCoy has not talked to anyone in the last few days. No phone calls or meetings with anyone connected with Harry Sheppard. Not even with his lawyer."

"We knew this already," said Justice Kingsley, tone impatient. "Did Mr. McCoy leave Miami?"

"Yes, he did," said Richard. "The apartment manager here has been keeping an eye out for McCoy. He arrived on time. One of his business partners was with him. Our man says neither of them left, but McCoy's car no longer in its spot."

"Which means he's now on the loose," said Justice Kingsley, his teeth clenched. "If Harry's men got to McCoy, he's going to end up identifying you. *With* the FBI listening in. Once you go down, Steven will, too. I should've known you couldn't be trusted to do this right, but of course Steven keeps insisting—"

"Sheppard and his cronies are all accounted for, sir," Richard said, voice tight. "Mrs. Kingsley's brothers are both in California. Liam Luce is on a plane to DC with Temple and Andersen. Alex's wife and the two boys are in their home in Long Island. Everyone else is right here at this meeting. Also, even if I get IDed as Brennan, no way will I rat out Steven."

"Grandfather, please," Steven begged. "Since there is a chance McCoy is with Sheppard, we'll get Rich out of here right now and make sure he's not IDed. We were being careful about it, anyway."

The plan was for Richard to wait there only until they were notified of McCoy showing at the door. Now...

"None of us will go down," insisted Steven. "In the event McCoy's merely delayed, we'll make sure he hears about the bank transfer the moment he walks in. Hell, we'll do it even if he *is* with Sheppard's people."

Once McCoy heard, he'd go to Ryan Sheppard to extort money. It was his nature. Harry would be told about it, and he would run to his father's rescue. He would go to prison for killing McCoy. Brad might or might not return, but without Sheppard, the network would remain with Steven.

"Do you understand no matter what happens here, Rich is also going to prison?" Steven asked the Kingsley patriarch. "For sex trafficking *or* murder. He's doing it for me. So *I* will be safe, and the network will stay in *my* hands."

"Some sacrifice," scoffed Justice Kingsley. "Even if everything works out the way you said, Brad's going to return. The plane

Liam Luce is on? Andersen's on it with Temple. They're planning to talk to President Clinton. Andersen claims he now has enough congressional support for a pardon. Lilah will soon be back in New York, and she's going to be the one fighting us for the network. Regardless of what happens with Harry, we will lose our hold on the network. Mr. Armor underestimated Lilah once and almost lost. He's doing it again."

"Almost," Richard said, the vein in his eye throbbing from the insult. "I still won."

"Only because of Brad's stupidity," dismissed the former justice. "When she returns, you're not even going to be around to fight Steven's battles for him. You'll be in prison for sex trafficking. There's also the Prince fellow. What's happening with him? Once should've been enough to tell you he couldn't be trusted, but you did exactly as you pleased again. What if he's turned informant? Steven will also be in jail with you. Thanks to your incompetence, he's going to lose."

"I won't let him," vowed Richard.

"If you mean what you say, get Harry," ordered the justice. "He's out here, isn't he? We'll get Lilah when she comes for revenge."

"Grandfather," shouted Steven. Heads turned. Lowering his tone, he said, "Rich can't just shoot someone out in the open. There won't even be an argument to make in court for any sentence less than hanging."

Godwin Kingsley gritted his teeth. "Steven, you're an imbecile. So is your friend. Why do you think Harry's in the casino with all those women hanging over him? He knows very well we might try to get rid of him some way. He's making sure we don't get a chance. Plus, we need to assume Harry's men do have McCoy. We *are* going down no matter what you say. Our only remaining option is to finish Harry off... right here, right now. If Mr. Armor really wants to sacrifice himself for you, he'll kill Harry. Mr. Armor is prepared to go to prison for the Luce murder, so why not for killing Harry? Lilah will die in her attempt to get revenge. There will still be the problem of McCoy, but he can be bought off or terminated if Harry's not around to cause problems." Eyes glinting, the Kingsley patriarch added, "But Mr. Armor will do nothing. You're a fool, Steven. For Mr. Armor, you were only a way for the chauffeur's son to make it big."

The colors in the casino merged into each other. Sounds rose in chorus, taunting Richard. *Chauffeur's son. Chauffeur's son! CHAUFFEUR'S SON!* Throat hurting, he swore, "Before we leave this place, I *will* get Sheppard."

"Stop, Rich," said Steven. "Grandfather's trying to goad you... I'm not letting you die for us."

"Quiet," snapped Gen. Potts. "Hector's on his way here."

"'Evening, Godwin," greeted Hector Sheppard. "General Potts. Almost time for dinner."

Flicking a glance at the blackjack table, the former justice said, "Your brother doesn't seem to think so."

Hector flushed. "He'll be there. Our Sabrina is married to Alex, and she wants him back. So Harry will be there and on time."

"Alex is my grandson," said the patriarch. "I want him back, too. But as a former justice, I must uphold the law. Nothing—no one—can be above the law. Not even family. Even if the government pardons Brad, I must make sure he doesn't get another chance to risk national security."

"I understand," soothed Hector. "Er... I need to speak with Rich and Steven."

The center of the slot machine section was not a good place for an emergency conference, but Richard didn't want to let Sheppard out of his sight. One way or the other, Sheppard was not going to walk out the hotel of his own volition. If McCoy didn't show, Richard would have to make sure Sheppard died.

"Listen," Hector said. "I have news..."

Five minutes later, Richard muttered, "I don't believe it."

The black man by the stage held a cell phone to one ear, the other cupped by a palm to block off the cacophony. Dante Maro was not merely Gateway's COO; he was also Harry Sheppard's friend.

"I called Harry's lawyer," Hector said. "He confirmed it. They got the news last week. The lawyer said, 'DNA will save the day.' It's going to save you, too."

"The *lawyer* confirmed it?" Richard asked, unable to believe his luck. The criminal defense attorney representing Harry Sheppard was no shyster.

Tone bewildered, Steven asked, "But why didn't he go to court right away? We would've heard if he did."

Richard cursed. "Sheppard delayed it because if there's other evidence putting McCoy in Brooklyn, the FBI's case against me will fall apart."

"Harry simply wants you to go to prison," Hector agreed. "Or he's planning to somehow use the info against you in the negotiations. Rich, I apologize for my brother."

Richard waved a dismissive hand. He needed to think this through. There were too many loose ends.

Steven huffed in relief. "Thank God. I didn't want McCoy—" He coughed, swallowing what he'd been about to say.

"We need to talk it over with the justice," Richard inserted.

"Of course," said Hector, backing away with a relieved smile.

Walking toward where the former justice stood with the general, Steven hissed, "What if Grandfather is right, and Sheppard's men have gotten to McCoy? If he knows enough to identify you, we're in trouble. Also, let's not mess up this new chance we have with the DNA. We need to get you out of here, Rich. Once we're in New York, we'll get McCoy's DNA to the cops. You'll be free of the sex-trafficking charges. Then, we'll figure out how to handle the rest of it... the Brennan connection and the other stuff. For now, we'll wait a couple of minutes and tell Hector we're canceling the negotiations. Sheppard's been behaving like a fool. Who'd want to negotiate under the circumstances?"

"I agree," said Richard, eyeing Godwin and Potts, Sr. "We need time to think through this new info. Perhaps we can use it to put Sheppard once again in prison. I see possibilities... the bank transfer and the money trail... we do need to discuss it with your grandfather. There are a few things I don't understand."

Hands clasped behind his back, Godwin Kingsley waited until they were within a couple of feet. "What did Hector say?"

"You're not going to believe this," Steven started eagerly. "But—"

"Hey," shouted a voice. "Major, wait up."

Still performing with the cabaret troupe, Sheppard dropped a note. The girls around him giggled.

Richard pivoted, and Steven with him.

Blond hair, gray irises, familiar features. Sneakers and jeans and black bomber jacket coated in dust. "Liam Luce," said Steven, tone wild. "He's supposed to be in DC."

Mouth twisting into a snarl, Will Luce's son moved to the side. Behind him was a slender man with a dark, curly mop. James McCoy. His blue eyes widened and fixed on Richard. His mouth opened. "Brenn—"

A deafening report. There was stunned silence for a couple of seconds, followed by screams. Red bloomed on McCoy's shirt. His shocked face looked down at the wound. His knees folded, eyeballs rolling back. With a heavy thud, the body hit the floor. All stares turned to the smoking weapon in Steven's hand.

On the stage, drums rolled. Cymbals crashed. The whirring and jangling of slot machines sputtered to a stop. The panicked shrieking gathered intensity, with some in the room running out, some seemingly frozen in place. Guards came sprinting in, shouting orders at the guests to clear the room.

The fake Elvis heroically carried on with the show. Passing his saxophone to one of the showgirls, Sheppard leaped down from the stage. The crowd scurried out of his path as he strode to where Steven stood. There was no lurching, not a single sign of intoxication in the trickster's gait. Liam Luce skirted the corpse on the floor and joined Dante, the two of them flanking Sheppard on their way to the Kingsley contingent.

David and Aaron Kingsley ran huffing and puffing to the scene, their confused gazes darting everywhere. Shouting over the cacophony, they kept asking what happened, but no one responded. At least Steven's mother wasn't present. Nor was his wife. Patrice Kingsley and the Sheppard parents were not around, either. Charles stumbled to the group, his giggle both drunken and fearful.

Sheppard halted in front of the Kingsley patriarch, Liam and Dante on his either side. David was staring straight at Sheppard as though seeing clearly for the first time in his life. The music continued, but a frightened hush fell over the rest of the crowd.

"'Evening, sir," Sheppard greeted the former supreme court justice, every syllable clearly articulated with no slurring. "It's good to see you again. You, too, General Potts. David... Aaron..." The con artist nodded in the direction of Steven but continued addressing the Kingsley elders. "Wish the circumstances were better. I showed up tonight to talk peace, but it looks like peace was not on the agenda."

Godwin's throat worked for a few seconds. "Steven," croaked the old man. "He... he..."

Sheppard smiled gently before turning to Richard. "It occurs to me," said the former petty officer, "we've been at the same events many times over the years, but no one ever thought to introduce us." Next to him, Liam Luce and Dante continued to stay silent. Laughing in low tones, the tricky S.O.B. shook his head. "I'm Harry... Harry Sheppard."

Then, the trio of men marched out of the hall, some of the skimpily clad ladies from the stage following. No one—not a single person—dared say a word to stop them. On the stage, Elvis held the last high notes of his signature song, "Viva Las Vegas."

Part XX

Chapter 60

A few days later, Christmas Eve 1997

Ossining, New York

The train whistle hooted, breaking the silence of the night. The rumbles got louder and louder as the locomotive chugged its way out of the station. Earth trembled, and the walls of the Berra residence vibrated. In the basement, the futon shook.

Hot, silky skin. Warm, jittery breaths. The minty taste of Erika's kiss. Michael was lost in a world of surging feelings, his entire being reduced to his senses.

Chugga, chugga, chugga, chugga, choo, choo.

Wildly shouting his satisfaction to the universe, he collapsed on top of his girl.

With a distant echo of a second whistle, the train's sounds died down. Michael was trying to gulp air into his lungs when there was a giggle beneath him, soft hands pushing against his shoulders.

"Sorry," he said and rolled to one side of the convertible futon, bringing her with him to lie across his chest. Her long curls draped across his sweaty arm.

The basement was dark, but the furnace kept it toasty. There was a ground level window peeking out into the backyard, but the sliver of a moon in the sky didn't provide much light. Thank God no one was in the yard to witness what happened. Nor was anyone else in the house, Officer Berra diligently performing her duties in Sing Sing.

"Merry Christmas, baby," whispered Erika. "Did you like my gift?"

"Oh, yeah," Michael growled. "Did *you* like it?"

"It was good," she said, raising her head to rest her chin on his sternum.

He frowned. "What do you mean good? Just good or really good?"

"It was really nice."

Nice? Not the word he was looking for. All the books said she should be practically swooning by now. Not batting those bright-blue eyes of hers at him. "You know," he started. "I read there are other things we can do."

She giggled again. "Like what?"

For a smoking-hot chick, Erika really didn't know much. Well, she had done *it* before. She even showed him the easy way to put on a condom. But from what Michael could figure out, her prior experiences were limited to a couple of fumbles in the back seat of a classmate's car. Between her father and older sister, very few boys dared anything more. Which was why she'd begged Michael to keep "them" a secret. Having made Officer Berra's acquaintance, Michael emphatically agreed. Plus, there was Ma. She would flip if she found out her "Mikey" was dating a seventeen-year-old. But Michael knew more about sex than she realized. More than Erika, too, it seemed.

"Like..." Michael said. "Hold on... lemme get my book."

She giggled a third time. The how-to manual said it wasn't merely about inserting tab A into slot B. Many possibilities existed. A few experiments later, her "yeah, babyyyyy" nearly drowned out the thunderous rumbling of the next train.

#

Later in the night

Erika dropped Michael off at the far end of the road. The security hired by his ma was top-notch, but Michael hadn't lived right next to a home guarded by the Secret Service without learning a few tricks. A five-minute jog across the shadows, and he was standing in his own yard.

No cars, no dogs in the distance, no birds. Everything was silent. Freezing wind ruffled his hair, stealing under his collar. Zipping his thick jacket, Michael hauled himself up the bare branches of the apple tree. It was an easy jump to the sloping roof, but his foot slipped, and he slid. Yelping, he struggled to get a handhold. His fingers hooked on something... the edge of a shingle. Ignoring the scrapes on his palms, he scrambled toward his bedroom window. It was dark, with the alarm disabled, just as he'd left it. Noiselessly, he opened the sash and swung a leg over.

Bright-white light flooded the room.

"Whoa," said Michael, teetering. He held up an arm to shield his eyes.

"Where were you?" asked Ma, tone hard. Sitting in the chair next to the fireplace was Gabriel, an apologetic look on his face.

The phone rang.

"Phew," Michael muttered a minute later, watching from the couch as Ma stalked up and down the living room, chattering excitedly with Noah. Ever since news of the DNA evidence came out, political support for Uncle Harry was going through the roof. By extension, the exiles were being seen in a more sympathetic light. President Clinton promised to discuss the pardon with his associates in the Congress.

At Michael's side, Gabriel yawned. "She ain't gonna forget what you did. Take my word for it."

"What did you tell her?" whispered Michael.

"You went to hang out with some hackers you met on SixDegrees," Gabriel said. Sabrina herself had joined the social network site and put forth only one condition for the boys to sign up. They could not share personal information. "It was the best I could think of at the time," added Gabe. "Or she'd have called the guards and the cops and everybody to go looking for you."

"Good excuse." Hackers didn't like to reveal their identities, so she wouldn't be suspicious.

"You're still going to be grounded." Glumly, Gabriel added, "Me, too." Narrow-eyed, he glared at Michael. "Hope it was worth it."

With two thumbs up, Michael grinned. "Totally."

"All right, bro!" said Gabriel, fist-bumping his cousin.

Ma came to an abrupt stop and pivoted toward them. "I'm going to let you go, Noah. Minor crisis at home."

Chapter 61

A few days later

New York, New York

Eight years had brought a lot of changes to the city. Funky new shops and ritzy restaurants lined the once-gritty Bowery Street. Pedestrians appeared fashionably dressed, hurrying home from work or to social engagements. Missing were the derelicts who frequented the neighborhood, the drunks and the addicts whose bodies rock 'n' rollers needed to step over on their way to the CBGB. The panhandlers who could turn muggers in an instant were also absent. Crime and vagrancy were down thanks to the current mayor. Still... the creative characters who expressed their art on the walls... the musicians, the writers, the weirdos at the street corners who swore the moon really was a hunk of cheese... where did they all go? The flophouses sheltering homeless vets were also torn down.

Parking the Harley in front of his apartment building, Harry waited for Liam to climb down from the passenger seat. Sunlight glinted off the plaque on the edifice to the right. Genesis—the name of the Sheppards' old company, the one stolen by Jared Sanders. The newly renovated structure housed veterans with no place to call home. Dante got Gateway to redirect earnings from Harry's stock toward the shelter. Their disgraced former employee still wouldn't see a penny of it, *and* it would be good PR for the company. Then, the Temple Foundation extended its financial support of the drug and alcohol treatment program meant for prisoners to include rehab and psychiatric aid for discharged military men. A few other non-profits also expressed interest in working with the foundation, mainly parent and teacher organizations involved in the support of troubled teenagers.

One thing did not change while Harry was away—the lack of an elevator in his apartment building. Jogging up the stairs to the fifth floor with Liam, Harry opened his front door and swept his arm with theatrical flourish. "Here he is! The man of the hour."

Grinning at the group in the room, Liam walked in. He'd spent the last three weeks in Las Vegas being interrogated by the police department. His gray eyes were shadowed with fatigue, and there was a thick stubble on his face, but the former ease had returned to his smile.

With backslaps and exclamations, Liam was welcomed and practically shoved into the couch by Dan and Shawn. Noah and Temple were at the small dining table, and the boys were next to the window.

"I stuck to my story," said Liam. "County police thinks all I wanted was to get McCoy to confess to my father's murder... which is true when you think about it." Only, not in the way the cops imagined.

"What was Steven's excuse?" Shawn asked.

"He said he'd called McCoy to the meeting to see if there was any way out of the sex-trafficking case," said Liam. "When he saw us together, he was afraid I was going to get McCoy to attack him and Armor."

Dan frowned. "The cops buy it? No one's asking for more explanation?"

"They will," Liam said, fierce satisfaction in his eyes. "But Hector already gave his statement about talking to Steven and Armor regarding the DNA." *The Big Apple Reporter* broke the news of the genetic evidence within minutes of McCoy's death. The entire media was now discussing it. But Harry's brother's testimony would prove the Kingsleys were aware of it before McCoy appeared in the casino. "So they can claim they already knew there was proof McCoy was not in Las Vegas, talking to the major about trafficking. It leaves Steven with no obvious motive to do away with McCoy, except self-defense. But yeah... the police are not gonna simply take anyone's word for it."

"The only other motive would be the Brennan connection, which is now unprovable since McCoy's dead," Harry said, throwing a glance at Noah. Patrice Kingsley could rest easy.

Since Harry never told her how he planned to make sure Richard didn't get implicated for murder, she would've been worrying about it over the last couple of years. Aaron Kingsley didn't know, either. Both wanted the exiles to return, but they also had other loyalties, and it was best for all concerned if neither was too deeply involved in any of the schemes.

With a slight nod, Noah said, "Since McCoy had already attempted to murder Neil and Dan and this new DNA evidence points to another killing, Steven does have the perfect justification for playing scared."

"Yup," said Liam. "What reason did I have for popping up with my father's murderer? It's not a secret I've been working with Harry. What if I believed Steven and Armor were behind my dad's death? What if I were trying to even the score? Etcetera, etcetera. The one remaining question is will the DA file at least a lesser charge?"

"Doubt it," Noah said. "I'm sure Godwin will do everything he can to make sure Steven doesn't spend even a day in prison. Or the network's board could be forced to take action against him, and Godwin wouldn't want it. After all, they didn't even wait for an arrest before kicking out Harry."

"I'm gonna bet the case will be closed soon," said Shawn. "The DA will label it self-defense and call it a day."

"There will be some sort of investigation of course," Harry corrected. "Short, but there will be one."

"*Very* short," agreed Dan. He laughed in exultation. "After all this time, the Kingsleys will be begging the cops to reopen the Luce murder case. Godwin's cash will pay to expedite the DNA analysis. They now have no choice. The Kingsleys need to prove McCoy was the one who murdered Liam's dad to show Steven did have reason to be afraid."

More elated laughter went around the room. Claps, cheers, and a "Hallelujah!" from Gabriel. To save his one remaining heir, the Kingsley patriarch would be forced to take back the bullet he fired toward Harry. Godwin Kingsley himself would make sure Harry was exonerated.

"What about the bank transfer leading to Gateway?" asked Harry. "Anyone say anything?"

Liam chuckled. "Nope, but I bet Steven and Armor are wondering what the hell happened."

Shawn guffawed. "Every single bit of info... every damn moment of the last nine years... since Cuba... they've been watching me... *me.*"

The Kingsleys' failure to pin treason charges on Lilah was attributed to his computer expertise. He knew he was under constant surveillance, physical *and* digital. Armor and Steven and the rest would've imagined themselves safe when Shawn made no attempts to unravel the virtual tangle which began in Gateway's bank account and ended in McCoy's. The enemy never realized there was someone hidden in plain sight, someone who sneered at the pitiful safeguards put up by financial institutions.

Ms. Sabrina Kingsley once designed a virus which Shawn deployed through a client's systems, using the setup to track certain cash movements. A tweak to the same bug... she didn't bother disentangling anything. A small redirection, and the fake cash trail circled back to McCoy's own account, leaving the Sheppards free and clear, allowing the authorities no reason to even investigate it and discover traces of her manipulation.

Whether or not there was actual DNA, Harry had planned to get Steven to do away with McCoy in an attempt to protect Richard. Once the enemy revealed the snare they prepared for him, Harry could destroy it while getting what he wanted from them at the same time. Any sooner, and it would have left open the trap laid for Harry. Now, Armor and the Kingsleys wouldn't dare try any new tricks and risk the cops linking the attempts to Steven's public shooting of McCoy.

Even if there had been no DNA, McCoy's death at Steven's hands would've been enough to open an investigation into the criminal's past, including any potential involvement in the Luce murder. The Kingsleys would make sure of it to bolster Steven's claims of self-defense. Surveillance camera footage from then would be reviewed by appropriate authorities. It would be proved McCoy was not in Vegas. Reasonable doubt would be created on the identity of Will Luce's killer, leading to a likely win on appeal for Harry. But as Noah once said... the hand of God made sure there was indeed DNA.

What Sabrina did with her computer virus also bought temporary reprieve for Harry in case Liam failed to get to McCoy before Steven's men. McCoy would've been told by the Kingsleys the plan to trap Harry started with the Sheppards. True to his nature, the criminal would've tried to take advantage of the situation, but with the false trail no longer around for the authorities to find, Harry wouldn't have to do a single thing to protect the Sheppard parents. It would buy him enough time to make sure the DNA information reached McCoy and the Kingsleys some other way. Perhaps by using the same DNA info, the enemy would try laying other traps, thus prolonging the game. No matter what, McCoy would've been sacrificed to get Armor out of trouble, which meant Harry would be absolved of the Luce murder at least.

Whether the Sheppard family deserved it or not, Sabrina had just saved their collective hides. They would never even hear of it, much less get the chance to show appreciation.

The former attorney general stood, taking measured steps toward Liam. "I'm not going to ask what bank transfer y'all are talking about. Nor do I want to know if you realized Steven would shoot to kill. You snuck out of the plane with the help of the Secret Service, so I don't even *want* to know. But what did you actually tell McCoy?"

"I said I was going to show him Brennan," Liam admitted. Once McCoy was safely locked in the room, Liam called Harry's phone, simply letting it ring to convey the message.

Noah nodded. "And Mr. McCoy thought Brennan would help him escape the Kingsleys. He never imagined anyone would pull a gun on him in front of a few hundred people."

"What about Harry?" Dan asked. "How long will it be until he's out for good?"

Noah smiled. "The cops are comparing DNA from the Brooklyn crime scene to samples obtained from McCoy's remains." No warrant was required to obtain evidence from a corpse in such cases. "As soon as there is confirmation, Harry will go free. Thanks to Godwin's pressure, the state will expedite matters."

Sections of the media had also turned particularly loud, demanding an accounting from the government for an innocent man being sent to prison for eight years. The press asked if it could happen to someone with the clout and connections of Harry Sheppard, how would ordinary Americans fare? How many more innocents remained incarcerated? A couple of major newspapers bluntly called Harry a political prisoner, put in Sing Sing by opportunistic leaders eager to show off their equal justice credentials. Those currently in power were just as eager to show they were working on the problem, which meant New York's most high-profile wrongful conviction would soon be overturned.

The information Harry gathered through Lupe's angels was also being put to use. The politicians on the list wouldn't dare ignore his request for support much less speak against him after recent events. None of them would even murmur in protest if the sitting American president solicited their advice on a pardon for Brad. Besides, thanks to Noah's diligent courting of the media, the same damned fool who married Lilah and wagered her life on a game with her enemies was now seen by a sizeable section of the public as a good guy tricked into a bad deal. Harry didn't have a choice except to play along if he wanted the pardon to happen.

"We should hear back from the White House any time now," added Noah.

"Good," said Liam. "We'll celebrate once it's all over, but I'm meeting Verity for dinner tonight." The siblings would mark the end of their quest for justice. With a fleeting glance at Harry, Liam mentioned the investment banker Verity was dating. The fellow was happy to hear of the resolution to the murder case.

Harry didn't say anything, but he nodded. After the last nine years, all of them deserved some semblance of peace and happiness.

Lilah would be home soon. The one remaining problem was her plan for the network. If Harry had been restored to his position as chairman, he could've forced Brad into an agreement to dismantle the structure as prerequisite for return of even the Peter Kingsley Company to his control. He wouldn't have the option of approaching the board to object since they would kick Harry out for it. Without Harry, Brad wouldn't have a prayer of taking control of anything.

If Patrice Kingsley had not visited Harry in Sing Sing when she did, Major Armor would've been sitting in prison in Harry's place for the murder of Will Luce, Steven booted from the network. Under the circumstances, the board wouldn't have much of an argument to make why the chairmanship couldn't be returned immediately to Harry. Perhaps the exiles would've already been back. Lilah would already be working on taking apart the empire she built. She would've been free to live her life as she pleased, with whomever she wanted. But now... *Some way,* Harry mused. He needed to find some way.

Chapter 62

Within minutes of Liam's departure, Noah and Temple also took their leave, as did Lilah's brothers, leaving Harry with the boys. Closing the door, he turned toward the two teenagers sprawled on the couch. "I told Sabrina you two can stay tonight. She's going to a Broadway play with Regina... Officer Berra. Her little sister is with them—Erika."

There was a sudden squeak from Gabriel, quickly suppressed. Michael's ears turned red.

"I'm assuming Gabe knows what you've been up to, Mike?" Harry asked. "If not, he can wait in my office while we talk. I got a computer last month he can play with."

Ignoring the offer, Michael asked, "How did you figure it out?" His eyes turned angry. "Did Ma or Uncle Shawn hack into my Hotmail account?"

"No," Harry said, opening the refrigerator. It was still winter, but tonight, he needed ice-cold beer. "You told me. Just now."

"Huh?"

Relishing the citrusy taste of the brew, Harry settled into the chair and hooked an ankle over the other knee. "Your ma says you haven't paid much attention to the girls in school since you broke up with Sasha. Sabrina thinks it's because you've been busy... school and your work in Ossining. She thinks you picked another job in town because it would be easier for you to visit me."

"I did," Michael said quickly.

With a short chuckle, Harry eyed his nephew. "Right... a fourteen-year-old boy taking the train two days a week simply to visit an uncle. Regina mentioned you met her sister. Then, I heard about your midnight jaunt. But I wasn't sure until I saw your reaction just now. Why all the secrecy? From what I hear, she's a lovely girl."

"Does the officer know?" Michael asked, trepidation in his voice.

"No. Your ma doesn't, either. Grandma Patrice is spending the evening at your home. They're making preparations for the triumphant return of our exiles. Sabrina still believes you were out with your hacker friends."

"What?" squawked Michael, sitting up.

Gabriel gaped at Harry. "You lied?"

"I bluffed," admitted Harry. "I didn't think a young man would take a boatload of trouble for just some buddies, either." At Michael's growl, Harry laughed a second time. "You two have a lot to learn about sneaking around. And Mike, you still haven't told me why you felt you needed to."

An annoyed huff or two later, Michael collapsed back. "Ma won't get it," he complained. "She thinks I'm a baby. She still calls me Mikey sometimes."

"Embarrassing," Harry agreed.

"Uncle Harry," said Michael. "You said there was a girl in Libya. A princess or something? When you were a kid, I mean."

"Yeah?"

"How old was she?"

"Around my age."

"Erika is, too. Except—" Michael sat forward, eyes anxious. "She's seventeen. God, she's hot."

Keeping his movements unhurried, Harry gulped a mouthful of beer. "Erika knows your age?"

"Yeah. And she *just* turned seventeen. She was sixteen only a few months ago. I'm now almost fifteen. See? Fifteen and sixteen. It's not too bad, right?"

"Not when you put it like you just did," Harry said. Sabrina wouldn't see it the same way. Nor would Regina Berra.

Tone ardent, Michael repeated, "My God, she's hot."

Gabriel nodded in fervent agreement.

"Tell me something more about Miss Erika," Harry invited.

Michael frowned. "What do you mean? She's—"

"Hot," Harry completed, trying not to laugh again.

"Not what I was gonna say," Michael countered. "I mean... she's nice, too. Sweet... too sweet, sometimes. She never argues. It's not as if I won't like her anymore if she... and enough questions about Erika."

Of course he wouldn't want an uncle—or even a father-figure—poking a nose into his romance. At Michael's age, Harry wouldn't have, either. Setting the beer to the side, he said, "All right... so let's talk about the irresponsibility of the stunt you pulled. In all our conversations, did you somehow miss the part where I was going to be in Las Vegas to negotiate with the Kingsleys?"

Michael muttered, "You were done with your negotiation."

"You, more than Gabe, have seen what the Kingsleys are capable of. What if you got caught? Forget the part about all our plans going down the drain. What if they hurt you?"

"I'm not a kid, anymore. I can take care of myself. Uncle Liam says I'm better with a gun than even Dad."

Liam had in fact told Harry he couldn't train Michael any longer. The boy's natural skills called for better tutoring than what a regular West Point graduate could provide, and Liam hired a retired instructor from the U.S. Army Sniper School. "Mike," called Harry. "You're still fourteen."

"Almost fifteen," Michael reminded his uncle. "And I've also been training for hand-to-hand combat."

Harry puffed out air through pursed lips. Finally, he said, "Confidence is good, but there's a difference between taking a calculated risk and rushing into a situation you're not equipped to handle. No, boxing and wrestling and shooting lessons do not make you prepared to face off with the likes of Major Armor. Your smugassery could've gotten you killed. Not to mention what might have happened to your ma if she went looking for you."

Michael blanched for a second. "What are you planning to do?" he asked after a moment or so. "Ma's already grounded me."

"Me, too," Gabriel added, tone morose.

Harry mused, "Obviously, making you clean Regina's garage is not going to work."

There was a surprised snort from Michael, followed closely by a chortle from Gabriel.

"I'll think of something appropriately horrifying," promised Harry. As soon as he found the heart to do it. Hell, if he could go back in time to his fifteen-year-old self, he'd be sneaking out every night to make out with his girl. If he knew what horrors waited around the corner, he'd have grabbed her hand and run. "In the meantime..." Harry went to the desk next to the long mirror on the wall and took out two small boxes. Tossing one to each boy, he said, "Don't catch any diseases. Don't get anyone pregnant."

"Uncle Harry," muttered Michael, his face bright red, but he tucked the condoms into his coat pocket. So did Gabriel.

Later, Harry and Gabriel sat on the fire escape, not giving a damn about the freezing December air. Handing out cans of soda, Michael clambered over the windowsill to join them. There were many going in and out of the CBGB, but unlike the punk rockers who used to frequent the bar when Harry first bought the apartment, the new guests were well dressed. Black velvet seemed to be ubiquitous on the women. Regaling the boys with stories of the bar and the Palace Hotel next door, Harry kept them in splits.

The boys argued over the chances of the U.S. soccer team in the world cup games coming up in a few months. They talked about their intended futures, Michael still firm about his plans for West Point. "Aunt Sabrina's pushing me about college," Gabriel grumbled.

"You're nearly sixteen," Harry pointed out. "Past time to start thinking about such things."

"I don't know." Gabriel shifted restlessly. "What if college isn't for me? I mean, *you* didn't go."

Contemplating the boy, Harry asked, "So what do you want to do? Enlist?"

Gabriel said, "No... I've been looking up stuff on the oil business. I'd like to give it a try."

"If... *when* we win the network back," said Harry, "you could do it, but it could be a long time until then. Besides, education comes in handy no matter what you do in life. I don't have a formal degree. But trust me... SEAL training teaches you plenty."

"I know," said Gabriel. "But lemme at least try working with my hands... start in the fields and know what it's like. As for getting back the network..." He grinned. "The Kingsleys are not the only game in town. What if I went and worked someplace else? I could use my mother's name... Ramirez. No one's gonna know I'm Victor Kingsley's son."

Dryly, Harry said, "Most people in oil sector are going to take one look at you and run a check on the ID. Your alias isn't going to last a week."

"We'll see," Gabriel said. "I speak Spanish fluently. I know the food, the culture, and some of my foster dad's old contacts could help. Gabriel Ramirez will probably get a job pretty easily. If not oil, I want to be a firefighter." When there was companionable silence for a couple of moments, Gabriel asked, "How do you tell when... ahh... a girl's more than hot? You know... when you think you want her to stay with you? I mean, like my dad never married my ma."

"I can't answer for Victor," Harry said. "I can't even answer for myself. It's one of those things you figure out as it happens."

Tone vehement, Gabriel said, "I'm gonna figure it out *before* I have a kid."

Wrapping an arm around the tall teenager with the buzz-cut hair, Harry hugged him to his side. "Some lucky young lady's out there in the world waiting for you."

Michael guffawed. "Blow her a kiss, Gabe."

"Shut up," Gabriel said crossly. Making loud air-kisses, he added, "You send some to *your* girl."

Michael of course tried to outdo his cousin with even more exaggerated smooching noises.

"Good God," Harry said. "Not an ounce of coolness between the two of you. Where did I go wrong?" When Michael snickered and teetered, Harry added, "Careful... I don't want to tell Sabrina you broke your neck just when we're getting everything sorted out."

"You think they've heard?" Michael asked. "About the DNA and everything?"

There could only be one "they."

"I hope so." Harry grinned, wondering what Lilah was doing. Did she know her exile was coming to an end?

"We're still keeping an eye on the Kingsleys... right, Uncle Harry?" asked Gabriel. "I mean... we're so close."

"Of course we will," assured Harry.

But wherever Lilah was, she would be safe. Steven was in enough trouble already with the McCoy killing, and anything happening to the exiles right when they were on the verge of returning would get the Kingsley heir into boiling hot water. With Brad's restoration to the throne a possibility, all his enemies would remain in their holes until dust settled.

Part XXI

Chapter 63

December 31, 1997

5 AM

Naini Central Prison, India

The khaki-clad constable marched close to the bars and yelled, "Hoda." There was complete silence from inside. "*Hoda,*" the policeman shouted, peering into the dark cell and the sheet-covered lump on the narrow cot inside. He made a face, signaling acute nausea at the smell of rotten eggs.

There was a grunt, and a hand appeared from under the bed sheet, pulling it tightly around a vaguely human form. The metal door opened with a squeak. A boot slammed into the patch of sweat on the sheet, right where the upper back would be. With an angry roar, the prisoner threw off the coverings.

"DSP saab has more questions for you," the young constable said, using the back of his hand to block his nostrils. "*Hai, Ram,*" the junior cop exclaimed, calling God. "You stink."

#

A few minutes later

The DSP's office was dark and dusty, its walls lined by metal cabinets crammed with crumbling folders. Hoda sneezed twice and muttered irritably. He remained standing as the DSP—deputy superintendent—waved the constable away.

Watching the young man exit, Hoda remembered the comment on body odor. Before Alex Kingsley trapped Hoda, he'd lived a happy life. His collaboration with the drug lord called Prince kept Hoda in reasonable luxury. He'd been well-fed with black hair and bright-black eyes... always neatly groomed and prone to wearing white. Then, the Kingsley son of a bitch showed up in India with his plans for an oil empire, tempting Hoda into believing he could break into the American drug market. Hoda didn't realize the damned bastard was merely a front for the Indian military. The sting led to the arrest of Hoda and his associates. Prince was the only one who escaped.

Now, Hoda wore a prison uniform. It was also supposed to be white. The hue of dirty cement. He also lost considerable weight, so the clothes hung on his frame. It was Alex Kingsley's fault Hoda was suffering in jail.

The Kingsley brothers were also suffering. At the beginning of their exile, Prince harbored high hopes of getting them to work with him. Hoda told the drug lord not to bother with conciliation, but the advice went unheeded. Prince learned his lesson after being thwarted by the brothers yet another time in Macau. All later efforts to locate the sons of bitches went nowhere. Perhaps Hoda shouldn't have sent the nasty I-told-you-so letter three years ago. But how else was he supposed to react after hearing for the umpteenth time he'd have to wait before attempting a jailbreak? Terrorist attacks were on the rise, and the Indian government was keeping a closer eye on entry points. Prince didn't want more of his allies in prison for helping an escaped convict flee the country.

Lies, Hoda muttered in his mind. *All lies.* Prince helped Priya, but Hoda was of no use to the drug lord outside Indian borders. Still, Hoda should've remembered not to taunt his former boss, and Prince wouldn't have cut off all contact. No matter. If Hoda could prove his continued worth, Prince would see the point in helping. Which was where the deputy superintendent came in.

When the door shut behind the junior cop, Hoda sat in the chair across the table. "The constable needs a lesson in manners."

Clucking soothingly, the DSP offered a small box. "Here."

"I don't smoke," said Hoda. "Filthy habit."

"Hope you don't mind," the policeman said and clicked open a lighter, holding the flame to the cigarette. Except for the khaki uniform and the small mustache, he looked as used to the good life as Hoda had been before becoming a guest at the prison.

"What's the word?" asked Hoda, getting impatient.

"The exiles got to India. I was able to confirm as much."

Incredulously, Hoda stared. "*Saala,*" he cursed. "You woke me for that? When are you going to be worth the money I'm paying you?"

"Wait, Hoda*ji,*" said the policeman. "The army man was here last night. General Mittal. Isn't he related to them in some way?"

Hoda's eyes snapped to attention. "Yes. Mittal's the woman's brother... cousin... something. Why was he here?"

"Not here in the jail. At the police club in town. I didn't seem him myself, but the IG... Inspector General... was with him, so every cop in the department is talking about it today. According to gossip, the IG went to college with Mittal."

"I don't like it," Hoda said. "Do they suspect something?"

The DSP blew a smoke ring. "Not about me. I don't see how." The man was greedy enough to take money from influential prisoners under his charge, and he was smart enough to keep his lifestyle modest to minimize the risk of being caught. As far as Hoda knew, all the money went into a foreign account. There were no trips abroad. Mrs. DSP didn't flaunt jewelry or drive flashy cars. Their kids went to the local school. There were no reasons for the authorities to suspect the man of being on the take. "Mittal was celebrating the end of a mission," continued the DSP.

Voice vibrating with rage, Hoda said, "Not 'a' mission. Mittal was celebrating Harry Sheppard's release from prison. He's going to win, isn't he? The bastards are going back home." The Kingsleys' suffering would end while Hoda's continued. Once they returned to the safety of America, he could no longer offer their location as a bribe to Prince. Even if he managed a jailbreak with the help of the DSP, there would be no drug lord waiting to get Hoda to a secure place. "I need to find them before they leave the country. It's my only way out."

Stubbing the cigarette on the desk's wooden surface, the DSP said, "You haven't asked me how I confirmed they were in India."

"Are you playing games with me?" Hoda asked, angry beyond belief.

"Hodaji," admonished the DSP. "Hear me out. The kid in the advertisement the *hijra* was bragging about knowing?"

After Hoda's break with his former boss, he asked the DSP to keep an eye on Alex Kingsley's known contacts in India. Sure, Prince's men were doing the same, but Hoda's aim was to beat them to the exiles or at least to info pointing to their location.

Long shot, but he was desperate. The transwoman named Rekha was one of the people the crooked cop kept under surveillance. In a drunken state, Rekha claimed she knew one of the child models in an old commercial, and her pals in the colony laughed at her for telling yet another tall tale. So did the DSP's informant who only mentioned it to him in the passing. Rekha was no Mahatma Gandhi after all and usually embellished whatever stories she made up with impossible to believe details. The fact she clammed up when asked how she knew the young girl was taken as further evidence Rekha was simply being her usual blowhard self.

Out of frustration at not getting anything useful, Hoda snapped at the DSP and reminded him Rekha was already familiar with other high-profile people. So perhaps they should check on the kid model before dismissing the idea she could be important.

The DSP grinned. "Guess what? She's not from the northeast as we originally thought. I mean, she *looks* a little mixed. I contacted the ad agency. Seems she's from Goa. And..."

"And?" echoed Hoda.

"She's related to Prince."

"Heh?" Hoda frowned. "I doubt the hijra actually knows anyone in Prince's family. She probably found out the kid's related to him and started jabbering."

"Could be," agreed the cop. "But my contact says this Rekha does know a couple of the hijras who work in the resort."

The resort owned by Prince's relative? Hoda had stayed there a couple of times. "Tell me more," he said.

The occasional communication the transwoman got from her home state had always been public knowledge. Her sudden and unusual reluctance to elaborate on her friends' work in the drag show or any of the celebrities they might have met was thought to be from fear of Prince. "Two years ago," continued the DSP. Priya, the actress/mistress of the drug lord returned to India. Everyone knew Prince brought her home in his yacht, staying safely in international waters where the Indian government couldn't touch him. During the couple of days the actress was at the resort, a commotion happened which involved an overdose. The cops used the address on the dead man's passport to inform next of kin of his passing, but no one showed up to claim the remains. The corpse was eventually buried with the other unclaimed and unidentified dead bodies. "I think it was Prince," finished the DSP, tone triumphant.

One second... two seconds... "Saala," Hoda cursed again, laughing this time. "We're talking about one overdose death in a place like Goa. And Prince sold drugs; he didn't use them himself."

"There's more." The Russian mafia was under pressure from one of their paymasters to find Prince, who became difficult to get a hold of around the same time. The Bratva decided to contact their flunkies in the local police department but didn't get a straight answer. "In fact," continued the DSP, "I can't find a single person who has communicated directly with Prince in the last two years. Connect the dots, Hodaji."

Could it be? "How do the exiles fit into the picture?" asked Hoda.

"I'm not sure," admitted the DSP. "One possibility is Prince found the exiles through the hijra. They started working together. Something went wrong."

"Dammit," said Hoda. "It means there's no one left to help me get out of India."

"Hodaji," reproved the cop. "Every problem has a solution. I tried asking a few questions... you know... about who paid the Russians. Seems Prince first contacted the Bratva because *they* were asking around about the exiles."

"The other Kingsleys," Hoda said, realization dawning.

"Yeah." The DSP nodded. "What's his name?" The tone of the question was carefully casual, and Hoda didn't think much of it at the time.

"Steven." Hoda had made it a point to study all the players. The diligence was going to pay off. Finally! "Contact the Russians," he ordered. "It's time for us to talk."

Chapter 64

A week later, January 1998

Goa, India

"I quit!" Tara yelled before stomping to the chairs lined along the wall in the dance hall. Making sure the squeaking of the rubber caps across the mosaic floor was as loud as possible, she dragged one of the seats toward her and collapsed into it before kicking off her sneakers. The shorts and tee were soaked in sweat, clinging to the boyish figure which stubbornly refused to fill out to match her height of five-five.

"On your feet, Private Tara," bellowed Maestro Alex, his waist-length dark hair tied into a bun at the nape. The silly makeup had almost worn off during the training session. Thank God there were no guests around to see him this time of the evening. Alex would put on his wraparound sunglasses and add a touch of lipstick when they left the hall. The saffron clothes remained the same from his Arjun days, including the bandana which now lay tossed over the back of a chair. "No Kingsley has ever quit in the middle of basic training."

"*I* am not a Kingsley," Tara pointed out quite pleasantly. "We Mathurs quit all the time. We quit jobs. We quit diets. We quit smoking. We quit college. We quit every chance we get. I come from a long line of chronic quitters, baby!" In fact, it was only the month before that Tara quit her very first boyfriend. The dumbass got a little too free with his hands and found himself with a broken nose for reward. At sixteen, she was still making up her mind on the whole sex thing. "Besides, what kind of basic training lasts two bloody years?"

"Because you refuse to cooperate," ground out Alex. "And don't curse."

"Because I didn't sign up for it," said Tara. "All this kickboxing and hand-to-hand combat and whatever." Not to mention the shooting classes she was forced to take at the local range every couple of weeks. "And I will damn well curse whenever the hell I want, wherever the hell I want."

"Tara!" snapped Alex. He huffed. "You need to do this. You know you do."

Yeah, she did, and the awareness was what always made her get up and continue even though she hated how pathetic she was at it. Tara was never going to forget the horrible day when Prince showed up. Lilah was totally unnerved by the thought something could've happened to a child because of her. It didn't matter how many times Tara announced she took full responsibility for disobeying orders and staying when she was supposed to have left the moment Victor showed on scene. Lilah kept asking Tara what on earth she'd been thinking. Her shaken papa agreed she needed self-defense lessons, and Maestro Alex immediately turned from dance teacher to this tyrant of a drill instructor.

Maestro... Tara sighed inwardly. After the Prince episode, she heard only bits and pieces of the whole story from the different people involved until she finally managed to corner Hema. There were still parts which didn't connect, information Hema either didn't have or wasn't about to share. The computer in the manager's office was linked to the internet, and Tara told Maestro they could probably check for more recent information on the Kingsleys. *The New York Times* and *The Wall Street Journal* started digital editions the year before, and such big newspapers surely reported on the network's doings. Lilah nearly choked when she heard the suggestion. Who knew which government agency could be monitoring whom... that sort of worry. Tara was told to keep her fingers away from the keyboard and her lips zipped about what she did know. She wasn't ever to call the exiles by their real names when anyone else was around. As far as the rest of the world was concerned, Maestro would remain a transgender woman.

Alex actually allowed everyone to think he was a woman only to keep Lilah safe. For years! And they weren't even married! Really, Tara wasn't quite sure how Lilah managed to... how could any red-blooded female stop herself from falling a little in love with a man like that? Mentally, Tara smacked herself on the head. What a bloody cliché, nursing a crush on her teacher!

When the training session was over, she followed Alex to the conference room in the office section where Lilah and Hema waited with Victor. The clinic where Dr. Neil worked was the group's usual meeting place, but Lilah refused to go the last few times. The help they expected from back in the States was late coming through, and Brad and Lilah ended up fighting about it each time they talked. The guy was nicer to the stray dog which used to hang around the clinic than to his wife. Brad even took the mutt home for good a couple of years ago.

So the men met at the clinic while either Victor or Alex stayed with the ladies, and someone would bring news back to the resort. At least this time, the mood wouldn't be quite so grim. According to *The New York* Times—the paper edition—their friend Harry was finally out of prison. The pardon was expected to be announced any day now.

Only thick silence greeted Tara and Alex when they walked into the little conference hall. Hema and Lilah sat quietly in chairs, the Nepali woman poring over a newspaper spread on the table. At one end was Victor, his face ashen.

"What's going on?" asked Alex, eyes darting between his brother and the two women.

Not saying a word, Lilah slid a magazine across. On the cover was a man who was surely Victor from a decade ago. He carried a full set of hair unlike the shaved style he sported now. At his side was a very glamorous chick wearing a bright-blue skirt suit with big ol' shoulder pads. "Victor Kingsley's Divorce Has Been Finalized," said the headline. "And He Doesn't Know It."

#

Later in the night

Curled in the recliner next to the window, Tara stayed silent as did the others while Victor downed bottle after bottle of beer. Alex had refused to let Victor return to the apartment he shared with Brad, insisting they rent one of the cheaper rooms until morning.

"My own fault," Victor muttered, sprawling across the single chair at the little dining table. Lilah and Hema were seated on the bed while Alex stretched out on the carpeted floor. "I lost my wife because I—my own *damn* fault. Which woman would want a husband like me?"

Many among the resort's female employees, certainly. The story put about by "Chef Vikram" and "Krishna" that they were about to get married had caused a lot of bellyaching in the salon. Of course with Prince dead, a broken engagement quickly followed with some equally ludicrous excuse about disagreement between the families. Any of the salon ladies would've offered comfort to Vikram had he been looking for any. Outside the group of seven, only Tara and her papa knew Vikram/Victor already had a wife back in America.

"Who the hell can blame her for wanting a divorce after nine years?" Victor continued.

Tara's glance flew to Maestro. He was married, too. His wife had also been waiting nine years.

"And I'm still here," Victor said heavily. "God help me, I'm still here instead of running to Luisa and begging her to take me back."

Alex hauled himself to his feet. "Dude..."

Victor held up a hand, his entire frame shuddering with contained emotion. "Don't worry, bro. I haven't forgotten. Family first. I won't risk Brad's life... not even for my wife."

"Not what I was going to say," Alex countered. "I... ahh... hell, I don't know what I was gonna say." Striding to the dining table, he wrapped his brother in a hug.

A muffled sob came from Victor. The shakes racking his body got more violent. Then, the tears started.

Much later, Tara was on her way home, escorted by Alex and the two women. The cobblestone path which led to the owner's residence and the rest of the staff buildings was lit well. The usual noise was going on in the main hotel grounds. "You think your Sabrina's still waiting for you?" blurted Tara. The moment the words were out, she cringed.

"I always assumed so," Alex said, his tone hesitant.

"Sabrina is not Luisa," said Lilah. "She would wait to tell you in person before divorcing you."

"Gee, thanks," muttered Alex.

Hema giggled, and so did Tara. "I bet she's not going to divorce you," Tara said, wanting to make up for the stupid question. "Not if she's smart. I'm not even going to get married unless I find someone like you, Maestro."

Alex seemed to catch his foot on something and nearly fell. Instead of helping, Lilah coughed a little. Regaining his balance, Maestro reached over and ruffled the curls on Tara's head. "You'll find someone young and handsome, who treats you like the star you are. He'd better... or I'm gonna have to pay him a visit. No one's messing with my child."

Child? And why did he use that tone? Why was Lilah coughing like... they couldn't know about Tara's crush, could they? How utterly humiliating if they did! She was between boys she liked was all. Someday, Tara *would* meet another handsome boy. Who knew? She might even let him get handsy with her. Maybe someone like Shah Rukh Khan, the Bollywood actor. He was so bloody cute and charming... all the girls in Tara's class wanted boyfriends like him who'd serenade them with mandolin music.

"Sorry," someone said, his accent Russian. When Tara looked up, an overtanned fellow with jet-black hair was blocking their way.

At her side, Maestro stiffened. The Russian fellow was not a tourist, and Maestro would know it. Tara had spotted the Russian and his associates many times over the last few years, when they were meeting at the resort's restaurant. He was one of the people her papa warned her against. Mafia, of course. Prince was gone, but Goa still harbored more than its fair share of the criminal element, including the imported variety. The Mathurs couldn't afford to piss off the whole lot by banning them from The Mermaid.

The exiled Americans also stayed out of the mafia's way as much as possible. Prince was offed before he got the chance to tell the Bratva he found the Kingsley brothers and Lilah. Still, their evil cousin was the one to contract the Russian mob, eventually leading to the deal between them and Prince. Which meant the entire mafia network was on the lookout for the seven people on the run. The exiles even discussed leaving Goa after Prince's death, but to Tara's relief, they decided to stay. After all, the mafia's foul reach extended to pretty much every major city in every country, and Goa remained the one place their enemies wouldn't imagine them picking as hiding spot. Even Prince found them only because of a series of terrible coincidences, starting with Tara's mother's death.

"Excuse me," Lilah said to the Russian. "May we pass?"

Tara had to grin. Lilah could ask for directions to the ladies' room and make it sound like a royal command.

The Russian fellow stepped to the side, letting the group go on. Not even ten seconds went by before there was a shouted "Hey!"

Tara turned to check, as did the rest. Alex put a foot forward, placing himself between the women and the Russian. "Can we help you?" Maestro Alex asked.

"No, no... just curious," said the Russian. He nodded at Tara. "You the model, right?"

"Me?" She shook her head in confusion. "Yeah... a long time ago. I don't do any modeling anymore." Fashion design was what interested Tara. She could already see her name in *Vogue* and *Harper's Bazaar* and the rest of the glossies as the creator of the most stunningly beautiful clothes the world ever laid eyes on.

"Why do you want to know?" demanded Alex.

The Russian smiled, his teeth gleaming. "Simply asking."

As the group neared Tara's home, Hema babbled, "He was curious about Tara. That's all. People are always asking about her. We still have pictures of her in the salon! I mean... it can't be about us. The pardon's supposed to happen soon. No one will try any funny stuff with us at this time." Tone uncertain, Hema added, "Right, Alex?"

"Yeah, probably," he said. "But I'm going to let the rest know... just in case."

Chapter 65

Two weeks later, late January 1998

Corpus Christi, Texas

"What's going on, Phillip?" Richard asked. He was supposed to be working, but the events in Vegas continued to niggle at him.

The itch started when he heard about the DNA, when Steven fired his gun, killing McCoy. Before Richard could figure out what was setting off the warning bells in his brain, guards swarmed the casino, herding the guests to safety. Sheppard and his entourage were already out, but the Kingsleys and Richard were forced to stay until the police arrived. Who knew what would've happened if it weren't for Godwin Kingsley's intervention?

The former supreme court justice could not let the network's board use the incident to kick Steven out as CEO and chairman. The replacement was unlikely to be another Kingsley. Perhaps it would be one of the Barronses. Perhaps it would be Harry Sheppard... if he were to be exonerated. Perhaps someone unrelated. Years' worth of work would go down the drain if Steven got arrested.

Godwin made several calls to bigwigs in Nevada law enforcement. He insisted Steven acted in self-defense. The Kingsley lawyers brought up McCoy's history of attempted murder... that of Daniel Barrons and Neil Kingsley. Hector confirmed he told Steven about DNA evidence being found in the Luce murder. Even Liam Luce's presence added to the idea McCoy was brought specifically to attack the Kingsleys.

The DNA would place McCoy in the Brooklyn apartment at the time of Will Luce's death. Godwin got the family lawyers working overtime to prove it. After all these years... after everything they did to put Sheppard in prison... Steven and Richard sweated bullets, hoping the genetic material would be a match.

They knew what the FBI planned. The feds would use the immigrant sex-trafficking case to put pressure on Richard to admit he helped McCoy pretend to be in Vegas while he was actually in Brooklyn. After all, if they were in separate cities, they couldn't have had a meeting to discuss the illegal immigrants working for Richard's company. The feds preferred to catch the bigger fish—the Kingsley heir and CEO of the network—and would let Richard off the hook.

Richard was never going to betray his best friend, but with McCoy already proven not to be in Vegas on the night in question, the FBI couldn't do shit to force a confession in the Luce murder. Nor could a dead McCoy testify against Rickie Brennan/Richard Armor. There was nothing linking the Kingsleys to Will Luce's death.

The district attorney waited until the results of the DNA testing were back before announcing he was closing the casino shooting case as a matter of self-defense. He didn't believe there was need for a lesser charge, either. Prosecutorial discretion... etc... etc.

Richard huffed in relief at the news. If the DA had been looking for political celebrity, he could've still chosen to go after Steven, but the former justice's name still carried such weight in the public mind that ambitious officials preferred not to antagonize him. Except of course when someone like Harry Sheppard blackmailed them into it with information obtained from strippers and prostitutes.

Sheppard was now a free man thanks to McCoy's timely death, but the criminal would've been of more use alive to the Kingsley brothers and their woman. It would've taken time and effort, but Sheppard could've forced McCoy to submit to a DNA test. In exchange for lesser charges, the criminal would've testified against Richard, and there was no reason for the major to have conspired to frame Sheppard in the Luce murder except to help his friend, Steven. In a couple of years, Steven would've been kicked out of the network, Brad back in.

No way Sheppard wasn't planning exactly this outcome. There should've been dismay on his face when McCoy was shot. Instead... the audacious introduction... the mockery in the laughter... and something else.

More than a month later, Richard was still trying to puzzle out the con man's behavior. Not merely puzzle out... the smirk needed to be wiped off the former SEAL's face. Permanently.

Phillip's arrival at the Texas office of Armor Drilling Company didn't help distract Richard's thoughts from Harry Sheppard. Settling deeper into the chair across the desk, Phillip demanded, "Where's Steven? He needs to hear this, too."

"Out talking to the men from Pentagon," Richard said, closing the folder in front.

"Still?" Phillip ptchaaed.

Steven planned to spend a week in Texas to brainstorm a way forward, but the feds called to discuss the ongoing trouble in the Middle East. As an officer assigned to the Criminal Investigation Command, Major Potts was sometimes involved in counterterrorism missions, and he was fully aware of the reason the defense department requested an urgent meeting with the network's CEO. A secret grand jury investigation of the latest religious fanatic on scene was going on in New York. The member companies of the network could provide intelligence which might prove useful in obtaining an indictment. Under normal circumstances, Steven would've been happy to help, but he needed to fix his own problems first.

There would've been no problems to fix if Richard and Steven succeeded in putting away their main enemy for good. Still, the nine years Steven was at the helm of the network had been enough time to tweak the organization's governing structure to better benefit its leadership. The board members wouldn't let Sheppard shove them around.

Learning the PR game was damned difficult for Richard, but he did it. Despite the media's adulation of Petty Officer Sheppard, most reporters continued to appreciate Richard's bootstraps story. They also made sure to mention his betrothed was someone quite ordinary and not a pampered princess like his supposed former lover, Mrs. Brad Kingsley. With the McCoy threat behind them, Richard had agreed to set the wedding date in March.

The immigrant worker issue was under active investigation, but it wasn't getting any traction in the press, while the charity arm of Armor Drilling continued to generate plenty of goodwill. Steven, too, attracted admirers for the way he was handling the network.

The legal system... even if the courts ordered Steven to return control of the Peter Kingsley Company, the larger network was another matter. Yeah, politicians were falling over themselves to help Sheppard, but with Justice Kingsley and General Potts on the other side, the government would be careful in voicing its opinion on the leadership of the network.

It would've been easier all around if the five brothers and the missus died in exile, but both Steven and Richard were prepared to fight to the bitter end. The chauffeur's son would face off with the Kingsley golden boy and his pal, Harry Sheppard. Richard possessed the skills, the weapons, and the determination to win. The petty officer would learn his biggest mistake was taunting Major Richard Armor.

"Damn," said Phillip, returning Richard's attention to the present. "I'm flying back in an hour. Never mind. You can update Steven."

"About?"

"You know the phone call he got?" Phillip asked. "The man who wanted his cell number? I thought I'd check... just in case."

Richard shook his head, indicating ignorance.

"You were there when Steven talked about it," insisted Phillip. "The caller mentioned a transgender woman."

"Yeah," said Richard, memory resurfacing.

"Well... turns out the fellow who called is a superintendent or something in an Indian jail," continued Phillip. "He was trying to make money off info he collected on Alex and the rest."

"Legit lead?" Richard asked.

"Seems so," said Phillip. "When Steven didn't call back, the super decided to hit up a different source for cash—one of the prisoners, a man named Hoda. Get this... Prince might be dead."

#

A day later

"Fractured vertebra," Richard said, flipping through the papers in the folder. "Evidence of heroin and MDMA in the system, but the victim fell from his chair and broke his neck, which killed him before the drugs could."

General Potts was seated next to Richard in Godwin Kingsley's home office, smiling proudly at his son's achievement. Across the desk from them, the former justice rocked back in his leather chair, saying nothing. Steven was on Richard's other side. Charles, as usual, was on the couch in the back, too wasted to understand anything being said.

"If Prince died of a broken neck," pronounced the general, "it was Victor who did the deed. No question."

"We have them?" Steven asked.

"We have them," said Richard, closing the folder and getting to his feet.

Chapter 66

The next day

Long Island, New York

Holding up a hand, Harry signaled Liam to wait. Verity's brother arrived at Temple's home mere seconds after the phone rang in the library, and the man at the other end of the line had important information to convey. With an impatient huff, Liam paced the carpet. As both Noah and the former president waited on the couch in jittery anxiety, Harry listened to Shankar Mittal's extraordinary story.

India's west coast... a spot on the radar screen of the nation's Narcotics Control Bureau... the Bratva contacted Goan police with a few questions about a drug lord familiar to both Harry and Shankar. After the conversation, a known player in the local mob telephoned someone in Naini Central, where Hoda was jailed, which was how Shankar got involved.

"Military intelligence was already monitoring Hoda's communications," continued Shankar. "We intercepted a couple of calls to the prison from a number in Virginia. Quantico, to be precise... your Criminal Investigation Command. Who there would be interested in an inmate of an Indian prison?"

"The CID," Harry said urgently. "Major Potts works for them. Shankar, we need to get Lilah and the rest out ASAP." There would be uncertainty while the exiles were detained by Indian authorities and the pardon worked its way through official channels, but it couldn't be helped under the circumstances.

"I will. Once you tell me where they are."

"What do you mean?" Harry snapped. "You just suggested they're in Goa."

Shankar swore. "So you don't know, either. It's a state with more than a million people and not only of Indian ethnicity."

Phone still held to his ear, Harry wheeled around. "Liam, check with Shawn where the Kingsleys are right now."

"I was trying to tell you," Liam said. "Major Armor is at the JFK airport, boarding the flight to Bombay."

Part XXII

Chapter 67

8:30 PM, Eastern Standard Time

January 30, 1998

Air India Flight 102, en route *to Mumbai (renamed from Bombay)*, India

In cattle class, babies squalled, and passengers lined up at the latrine, enviously eyeing the curtains shielding the well-to-do from the *hoi polloi*. Three rows into the luxury section was a blond man with very little gray in his hair, his posture reminiscent of a warrior. Ignoring the clinks of silverware and the saree-clad flight attendants, Richard tilted his chair back.

The Kingsley patriarch had made it clear there would be no corporate jet on this mission. If there were, Richard would've been in India by now, but there could be no official documentation of the family's involvement in the operation. The pardon was expected to happen within days, and the deaths of the exiles at this point would almost certainly create political uproar. They were no longer considered traitors to the nation. The section of the press friendly to Sheppard hammered home stories which cast Lilah Kingsley as a heroic figure standing up to a corrupt elite. Charles's attack on her in Cuba was mentioned time and again. Thanks to Sheppard and his propaganda, Brad was being seen by a significant chunk of the public as a good man who was taken advantage of by his evil cousins.

If all seven of them were to die in one stroke with evidence of a Kingsley-sanctioned visit to India by Major Armor... Sheppard wouldn't have to do a single thing to make anyone pay for his girlfriend's demise. The world's attention would immediately turn to Steven. He'd be out of the network in a matter of weeks, and the U.S. government would start looking for connections between him and the Russian mafia.

Flying private or not, Richard needed to be in Goa make sure the operation went according to plan. He *wanted* to be the one hunting down his enemies. The Kingsley golden boy would soon learn who was the better man. Before Petty Officer Sheppard died, he would hear exactly how his beloved and his best friend met their ends.

Taking the map from inside his jacket, Richard spread it out on the tray-table. The blue of the ocean... the shore... a red circle was drawn around the name Vagator.

"Here you go, sir," said the sweet-voiced flight attendant, handing him the Bloody Mary he'd requested. "Oh, you're visiting Goa? Beautiful place... especially if you have company."

A quick glance showed him an enticingly painted face. Her tongue darted out, running over the edge of her upper lip as she waited for his response to her unspoken invitation. "Some other time," he said. Richard had more important things to occupy his mind than her muffled gasp of embarrassment as she scampered away. He had an appointment with another gorgeous woman.

Sipping the sour drink, he flipped the map over and studied the address written on the back. He'd be in Goa in less than twenty-four hours. Thanks to time zone differences, he'd skip a day and land in the city on Sunday, the 1st of February, a little before sunrise.

\#

Same time

Interrogation Room

Naini Central Prison, India

Concrete walls, wooden desk with chairs, a table lamp which could be turned to shine directly into the prisoner's eyes... the cops had not yet tried the trick with the lamp. Hoda shivered, his shirt and pants still wet from the last dunking. It was almost daybreak, but he hadn't been allowed to sleep. Any time he dropped off, the bastards threw him into a tub filled with ice-cold water. "I have no idea what you're talking about," he insisted as loudly as he did since he was dragged from his cell to this room.

There was a ringing curse from the man in the dimly lit corridor outside the bars. Lieutenant General Mittal resumed his stalking. The son of a bitch looked much the same as he had more than a decade ago, with crew-cut hair, neat mustache, and muscular frame. Unlike the day he arrested Hoda, Shivshankar Mittal was not in the disguise of a mild-mannered secretary. He was wearing military fatigues.

"We *know* you talked to someone in America," the IG repeated, tone impatient. "If you tell us the address you gave, I will personally make sure your sentence is commuted."

Liar, muttered Hoda. Just like the third man in the room—the crook of a DSP.

First, Hoda hadn't been able to understand why the cops were claiming some American fellow called him at the prison. For one, international calls were sure to be monitored, and Hoda wasn't fool enough to try it. For another, he didn't want to deal directly with the Kingsleys and got in touch with the Bratva through the DSP. The criminal kind was more trustworthy in such transactions than the rich who pretended to be law-abiding.

Watching the DSP's fingers tremble as he reached for his cup of masala tea, realization came to Hoda. The weasel remained true to his nature. Before ever talking to Hoda about it, the DSP tried to sell the information on Alex Kingsley to his cousins. The Kingsleys would have offered more money, of course. The DSP would've used a payphone to make his call, giving the Americans Hoda's name and the prison number instead of his own. So the crooked cop would escape trouble if anything went wrong.

The Americans didn't respond, and the DSP brought the same info to Hoda. A few days ago, someone in the States deigned to return the call. By then, the DSP and Hoda confirmed the location of the exiles through the Russians. Unfortunately, the calls were intercepted by Mittal and his cronies. They were afraid of the enemies getting to the exiles before a pardon came through. Since they believed Hoda alone was responsible, he was at the receiving end of their tender, loving interrogation tactics. The rat of a DSP escaped.

"The IG is a man of his word," the DSP now said. A sheen of sweat covered his face. Silently, he begged Hoda not to snitch. After the IG left, there would be promises. A share of the Kingsley cash payment, most likely.

Reward or not, Hoda had no intention of exposing the DSP to the bigwigs. With Prince gone and the Russians now on Mittal's watchlist, all hope of reprieve was lost, but even if Hoda needed to die in this prison, he'd make sure Alex Kingsley paid.

"Like I said before," Hoda wheezed, "you're mistaken. I don't know anything about any Kingsleys."

\#

11 PM

January 31, 1998

The White House

Noah Andersen had requested an emergency appointment, but President Clinton's secretary showed the visitors to a plush room, apologizing for the boss's tardiness. After an hour, the president was still closeted with his senior staff. There was trouble brewing, threatening the political life of the incumbent of the Oval Office. Every news channel featured breathless journalists reporting on the scandals involving Bill Clinton.

From his position by the window, Noah threw a glance behind where he left the rest of the group. Making sure no one was listening, he muttered into the cell phone, "Patrice, I'm trying, and so is Harry."

"Don't you understand?" she asked, tone frantic. "If Richard gets to them, Alex and Victor will try to stop him. No matter who wins, *I* will lose a child or more!"

Teeth clenched, Noah started, "All these years, and you never thought of..." He took a deep breath. "All right. The plan is if Mittal cannot find the location, he's going to follow Richard to our exiles."

"What happens after they're found? The general will protect Brad and Lilah and the rest, but he's not going to care about Richard. Please tell Harry... *he* needs to find them before any general. Don't let my sons kill each other. You owe me. Harry does, too."

Noah sighed. "You're still holding on to your grudge against Ryan. As I said... Harry is trying to help you. And when this is over, we're going to talk... you and I and Harry. Richard is clearly willing to kill in support of his friend. He's even willing to take the entire blame for it, or he wouldn't be going to India by himself. If he doesn't succeed this time, there will be another attempt... and another. Harry and Brad and the rest might decide enough is enough and strike back. You *will* at some point end up losing a son. The only way to stop it from happening is to talk to Richard and hope he listens to reason." The major would also need to show the sense to keep things quiet. If Godwin were to suspect Richard might switch sides, the chauffeur's son could possibly be held responsible for all of Kingsley wrongdoings. The other culprits would escape.

"'When this is over'?" Patrice parroted. "First, let it be over. Make sure all of them—Peter's boys *and* Richard—come home alive. I don't want anything happening to any one of them... especially not at each other's hands! They're family. How is it difficult to understand?"

"Family?" With a huff of exasperation, Noah ran a quick eye over the group in the sitting area. Gabriel, Patrice's oldest grandson, was sprawled on the chintz-covered armchair. Temple was on the settee across. The secret service personnel stood within arm's reach. Even inside the White House, they couldn't leave the former president unprotected.

A young man came out of the inner offices, covering a yawn with the back of his hand. His fatigued gaze went to Temple.

"I'll let you know as soon as I hear something," Noah said and hung up. He reached Temple the same time as the young aide.

"I'm sorry, sir," the aide said to Temple. "I don't know if Mr. Clinton's going to have time for you tonight."

"We'll wait until he has time," said Noah.

Trying again, the aide said, "Perhaps Mr. Temple could rest in a guest room? I'll call when the meeting's rescheduled."

"He wants to be here," Noah insisted. Even if the former president couldn't talk, out of all of them, he had the best chance of getting an audience with Bill Clinton.

Once the aide disappeared down the hallway, Gabriel said, "I wish I could've gone with Mike and the rest."

As the lawyer for the exiles, only Grayson Sheppard was needed in India to make arrangements for their return, but Sabrina and Michael were adamant about going along. In the military quarters arranged by Shankar Mittal smack in the middle of the naval base, all three would be safe. Shankar even managed to get them emergency visas. Gabriel couldn't go. Sabrina hadn't been able to adopt him in Victor's absence, and without a parent's signature, a minor couldn't get a passport.

As for Harry... several of his connections in the government contacted him after news of the DNA evidence broke. They all offered help. So did an influential old friend, one of the Saudi princes. Regardless, Harry's passport had not yet been reinstated, and he was admonished by his lawyer not to break even a speeding rule until then.

No one was surprised when he went missing five minutes after learning about Major Armor's trip to India. Not a single person knew where Harry Sheppard was at the moment.

#

8 AM, local time (3 AM the same morning in DC)

January 31, 1998

Heathrow Airport, London

Michael slurped the last of the orange juice before tossing the cup into a trash can. At least it took the edge off hunger. His tummy had been churning nonstop since they left New York, but he couldn't choke down a single bite of food. Nor could his ma. She was currently taking a nap in one of the chairs.

Travelers streamed around Michael. A female voice made an overhead announcement, asking for some passenger or the other to proceed to the gate for immediate boarding. Tucking his hands into the pockets of his coat, he stared through the glass wall at the white Airbus with red lettering on it. "Is it the one?"

Grayson Sheppard glanced up from his cell phone. "Probably."

Major Armor was on the plane. Lilah's brothers and Uncle Liam were tracking the movements of all the Kingsleys and their sympathizers. Mr. Dante was sticking like glue to Uncle Hector. Out of all their enemies, only Richard Armor had left the country.

"Why can't the cops arrest him?" Michael fumed. "He's going there to kill my dad."

"There's no proof," Uncle Gray said for the umpteenth time, his tone still patient. "We can't ask Indian police to arrest the major before he actually does something. Creating an international incident at this time might give politicians back home an excuse to withdraw support for the pardon. Don't worry... Armor will be watched. The moment he tries to do anything to our exiles, he'll be caught. But I wish... nothing's certain until we see the president's signature on the piece of paper." Grayson tried to smile. "You're a kid... you shouldn't have to listen to all this."

"It's all I've heard most of my life." Mussing his hair in agitation, Michael said, "Don't start hiding things from me now, Uncle Gray. Is there a chance Uncle Brad won't get a pardon?"

"It's not done until it's done. Plan is for General Mittal to keep our exiles in Indian government's detention until Noah calls us with an update. We think it will happen in a day or two, but what if some bureaucrat in New Delhi decides to hand them over to the Americans before? What if something goes wrong, and the pardon doesn't happen?"

After a few seconds, Michael said, "Dammit."

"We'll cross that particular bridge *if* we get to it," Grayson stated. "Armor is our more immediate problem."

"How long will it take the major to get to India?"

"Ten hours, give or take," said Gray. "But to reach Goa, Armor will have to catch another flight from Bombay... I mean, Mumbai. We'll get to them long before Armor."

Despite Harry's impending exoneration, Gateway refused use of their private aircraft. So did Andrew Barrons. Grayson, Michael, and Sabrina took the first flight they could get. Only economy tickets were available at this late hour. It didn't bother Michael or Sabrina, but the old lawyer was clearly exhausted. Thankfully, General Mittal would have a helicopter ready to take them to Goa.

"The general's not going to wait for us," continued Grayson. "Once he knows where the exiles are, he'll ask the Western Naval Command to extract them."

Michael needed to be there... he didn't know what he could do to help, but he wanted to be in the city. If they could use Gateway's jet...

Michael glanced in the direction of the private jet terminal. A form at the periphery of his visual field snagged his attention. Striding toward a waiting airport employee was a bearded man clad in a black-and-white business suit, side curls visible under his black hat. "Avraham ben Terah," he introduced himself to the female employee.

The woman nodded. "We've been expecting you, sir. The Saudi aircraft is ready and waiting."

Michael's eyes narrowed. Something about the man... something familiar...

#

10: 30 AM

January 31, 1998

The White House

Pacing the carpet, Noah said, "I'm beginning to think they haven't let President Clinton know we're here. I can't imagine he'd keep a former president waiting all this time."

Both Temple and Gabriel were leaning back in their respective chairs, clearly fatigued but neither sleeping. The security personnel were, as always, alert.

"Could it be the Kingsleys?" asked Gabriel.

Noah came to a sudden halt. "Godwin could have one or more of the aides in his pay. It's been known to happen." Fury built. "I'll see how he's going to keep us out. Let's go, Temple.

We'll find out if the Secret Service opens fire on a former president and a former attorney general."

"Wait," said Gabriel, nodding toward Temple's guards. "Can't they help? I mean... they would know high-up people who can check with Mr. Clinton's security, right?"

A little while later, the lead officer of Temple's detail conveyed the information Mr. Clinton was already busy with the day's appointments, but the president promised them time in the evening.

Noah groaned. By then, it would be morning in India. Richard Armor would have landed in Goa. He'd head straight for Lilah.

#

Same time

Interrogation Room

Naini Central Prison, India

"Who told you where they were?" asked the IG, his form wavering in front of Hoda's eyes. The cop's voice echoed eerily between the concrete walls.

The source was right in the room... the corrupt DSP. Giggling maniacally, Hoda countered, "Who told whom... whom..." His throat hurt with thirst. Sharp hunger clawed his abdomen. The clock on the wall said it had been more than twenty-four hours since the grilling began. The rest of the inmates would've already had supper. His partner in crime—the DSP—hadn't dared leave. He looked just as beat as the IG. Just as beat as Hoda himself. Hoda yawned. "Don't know what you're talking about."

"Listen, you sonuva—" Mittal bellowed from beyond the bars.

The IG held a hand up, silencing Mittal. Flipping through the pages on the table, the cop said, "These are the phone calls you got in the last year. Who called?"

"Friends," said Hoda, his voice thick.

"Some of the calls were from Mumbai. Which friend there called you?"

"None of your damn business," Hoda said.

A hard fist landed on his jaw. He tumbled to the floor, chortling in satisfaction.

#

5 AM, local time

February 1, 1998

Naval airbase, Goa

The sky hadn't brightened yet, but sounds of the workday already echoed into the guest apartment at the base. Lights floated along the dark waters of the sea. A brisk wind battered Michael's face and body as he peered into the horizon from the second-floor balcony. "Coastguard?"

"Fishing boats," said General Mittal. He'd reached the airport the same time as the Americans, accompanying them to the guest apartment. The man was sharp-eyed, slightly impatient in his tone. "Get back in here," he snapped at Michael. "We have work to do."

Crunchy buttered toast was served by a male aide who looked as military as the general. Hot, sweet tea was poured into porcelain cups. "The call you were waiting for came through," the aide said to the general. "Mr. ben Terah said he'll be at the base as soon as he can. There was trouble in Mumbai... some issue with his passport. He asked for the airport officer you mentioned, but it's taking time. Papers to fill out, etcetera."

"Damn bureaucracy." The general nodded. "Please call back and let him know the equipment he requested is ready to go the moment *we* are." Under his breath, Mittal added, "Avraham, I hope you didn't forget how to fly in the last nine years."

When Michael glanced at Ma and Grayson, there was no sign they heard the muttered name.

Turning to Michael's ma, the general said, "Sabrina, I need your expertise. My friend wasn't able to convince Hoda to talk. But we do have some Mumbai numbers from which he got phone calls over the last year. Unfortunately, we don't have time for a warrant for the telecom company. Lilah's brother—Shawn—tells me you can help."

There was a gulp from Grayson. "I don't want her doing anything illegal."

"Let's worry about legalities later," said Ma. "I need a compu—"

"Everything's right here," said the general.

In what Michael thought was a second bedroom, there was an array of computers arranged on a long desk. A couple of swivel chairs stood waiting. The three phones and the fax machine were silent, but a familiar hum thrummed through the air. Cyberspace beckoned.

"Ma," called Michael. "Let me, please."

There was an irritated "ptchah" from the general. "There's no time to wast—"

"I understand, sir," said Michael. "But I'm as good as her."

With a huff, Sabrina drew herself up. "You might *think* you're..." After a moment, she deflated. "Dammit, Shankar. He *is* good."

The general scratched his jaw as though unsure. Finally, he said, "Just get me the names."

Ma warned him, "If there's any trouble about this, *I* did it all, not Mikey."

"Ma," exclaimed Michael. Pivoting to the general, he said, "I'm Mike. Michael Harry Kingsley."

Both Sabrina and Michael worked the equipment, referring now and then to the list provided by the general. They conversed very little, the clicking of the keyboards making enough noise to compensate. Behind them paced the general, leaving Uncle Gray to rest in the other room.

A shrill double tone tore through the familiar clatter. Behind Michael, the general barked "Hello!" into his cell phone. There were a few angry exclamations from Mittal, followed by rapid-fire Hindi. When he hung up and threw the phone onto the table, Sabrina swiveled around in her chair.

"More problems?" she asked.

"I'd say so. We've lost Armor."

"What do you mean lost?" asked Grayson, appearing at the door.

"He landed at the airport in Mumbai," explained the general, "and went to the men's room. Didn't leave, but he's not in there anymore. There are no other doors, no windows. Still, Armor seems to have disappeared."

#

9:15 AM

A few miles away

"Drug raid?" Alex echoed the cop who was at the main gates of the resort. When he and Lilah escorted Tara to her Sunday morning shooting lessons, they weren't expecting to return and find policemen swarming the grounds and a noisy crowd gathered on the street. "But why?"

The khaki-clad constable sweated profusely under the bright sun and clearly was in no mood to answer questions. He waved the baton, forcing the group of three to step back. "Ask the damn manager when it's done."

There were shouts of anger from the guests waiting to return to their rooms after a hard night of partying. "My father's the manager," Tara was trying to say, her voice drowned out by yells from the increasingly irate crowd and the questions barked out by TV news crews.

"Cameras," Lilah said near Alex's ear.

The media... the exiles were so close. They simply needed to stay hidden for a few more weeks while the pardon process went through. The news of Harry's exoneration already made them relax their guard too damned much. Not enough to discard their disguises. Still... Alex growled to himself. Neil and Scott breakfasting in the kitchen with Victor was not a major risk, and Brad and Hema were only doing their assigned jobs in the resort.

There was the Bratva, but Steven wasn't stupid enough to try any tricks at the moment. The press was kept outside the gates and wouldn't be able to snap pictures, accidentally or otherwise. Also, the cops were looking for drugs, not missing Americans.

The five people trapped inside would be all right. If Alex and Lilah hung around the gates, they were more likely to be caught on camera. The quasi-religious clothing they always sported might withstand a quick glance, but he preferred not to take the chance. They needed to get to the safety of the ladies' hostel.

"Maestro," Tara called, tugging at his hand. "My papa..."

"Sir," Alex tried to catch the cop's attention, but the crowd was too loud. "We live—" A thought occurred. Such raids usually involved guest areas, but the ladies' hostel could also be searched.

The cop guarding the gates shoved someone—a reporter, from the microphone in his hand. He stumbled onto his female colleague. More people fell. Shouts of anger rose. A hand each on Lilah's and Tara's upper backs, Alex moved them to the side.

"We need to leave," Lilah said urgently. "If the situation gets worse—" The more chaotic the raid got, the more attention the media would pay.

Alex nodded. "Yeah, and the... ahh... luggage..." His sniper rifle and the submachine gun were safely concealed below the false bottom of his bag, which itself was hidden under loose tiles below the cupboard in his room. Still... "Tara, let's go." Wrapping an arm around the girl's shoulders, he hustled her out.

"B-but," she sputtered. "My father..."

"He'll be all right," Alex soothed. "The resort itself is not involved in anything." Prince's death put an end to that particular problem. Unfortunately, Mathur and his money didn't carry the same clout with the local police. The Mermaid was forced to deal with the same corrupt officials who made life difficult for ordinary Goans. "A guest or two might get picked up," Alex continued. "Nothing more." The bad publicity would last a few weeks until the media moved on to the next sensational story.

"There's a phone booth on the main road," Tara said. "Let's call Papa's cell."

"He might not be allowed to answer," Lilah warned.

"Standard operating procedure for government agencies," agreed Alex.

"So what do we do now?" asked Tara.

It was a ten-minute cab ride to Arpora, where Neil had his alternative medicine clinic. He didn't see any patients on Sundays, so the place would be empty. The tattoo parlor next door would be open, but business was slow in the mornings for most establishments catering to tourists. The three of them could stay safely hidden until the raid was over.

#

10:45 AM

Naval airbase, Goa

"I have something," called out Michael, drawing a thick red circle on the map of Mumbai.

Sabrina swiveled, her eyes eager. In two strides, General Mittal was standing next to Michael, peering over his shoulder.

Michael explained, "There were calls to the prison from four or five different numbers in this neighborhood. There was a pattern, too." He jabbed at the paper with the tip of his finger. "One, two, three, four. As though—"

"Someone was using the devices in the specific order," the general interrupted, tone thoughtful, "to make law enforcement think the calls were from different people."

"Yes, sir," Michael said. "I tracked down some of the other calls made by the same devices. No pattern there. None whatsoever. Very few repeated numbers."

The general's sharp gaze pinned Michael. "Public telephones." With a curse, he added, "In and around the Chhatrapati Shivaji Terminus. It's going to be a long time before we can track down the fellow."

"Terminus?" Sabrina asked. "Buses?"

Mittal shook his head. "Trains. It's probably the busiest railway station in all of India."

"Alex mentioned a really busy train station in Bombay once," said Sabrina. "But the name was different."

"Victoria?" the general asked sharply. "VT station?"

"Maybe... I don't quite... but it could be. It's where he met Rekha... you know, the trans—"

"I know who she is," said the general, suddenly bristling with excitement. "Victoria Terminus was the old name of the place. We need to locate Rekha."

Before they could do anything about it, Grayson Sheppard came to the door. "He signed it."

"The pardon?" A hand to her mouth, Sabrina covered her startled sob.

Like the general, Michael pumped his fists in the air. The elation was followed by disappointment when Gateway's office in

Mumbai refused to hand over Rekha's phone number. The general's men could physically go to the woman's place, but it would take time they didn't have. Waving violently at the general, Sabrina asked him to stop arguing with the manager. A dozen keystrokes later, she was in Gateway's systems.

In fifteen minutes, the general hung up from another call. "It was from my Mumbai man," he explained. "Rekha denied contacting Hoda. She was... er... loudly unhappy about the suggestion she'd sell Alex out."

With a sound of despair, Sabrina collapsed back into her chair.

"But," continued the general, "Rekha told us where to find him."

Things got kind of blurry all of a sudden... exclamations, shouted commands to the aide to inform hangar staff the general would again be using a helicopter. When the aide marched out, Ma said to the general, "We're going with you."

The general eyed both her and Michael. "You'd probably be safer with me. Grayson, you, too. It would've been best we kept the navy's involvement to a minimum. I don't want anyone else getting into trouble with the defense ministry over this. Unfortunately, the pilot I was expecting... not sure he'll be here soon enough... any of you know how to use a gun?"

"Sort of," Sabrina said, flushing.

Michael rolled his eyes. Even if the weapon were right up against the target, she wouldn't be able to shoot. And Uncle Gray had cataracts.

With an exasperated grunt, the general asked Michael, "What about you, boy? You're Alex Kingsley's son. I hope you know at least how to point, aim, and fire."

Tone deliberate, Michael said, "I'm better than Dad."

At the startled look on the general's face, Ma apologized, "He takes a little getting used to. Liam does say Mikey's almost as good as Alex, but my son's not shooting anyone."

"Mike," corrected Michael. "And I'm better. Not 'almost as good.' My instructor agrees. He used to teach at the sniper school in Fort Benning."

"Let's hope we don't get the opportunity to test your skill," said the general. Before Sabrina could object further, he held up a soothing hand. "Only making sure your boy can protect himself—and you—in a pinch."

In a couple of minutes, the aide returned with a colleague. "There's a situation at the resort, sir," said the newcomer. Apparently, India's Narcotics Control Bureau kept an eye on hotels in Goa for evidence of drug trafficking. Two days ago, somebody high up in the agency received a tip about international criminals using The Mermaid as a hub for heroin smuggling. "According to the local chief, the call came from someone in the U.S."

"Get me the NCB director on the line," ordered the general.

Watching him talk on the phone, Michael hopped from foot to foot. His ma was in her chair, eyes closed and lips moving as though she were praying. Face ashen, Grayson was also seated. The two aides continued to walk in and out.

When the general finally hung up, both his men were waiting with updates. "The helipad at the resort has been cleared for landing," said one of the aides. Sabrina sat up, as did Grayson. "Out of the five men, four are inside the main building. Our people are securing them as we speak. The girl—Hema, I believe—is also in the main resort. Two are missing, along with the owner's daughter."

Sabrina clapped a hand to her forehead. "Lilah."

The aide nodded. "And Captain Alex Kingsley."

Chapter 68

A few minutes ago, around 11:15 AM

Elsewhere in Goa

It was too early in the morning for tourists to gather on the beach, but the maze of a neighborhood where Neil ran his alternative medicine clinic enjoyed relative peace even in the thick of rave party madness. Only the sounds of birds and the distant honking of vehicles echoed into the tiny single-story building. At the doctor's desk, Lilah sat and willed herself to relax. The ceiling fan whirred, circulating air. Her sunglasses and scarf were already off, and the saffron-colored tunic and loose pants were thin enough, but she continued to sweat.

The half-door to the waiting area remained shut, as did the bathroom at the back of the exam room. The phone on the desk had rung a couple of times, but both were patients hoping to be seen on a Sunday. As expected, calls to the resort didn't go through. The cops conducting the raid wouldn't allow communication with the outside world until every nook and cranny was examined. Lilah, Tara, and Alex were in for a long wait.

There were several old newspapers strewn on the tabletop—all carrying articles about Harry's release—but Lilah couldn't focus enough to read them again. Something was bothering her... if only she could pinpoint what.

Curled up in a chair next to the barred window on the right was Tara, sketching furiously. The girl had a pattern. She danced until she tired whenever she remembered her dead mother, drawing designs with the ferocity of a hurricane when she was otherwise agitated. Young Tara was worried about her father. There should've been nothing on her mind beyond schoolwork and friends and her future, but she already witnessed more violence than most adults did in their lifetimes—thanks in part to Lilah.

The door to the supplies closet squeaked open, Alex peering in. Brooms, a mop, cleaning liquids, towels... he couldn't be planning to do housekeeping to kill time. The clerk would've taken care of it after Neil's last session the night before. The tiled floor almost gleamed, and a faint smell of bleach still clung to the air. Alex's eyes were on the number-locked steel vault at the back which held the spare weapons belonging to the exiles.

Tugging off his own printed saffron bandana, he tossed it onto a chair. The dark wraparound glasses he wore outside were already resting on the same chair. The waist-length dark hair stayed twisted into a man-bun at his nape these days. Alex went to the left where the medicine cupboard was. "Just making sure," he muttered. "Prince juniors..." Who knew if there were more of them in Goa? Disinfectants, anesthetics, disposable surgical instruments... in a pinch, anything could serve as a weapon. In fact,

Neil and Scott faithfully cut up Coke cans and crammed them with the color powder Indians used every Holi, the celebration marking the beginning of spring. A wick was threaded through the lids. Besides the do-it-yourself smoke bombs, the vault also held leftover crackers from Diwali, the festival of lights.

Lilah sighed inwardly as Alex resumed pacing. Perhaps it was the possibility of Prince juniors that was troubling her. She couldn't see why the drug raid would. In her eight years in Goa, other hotels were raided by the narcotics agency. With Prince's clout gone, The Mermaid was seen as fair game. *Nothing more,* she assured herself.

Her eyes went to the newspapers on the desk. Perhaps it was *The Wall Street Journal* interview with Harry which triggered her unease. Most of the journalist's questions pertained to Harry's experiences with the criminal justice system and the expected pardon for Brad. Harry stated his intention to sue the network's board to be reinstated as chairman. Even with the pardon, the signature of the chairman was necessary for Brad to return as CEO of the network. When Lilah left on her exile, the plan was to use the clout of chairmanship to force the five Kingsley brothers into dismantling the oil empire. No, they wouldn't like it, but without Harry, they wouldn't even get their own company back. Now... it could be years before Harry won the lawsuit... *if* he won.

Lilah shook her head. The complication was not something she was unaware of for the last eight years. It certainly didn't explain why she was so jumpy all of a sudden. There *was* the last part of the interview, the fluff toward the end. Questions on his friendship with Alex... gossip about a love affair with one of the correction officers at Sing Sing which Harry bluntly denied... and his marriage to Lupe Valdez.

Rolling her shoulders, Lilah stood, took a few steps up and down, and sat back. The thought of Lupe's death always made Lilah jittery. She'd agonized over it for eight long years without stumbling on an answer. How far was she willing to go in this war against the Kingsleys? Hema saved Lilah from the rapist congressman and barely escaped death. Who knew what fate would've waited for Tara if Prince won the confrontation? Was surrender the only way to minimize collateral damage?

Lilah rummaged through the pile of newspapers. There it was... the *Journal.*

"Any leads on your wife's murder?" the reporter had asked Harry.

Wife... Harry found time to marry while the friends he was supposedly fighting for were running for their lives, and he chose a woman whose identity centered around her sensuality. A woman who sacrificed herself in a war which was not even hers.

According to the interview, a portion of her ashes were kept aside by Liam because Harry wasn't allowed to travel outside the country in the aftermath of the two murders. As soon as his passport was reinstated, he would fly to an undisclosed destination to honor her memory in a manner which would've pleased her.

Her memory wouldn't have needed honoring if she didn't deliberately choose to put herself in harm's way. *Why?* Lilah asked for the millionth time, but the spirit of the dead woman did not respond.

#

No matter how many times Tara told herself Papa would be fine, the heavy weight within her chest refused to dissipate. She couldn't lose her father. Mama was gone, and Maestro would soon be leaving. The police wouldn't put a resort owner in jail because a guest or two got caught with drugs, would they? But what if the officers stumbled on evidence connecting The Mermaid to Prince?

Tara continued sketching, but her fingers trembled. She didn't have any family left except Papa. Oh, there were dozens of Mathurs in Goa but none who could be trusted not to steal the resort. Tara never met most of her mother's relatives in Mizoram, and the grandparents from both sides were dead. If her father got sent to prison... there would be lawyers... courts... what the hell was Tara supposed to do all by herself? She had plenty of friends at school, and the nuns in charge liked her. Maybe she could hide in the convent until Papa got out of trouble. A convent! What kind of food did the sisters eat? Not anything good if their clothes were any indication.

She drew the last curl on the pencil sketch of Jack and Rose at the bow of the *Titanic*. The drag queens were so whiny about Tara's refusal to stitch replicas of the movie's gowns for their weekly show at the resort. Well... they were now aware Tara Mathur only did originals. She put her initials at the lower right corner of the sheet, on the hull of the ship. The paper was thin and flimsy... not as if a clinic needed to keep art-quality notepads.

Flipping the leaf, Tara stared at the empty page for a few seconds before glancing outside. From her chair, she could see up and down the narrow gap between the clinic and the building which housed the tattoo parlor. A part of the street in front would become visible if she craned her neck ever so slightly. Most tourists would be snoring in their beds this time of the morning, all pooped out after a hard night of partying, but there were always one or two chirpy early risers.

Tara frowned. The fellow in khaki shorts behind the black couple... Europeans far outnumbered American visitors to Goa, but she saw enough of them to spot at least the male ones. The combination of khaki and lighter cotton seemed to be a national favorite. Some outfits were particularly ghastly, but she tried not to hold their fashion choices against them. After all, Tara also preferred comfortable jeans or shorts with a tee. Her dark curls were okay... when she remembered to brush them into some sort of order.

The chap on the street sported dark tresses, too. He seemed somewhat browner than other white guys... not simply more tanned. She peered. Bronzer? The skin tone was *way* even... not natural. Now that she looked closer, his hair was also wrong. Dye, for sure. Tara frowned again. There was something familiar about him. The form, the stance. Without glancing down, she started sketching again.

The old rotary phone on the desk rang, but Tara was too busy to pay attention. It would be yet another patient, asking if the doctor would make an exception and see just one patient just this one Sunday. The people at the resort didn't even know Tara, Alex, and Lilah took refuge at the clinic. Yeah, Chef Victor or one of the others might guess, but it would be a few hours before they were allowed to make calls.

"Hello," said Lilah's voice. Alex was also talking, perhaps urging her to cut the conversation short... just in case the resort was trying to locate them.

"Maestro," Tara called, uncurling herself out of the chair. "Can you take a look at this?" She thrust the notepad toward her dance teacher. The man on the street looked a little like Alex, and it couldn't be a coincidence... could it?

Alex was on the line now, listening in silence to whatever the caller was saying.

"Maestro," Tara insisted. "You *need* to see—"

"In a minute," said Lilah, holding up a hand. She was standing as well, sweat plastering tendrils of red-dyed hair to her forehead.

"But—" The fellow was still hanging out by the gate. Correction: he was hiding behind a parked van.

"They want you there," said Alex, hanging up.

"Heh?" Tara asked. "Who?"

"The Narcotics Control Bureau," said Alex. "It was your father's lawyer who called. You own half the place, so the cops are insisting on interrogating you. Apparently, a couple of female officers are on their way to pick you up. The call was to make sure we stay put."

"I don't like this," said Lilah. "Are you sure it was Mathur's attorney? Tara, do you happen to know your father's lawyer?"

An alarm started buzzing in Tara's head, driving out all other thoughts, all confusion about strange men on the street. "I... lawyer... I think maybe Sharma Uncle... not sure."

"That's the name the fellow gave me," Alex said. "We could try to call back to verify, but I doubt anyone will be allowed to pick up. The cops won't care if we have doubts."

"If this Sharma is a lawyer, he probably has a cell phone," said Lilah. "We can at least try."

"I don't know the number," Tara said, swallowing hard. Her tummy was churning, like she was going to throw up any minute. "His office... shit, it's Sunday... they won't be open. I know where he lives, but it's near the basilica." A good forty-five minutes by car.

"So let's go there," said Alex. "His family can verify for us if he's at the resort. The guys at the tattoo parlor can let the officers know where we went. They can either follow us to Sharma's residence or wait for us to get to The Mermaid."

Which would be nearly two hours from now... her father would be worried sick when she didn't turn up at the expected time. "Maybe Papa can't sign anything without me," Tara muttered. "I can't just ditch him and hide someplace. I should be at the resort, helping him."

"Tara," called Lilah. "There's little you can do legally until you reach the age of—"

"I don't care," said Tara. "My father needs me, and I'm going." Tossing the notepad to the chair, she strode to the half-door and pushed it open. "All three of us should go before the policewomen get here. I mean... what if they don't let you two go with me? Let's just leave them a message we're on our way and get started. You're a lawyer, Lilah, and Papa trusts you. Who gives a shit if Sharma Uncle is not actually there?"

"I don't know enough about Indian law," said Lilah.

"I really think—" started Alex.

"No way." Tara shook her head violently. "I ain't hiding. The raid is my problem as much as my father's. Maestro, could you *please* try calling the resort again? I'll wait for you at the gate." She jogged out before the other two could respond.

#

Alex huffed. "I'll call the local precinct. They should be able to get in touch with the team inside the resort." With his free hand, he patted the firearm belt under the tunic. He would have to hide the pistol somewhere in the vicinity of The Mermaid before going in, or the cops would confiscate it. The spares in the clinic could serve as replacements if needed. His sniper rifle and the submachine gun were safely concealed in his room at the ladies' hostel. If the police stumbled on the heavy-duty weapons...

Lilah was still staring at the half-door through which the young girl exited. "Her problem as much as her father's," she murmured.

"Heh?"

"What Tara said... she knows it could be dangerous to go to the resort right now, but she's willing to take the risk. Because it's *her* fight, and she trusts you and me to have her back." Picking up the scarf as though in a daze, Lilah once again wrapped it around her hair. "Perhaps all of them see it as their fight."

"Who are you talking about?" asked Alex, only partly listening as he waited for the call to be answered.

"Hema, Tara, even Mathur..." Shaking her head, Lilah added, "Let's focus on the current trouble. We're probably worrying unnecessarily. Mathur would have called the lawyer already, and the officers would've tried to track down Tara. So the call was likely legit. The attorney will make sure she doesn't get into trouble. Alex, I'm worried about the media crews. I mean... every camera in the place is going to be on Tara when she reaches the resort. *We* will be right behind."

"Dammit," said Alex. "Maybe we can get someone else to—"

"Hello?" snapped an impatient male voice on the phone. "Anjuna Police Station."

"Ahh... hello," said Alex. "May I speak to the officer in charge? It's about the raid at The Mermaid. We got a message..."

As he continued explaining, Lilah wandered to the chair occupied by Tara and picked up the discarded notepad.

"We cannot interfere in an ongoing investigation by another agency," said the fellow at the other end of the line.

Lilah flipped a page.

"I'm not asking you to interfere," stated Alex. "We simply need some assist—"

A momentary stillness, and then Lilah jerked back as though in shock. "Alex!" she shrieked.

"What?" Alex asked, tossing the phone back onto the cradle.

"Armor," Lilah said, holding up the book.

"Ar—*Armor?*" They both rushed toward the front door. "Fall back," Alex shouted, drawing his gun. He galloped out only to screech to a halt.

"Alex Kingsley?" someone inquired from the gate. Eyeing Alex up and down was the Russian mobster who once asked Tara about her modelling days. The man laughed. "You're *Captain* Alex Kingsley? Some captain!"

Chapter 69

"Tara," shouted Alex, desperately scanning the terrain for her. And where was Armor? Did he get the child, holding her somewhere out of Alex's reach?

The Russian and his two comrades continued laughing. Wind gusted, sending the leaves of the coconut palms rustling. A cawing raven landed on a swaying power line, watching the unfolding scene with its head tilted to one side.

The second-hand van meant to be the exiles' emergency escape vehicle was still parked in the small yard. Only a couple of tourists could be seen on the street, and they were already at the end of the block. The souvenir shop on the left wouldn't open until late afternoon when partiers returned to the beach. The door to the tattoo parlor on the right was ajar, but no customers were waiting to get inked, and the artist couple who ran the place were likely in their office, catching up on paperwork. Other businesses, the one or two private residences on the block... no one was outside. No one in the neighborhood would know what was happening unless Alex did something to alert them.

"Tara!" he shouted again. Forget calling for help... forget using the weapon... Alex didn't dare say a word to the three gangsters and put the girl at risk.

"You looking for the kid?" asked the Russian, his chortles finally dying down. "She's right here."

Yet another of the thugs who frequently hung around The Mermaid joined the group. This one was local and well-known for acting as intermediary between his Bratva colleagues and the Goan police. His fingers were wrapped around Tara's right arm, almost dragging the stumbling sixteen-year-old.

"I thought I'd have to work for it," the Russian said, his tone gleeful and brown eyes wide with anticipation. "But the girl came running straight to me."

At least she was not in Armor's custody. Where the hell *was* he? If Tara didn't leave the bastard's picture as unintended warning, Alex wouldn't have drawn his gun before sprinting out. He might have been dead from the Russian's bullet by now, and the criminal would be inside the clinic, hunting Lilah.

Alex started on a sudden realization. Armor could've issued orders from the safety of the U.S., instructing the Bratva to kill all seven of the exiles. The ensuing media furor would provide him and Steven with proof of their enemies' demise. Unfortunately, international attention would end Steven's reign as CEO if the connection between him and the Russian mob came out. Armor was in Goa to make sure the mission went as planned, with no harm done to Steven.

There was a strategy to deal with all the exiles. Whatever it was, Alex and Lilah were clearly designated as the first to go.

The major was hiding somewhere to avoid getting caught by the Indian authorities in case the Russians failed to deliver. If Alex turned out to be armed—as he did—the faceoff would be prolonged, increasing the chances of the criminals' defeat. Even if Armor managed to escape the scene before any cops showed up, being spotted by a random passerby would get him—and Steven by extension—into trouble. So the major was waiting in the shadows for Alex and Lilah to be delivered into his hands. Perhaps the son of a bitch would pull the trigger himself. After the defeats Armor was handed in Macau and Beijing, after the humiliation of Harry's exoneration, the bastard would want validation.

There was a scuffling sound behind Alex, where the clinic door was, but he didn't turn to check. Lilah would know better than to venture out unless it became absolutely necessary. She would call the cops. Perhaps she did already. Thank God the phone was still working, which meant the clinic wasn't where the Russian expected the confrontation to happen, or the lines would've been cut. The drug raid at The Mermaid... did the thug believe Alex and Lilah would hide in the ladies' hostel with Tara?

Regardless, Armor had to know they'd call for help. The Russian mob might have accomplices in the local precinct, but there was no way to make sure the mafia plant was the one who answered Lilah's call. Armor would've planned to complete his task and escape before the police possibly showed up.

The enemy was on a clock. But if Armor thought he didn't have enough time to kill without leaving witnesses, he could order the Russian to fire his gun no matter who was watching.

"What do you want?" Alex barked. Perspiration drenched his clothes as he made quick calculations. If he could somehow get Tara back inside... the front door was heavy duty, and the windows were barred, so she and Lilah could possibly fend off the thugs until the cops showed up. At four-to-one disadvantage, Alex wasn't likely to make it, but Lilah would. She would keep Tara safe until they were rescued.

"Tell the broad to come out," said the Russian. "Now!"

Somewhere not too far away, an engine thundered to life... a motorcycle? There was another sound, the distant rumbling of an approaching helicopter. Alex didn't bother looking for the source of either noise. Motorbike riders were common in Goa, and while navy choppers frequently flew the skies, they were hardly likely to spot the drama going on in one side street. "Leave her out of this," said Alex. "She has nothing to do with your boss's gripes against us."

The Russian's eyes narrowed. Of course he didn't have a clue Alex knew about Armor's presence. "Enough stalling," the Russian bellowed over the rising cacophony. "Get the woman out here, and I'll let you and the girl go."

Alex snorted. "Sure you will."

Armor would be getting worried by now. The only reason he hadn't yet given the order to shoot his old rival was he couldn't tell how Lilah would respond. The major was clearly hoping Lilah's affections for the girl would lure her out, but he wouldn't be certain of it. As far as Armor knew, if he shot at Alex, Lilah might lock herself in regardless of danger to Tara.

A diversion... Alex needed some kind of distraction to get the girl back in the building... to secure both her and Lilah while he held off Armor's thugs.

The bike on the street continued its rumbling but didn't appear in Alex's visual field. The staccato roar of the chopper got louder. Even the thwacks of the blades were audible now. Alex chanced a glance up. The helicopter was flying low. Too low. And it was hovering. Did the pilot notice something suspicious? Or was he working with the enemy? Where was the biker?

The Russian, too, took a quick glance at the royal-blue helicopter. The white lettering on the tail said, "NAVY."

"You're wasting time," yelled one of the thugs. "Get the woman out here if you want the kid to live."

Nope. The pilot could not be in the Bratva's pocket pals if the concern on the Russian's face were an indication. "No," Alex spat. "You may be able to get my brothers and me, but the Indian navy will take care of you before you get anywhere near Lilah."

The Russian snarled. "Not unless they've started hauling sharpshooters around on routine patrols. I can take you before the pilot gets help. My men will deal with the girl and Mrs. Kingsley. Move it or all of you will die."

"Use this," Lilah's low voice said from behind the door to the clinic. "Quickly!"

Not glancing away from the criminals, Alex extended his hand backward. Hot metal, a sizzling sound... he didn't need to look down to know what it was. Within seconds, the DIY grenade flew across the air. The flame scorched through the alcohol-soaked fabric wick.

"Get out of here," bellowed one of the criminals, lurching backward. "Molotov cocktail!"

More and more cans were handed to Alex in quick succession. He hurled them in the direction of the enemy. Screams... yells of disbelief... shouts of alarm from the building to the right... the flames disappeared inside the Coke can.

"Tara!" Alex yelled, hoping the kid retained enough presence of mind to use the confusion to escape. "Now, champ!"

Colors exploded. Pink, blue, yellow, red... instead of fire, dense clouds of powdery smoke chugged out of the cans, filling the air. "Holi's next month," someone yelled from the tattoo parlor.

"Bloody bitch," shrieked the local thug. "Stop biting!"

"She kneed me," yelled someone else.

A skinny form came hurtling through the fog, halting by Alex's side. "Maestro," gasped Tara. She was coated in powder of all hues. Some of the dust drifted toward Alex, settling on his hair, his arm, his clothes.

"Do not retreat!" hollered the Russian, staggering through the smoke with his gun in his hands. He, too, resembled a strange creature... a beast of many shades. "It is *not* a damn bomb." Only two of his men stopped, but it was two too many.

Alex mumbled a curse. He was still outnumbered. "Inside, Tara!" he snapped.

"You asked for it," said the Russian, raising his arm.

More screams came from the owners of the tattoo parlor. "Are you crazy?" one of them shouted.

"Call the cops!" screeched a second female voice.

"Tara!" Alex bellowed. "Inside... now!" Bringing his wife's lovely face to his mind, Alex bid goodbye. Everything faded from his field of vision except the Russian thug's brown eyes. Small muscles tightened in Alex's hands. A slight pressure on the trigger.

A loud report... a whoosh followed, then a thunderous crash.

Startled, Alex darted a half-glance toward the source of the noise. The coconut tree? Large and hard-shelled coconuts rolled on the ground. The Russian's attention was on the helicopter. The two tattoo artists were also staring at the sky. There were more people on the streets now, all shouting, screaming.

"Maestro," cried Tara.

Lilah came running out, her own pistol in one hand, grabbing Tara's shoulder with the other. "Get inside!" Lilah screamed.

Another explosion came from the heavens. This time, a branch fell. A dark form leaned out from the open hatch of the chopper, wind billowing his black shirt. His hair whipped all around his face. In his hands was a rifle. He turned, pointing it in Tara's direction.

The girl's mouth opened and closed, eyes widening in horror. "Maestro," Tara said, her thick voice hardly audible over the thundering of the chopper's engines. "Save me."

Whoever he was, the shooter already demonstrated his skill with the tree. He was now compensating for the wind. He might be pointing at Tara, but his target was the Russian. "Fantastic," murmured Alex.

"What?" yelped Tara.

When Alex swiveled back, the Russian's eyes were darting between his target and the unknown shooter. The criminal had recognized himself as the shooter's mark.

The Russian and his comrades wouldn't dare fire back, either. The navy didn't normally involve itself in local law enforcement matters, but the stance would change the moment one of its own was killed by the mob. The Bratva certainly wouldn't want the Indian military after them, and any gang member who invited unnecessary attention wouldn't live long. The Russian's two remaining mates were already backing away.

"Your friend up there..." bellowed the Russian. "I'd ask him to stop. Your brothers are still in the resort... my men have them."

Alex snarled. "I'll take my chances." Even if he ended up dead, and the rest of the Kingsley brothers died in the resort, the chopper crew was clearly not a part of the enemy team. They would make sure nothing happened to Lilah and Tara.

"Yo, man," called one of the criminals. "Let's get out of here." There was a black van with tinted windows waiting on the street.

The thug who ran before was back to collect his comrades. "The police are going to be here any minute. Let's go!"

As they backed away, Alex gave chase. Armor... he was in the damned van. He had to be. If he were dragged out, if the Indian government exposed him for the criminal he was, Steven would soon fall.

Sprinting, Alex took a shot. One of the thugs screamed, but he didn't stop running. Nor did anyone turn to return fire. Keeping out of the navy's clutches seemed to be their main goal now. The shooter in the helicopter... what the hell was he waiting for? Why wasn't he helping Alex?

The van door slammed. Tires screeched.

Alex fired again. Two bullets down... four left.

The vehicle rammed into an electric pole, sending up metallic sparks. Cawing in alarm, birds flew off the swaying wires. The van swerved back onto the road, speeding away.

"Shit!" roared Alex, watching the vehicle disappear. "Shit, shit, shit."

#

Wiping sweat off his forehead, Alex limped back in the direction of the clinic.

"Are you fucking crazy?" yelled one of the artists who owned the tattoo parlor. "Shooting at the Russians! Go inside and wait for the police!" Nobody—absolutely *nobody*—wanted to mess with the mafia.

"Did you get the license number of the van?" Alex bellowed over the noise of chopper blades, already knowing the information was not likely to be of much use. The thugs would no doubt ditch their getaway vehicle, and Armor would've traveled under an alias. Looking around at the small number of spectators on the street, Alex tried again, "Anyone?"

"Ask him," said a woman, her finger pointing up.

The helicopter was still hovering over the scene with everyone on the ground now staring skyward. The shooter... he could've ended the problem of Major Richard Armor today but chose not to. Or the chopper crew didn't have a clue who was in the van. They somehow spotted what was going on and decided to help but didn't intend to kill anyone, criminal or not.

"Alex," Lilah shouted from the door of the clinic. "Are you all right?"

As she and Tara sprinted across the tiny yard to join Alex, the chopper tilted about in the wind and fell a couple of hundred feet.

"What the hell?" muttered Alex.

Stopping short by the clinic's gate, Lilah, too, stared up. "Is he trying to land here? There's no space."

A rope fell from the door, twitching in the vortex of air set up by the blades. Eyes on the shooter, Alex said, "He's coming down."

A horn blasted some distance away, the enthusiastic drums of a recent chartbuster rolling out of the vehicle's audio system. Paying no mind, the shooter descended on a harness. The air seemed to shimmer in anticipation as the hero of the hour landed feet first. He stumbled forward a short distance before unhooking himself from the harness. Once he signaled the pilot, the chopper turned back, the sounds fading as it vanished into the horizon.

The shooter was not in uniform... just ripped jeans and a black tee with a hole in one armpit, brown combat boots on his feet. Collar-length dark hair whipped about in the wind. Protective glasses notwithstanding, the smooth fullness of his cheeks revealed his youth. Too young and too unkempt to be military, but there was no denying his skill.

Taking his glasses off, the shooter tucked them into his back pocket. Nor did the boy appear Indian.

Murmurs rose from the crowd, but Alex continued to stare, trying to figure out where he saw the lad before. Everything about him was familiar, yet not. The eyes...

"Mikey?" asked Lilah, her husky voice high in amazement.

An exasperated look came over the boy's face. "Mike," he corrected. "Michael Kingsley."

Part XXIII

Chapter 70

Two days later

(9 years after the exile began)

Out on the Arabian Sea

Squawking raucously, a flock of seagulls flew past the ultra-luxury liner designed solely to attract the mega rich of the planet. Fingers gripping the railing, Lilah leaned far over, tempted to leap into the frothy ocean. It had been so long... she was already dressed for it. Swimsuits were provided to any passenger who might request one, and the crew produced a bikini in dusty red just for her. The matching sarong-style wrap fluttered in the mild breeze, its printed fabric flapping against Lilah's legs.

She swept aside the tendrils of hair whipping her face... tresses newly dyed to their former blue-black glory. The brown contacts had been switched for clear prescription lenses, revealing the hazel color of her irises. Lilah never realized how much she missed being her old self until she opened the package Sabrina brought along. One look at the cut-glass bottle holding the lotus oil perfume, and Lilah nearly cried.

A chorus of oohs and aahs rose from the group on Lilah's left as a dolphin somersaulted into the air, nosing neatly back into the deep-blue waters. The spectators were mostly wealthy Europeans who liked to brag about experiencing ethnic culture. Some seemed to imagine Lilah was one of the marvels to be gawked at. She'd so far been accosted by a French movie star and the deposed dictator of a small island nation as well as a gaggle of young royals who wanted an introduction to the movie star-gorgeous Neil. The rest were gracious enough to give space to the newly resurfaced Lilah Kingsley, but curiosity was writ large on every face. There were more than a few surreptitious camera flashes even as she stood watching the dolphin. The grinning creature was joined by a partner, and without any prompting, the duo put on an energetic performance for the human visitors.

"C'mon, sis," said Dan, and he grabbed her hand, pulling her behind him to the long, white-clothed table arranged specifically for their group.

With a loud report, Shawn uncorked the champagne bottle. Everyone crowded around Dan and Lilah, singing "Happy Birthday to You." Two weeks had passed since their actual birthday, but it didn't matter. This was the time to celebrate all the birthdays they didn't get to wish each other. At the sight of her twin's grin, her heart soared in joy. They'd catch up—her and Dan and Shawn—as soon as the madness settled.

How the two men managed to get places on the ship for so many at such short notice, Lilah didn't know. Those who had been eagerly awaiting the return of the exiles flew to Goa as soon as they heard the news. Shawn and Dan, Patrice, Mr. Temple and his friend, Noah Andersen, Uncle Gray, Dante, Sabrina, and Michael. Hema spent only a day on board before returning to the resort to bid goodbye to the ladies she worked with all these years. Shankar also took the boat back in the morning, partly to explain his involvement to his superiors, partly to pick up the two people who were expected to arrive at the naval airbase anytime now. With

Victor's signature, Gabriel's passport application was rushed through. Liam had volunteered to stay behind to accompany the boy on the trip. Last Lilah heard, they were in Mumbai, impatiently waiting for the connecting flight to Goa.

Tara and her papa were also present at the party. And yeah, the phone call which drew the girl out had been genuine. Terribly timed, allowing Armor's thugs to snatch her as hostage. How the major otherwise planned to lure his intended victims was anybody's guess, but Alex ventured a couple of ideas about the enemy's overall strategy.

The tip which led to the drug raid was probably called in by Armor or the other Kingsley hanger-on, Phillip Potts. Every cop who was a part of the team couldn't have been on the take, but there were surely one or two who would plant evidence implicating Brad.

Tara's Sunday morning shooting lessons were not a secret. When she returned with Alex and Lilah, the three of them were expected to take shelter in the ladies' hostel, where they would be shot by the Russians. All seven exiles—mere days from a pardon—dying at the same time would raise suspicions, but two during a mafia incident? The U.S. government could well be persuaded not to look beyond the Bratva for explanations. Harry wouldn't believe it. He would of course retaliate and be killed in the process.

Despite a pardon from Washington, Brad would've landed in an Indian prison for the planted drugs. A convenient accident... perhaps a suicide... he, too, would die in a few months. Of the three remaining Kingsley brothers, only Victor would've been considered a threat, and he'd be taken out in another well-timed accident.

Unfortunately for the enemy, the ruckus created by the media caused Alex, Lilah, and Tara to head to the clinic instead of the hostel. Even well-planned missions couldn't account for every variable, and Armor would've had only a couple of days to put together this operation, or he might have arranged an assassin in the clinic building, too.

Unknown to Armor, communications between Naini Central and the Criminal Investigation Command in Quantico were intercepted by Shankar Mittal. Spotting Armor on the street, Tara sketched his picture. And of course, young Michael Kingsley showed up.

Both Shankar Mittal and the pilot of the chopper told the boy not to shoot anything with legs. Michael was to demonstrate for the thugs he could take them out if he so wished... nothing more. He wasn't allowed to open fire at the getaway car. A teenaged boy, an American, killing someone in Goa? The repercussions would not be good for Michael or any of the adults who accompanied him. Which meant Armor was probably back stateside by now while all his enemies celebrated.

Well, almost all. Besides Liam and Gabriel, there was one more person missing from the party. Lilah knew he was around, but she hadn't spotted him in the last hour—the pilot of the helicopter which showed up in the nick of time to save her, Alex, and Tara.

"Ladies and gentlemen," called the DJ, "Enjoy Los del Río!"

"Macarena" blasted out from the sound system.

Holding two glasses of bubbly, Sabrina danced her way over. "It's your birthday, Lilah. Eat, drink, and be merry."

"You look like a tipsy mermaid," Lilah said, laughing. Sabrina always looked good in blue-green colors, and her generous curves showed off well in the two-piece.

"A *sexy* mermaid," shouted Alex, coming up behind his wife to slide an arm around her waist.

A shadow passed across Sabrina's face, but when he nuzzled her shoulder, she sputtered like the nineteen-year-old she'd been when they met. Uncaring of the audience, they kissed. There was desperation in the way they clung to each other. Despite the separation, despite the tears and the anger and the unasked questions, there was love between them. Real, solid love.

Fatherly longing was in Alex's frequent glances at the son who showed up from the sky with a weapon in his hands like the archangel he was named after. Whereas Michael seemed quite determined to give his dad the royal ignore.

"Lilah," someone called from behind.

She bit back an unladylike curse. Noah Andersen, the former attorney general, had been trying to corner her into a conversation since he and Temple arrived the night before. No matter the sins of her former mentor, Lilah wanted to talk to him. She wanted the reassurance he still recognized her even if they couldn't actually communicate. But not with Andersen hanging around. Whatever the crafty old fellow did to make up for his hand in wrecking her personal life, Lilah was finding it hard to forgive.

"Don't run away," Andersen requested. "There's something we need to discuss."

"Another time," Lilah said abruptly, grabbing the white coverup shirt she'd left on the back of a chair. "I want to talk to Tara before we leave."

"She went to the buffet table with Michael." Tone urgent, Andersen said, "You really need to hear this."

#

"Can Brad do that?" Lilah asked, hot anger surging. Heaving herself off the armchair in her suite, she paced the carpet. "We have a pre-nup."

"It only protects *your* position," Andersen pointed out, seated on the small couch. "There's nothing in it stopping *him* from quitting."

Brad once talked about surrender, but it was when they were on the run. Now, he could return home a free man and fight Steven for the network. All their other enemies were defeated.

Two years passed since the death of Prince, and Brad never uttered a word. He'd listened to Victor's account of what happened, merely nodding in response. Lilah was fool enough to hope they were done with the episode. Instead, incensed over her manipulation of his brothers, Brad was prepared to cede to the hated cousins than allow her to win. There was nothing stopping him from telling Steven to keep control of the company and the whole network. It wasn't a sale, which would be subject to the regulations of the American government. A mere continuation of *status quo,* and the feds might just decide to let it pass.

All these years... all the sacrifices... Godwin would triumph. The old fellow couldn't have many more years left to live, but he'd make sure Kingsley Corp ruled the world.

Twirling a pen, Andersen continued, "We're lucky Brad called me first. He claims it's not only about possible infidelity on your part. According to him, your actions put his life in jeopardy several times."

"My actions were what got us out of trouble." Lilah played the Indian Defense for the last nine years. Each successive enemy believed he was within reach of victory, not seeing her army waiting in the shadows to deliver the death blow.

"Brad says he wouldn't have gotten into trouble to begin with if it weren't for you. Besides, he has qualms about hauling Godwin to court... which is what will happen if you pursue legal action against Kingsley Corp."

"They still believe Godwin's on their side," conceded Lilah. "At least emotionally. Victor, Alex, Neil, Scott... all of them think it. Even if it were true—which it isn't—Godwin's supporting a criminal. What about justice for the five of them, for the employees who trusted us, for our business partners? What about justice for *me?* I was assaulted!"

"Justice is perhaps not the primary motive at play here," Andersen said. "Anyway, I did bring up the pre-nup with Brad. Imaginative argument, but it got him worried. I told him while the government would likely not interfere, *you* might still have a case for pursuing legal remedies if he tried permanently signing over control without your consent. He'd be out, but it could possibly be considered a violation of the pre-nup clause which relates to your position in the organization."

The marriage contract was tilted in Lilah's favor, but at the time it was signed, Brad and his brothers desperately needed support from the Sheppards and the Barronses in their corporate battle against the Kingsley family. She would own one-sixth of the stock in the Peter Kingsley Company for her lifetime and would be the CFO. In the event of divorce or separation, Lilah wouldn't lose the voting rights on her stock or her administrative position. She couldn't even be fired without evidence of severe incompetence, or the company would be forced to fork out more stock as compensation. In case of her death, her beneficiary couldn't be Brad or anyone in his immediate family. Lilah didn't know at the time she would never be a mother, but the contract decreed her children would have their inheritance held in trust by someone outside the Kingsley clan. Brad, on the other hand, did not enjoy the same protections.

Andersen held up his pen. "Brad can't fire you without presenting a paper trail of bad decisions on your part, but Steven could. *He* is not bound by the contract Brad signed with you."

"A roundabout way for Brad to break the pre-nup," Lilah said, sitting back in her chair. "I would have the stock but would no longer be CFO. No say at all in the day-to-day activities of the business."

"A court be persuaded to see it exactly that way," said Andersen. "An illegal transfer from Brad to Steven, made with possible illegitimate intentions. Also, one of your arguments in Gitmo was that Brad never got consent from you as CFO and major shareholder before getting into a deal with the Iranians. It wasn't simply a breach of the company charter. What he did could be considered his first violation of the terms of the pre-nup."

"I didn't mention the pre-nup in Cuba because I didn't believe it applied," mused Lilah. "But perhaps—"

Andersen nodded. "You could argue it retroactively and claim repeated infringement of your rights in the business if Brad tried to permanently transfer control of his stock to Kingsley Corp or any other entity."

"So if the court agrees he broke the terms—twice, in fact—I could be entitled to compensation."

"Which would mean part or all of Brad's shares could be handed to you, thus leaving you with perhaps one-third of the company. Even if one of his brothers tossed support your way, you'd be in control of half the stock. It might be enough to make you CEO."

"I could do exactly that," she speculated.

"You could," Andersen agreed. "You're a lawyer. What do you think your chances are?"

"Less than fifty-fifty," she admitted. "Even then, I'd have only my shares and *maybe* Brad's if I won them back from Steven. Without Brad's say-so, his brothers won't cooperate. He imagines me as a *femme fatale* who lures every man around into doing my bidding, but none of those four will support me in a business dispute which pits me against their precious big brother. But my specialty is constitutional law, not divorce. I'd hire a shark."

"Brad would hire one, too. The battle could take years. The Kingsleys would be controlling the business the entire time. You would end up fighting both sides."

"I'll get a stay on the transfer," Lilah said, her voice vibrating in frustrated rage.

"Wait," said the former attorney general. "What I said has stopped him for the time being. I also told him not to mention the idea to anyone else—including his grandfather—because it might be considered further evidence of collusion to defraud." On an awkward cough, Andersen added, "Brad now figures his chances at thwarting your ambition—as he calls it—will be greater if he can prove infidelity on your part and fight the pre-nup itself in court. Trust me... if he could bring Prince into it to prove how you endangered him, he would. Unfortunately for Brad, divulging anything about the Prince episode would get his brothers also into trouble. I told Brad even informing me was problematic since I would be obligated as a lawyer to notify the authorities. Lucky for us the feds aren't terribly unhappy at the death of the criminal and won't investigate further. Still, Brad understands his hands are tied on the issue, so he's planning to go after you for adultery."

Lilah snapped, "I haven't done anything."

"I get it. Thing is Brad believes it, and he's convinced you're pining for his brother. How much angrier do you think he's going to be if the truth comes out?"

"What truth? I consciously set aside all prior relationships when we got married. I had every intention of making it work with Brad. He was the one who—"

"He's not going to see it the same way," Andersen insisted. "We're lucky Godwin can't use the info against you."

Temple worked with Andersen and the Kingsley patriarch on the Kingsley-Barrons-Sheppard alliance. All three men were aware of what was going on in her life from the time she escaped the fire at the Egypt-Libya border. If Godwin chose to divulge what he knew about her past, including her relationship with Harry, Brad might conclude it was kept a secret from him by his own grandfather.

"Godwin can't say anything," Andersen repeated. "But what do you want to bet Steven and his friends have thought along those lines? I doubt Godwin's said anything to them they might eventually use against him, but it's not a stretch to imagine Steven getting the idea from the tabloids. He and Charlie and Richard... they know Brad... and they would love to drive a wedge between the five brothers and Harry. The only reason Steven hasn't tried anything of the sort is Brad won't believe it coming from his cousins. Not as things stand right now. But the moment you give Brad reason to doubt, what Steven says is going to seem credible. Godwin could then build on it without having to reveal his own role in the whole scheme."

"Options?" Lilah asked.

"Only one," said Andersen. "Do not give Brad any openings to claim infidelity on your part and go to court to break the pre-nup. Not one single opening. Besides, if he thinks you're all alone, it might make him happy enough to forget about spiting you... less reason to give up the business to Steven. Yeah, the emotional dependence on Godwin will still be a problem, but we'll work around it. None of us will say anything negative about Godwin."

"My opinion of Godwin is not a secret for Brad and his brothers," admitted Lilah. "Only Alex knows my reasons, but they're all aware of what I think of their precious grandfather."

Andersen sighed. "The direct approach would've worked if the people listening were willing to hear. Which is why Harry and I will need to tread carefully."

"Godwin's not going to be the only roadblock," she mused. "The original plan was to—"

Andersen nodded. "I know. Harry was chairman. He would veto any attempts to get Brad reinstated as CEO until there was an agreement to take down the network. Now..."

Now, Harry would first have to sue the network's board to be reinstated as chairman. The legal proceedings could take years. Lilah would be trapped in her role as Mrs. Brad Kingsley all the while. Some other way... there *had* to be some other way...

"Remember," Andersen said. "Not one opening for Brad to break the pre-nup. No matter how long it takes."

"Does Harry know?" Lilah asked abruptly. "Is that why he hasn't talked to me?"

"He knows." Tone chiding, Andersen added, "But *you* know very well you've been doing the vanishing act each time he's within fifty feet."

After the encounter with Armor, there was another call on the clinic's phone. Shankar Mittal was on the line, asking Alex, Lilah, and Tara to wait with Michael until a military truck arrived to take them to the resort. There was a second man talking in the background, the pilot of the chopper. His rich, deep tones sent Lilah's heart thudding. She bolted to the bathroom, pretending not to hear Alex's excited voice greeting his brother-in-law.

Sabrina had also arrived at the resort within an hour, and she muttered something about fake passports. Some diplomatic sleight of hand was required to make it appear as though her brother traveled the legit way to India. With politicians and old friends from the CIA and even foreign governments now openly showing support, the state department was expected to let Harry go with a slap on the wrist. It still took him twenty-four hours to soothe annoyed national security officials and join the group on the cruise liner. Lilah had watched from behind a glass window as he climbed aboard, dressed casually in chinos and a light-yellow Polo shirt. There was a satchel draped across his torso... with the urn carrying his dead wife's ashes as one of the other passengers whispered.

Lilah had turned and left the restaurant, confining herself to her suite for the rest of the evening. There were no knocks at her door, no phone calls to her cabin. No one butted in when she spent the next morning talking to her brothers. Not until Andersen cornered her at the birthday celebration.

The elderly lawyer asked, "How long are you going to hide from him?"

Chapter 71

Security was tight in the private gambling room, with the brand-new technology of body scanners checking for cameras and listening devices even before a guest could get to the door. Dark and moody saxophone music greeted Lilah when she walked up to the ornately carved entryway. So did wisps of cigar smoke. Glittering chandeliers and silk-lined walls screamed wealth and opulence, and there was none of the constant ringing and clinking ubiquitous to casinos. Leather chairs were set around six tables or so of real mahogany. Waiters walked in between, serving drinks to the high rollers as they conversed in soft murmurs.

Pausing at the doorway, Lilah glanced at the other women in the room and smoothed down the spaghetti-strap gown in shimmery crimson. Nearly a decade of living frugally made her wince at the prices onboard, but it was worth it. The only thing she did with her hair was arrange it in a loose twist with tendrils curling around her jaw, and jewelry was limited to the tiny diamonds in her ears. In her right hand was a matching clutch.

A server materialized next to her elbow. "Madam?"

There were a couple of low tables by the portholes, where non-gamblers could sit with wine and food and enjoy the ocean. At Lilah's request, the server led her to one of the spots, her black stiletto heels making hardly any sounds on the richly carpeted floor.

On a small notepad, the young man scribbled her request for sauvignon blanc and goat cheese. The hefty bodyguard—the one hired as soon as the pardon came through—followed her in only to take a quick look around before retreating to a strategic position near the door. He would keep a vigilant eye on her but stay out of earshot unless she shouted for help. Perhaps she should've felt a bit more gratitude, but she didn't. Not after Noah reminded her the security firm was retained by Brad and couldn't be trusted not to snitch. She could've gotten the guard replaced, except a replacement would also carry the risk of—

"Here you go, madam," the server announced. "Would you like me to pour?"

"We'll take some baklava, too, if you have it," said someone else.

Lilah stilled for a moment in the joy of hearing his voice. Averting her eyes to the porthole, she focused on the blue waters of the sea. The sun was hovering on the western sky, its yellow now tinged the orange-red of approaching twilight. Noir jazz continued to play on the overhead system.

"Baklava?" asked the server, his tone uncertain. "I can certainly check."

"If not, just leave the wine and cheese here," Harry said cheerfully. "We'll make do."

Gaze pinned on the view outside, Lilah swept the glittering clutch to the side to make room for her order. Black pants and an off-white dinner jacket appeared in her field of vision as Harry settled into the chair across. When he handed her the flute glass, she saw the dull gray chain wrapped around his wrist, a miniature Eiffel Tower hanging from it. She still didn't look at him. Even when their fingers brushed, she didn't say a word.

"How have you been?" he asked.

As though they were casual acquaintances, meeting by chance! Wryly, she said, "I had a place to live in, food to eat... nothing to complain about, I guess. And you?"

"The same. No complaints." Tone bordering on bragging, he added, *"New York State* paid for my food and housing."

Lips pursed, she finally turned to face him.

"Hey, it wasn't so bad." He reached across and poked at her cheek with a finger. "Worth at least a tiny smile." She sputtered, and he laughed with her. "For the last two days, I was thinking of what I'd say to you... what you'd say to me. It was going to be very poetic."

"And?"

"One look at you, and I forgot everything."

She arched an eyebrow. "Really? It's been almost ten years. More probably you forgot what I look like."

With a shrug, he said, "Ten years, fifteen, fifty... you're still Lilah. I'd know you anywhere, however long it has been. Did you think I wouldn't track you down at some point?"

"Did you think all it would take was showing up?" she countered. Her hand rose as though to stroke his hair before dropping back to her lap.

"Uhh... no."

"Then?" she asked, sipping wine. Faint lines surrounded his eyes, lines which weren't there when they last met. Maturity sat well on him. Tabloids always gushed over the charm, the edge, the power radiating from the man. Harry hadn't lost any of his old mojo, but there was a new aura of control about him, leaving the air charged with a compelling energy.

"Tell me what it will take," he said. "I'll do it... and I'll accept whatever you're willing to give."

"What if I have nothing left to give?"

"You exist. It will be enough."

"Oh?" she asked, sudden anger reverberating in her voice. "Put your money where your mouth is. Get your cards out."

"My..." He frowned. "What do you mean?"

"Your cards... you have them, don't you?" From the day Harry learned to play poker, he carried a deck somewhere on his person. Those who lost to him—including Lilah—accused him of cheating, but no one ever found a thing wrong with his cards. "Or we can ask the staff."

"No," he said, shaking his head in obvious bemusement. "I have my own. What do you want to play?"

"What do you usually like to play?" Lilah asked. "Five-card draw?"

With a wary nod, Harry said, "All right."

When he took out his deck and shuffled, she dug into her purse and tossed a note onto the table.

"A dollar for ante?" he asked.

"No," she said deliberately. *"I* am putting up one dollar. *You* are going to put up your shares in Gateway."

Harry stilled. "My... uhh... the board hasn't released control yet. Besides, the SEC might object." The Securities and Exchange Commission regulated transactions involving even private stock.

"I don't really care... all your shares in Gateway."

He contemplated her in silence for a few seconds. "Okay," Harry finally said. "All my stock." He scribbled his IOU on a napkin, placing it next to the dollar note.

Shuffling, cutting, dealing... Lilah let him handle it all, not even glancing down at the cards. The other guests in the room would be too busy with their own sky-high bets to pay attention. None of the waitstaff was around to pick up any snippets of the conversation. The guard was also too far away to hear what was being said. All he'd see were two old friends catching up over a poker game.

When it was time to bet, Lilah once again said, "One dollar."

With a wry grin, Harry asked, "What should my bet be?"

She shrugged a shoulder. "One dollar... two... whatever."

"All right." Neither checked the cards or wanted any new ones. The bets remained the same. "Showdown," Harry murmured.

His was a rather mundane hand—three of a kind. Lilah turned her cards over one by one, bothering to look only when she was done. Jack of spades, queen of spades, king of spades, and ace of spades—a royal flush.

Inclining his head, Harry said, "Congratulations. You now own all my stock in Gateway. What do you plan to do?"

"Sell it for pennies," she stated, keeping her tone steady.

He coughed a couple of times. "Please invite me along when you tell the board. May we talk now?"

"Not yet," said Lilah. "I want to play more. Deal, please."

"The ante?" he asked.

She tossed another one-dollar bill onto the table. "Every share you own in any company, all your properties, your bank accounts."

Shuffling, cutting, dealing, betting... his straight to another royal flush for her. "Selling for cheap again?" Harry asked.

"Donating to charity," said Lilah.

Huffing out a breath, he asked, "What next?"

"Your apartment."

"Homeless and penniless?" Laughing mildly, Harry added, "Habibti, you're gonna have to feed me."

"Deal," Lilah snapped. In a couple of minutes, she demanded, "Your guns and your knife." One of the articles on Harry had mentioned the Ari B'Lilah being returned to him soon. "And your bike."

Harry winced. "Don't tell me... the scrap yard?" At her glare, he held up both hands. "All right, all right. The Harley, too." When it was over, he said, "I don't have anything else to play with except the clothes on my back."

"Not quite," said Lilah. She could almost feel the nastiness in her smile. "There *is* one more thing... your wife's ashes."

All traces of amusement vanished from Harry's face. "My wife's... Lilah, I... you..."

A second, two seconds, five, ten, fifteen... she waited for him to tell her he couldn't, that it was outrageous of her to even ask. The saxophone music in the background peaked on a jagged chord before returning to the intense and raw longing of its opening notes.

"Fine," said Harry. "The ashes it will be." He would of course do the same card-counting he always did, this time making sure *he* won.

Except... Lilah stared down at the royal flush in her hands, not quite certain what to do next.

"I'll bring the urn when we're done here," Harry murmured. "It's in my cabin. There's also a message which goes with it. You can have it now."

Thoughts foggy, she glanced back up. "Message?"

Harry dug into his jacket and brought out a folded piece of paper. "It's a letter for you."

Puzzled, Lilah took the note. The edges of the ecru-colored sheet were slightly torn as though the letter had been opened and read multiple times. It *was* addressed to her. A note written by a dead woman.

Dear Lilah,

If you're reading this, it means you escaped, but something happened to me. Sounds like some stupid fucking soap opera when I write it.

I feel like we're sisters. Or could've been if we met. We could've helped each other. You could've kept me from some of my poor choices, and I could've taught you how to show the middle finger to a couple of people in your life.

I never had a sister before, not one who counted, anyway. But sisters should take care of each other, right? So fight the good fight for me, dear sister. Finish the race. Keep the faith until the end.

Yours,

Lupe Valdez Sheppard (Ha! Couldn't resist)

P.S. Make them pay for whatever they did to me.

"Liam and I tried to piece together what happened the evening she was killed," Harry said, taking a sip from his wine glass. "Charles Kingsley visited the same night, but club records indicated he was gone before the time she called me about Will Luce. She saw something... heard something... when she called again, I'd already left for Brooklyn. Maybe the phones were tapped, but she could've walked out the front door and asked any damn cop for help. So there was someone in the club, spying on her. Someone working for Drummond. Liam and I believe it was still Charles, but we have no way of proving it. At some point, she wrote this letter and climbed out of her bedroom window. Then, we heard about Drummond being found in Beijing." With a violent grunt, Harry quaffed more wine. "Given what we knew of Lupe's connection with Drummond and this note she left, Liam and I concluded she sensed some threat from him... to you."

"Connection to Drummond?" The Kingsley brothers never mentioned it. Alex also didn't say anything of the sort when he admitted to visiting Eden.

"Yeah." In a few short sentences, Harry explained the outline of the arrangement between Lupe and the disgraced congressman, adding that the deal was not public info. The details of what happened between the two were not divulged, but Lilah could imagine.

"Fight the good fight," she echoed the words from the letter. "It was *her* fight all along."

Like Tara, Lupe, too, had encountered monsters, and she wanted them destroyed. Every man, woman, and child who helped the exiles fought for themselves on some level. They were driven by the need to see justice done, perhaps for past wrongs, perhaps for the gross misuse of a military uniform they revered, perhaps for a chance at a future free from fear. No bribery, no coercion... no leader could force them into a battle they didn't want. Nor did any leader have the right to order them to a safe corner while she fought their battles for them. They were all in this together, their collective anger against a corrupt elite Lilah's sharpest weapon, their trust her shield.

Sudden tears blurring her vision, Lilah smoothed out the paper on the table and tried to read again. She didn't need to go to the mountains for answers. First, a young girl, then the spirit of a sister Lilah never met brought her the clarity of thought she sought.

"Poor Lupe," Harry said. "She had so many dreams for Eden. This place... Goa... she would've loved to be a part of the scene here. In the end, all I could do was have Liam scatter her ashes wherever she planned to open a club. I asked him to keep some aside for you and me to say final goodbyes when we could. Please, Lilah? Will you do this for her?"

#

Two hours later

A few quick phone calls got the group together on the promenade. Fortunately, Liam had arrived earlier in the evening, Gabriel in tow. Verity's brother deserved to be present for this final tribute they were paying his friend. Lilah announced she had a moral obligation toward Lupe to do the last rites herself. After all, Lupe sacrificed her life to save Lilah's. No one objected, not even Brad. Lilah's guard was left behind for the perfectly valid reason of there being no room on the two-seater power boat.

With shadowed forms watching from the railing, Lilah donned the orange life vest over her gown and settled herself in the launch. Needles of lukewarm water sprayed onto her face as Harry drove farther into the dark ocean. The music from the cruise liner grew muffled.

"This should be a good spot," Harry finally said, powering off.

The brightly lit ship was still visible, and the single lamp at the helm of the small craft would tell the audience where they were. With the back of her hand, Lilah wiped the droplets from her lashes. Wind gusted briefly as she took the urn from the satchel on her lap. A tiny shiver went through her body.

Harry shifted to face her, the warmth of him radiating across the few inches between them. The breeze ruffled his hair from behind. "I'm not going to lie to you," he said, keeping his decibel level low. Only the half-moon in the sky and the stars and the waves around would hear the conversation in the boat. "If you hadn't been around, if we never met, if you weren't born... but you were, and we did, and there will never be anyone but you. Lupe... she was... I'm grateful to have known her."

If Harry hadn't been around, if they never met, if he were never born... in silence, Lilah remembered an encounter so long ago in Venezuela. She'd put aside any romantic feelings she harbored for Alex the moment she heard about his marriage to Sabrina, but Lilah finally understood what it was that drew her to him to begin with. Had Harry lived with the knowledge all these years?

Dipping her free hand in the water, Lilah let tiny wavelets tickle her fingers. Life was bewildering, she murmured, taking them on detours they didn't intend, forcing them time and again to learn their relationship anew. Life was constant, Harry countered, all paths leading them back to each other, at every age, in every form, for all eternity. The sucker punches thrown at them by the world, the accidental self-jabs, the mistakes, all melded into their very beings, yet they still somehow fit together. She nodded. Harry's memories of Lupe were now a part of Lilah, a poignant pain that she treasured.

Uttering a short prayer, she placed the urn on the waves. The cork on the champagne bottle popped open with a loud report. Clinking glasses, they toasted the life of Lupe Valdez. On the promenade, Liam and the rest would be doing the same. Music and laughter reverberated from the ship as the ocean carried the ashes deeper into the velvety night.

Harry's fingers were already on the boat's ignition when Lilah said, "There *is* a way."

"To do what?" he asked.

"To force Brad and his brothers to take down the network even if you're not chairman."

Chapter 72

Next morning

Lilah took a deep breath before exiting her cabin. A business meeting after so many years... office attire, folders, computers, market numbers, messages from partners... it was almost surreal.

As expected, the guard followed her all the way to the conference hall on the cruise liner. Halting at the closed entrance, she instructed the fellow, "Please remain here."

Not only him, all the bodyguards waited outside the doors, including Temple's security detail. No one but the core team would be allowed at the meeting. There would be no ship staff, no assistants, no outside lawyers, and certainly no press. With control of the entire oil network at stake, leaks could not be allowed. Except of course, the Kingsley brothers could be trusted to leak every word said today to their precious grandfather.

Stepping in, she did a quick visual sweep of the hall. It was luxurious, with elegant wallpaper, matching carpet, wood-and-leather furniture, multiple maps, a flat-screen television, and phones at every seat. Patrice and Sabrina were already in their places. The two ladies were never actively involved in the company or the network, but any fallout from the war with the Kingsleys would impact them. They deserved to hear what was being planned.

At the head of the table was Dan, Shawn on his right. Lilah's adoptive brother was conversing with Victor. Wrong... Shawn seemed to be mediating some argument between Victor and Sabrina. Alex and Scott were across from the bickering duo, talking to Harry and Dante. As though aware of her gaze, her best friend looked up.

With only a quick nod of acknowledgment, Lilah averted her eyes and continued her inspection of the room. Neil was with Patrice and Liam. Mr. Temple was of course present, as were Noah Andersen and Grayson Sheppard.

Finally, she saw Brad seated at the other end of the long table with the dog he adopted in Goa lying next to his feet. He was back to sporting the stubble beard from nine years ago. Except for him, the Kingsley brothers had completely shaved off their facial hair. Alex kept his man-bun for two days on his wife's pretty plea, but it was now replaced by a short and sharp style. All five wore business suits.

The place next to Sabrina was occupied by Mr. Temple. The only empty spot seemed to be between Brad and Grayson. Gritting her teeth, Lilah strode to the chair and seated herself.

Nine years, she reminded herself. She'd spent a long time on the run. She could survive another year or two pretending to be the loyal wife. Only when the Kingsleys were defeated and the network was broken apart would she be free.

"'Morning, sis," called Dan, grinning widely at her.

Lilah grinned back, noting the anxiety lingering in his dark gaze. It would be a while before he allowed himself to relax about his twin's safety.

"Seeing we're all here..." started Grayson. He gave a brief recap of the changes in the network's governing structure. Everyone at the meeting knew the info already. The dossiers were delivered to their rooms the night before. "...the offer to negotiate with Harry turned out to be a sham. Steven is not willing to give up control over the network. He's not even willing to return the Peter Kingsley Company. The network's board has authorized him to withhold transfer of power over both entities. As of today, Kingsley Corp remains in charge."

"Kingsley Corp," Brad stated. "Not Steven himself, which means Grandfather would have a say... except he'll be forced to argue for Steven."

Grayson cleared his throat. "Yes. Steven is the CEO of the company and the network even though Kingsley Corp is the business entity which controls everything. Godwin does have authority, and we must expect him to exercise it in favor of the organization he works for. It's his fiduciary duty... in theory. By extension, Godwin will be advocating for Steven."

In theory... Lilah shook her head. The five Kingsley brothers wouldn't hear that part. The former supreme court justice who forced a division of the parent company despite not holding a single share was now deemed powerless against Steven. Peter Kingsley's sons refused to assign any fault to their grandfather.

"So if we go to court against Steven, we must be prepared to argue against the entire Kingsley family," finished Brad.

With a nod, Grayson said, "Any legal move from our part will necessarily involve all the senior executives of Kingsley Corp. It would include any lawsuit against Steven and Charles for what happened in Cuba... the assault under custody, violation of rights, so on and so forth."

"I don't like the idea," Victor said. "I mean... are we seriously going to blame Grandfather and Uncle Aaron for what Charlie did?"

"I don't like it, either." A mild flush worked its way up Brad's neck and face. "Which is why it's important to consider peace. All of us would prefer to get our property back in its entirety, of course. But what's the point of winning if it means damaging all the relationships, the family that made us who we are? Besides, there's uncertainty in going to war. Even if we win, there will be people who resent us for it. More enemies... it will be a never-ending cycle." Pausing, Brad huffed. "Unfortunately, Steven's not going to be satisfied with anything less than complete surrender... which means we'll be back to where we began. Either we give up everything or we fight for everything. I wish we could somehow convince Steven to work with us."

"Brad," called Harry. "As Grayson said, I already tried to negotiate with Steven. It never even got as far as talking. His aim was to get me arrested again. Peaceful coexistence is a great concept... but only if all parties agree to it. Steven clearly doesn't."

Lilah hadn't needed the morning reminder from Andersen to know the tack Brad would take at this meeting. Nor did she forget the role she was supposed to play in the discussion. It was still not easy to refrain from responding, from snapping out loud that coexistence would result in the network being left intact with a power-hungry old man controlling the whole structure from behind the scenes.

Besides Harry and Noah and Temple, no one in the room knew Lilah intended to do away with the network. Not Brad and his brothers. Not *her* brothers, either. She never got a chance to discuss her plans with Dan before leaving on the exile, and Harry was imprisoned before he could plot out a detailed strategy for the few people in their circle whose allegiances were undivided. After the arrest, getting him out and bringing the fugitives back home had been everyone's primary concern, and anything that might come after was relegated to the backs of their minds. Didn't matter. Lilah's twin surely realized she wasn't going to return to the façade of a happy family running the oil empire, and he would support her whatever her decision.

Still, he and Shawn stayed quiet at the calls for peace, as did Patrice and Sabrina. Dante was included merely as a trusted advisor, and he couldn't make any official pronouncements while still on Gateway's payroll. Noah was studying everyone, making notes on his scratchpad, and who knew how much Temple understood?

"But Harry," argued Brad, "you went to Steven before the DNA proved you innocent... before the pardon. Now, you could go to court to get reinstated as chairman, so Steven might see sense in negotiating. We should consider talking to him again."

"I am definitely going to court," said Harry, "but a win is never guaranteed. It could be years before we get a verdict. Also, Steven knows his grandfather will stand by him... stand with Kingsley Corp. So will General Potts. Both names command respect in the public arena. There's Major Armor. He's been doing a lot of PR work... philanthropy. The government's not supposed to lick its finger and check the wind direction, but you can bet it will. It's one thing to issue a pardon involving a single individual and something else altogether to take sides over control of the entire network. Sure, our side has goodwill, but political pressure on the board will end up being equal with Godwin, Potts, and Armor on Steven's side. So why would he worry about me returning as chairman? Even if I do win in court, Steven's done a lot of restructuring in the last nine years... bribing the board members with power. You got the details from Grayson."

The board members would be even less likely to cooperate if they realized Lilah planned to dismember the network. Not only the companies which were part of the structure, there were many now with their interests tied to the vast empire, and they'd fight for its continued existence. Harry would have to play his cards very, very carefully to give her the victory she wanted.

"If we could show the board proof of what Steven did..." pondered Alex. "Not only the trick he and his uncle and Major Armor pulled in Cuba... I wish there were some evidence to connect them to McCoy."

Across the table from Alex, Patrice held folded hands to her face as though praying.

With a half-nod at Harry, Liam said, "Life would've been a whole lot simpler if we could pin the blame for my father's death where it belongs—on Steven and Richard. Unfortunately, too big a risk." He didn't specify how they would've done the pinning or what risk.

"Yes," agreed Harry. "Too risky. Brad, I'm not against peace. If it's what you and your brothers want, we can certainly initiate another discussion with Kingsley Corp. Sorry to say peace doesn't seem possible as long as Steven continues to enjoy support from the board. We should proceed on the assumption there will be war."

"This is crazy," said Victor. "Going to war with Grandfather? What about Uncle Aaron and the rest of the family? What's their mistake in this whole mess? I'd rather lose the whole damn network to Steven."

You, too, Victor? Lilah asked silently.

"And why are we jumping ahead?" Victor continued. "Remember, Grandfather doesn't have to take sides in an informal negotiation. Harry, if you go to Kingsley Corp again with a proposal our grandfather agrees with, Steven will at least make a show of considering it. Board members and so on will want him to. Who knows? It might even work. We have all done things we regret. Don't we deserve second chances? Forgiveness?"

"Steven, too?" Harry chuckled. "How about Charlie? From what I remember, you threatened to break Steven's thigh."

Steven had invited Lilah to sit on that thigh. Charles's hands tore her clothes, sliced Lupe's throat. There was a low growl from Dan, and Liam muttered something under his breath.

"Are you chickening out?" Harry taunted the boxer-turned-chef.

Bristling, Victor sat up. "Not what I meant. I'd be happy to go to war with—" Glancing toward his mother, he swallowed whatever epithet he was about to use. "All I'm saying is we can give a little. Isn't it the whole idea of diplomacy? Both sides lose; both sides win."

Harry inclined his head. "Just making sure you haven't changed your mind about what your cousins did. And far be it from me to ignore a potential diplomatic solution. As I said before, if it's possible to reach a deal without compromising our interests, we'll do it."

"I'm worried we're just wasting time with peace offers," Alex said. "I do want to get the business back. We built it with our sweat and blood... but I can't imagine going to court against Grandfather. Thing is I also don't see the point of talking peace with the likes of Steven and Armor. They didn't think twice before assaulting Lilah. What kind of damn bastards attack women? And a woman in their own family!" He shook his head. "Then again, there's Grandfather... and General Potts. He was our dean! The man couldn't have been nicer to any of us when we were in West Point. He taught me everything I know. I mean... he was part of the trial in Cuba, but what else could he do as the head of Army Intelligence and Security Command? He couldn't ignore potential treason. For the general, his first loyalty will always be to the country. Same for Grandfather. Both of them left the court when Lilah exposed what bullshit Armor's arguments were. They realized we did nothing wrong. But Grandfather's hands are tied now, and the general won't argue against Kingsley Corp unless there's national interest at stake. So how am I going to... what the hell are we going to do?"

Lilah raised a silent eyebrow. So Godwin *and* General Potts were to be absolved of their crimes. According to the five Kingsley brothers, all the blame lay with the evil quartet of Steven and Charles Kingsley, their uncle Stanley, and Richard Armor.

"I wouldn't be so quick to forgive Potts," Dan warned, tone firm. "Alex, the general might have been 'nice' to you Kingsleys, but I won't forget what he did to Lilah. You wouldn't, either, if she were actually your 'family.' Potts made sure I couldn't stop what was happening." The Barrons heir was detained on a false bomb threat and didn't even know what was going on with his twin. "Potts most certainly was aware of what a sick bastard Charles was, but the son of a bitch was still allowed to escort my sister. Because of it, she was—"

"Dan," called Neil. "I get what you're saying, but we shouldn't allow our emotions to overcome logic. Let's look at this in terms of likely outcome. What kind of support do we have?"

With a short laugh devoid of humor, Dan said, "Lilah will always have my support. If she decides to stick with you lot, I'll be forced to as well."

Thank you, Lilah whispered in her mind. The greatest blessing God bestowed on her was perhaps her brother.

"Barrons O & G will also stand by Brad," added Dan. "I'll make sure of it no matter what Andrew thinks."

From what Lilah understood, he spent the last nine years cultivating Barrons board members. Those who refused to be cajoled, he found incentives to offer. The information obtained through Eden's Angels served as his weapon. If only it were enough to bring the *network's* powerful board to its knees.

"For what it's worth, so will I," said Shawn. There was a computer program he mentioned earlier to Lilah, something designed to track the financial transactions of certain businessmen and politicians. She had a feeling it was the handiwork of a programmer she knew very well.

*Blessing*s, corrected Lilah. Andrew Barrons disowned his son in favor of the twins he adopted, but Shawn turned out to be an incredible big brother to both Dan and Lilah. The tabloids gave Sabrina enough grounds to loathe Lilah, but Harry's sister stayed a true and loyal friend.

"Count me in," said Liam. There was Will Luce's son, driven, presumably, by his need to see justice done.

"Thank you." Neil nodded. "So we have one big company on our side and a few good friends as opposed to... almost the entire network with Steven. Yeah, Harry's with us, but Gateway will go with Steven. I don't see how we're going to win."

"Doing the right thing is more important," said Scott. The confusion in his twin's eyes was obvious. It was perhaps the first time they disagreed in public. "Winning is good, and I... ahh... don't want to hurt Grandfather, but Lilah... Charlie's not a good man. We shouldn't forget no one did anything to stop him. Not Grandfather or Uncle David or General Potts. Charlie didn't get any punishment."

"He was given a dishonorable discharge by the military," argued Neil. "What else do you think should've been done?"

"Other-than-honorable," corrected Scott. "Victor told me it's not really a punishment, but dishonorable discharge would have been. General Potts got the military not to punish Charlie. It's not right. The general wouldn't have done it unless Grandfather asked.

He asked because of Steven, I'm sure. But not right at all." Blinking through his round-shell glasses, Scott turned to the eldest of the brothers. "Brad, you want peace, but I can't agree. Sorry. I don't like Steven. He and Charles hurt Lilah. Harry, if you talk to them, don't try to make peace. We should go to war."

Everyone in the conference hall stared at Scott in varying degrees of surprise. The astrophysicist was always supportive of Lilah, but he never went against his brothers. Not overtly and not until today.

"Thank God," Sabrina muttered, echoing Lilah's own thoughts. "At least one out of five is making sense."

"Yeah, thank God." Shoving his chair back, Liam got to his feet. "Scott's right. Why are we even debating this after the last nine years? Remember what all of us went through because of the Kingsleys."

There were murmurs of agreement from Grayson, from Dan and Shawn, even from Noah Andersen.

Clapping one, two, three times, Lilah stood. "Brad wants peace. Other than Scott, all the brothers want peace. Godwin wants peace. The entire Kingsley family wants peace. What a wonderful group of people, always looking for peaceful resolution of disagreements. Except for Steven and Charles, of course."

All the noise in the room came to a sputtering stop. Every eye swung toward her.

"Peace," she repeated. "Or do you mean business as usual... with the rich and the well-connected colluding to keep power in their hands instead of fighting over it? The version of peace under discussion here has nothing to do with justice or fair play or the common man's right to life, liberty, and the pursuit of happiness."

"Not true," objected Victor, shaking his head. "Corporate wars affect the regular Joes, too. A truce is better for all concerned."

"Oh?" Lilah laughed a little. "Didn't you just say you're willing to give up the network to Steven to save the family? Natural extension of the same idea would be you looking the other way if he and his buddies attacked more women. Maybe an employee or two. Maybe a partner. Attacking *me* is clearly not where you draw the line, so how does the regular Joe benefit from your truce?" Steven was being careful for now, but he knew other contenders to the throne were still alive and could use his misbehavior to oust him. Once Brad was out of the way... the day Harry died... the moment Lilah ceased to be a problem... "And who are you to offer forgiveness for an assault perpetrated on *me?*"

"I—" Victor's throat worked. "I didn't mean—"

She turned to Alex. "How nice of you to finally acknowledge me as family! Too bad I'm still a rung below your grandfather and your dean. If it means saving them embarrassment in court, you're quite willing to overlook Cousin Charlie's little mischief." The decorated veteran might have dressed like a woman for the last eight years to protect her. He might have been willing to sacrifice himself to save her and Tara. Yet when he was forced to pick a side in a zero-sum game, Alex picked his actual family. So did Victor.

"It's not what I said—" Alex began.

"Where was this concern about losing all these years, Neil?" Lilah asked. "When Brad was in danger, you were quite happy to depend on Harry and Liam and my brothers. Now that the pardon's come through, their support is not enough?"

Face bright red, Neil looked down at the papers in front.

"And you, Harry." Walking around the table, Lilah took measured steps toward where he was sitting. Liam put half a foot forward as though to head her off, but she brushed him aside. "You," she repeated, pointing a finger at her best friend. "Before you go to Kingsley Corp to discuss *peace* and *coexistence*, perhaps you can remind the people in this room of the reason behind the original Kingsley-Barrons-Sheppard alliance."

Hands on the table, Harry heaved himself up.

"I want all of them to remember Sanders," she said, keeping her tone controlled. "How he dealt with the companies which opposed him. I want them to remember Steven and Armor and how far they were willing to go to steal the network. I want them to remember what absolute power means in the hands of a criminal like Steven."

"No one's forgotten any of it," said Victor.

Ignoring the interjection, Lilah grabbed her French braid and shoved it in Harry's face. "This is the hair by which Charlie dragged me to court. I want everyone here to take a good look. Those who saw me that day... I want them to remember the bruise on my face... the blood on my clothes..." Angry tears sprouted at the memory, one or two spilling to her collarbone and trickling down. She knew what she was going to say even before stepping foot into the room, but the fury from that long-ago day still threatened to break through. Swallowing hard, she continued, "Harry, remember all of it when you go to the Kingsleys on your peace mission."

An answering rage flared in his eyes. "They will pay. Charles, Steven, Armor... everyone."

"Will they?" asked Lilah. "Who's going to make them pay when the talk is all about peace?

There was a muffled sound from one of the brothers... perhaps from Neil.

"Tell me, Harry," Lilah demanded, not taking her gaze off him. "Doesn't the SEAL creed teach you to serve with honor? Doesn't every branch of the military do the same? There are men in this room who're considered heroes by large portions of the media... defenders of our nation... those who once promised to shed their own blood to protect ordinary men and women. You're now rich. You're powerful. When did such elite heroes decide it's okay to ignore crimes as long as it suits their purposes? Why are we negotiating peace with criminals who haven't shown a single ounce of regret for what they did?"

"I will never forget what the Kingsleys did," Harry swore. "Unless they're prepared to make honest amends for all of it... unless they agree to do exactly as we ask... there will be no peace." His eyes repeated the pledge from the night before. "Exactly as we... as *you*... ask."

"Give it your best shot, Harry," urged Alex. "Steven's a damn... he won't listen to reason, but do your best, all right? I get what Lilah's talking about. Still, one greedy S.O.B. should not be enough reason to destroy the entire family. War must be the last resort."

"All other options must be exhausted first—diplomacy, sanctions, and so on," agreed Harry. "Which is what we're going to try. Steven had better listen to his father and grandfather. I'll talk to Godwin... and to Aaron and David and General Potts. If they cannot change Steven's mind, war *will* become unavoidable."

Godwin Kingsley was unlikely to change his own mind, let alone Steven's. Neither man would agree to take down the Kingsley banner flying over the oil empire. Harry would have to manipulate discussions to the point where the Kingsleys did exactly what Lilah wanted.

"A just war—corporate or otherwise—cannot be anything but the last resort," Harry added.

"This *is* a just war," said Lilah, "but not only because we ran out of ways to make peace. Our cause is just. This war belongs to the men and women who didn't have a voice until we promised to speak for them. The network was formed with their welfare as pretext, but they're not fools. They know it could be used to keep them down. It already was... see what happened to Lupe. Think of what could've happened to Hema and Tara."

Yet there were other just causes before, and the conflicts over those causes turned out to be meaningless. Righteous rage was never enough to justify a clash of this magnitude.

"This is a just war," Lilah reiterated. "Because we're not merely fighting *for* the men and women who stand to lose their freedoms if the enemy wins. We're fighting side-by-side. They know they cannot win on their own, but together, we have a reasonable chance of success. They see us as the leaders of their army because they trust us to do the right thing. They sacrificed everything—their careers, their future, their *lives*—so we'd survive to fight another day."

The private who testified in the court in Cuba, the two boys who got the exiles to Ecuador, Hema... even young Tara. The girl refused to cower in fear of Prince because she correctly saw the battle as a struggle over her own future. It was *her* fight, not merely

Lilah's. Tara refused to hide in the safety of the clinic, letting her father handle the corrupt cops on his own.

Lupe Valdez was one of the warriors on their side... the first among them to fall. She was not cannon fodder, certainly not collateral damage.

"Lilah," Alex called. "Hear us out, please."

"Hear *me*." Seizing the chair Harry vacated, Lilah pulled it back and sat, her legs crossed. "Listen to *me* now, all of you. Your decision doesn't matter. Whether or not even one of you five stands by my side bears no relevance. This struggle belongs to every man, woman, and child affected by the network, and they will not quit."

More than eight years ago, Lilah watched an ordinary chap carrying a shopping bag walking into a street in Beijing. He stood with his arms aloft, and the world held its breath as the march of the Chinese military was brought to a halt by the determination of an average citizen. The media christened him Tank Man. No one knew his real name even after all this time. No one knew if he remained alive. The one thing Lilah was sure of was that he didn't martyr himself only for the protesting students. Tank Man stood up for his own freedoms as well, for his own hopes and aspirations. Surrender was not an option for him *or* for Lilah.

"Even if the elites in this room refuse to fight," she continued, "even if you somehow manage to talk Harry into peace, there will be other leaders ready to take your place."

Lilah glanced at the faces around the table. Brad was staring straight ahead with a stony expression, but the rest were looking at her. The former president remained a mute witness to the chaos in the room.

"The spirits of my parents will be with me," she said. "My teachers, mentors... my brothers already announced their intentions. The children... brave young Michael will lead my troops. None of us will quit until it's done. Because we have a responsibility... a duty toward those who trusted us with power."

"Fight the good fight," Harry murmured. "Finish the race. Keep the faith." He dropped to one knee next to her chair. "Lilah, I give you my word... there will be no compromise with Steven which does not involve him giving up control over the network. However, we do need to make a genuine attempt at peace. Until then, there will be no support for war."

Not from the Kingsley brothers, not from the businesses which were a part of the network, not from the government, not from the public. So at the end of his peace mission, Harry would make sure Steven Kingsley rejected all offers of truce. Godwin would hide behind Kingsley Corp and claim helplessness.

The loyalty of the Kingsley brothers would always be with their grandfather. The only way around it was to force them to choose between Godwin and someone else they loved dearly... someone like Brad. Peter Kingsley's sons would be left with no choice except to approach the American government to break up the network or risk their older brother's life and freedom yet again.

The greed and arrogance of the Kingsleys would lead them into a conflict which wouldn't end until the clan was destroyed. The confrontation Lilah sought would happen. The United States Congress would declare war on the network on her behalf.

There was a shuffling sound from the other side of the table. The former president stood. "War," proclaimed Temple, struggling to spit out the syllables. "There *will* be war!"

THE END of Book 5

For a sneak peek at the next exciting book in the series, please head over to www.JayPerin.com

Want to know what happens next to Harry, Lilah, and Alex? Order *The Spanish Sacrifice* today to continue with this exciting tale!

Afterword

Let me start by acknowledging Tank Man. Sir, my politics began the moment I watched you walk into that street.

As mentioned previously, the One Hundred Years of War series is an adaptation of *Mahabharata*, the Indian epic mythology.

Repeated comments from prior books:

1.   My thanks to the writers whose works on *Mahabharata* I've enjoyed and learned from and to fellow myth enthusiasts from various discussion groups. Thanks to my friends who have patiently sat through my arguments on various plot points.

2.   For the purpose of this story, Temple was president from 1979 to 1986. Reagan-Bush (take your pick) from 1986 to 1992. Yes, I realize that doesn't make it eight years, but it can't be helped because I want to end the story the year I want it to end, so Temple's presidency had to come at this time. Also, I didn't want Temple identified with either a real president or with one of the political parties. Right now, he straddles Carter (D) and Reagan (R) administrations.

3.   I did not use real characters except peripherally. That, too, only for things they were actually accused/guilty of doing.

4.   I tried to stick to historical facts throughout the story,

including the minor details, but some changes were inevitable.

5.   As far as I can figure out, the U.S. Supreme Court did not have an internship program in the 1940s. Please consider it literary license. Columbia did have female students in their law school.

So that's it. See you again when *The Spanish Sacrifice* releases.

Sincerely,

Jay Perin

P.S. As always, if you liked the story, do tell others about it. Also, writers thrive on reviews. They help us figure out what worked and what fell flat. They help other readers make up their minds. Please do leave a comment on any of the sites.

Visit www.EastRiverBooks.com for a bunch of interesting stuff.

www.ingramcontent.com/pod-product-compliance
Lightning Source LLC
Chambersburg PA
CBHW051305190726
48290CB00001B/16